WAITING
for the
NEWS

GREAT LAKES BOOKS

A complete listing of the books in this series can be found at the back of this volume.

PHILIP P. MASON, EDITOR
Walter P. Reuther Library, Wayne State University

DR. CHARLES K. HYDE, ASSOCIATE EDITOR
Department of History, Wayne State University

Advisory Editors

WAITING
for the
NEWS

LEO LITWAK

 Wayne State University Press   Detroit

c.3

Library of Congress Cataloging-in-Publication Data
Litwak, Leo, 1924–
    Waiting for the news / Leo Litwak.
      p.   cm. — (Great Lakes books)
    ISBN 0–8143–2274–3 (alk. paper). — ISBN 0–8143–2275–1 (pbk. :
alk. paper)
    I. Title. II. Series.
PS3562.I79W35   1990
813′.54—dc19   89–5577
                                                        CIP

SEP 1 0 1994

To the memory of Isaac and Bessie
and to Daniel Litwak

The Origin of *Waiting for the News*
Jake Gottlieb and His Model

I WRITE this introduction more than twenty years after the original publication of *Waiting for the News*. The elation I felt when I received the first advance copy will probably not be duplicated. The timing then was perfect. It was August, 1969. The family had gathered at Myrtle Beach in South Carolina to celebrate my parents' fiftieth wedding anniversary. There were fourteen of us, the three sons, their wives, grandchildren, the spouses of their grandchildren, a great grandchild. We occupied two large cottages on the beach. These were carefree, joyous days filled with barbecues and drinks and cardplaying and reading and forays into the mild surf and journeys to the penny arcades and schlock shops and movie theaters off the strand. I waited for a quiet moment and produced my copy of *Waiting for the News*. I read the simple dedication, "To Isaac and Bessie—Fifty Years," and offered my parents *Waiting for the News.*

My father was then seventy-seven years old and still president of Local 285, Laundry and Linen Drivers, a union he had founded in 1934 and affiliated with the Teamsters.

He said he couldn't think of any better gift. He thanked me and kissed me. He took the book down to the beach with him that morning and began to read. I expected him to be even more pleased when he discovered he was the model for Jake Gottlieb, the labor leader at the center of the book.

He read beneath a candy-striped umbrella. He was clearly absorbed. When the sun shifted his legs were exposed and turned deep red but his attention didn't stray. My mother insisted he take a break for dinner. He resumed reading in our cottage and wouldn't stop for the nightly card game. He returned to the beach the following morning and by midday he had finished. He closed the book, put it down, and I waited for his opinion. He didn't say anything. I thought he might be so powerfully moved he needed time to formulate his judgment. Two days passed and we talked about everything else. He picked up other things to read, and he still didn't say a word about the novel. I began to feel irritated and depressed but I was resolved to wait him out though his silence already seemed a judgment.

Finally my ten-year-old nephew approached him.

"Grandpa, what did you think about Uncle Leo's book?"

He looked away, considered his response. "There are one or two things I would have left out."

"Like what, Grandpa?"

"There is too much sex."

By almost any standard *Waiting for the News* is not a sexy book, and I couldn't take the judgment seriously. Something else had offended him, and my brother Danny told me later what it was. "It's a tragedy. How could you put him in a tragedy?" Hadn't it occurred to me that my father would be upset being placed in the shoes of a man he so closely resembled?

I told my brother I hadn't placed my father anywhere. It was Gottlieb who was in the novel, and he was my invention, a mere fantasy, and I could put him wherever I pleased.

"Pa takes everything seriously," Danny said. "For him there is no mere fantasy."

Which is to say he was anchored in the real world.

He didn't trifle with the way things were. He asked for the unvarnished truth. He once told us, "My childhood was very serious. I was brought up on the Testament, the Talmud, and the Commentaries. I didn't play games."

On the other hand, he was hearty, and zestful, and life loving, with a raucous sense of humor. He enjoyed cards and chess. But he kept his eye on cardinal matters and had little interest in fantasies.

He later let me know he couldn't understand why I had to distort the way things were—fabricate a union, give birth to its membership, locate fantasy strikes and violence in an imaginary Detroit—and direct it all toward something terrible. Why hadn't I just considered his life? There I would have found drama enough.

More than enough, I said. His life was larger than anything I could imagine.

"Why shouldn't the facts speak for themselves?" he asked.

What would they say?

And he told me. He told us all. He repeated the story I knew almost by rote and yet could listen to again and again. We taped what he said and here is some of it.

I made my father unhappy. I, his oldest son, revolted against him at the age of thirteen. I questioned the foundations of his faith. I openly violated religious laws. Being young, I didn't spare his feelings.

I wanted to escape the czarist regime and get better conditions for Jews. I wanted territory that Jews could call their own. I wanted to change the economic structure of Jewish life. Instead of being a nation of middle men—of storekeepers—my dream was to create a nation with the normal range of classes. I wanted Jews in agriculture, industry, academics, science. That could only be achieved in a territory owned by the Jewish people.

I wanted to build a new nation, an independent Jewish nation. It was my dream. I preached it in the synagogues and in the streets.

I made application to the only foundry in Volynia, a steel foundry. I had quite a problem getting into the foundry because of my age. I was the only Jew who applied to the foundry. I picked the hardest job that a Jew could aspire to. I worked at the open hearth. I stoked the fire with coal. My mother was upset that I was a manual worker. I was the first one to do manual work in our family. I was entirely black—my shirt, my coat, my face, my hair.

When I was fourteen years old I joined WTO, the Jewish Territorialist Organization. We had to take an oath, "We raise our hands to the East and we swear to walk the world to reach the eternal land." The Black Hundreds were coming to Zhitomir to oppress the Jews, and we established self-defense for our neighborhood. The commandant of self-defense was a man named Joseph, from Homel in Lithuania. He was a terrific organizer. We bought guns from Kruzow, a gun seller though no one was permitted to own guns. Joseph taught us how to shoot. We used to go into the woods and to the dachas. Our main weapon, though, was a two-edged knife called a kinzow.

We met once a week in private homes. There were about forty-five in my cell. Small arms were distributed to defend against the Black Hundreds. My work was to organize the Jews for self-defense.

When the pogrom started, my mother and father tried to keep me in the house, and I pulled out my knife and they let me go. The Black Hundreds were in Kamenka, separated from us by a brook. We were outnumbered two to one. We were joined by gentile intellectuals, students, some of whom lost their lives in our behalf.

On one occasion the Black Hundreds reached the center of the Jewish neighborhood. Fifteen of our people were killed, including two non-Jewish students fighting with us. The Black Hundreds looted stores and businesses. They were armed with guns and knives and stones. We were organized in tens for reasons of secrecy. We used whatever weapons we could find, even stones. Black Hundreds were also killed.The soldiers and police came to their help. They put themselves in military formation between us and the Black Hundreds. Maybe 150 police, 300 Black Hundreds, and 150 Jews were in our skirmish. The Jews gave a good account of themselves. Ten of our people lost their lives in another skirmish. The government signaled to the Black Hundreds to stop fighting. These pogroms were organized by the government. The pogrom lasted two weeks.

I was sixteen years old in 1908 and an agnostic. My mother and father were very upset. They were pious and didn't believe in fighting the government. The great majority of the Jews in Zhitomir were pious and believed that Jews should protect themselves only by prayer. While the religious Jews ignored our struggle, Blinow, a gentile, gave his life for us. He denounced the Black Hundreds, and they killed him in the Square. I understand there is a monument to him there.

Someone informed on me, and I was arrested by the security police. They came at three in the morning and searched my house for weapons and literature. There were perhaps a dozen uniformed police. My father opened the door. My mother put my gun in her boot and put the boot outside. They searched everywhere. They found nothing illegal. The gendarmes asked me questions. I denied everything. I denied I belonged to any party. I didn't compromise anyone associated with me.

There was no justification for the arrest, but they arrested me anyway, and I was jailed with the political prisoners. When I protested the treatment, the chief came into my cell and said, "Why are you complaining? You're fighting for the people, then suffer for the people." I was in jail for four months before I was sent to Yarinsk.

The jail in Zhitomir was in the middle of the town, surrounded by a high fence, like a fortress. There were about fifteen people in my cell. Once a week we could talk through the windows. They told me I was sentenced to two years in Yarinsk, near Kursk, on the edge of Siberia. I was then sent to the Kiev fortress for a few weeks. When they took us to the railroad station for transport to Kiev, they chained our hands and marched us through the streets of Zhitomir. My parents marched with me to the railway depot. There were crowds marching along with us on the sidewalks. It was very rough treatment in Kiev. The food was very poor. There was a can in the cell for a toilet. There were maybe thirty in my cell.

The prisoners organized themselves according to party and even in jail the ideological differences were extreme.

From Kiev I went to Sumarow and Tula in central Russia and then to Moscow. In the Moscow jail I became sick with typhoid fever. I was in the hospital for three months, and the criminals who were the orderlies took our food. I was so hungry I stole bread to survive. We had to be careful who we associated with in prison because the government planted stool pigeons among us. The guards had instructions not to converse with the prisoners. There was a deep dislike between the criminal prisoners and the political prisoners, and they didn't associate with each other. The criminals were treated like cattle while we were treated with respect. They didn't give us prison uniforms. We wore our civilian clothes.

It took several days to reach Yarinsk. We traveled in a special prison train, barred and guarded. I arrived in the springtime. Yarinsk was a poor, god-forsaken village, populated by the Great Russians, the real Russians with some mixture of Mongolian blood. The local people were fishermen and farmers. It was a small village, about the size of a resort town, located in the tundra, a treeless wasteland. There were long days when it never got dark. We also saw the northern lights.

I was in Yarinsk for a year and six months. I had a room in a peasant's house. I used to buy a cow's head, chop it up, make a stew and it would last me for days. For breakfast I had bread and butter and tea.

During the day we had lectures and discussions. There were representatives from all the parties. There were perhaps two hundred exiles in Yarinsk. We were not permitted to work because the government didn't want us to mix with the local population. We were forbidden to leave the town. We received written instructions, detailing our duties and limitations. Our meetings and lectures were not supervised. It was an intellectually lively place, full of arguments between various political parties.

The government gave us eleven rubles a month. A ruble in those days was equal to fifty cents. The room cost us two rubles a month. We had thirty-eight rubles for winter clothing and twenty rubles for summer clothing. I had to be careful when I shopped. For twenty-five kopecks I could buy three pounds of potatoes. Potatoes were the main item of food. We could buy a rabbit for forty kopecks, and the rabbit could last three days.

Before my exile ended I sent a letter to Stolypin, the prime minister, asking permission to join my sister in Archangel. They gave me permission to spend six months near there. It was a bit warmer there than Yarinsk and more civilized.

After I returned from exile I worked for my uncle, and in 1913, when I was mobilized for military service, I left the country.

He came to this country in 1913 at age twenty-one, one life done and several more to go. He arrived in Galveston, examining Texas as a place for Jewish settlement. The Jewish community there shunted him off to St. Paul. He went to Detroit when he heard Ford was hiring for the River Rouge plant and got a job on the assembly line making radiator caps. He left for military service in 1917, served in Europe and after the war returned to Ford. In 1920 he became a truck driver and his union organizing began.

Local 285 was his child. It was his child as a work of art is an author's child. He wasn't modest. He claimed paternity. "It's my child," he told the *Detroit Free Press*. "I built this union. I built it single handed."

He fought to bring it into existence, risked his life to establish it, guarded it from the intrusion of the mob, resisted a Communist effort at takeover. His honesty was legendary. The Kennedy investigation of corruption in the Detroit Teamsters concluded, "Isaac Litwak wouldn't take a cigar." A member of the employers association, no fan of his, told the *Free Press*, "You can't even buy him a cup of coffee."

His integrity was uncompromising. Employers tried to work around him and contact other officials in the Teamsters but he didn't allow it. He was at his best in a knockdown battle. He risked his life without apparent fear.

His friend, Jimmy Hoffa, had the political grace my father lacked. He was a different kind of labor leader, shrewd, adaptable, dangerous. He didn't scruple at accumulating power. At the same time, he was loyal, gregarious, intelligent, charming, pragmatic, and popular with the rank and file for whom he secured solid contracts. My father respected Hoffa as a remarkable, if sometimes ruthless, labor organizer who had vastly expanded the Brotherhood of Teamsters. No labor union had greater power to affect the nation's economy. Hoffa valued my father, and they stood side by side during the labor wars. They walked picket lines together and, when my father refused to disband a picket line declared illegal, they went to jail together. My father refused to let the mob operate in the laundry and linen industry. He was beaten up on our front porch. He was pulled from his car while it was stopped in traffic and assaulted. Hoffa warned him of serious death threats, and he moved from the house accompanied by a bodyguard provided by Hoffa, carried a pistol, slept in hotels, and without Hoffa's help he might not have survived. They were friends to the end.

Still, he wasn't comfortable with Hoffa's narrow understanding of brotherhood. He felt that the wrong people influenced Jimmy, diverting him from his true calling as a labor leader.

The contradiction between his own dream of brotherhood and what existed in fact sometimes wore him down. This is the text of a card he sent me when he was seventy-four years old. The greeting on the front said, "Happy New Year."

Dearest son Leo. I can't explain the reason why in spite of the urge to talk to you about many things, the urge vanishes when we come face to face or when I write to you. For this reason my letter to you will be very short. Life here is as usual. I keep busy with union matters, but I am skeptical about the long-range usefulness of my trade union activities. It does not give me any real spiritual satisfaction. Very often I feel quite empty, with no real, valid purpose. I know you have your own troubles, but you do not talk about them. Maybe it is much better not to talk, because there is no answer. In the meantime on the occasion of the Jewish New Year let me wish you and the ones dear to you the very best.

I think everyone who knew him would be surprised by this moment of despair. In his life there was no evidence of it. He'd come through everything—the rejection of faith, labor wars, world wars, the loss of family in the holocaust—and his energy never flagged. He seemed fearless and indomitable. His achievement had been more than respectable. He was responsible for innovations in labor contracts that were considered trendsetters throughout the labor movement. The Detroit newspapers referred to him as a labor legend. And yet he'd dreamed of having a larger effect. His local had a membership of less than seven hundred at its height while Hoffa controlled legions.

Four years later, when he was seventy-eight years old, he rallied his people against a united linen industry. Half-page advertisements in the Detroit papers appealed to workers and clients not to submit to "Isaac," whose policies, they said, had brought the linen industry close to ruin. In his own ads and broadsides, he answered that strangers had come to Detroit to take over the industry. They meant to undo forty years of union progress, and he would never allow it. A strike and lockout began in December of 1970 and persisted through the winter in what became the longest strike he'd ever undertaken.

The old man walked the picket lines with his troops through a particularly ferocious winter. Finally his back gave way. The pain brought him to his knees. He lost sensation in one leg and never fully recovered.

I visited him while he was convalescing from a back operation. He was in constant pain, and I hoped I could distract him. I told him to close his eyes and imagine Myrtle Beach. Think of the sun and the hot sand and the gentle surf. Imagine the sand covering his numb leg and his throbbing hip.

He closed his eyes. There's no beach, he said.

"Imagine one."

He closed his eyes but no beach came to mind, no sea, no ease for his legs. He couldn't allow a real pain to be removed by an act of fantasy.

He retired at age eighty in a huge affair at the Latin Quarter night club. There were nine hundred diners in attendance. There were city officials, representatives from the Jewish community, the local Teamster hierarchy, judges, his entire rank and file, all his family. Jimmy Hoffa, released from prison, was the main speaker. He reminisced about the old days when he and Isaac were happy warriors. He anticipated more wars and more victories, but that wasn't to be.

I came to stay with him at my brother's house when he was dying of uremia. One night his bedside bell rang violently. "Leo!" he called, "come quick! He's here!" I ran to him. A hall light cast shadows across the ceiling above his bed.

"Who is it, Pa?"

"In this room. He was so big. He touched the ceiling."

"Who, Pa?"

"The angel of death. I wanted you to catch him and hold him."

The angel of death appeared as vivid as life and perhaps it needed someone with a habit of fiction to understand that it was an invention of the mind.

Long before he died my father became a fan of *Waiting for*

the News. He began to enjoy being identified with Jake Gott-lieb and that pleased me as much as anything. As Irving Howe wrote in his review of *Waiting for the News*, "Jake had an out-sized glory. . . . His power is more than personal, it derives from historical drama. He lives by some idea of what a man should be—and is that not at least the beginning of heroism?"

My father lent Jake Gottlieb his power and if, with the reis-sue of *Waiting for the News*, others can experience that act of grace, our book will have done its work.

WAITING
for the
NEWS

I

———◆◆◆———

My pa, Jake Gottlieb, had prepared himself for a great destiny. He had had in mind such models as Eugene Victor Debs, Vladimir Lenin, Judah Maccabeus. Yet in 1939 at the age of forty-seven he found himself a liege of Hyman Kravitz, whose insigne was a skeleton globe with blue longitudinal ribs and a red slash across its equator, bearing the name, "Atlas Laundry and Linen Supply Service." My pa wore the insigne on the back of his blue shirt and on his overseas cap. It spread across both sides of his truck van, accompanied by the motto, "Put your burden on our shoulders."

He counted dirty sheets. He scattered roaches. He bore the burdens of others on his shoulder.

Sometimes Ernie and I accompanied Jake on his route. He introduced us to places we otherwise would never have seen. We entered utility rooms of show bars, past marquees that featured bosomy ladies. Our pa dumped bins of dirty linen onto spread sheets. While porters mopped empty barrooms, we sorted napkins, tablecloths, towels, uniforms, bloody aprons. We listened to the scrape of buckets on the floor, the squeal of a ringer, the sound of water draining into buckets, the slap of mops dragged across tile floors. Once I heard the click-click of high heels, an early-rising performer coming for rehearsal, wearing slacks, sweater, a kerchief—the skin a disappointment but not the breasts. I recall the piney odor of a cleaning compound.

When my pa stooped to gather in linen, I saw the globe of Kravitz spread on his back. He knotted the corners of the sheet with swift crossings. Powerful tugs formed a bundle the shape of a giant pumpkin. He gripped the bundle by its stem, the world spreading on his back again—the red sash binding the ribs—and hoisted fifty pounds of dirty linen. He gripped the bundle with one hand, the other dug into his waist, his jutting elbow forming an anchorage for his unstable load. The top of his van mushroomed with bundles secured by a chrome railing. It was an eight-hour day for Jake Gottlieb, five and a half days a week with considerable overtime at no extra compensation.

Why did he labor under the colors of Kravitz when he had such great ambitions? Ernie and I knew that those were tough years and that Jake Gottlieb had growing boys to feed, both wolves. Ernie was fifteen, and I was fourteen, and we had big appetites. Why wasn't my pa crushed by those bundles on his back? Why didn't he sink under the globe he carried? Why didn't he admit it was a defeat to be serving Kravitz?

I saw Jake Gottlieb stretch on his toes, balance a bundle in the palms of his hands, his face beet red before he released the bundle, casting it up to the roof carriage, and I vowed that someday I would free him from his burden.

This laundryman had grand designs. He left a trail of discord halfway around the globe, an advocate of revolution. At sixteen he had already served time in Siberia, thanks to the Czar, then fled Europe, conspiring all the way. He later returned as one of General Pershing's legionnaires. I have photos of

6

Jake as he appeared during his triumphal return to the continent that had expelled him. He wears a dirt-brown uniform and puttees, a level-brimmed campaign hat—a stubby, powerful man who lends style to the drab outfit; chest out, chin in, eyes forward, hands rigidly along the seams of his flared trousers, younger than the Jake Gottlieb I spent my life recognizing, but still recognizable. The scars don't yet show. They'll soon appear. He settled in Detroit after the war and was hustled from the Ford River Rouge plant when he was caught haranguing the assembly line. He was forbidden to operate in the auto business under the name of Jake Gottlieb and continued to work as Jake Love. He drove a truck hauling slag from a foundry. The slag haulers' union was rubbed out when its only member, Jake Love, was kicked off the premises and a scar was etched on his bald dome.

When we were very little, Ernie and I sat on his lap, each of us straddling an enormous thigh, and I considered the scar up close. It was located above the eyebrows, which flourished, like black pennants, on heavy ridges, a white scar, the beginning of a bold signature. It crossed his tan, freckled dome, an inscription made by a company cop using a billy. When I traced the scar with my fingertips, perhaps completing the signature, Jake grabbed my hand and kissed it. Then, playing it fair, he tried kissing Ernie, too, but Ernie refused to be touched, and broke away. My pa told me then, "Now everyone can see I'm smart; it shows where they pounded sense into me."

No one ever managed to persuade my pa by threatening him with scars. His marvelous smile would spread his cheeks and give you a clear view of the repair to his front teeth. Caught by hoodlums late one night as he came up the stairs he lost his front teeth; yet his smile remained wide open. He wasn't made cautious. He offered easy access for anyone who wished to finish the wreck of his bite. "Boys," he told us, "it only hurts before they give you the scar. Afterwards, they can't do you any more damage. I say to them—all the bosses

7

and goons and hoods—'Be my guest.'" He had a profound voice, a bass baritone, and his laugh issued like a cannon barrage.

Despite thirty years of vain effort in behalf of revolution, he wasn't finished trying. He invited new scars. It was too late to be choosy about footholds; he was desperate to begin his climb upward. Atlas was the place where he intended to start. He had plans for Atlas that Hyman Kravitz knew nothing about. Jake meant to organize Atlas and end the tyranny of Kravitz. He meant to remove that globe from sore backs.

II

---••◆••---

THERE WAS in our old Detroit neighborhood a restaurant called
The Cream of Michigan, famous for its barley soup and dairy
dishes. It was a humble place, in a humble neighborhood,
planted among haberdasheries and grocery stores. The Cream
of Michigan didn't confine its service to the cream. It's true
that you could find affluent gents from the suburbs with monogrammed hankies in the breast pockets of English-cut tweed
jackets who sought the corn bread and barley soup of their
youth. But The Cream of·Michigan was patronized mainly
by neighborhood people, men of the working class. It was also
the special preserve of the Jewish toughs, our hoods, who
occupied the counter and the front tables. When we passed
behind them and glimpsed a rear view, we saw bulls at a
feeding-trough, with enormous backs and necks and jowls. They
wore fedoras on small domes.

We knew a man who was a doctor to these hoods. This
doctor entered The Cream of Michigan one day. He heard

9

a quarrel and turned to look: a behemoth descended from his stool, grabbed a little guy who had irritated him, and with a twist and a twirl heaved him through the plate-glass window. The little guy crawled to the streetcar tracks, where, as the doctor put it, "He exsanguinated." That was a new style for our people, our own hoods and killers. And after all the pretty talk is pared away, what were Arthur and his knights? The cowboys of the West? Stenka Razin? Robin Hood? Admired butchers! It wasn't a style Jake cared for. The Jewish hoods were killing Jews, not dragons. It's not that they lacked sentiment. The juke box at the rear of The Cream of Michigan played "Main' Yidishe Momme" among other fine pieces, and these hulks grieved for mothers. Yet they could blot the tears, honk their noses, get down from their stools, and heave you through plate-glass windows. While you exsanguinated, they finished their barley soup. Jake scorned these bums. He had no quarrel with sentiment: in memory of his own mother he could also weep. These oxen, though, when they were finished weeping, were ready to pound your head with fists like boulders. They struck without sentiment, not even with hard feelings, and resumed slurping their soup. The incident with the exsanguinating man was rare, since most of the damage they inflicted was off the premises.

There was one among our hoods, Happy Weinberg, whom we kids most admired. Weinberg had a sunny disposition and a freckled red face as tubby as the moon. When Happy grinned, you saw white and gold. He had a laugh that was so exuberant you had to join in. He was fond of children; he let them hang around while he played pool. He probably got a boost out of the appreciation of children. I wouldn't have been surprised to find Happy watching cowboy movies on Saturday afternoon. I don't mean to represent him as a moron who happened to be a hood by accident—a buffoon first, secondly a bruiser. That isn't my intention, because that big, sunny face with the merry eyes might very well be focused on a brutal scene such as a girl being handled while her cowed escort is invited to be a bystander. If Happy gave a hard goose to your sister, you kept your mouth shut. Happy could unloose that infectious laugh while some frightened tailor was being slapped around. It was a good laugh, a real "ho-ho" that used all two hundred and fifty pounds of Happy. He was able to laugh at how absurd men look when they are being tormented. We kids didn't despise him for that. Weren't we instructed to be cool when murder was done? I'm speaking, of course, of our other models, Tom Mix and Buck Jones and Bob Steele and the Manassa Mauler and Achilles and Joshua and Sergeant York, not to mention Mickey Mouse and that crowd. His cool meanness, his cheerful sadism, made Happy all the more admirable to us kids. Not to Jake Gottlieb, however.

He walked past the counter at The Cream of Michigan as if the hoods didn't exist. He wasn't about to surrender a first-rate restaurant because hoodlums shared his appetite for good barley soup. With Ernie and me in tow, he marched to the tables in back and let people know that Gottlieb was around. He ridiculed the hoods. His comments were loud and clear.

We often accompanied Jake to The Cream of Michigan. The prospect that he might offend Happy and his cohorts scared me. These men needed little cause to heave you through plate-glass windows. Ernie made no effort to disguise his anguish. Happy Weinberg had an unpredictable sense of humor. He might laugh off Jake's abuse. He might even enjoy our nervy pa. But he had a buddy, Whitey Spiegelman, who was dangerously sensitive. This Spiegelman wasn't to be teased. Ernie feared that Jake was ignorant of Spiegelman's possibilities. Such ignorance was a threat to us all. Spiegelman resembled a clerk. He was scrawny and bald and doughy-nosed. If a defined chin is evidence of power, he could be classed as timid and meek, for he had no chin. Yet, despite appearances, he was a dangerous man. We heard stories of sudden furies provoked by trivialities. He swarmed over his opposition, flailing like a windmill, not stopping until his tantrum had run its course. He may have lacked Weinberg's heft, but he was relentless. He had exceptionally skillful hands. We saw him perform card tricks. We watched him move around a pool table, bending, sighting, then stroking quickly. It was foolish to provoke such a man.

One Sunday afternoon we accepted Jake's offer of a meal at The Cream of Michigan. Again we had to listen to Jake's daring abuse, but when nothing came of it—the restaurant was crowded and every kid's pa had a big voice and every table had someone putting on a show—I relaxed and ate. I felt wonderful relief and became sassy myself.

We loaded up with food as we left. We were outside the restaurant when Happy Weinberg summoned Jake. He was waiting by curbside, leaning against the open door of a new Hudson. Spiegelman was at the wheel.

"Gottlieb, you old bastard. Say hello to a friend." It was an exuberant, high-pitched voice, a friendly tone that offered no threat.

Jake handed one package to Ernie and another to me and faced Weinberg with folded arms. "Do I know you? We've been introduced?"

"You're Gottlieb, the laundryman, okay? Meet my pal Whitey Spiegelman." He leaned into the car and explained to Whitey Spiegelman that Jake Gottlieb was a friend. Spiegelman didn't seem impressed.

"I'm no friend of yours," Jake declared, offering a statement of policy, not merely fact. Did he take that strong line because his sons were present? We knew that Jake's tone was always pitched to an audience. Couldn't he, out of concern for us, have retreated on this occasion? I have a photo of Jake taken about that time, an impressive profile, a face that would attract a sculptor who wants to make something out of a coarse-grained stone. A heavy face, a big chin, the short neck making a firm pedestal for the large head.

Happy bent down and faced me at eye level. "I see you boys around, don't I? You're Vic, right?" I was thrilled that he knew my name. "And this here is Ernie, who hangs out with Lenny Mitchell. Lenny Mitchell is my buddy, do you know that? I take care of Lenny Mitchell. Well, you boys got some daddy. What big ideas he got! Don't be surprised if one of these days you find out that me and your pa are in business. Weinberg and Gottlieb. How's that for a team?"

Jake said, "I got no business with you."

Happy straightened up and clapped Jake's shoulder, a good swat. "Don't be in such a rush, Gottlieb. I can do you favors."

"Why should you do me favors?"

"We got mutual friends."

"What friends?"

"Hy Kravitz."

"He's no friend."

"He speaks nice about you."

"By the time I'm finished with Kravitz," Jake said, "either he'll be out of business or he'll be paying a living wage. You tell that to Kravitz."

"It would be a special favor to me, Jake, if you talk nice to Kravitz. A friend of Kravitz is a friend of Happy Weinberg."

He only asked that Jake be reasonable and talk to Kravitz.

"You making threats?" Jake asked.

Happy appealed to us. "Did you hear me say anything, kiddies? What a touchy pa you got."

If Jake wanted to demonstrate that he didn't fear the most dangerous hoods on Twelfth Street, he had proved his point. What he said next made me dizzy.

"Listen, bums, with such arms and shoulders you should be standing in the front lines, breaking Nazi skulls. Instead, you specialize in old tailors. Tell Kravitz if he wants to speak to Jake Gottlieb, he can talk to him face to face. He don't have to use third parties."

Weinberg didn't need to make threats. His reputation made threats for him. If he greeted you, you were threatened. His tone of voice was irrelevant. I knew my pa had been threatened, and I trembled.

"We hear stories about them," Ernie told Jake afterward. "You don't fool around with Weinberg and Spiegelman. They can do terrible things."

We were under the spell of Weinberg's threat when Jake pulled us into the doorway of a closed Woolworth's.

"Listen, I'm in dangerous work; I don't hide that from you. Those bums mean me no good. But I assure you, boys, it doesn't give me a second of worry. I have been banged on the head; I have been hit in the face. No one intimidates your pa, Jake Gottlieb."

"These guys are serious," Ernie said. "Nothing is beyond them. Anything goes."

Jake clapped our shoulders. He fixed us solemnly. It was an occasion he meant us to remember. I felt, as I'm sure Ernie did, that this was one of Jake's stagey moments.

"Boys, if anything happens to me, Kravitz will be responsible. Remember that."

Ernie asked, "What do you mean, 'Remember?'"

"Remember what I told you. Act according to your conscience. Never forget you are the sons of Jake Gottlieb."

Ernie was almost already to explode. "Of course we won't forget. What a thing to ask!"

"And act accordingly."

"Act? What do you expect us to do?"

"I shouldn't have to say more." Did he imagine himself the papa of Mafiosi? "I only ask that you remember," he said. "Take an oath. Swear that you will do your duty by your pa."

We stood among the Woolworth displays, sales on swimsuits, sun-tan lotions, mosquito repellent, bug sprays, picnic utensils —reminded of the common pleasures of ordinary life—and Jake demanded that we take an oath appropriate to the barren hills of Sicily or ancient Israel but not Twelfth Street.

"Swear!" he ordered. "If something happens to your pa, swear that you'll remember."

"What could happen? What?"

"You heard what this bum Weinberg said."

"It's foolish," Ernie said. "I won't swear."

Why was Ernie so obstinate? All he had to do was swear, and Jake would be pacified. He insisted that we swear. He wouldn't budge from the spot until we did. However reluctantly given, he wanted our oaths. He wanted guarantees that his two sons would follow in his tracks and accept the consequences of his actions.

We squabbled in the doorway of Woolworth's. The threat of Weinberg no longer oppressed us. We fought each other.

"It's stupid! It's false! It's just melodrama!"

"Swear!"

We ignored inquisitive looks from passersby.

Finally I said, "Yes, pa, I swear." I said it to give him pleasure. Yet what wonderful relief when I took the oath. That was always Jake's effect on me. He oppressed me; then he liberated me.

So Ernie also agreed. "Okay. I will."

"You'll what?"

"I swear."

We swore that if anything happened to Jake Gottlieb we would hold Kravitz to blame. The next time that Jake faced Kravitz and was threatened, Jake would warn him, "Anything that happens to me, happens to you. My boys will see to it."

He hadn't won Ernie's good will, and so he wasn't satisfied. He stopped the car before turning into the driveway. Again he gripped our shoulders and held us tight.

"I hide nothing from you. You are of an age to be men and you got obligations. Your pa now speaks to you as men. You can see from our meeting with those hoodlums that I have enemies. They are dangerous, and they have no affection for Jake Gottlieb. That suits me; that's my pleasure. I don't want their affection, not a tiny bit. Such enemies give me no trouble. Not when I got two sons to take up my cause. So pay attention. I want you to swear an oath. If anything happens to your pa, remember that Hyman Kravitz is the man. Get Kravitz."

We took the oath. We swore, and not for the last time. Jake was in a risky business and he wanted guarantees of loyalty. "Who knows how long I'll be around? Can you blame me if I want your attention?"

Ernie blamed him.

How could we take the oath seriously? Our pa often assumed histrionic poses. Ernie tried to put the oath out of mind. "It's foolish," he told me. "He hams it up."

We number ourselves to Jake's meaning. He set himself against Happy Weinberg, and that was no match. Happy Weinberg at two hundred and fifty outweighed Jake by seventy pounds. Happy Weinberg, every day of his life, every hour of every day—including the night hours when he had bad dreams—plotted the most brutal use of his two hundred and fifty pounds. He was familiar with guns, brass knuckles, knives, pipes, blackjacks, bare hands. He saw all the world's furnishings as possible weapons. He studied each man he met with the obsession of a general who must consider any terrain he enters as a potential battlefield. Men were Happy Weinberg's battlefield. As for Jake, I never imagined his massive arms and his barrel chest as tools of war. He dreamed of the day when the lion would be couched with the lamb. He couldn't sustain any ferocity. He only had moments. If he conquered you, he assumed your burdens.

Jake let everyone know about his meeting with Happy Weinberg.

"They have me marked," he boasted. "Spiegelman, Weinberg, the whole Cream of Michigan crowd. If they didn't know I had a big mouth and sons to avenge me, I'd long ago be planted in a wooden box."

Listening to him, you could lose respect for his achievement. "Why doesn't he keep it to himself?" Ernie asked. "Why do we have to be told? What does he expect from us?"

"Shouldn't we share his troubles?"

"Even Weinberg and Spiegelman have their pride. There's no reason to insult them."

Jake believed in a Homeric style of history and told whoppers in the manner of the Greeks. It didn't bother me. It was a respectable tradition. Didn't Achilles boast each night at the campfire? Didn't the heroes proclaim their pedigrees, cite their credits, advertise their power before launching spears?

Despite the bragging, spears were launched; the glory was merited. It wasn't a style for those raised in the laconic tradition of Gary Cooper, whose silences, by the way, I always thought hammier and stagier than the bragging of more natural men. Jake's style suited me, if not Ernie.

I had terrible dreams. I woke up and saw Ernie in the cot opposite mine evidently in the same fix. Our nightmares had the same source. Jake made us swear, and the oath lay on our hearts like hot brands.

I remember a dream that Ernie and I must have shared. I dreamt that I rowed behind swimmers, crossing a lake. Jake was in the lead, flinging himself far ahead of the others. I rowed desperately to keep up. Fog closed us in. I thrashed the oars trying to keep Jake in view. I lost him. I rowed on and saw him floundering. He was stiffened with cramps. His enormous chin stretched to keep above the water. His eyes rolled. He grasped the side of the boat and tried to enter. He didn't have the strength. I couldn't reach him. He said to me, "Don't worry yourself, sonny. It's all right." Then he went under.

It was Ernie's shout that awakened us. I jerked up, ready to yell, and saw Ernie hanging over the edge of his cot, clutching for the man who had sunk in my dream.

Jake tried to comfort us.

"Your ma tells me you have bad dreams. She says you wake up at night."

Ernie didn't want any inquiry into his dreams. He said his dreams were his own business.

"If our talk the other day has given you problems, I want you to forget about it. Put it out of your mind altogether. It wasn't my intention to give you worries."

"Of course that was your intention," Ernie said. "How can you deny it? Can you ask us to take such an oath and then tell us not to worry?"

"All right," Jake said. "I made a mistake. Put it out of your mind. Forget it altogether."

"It's too late," Ernie said.

"I exaggerate always. It's in my nature. You know your pa, boys. He gets excited."

I didn't want to be let off. I knew the reputation of the Cream of Michigan crowd as well as Ernie did. They were interested in Jake, and we ought to be worried.

Ernie said, "If only I could understand why you were so rude to Happy Weinberg when he admits that he admires you. Couldn't you have turned him down in a nice way?"

"I should be a gentleman, you mean. You picked the wrong pa, sonny. Jake Gottlieb speaks his mind. His tongue don't go around in circles."

Though they both may have had good intentions, they marched inexorably into conflict. Jake said that it wasn't his policy to stick his head in the ground in the face of danger. He feared no man. He dared Weinberg to do his worst. "This Weinberg you admire so much, this bum you call 'Happy,' this ignorant hoodlum, is nothing. I don't negotiate with this pig. He's nothing; I offer him nothing. He gets no respect from me. I treat him like he belongs in the wild woods or the pig sty. Nothing; a cipher. What someday you got to understand is that it's your pa, Jake Gottlieb, who is something. Don't go looking so far from home if you want someone to respect. Try respecting your own pa."

Ernie wanted to speak what would be most damaging; he also wanted to restrain himself from speaking. He said finally, "Why don't you let someone else blow your horn?"

Jake stopped and caught Ernie's arm. "Who?" he asked. "Who will do it for me? My sons? Can I rely on my sons to speak for their pa? There's no one else to do the job, so Jake Gottlieb advertises himself. Otherwise he would never be heard from."

"Why should anyone be heard from? I don't want to be heard from."

Jake shook him. "I worry about you. You got no sense. I'm worried that you'll bury yourself. You'll smother because

18

you didn't have the nerve to fight." Jake shook him again. "If you hide your talents, who will see you? No one will come looking. Don't count on the generosity of strangers when you can't depend on your own children. Men will step on you just to be rid of the competition. They'll pretend they didn't know you were underfoot. You better make a sound. Yell out. Tell everyone who you are. You got plenty to brag about, a strong, intelligent boy·like you, Gottlieb's son."

My brother said, "I'm nothing. I got nothing to brag about." He made nothing of himself in order to torment Jake.

"You're plenty. You're Gottlieb's son."

"A man shouldn't have to boost himself."

Advice poured in from every quarter, Jake observed. Employers advised him to drop dead. Cops advised him to go back to Russia. Now even beardless kids got into the act. "Everybody in the world has an idea how Jake Gottlieb should behave. I'd love to pay attention but by hearing ain't so hot. It's my tough luck to have a bad character that I grew up with. Now I'm stuck with it. You don't divorce your character like it's your wife."

He said to me afterward, "Your brother got no respect."

"He worries for you, pa."

"My worst enemy don't show such contempt."

"He boasts about you. He feels terrible after an argument."

"I leave you no fortune. I got nothing in the bank. I invest everything in a reputation. All I leave you is the honor of being Gottlieb's son."

What more could he give? It was true about his character. He had been fashioned in fires so intense that all of the easily worked material had been consumed and only what was fiercely tempered and unworkable remained in his construction. He was reconciled to himself. That was the source of his enthusiasm and his energy. He wanted to be no one but Jake Gottlieb. He thought Jake Gottlieb as splendid a character as there was on the scene, adequate to any war, ready to assume the station he deserved but which was denied him by men and history. He wanted Ernie to acknowledge, despite the smallness of his achievement, his true size. I saw my pa, Jake, as monumental. You could get your bearings by sighting him. He commanded us to remember him. Ernie wanted to hold out, but he took the oath. I'll never let Ernie forget. We swore, more than once.

I was never reconciled to my brother's inconsistencies. Even at fifteen he was a powerhouse, sloping shoulders, heavy thighs, a long torso. He worked on his body so that it might become the image of his dreams. He was the shape and size of a budding hero. Yet, though he dreamed of heroes, he had no faith that they would come into existence.

A student of the stars, he was intrigued by Greek myths and looked into the night sky expecting to find representations of heroes. But what was up there? Only the sketchiest semblance. You could see the Dipper for what it purportedly designated, but you had to strain to see Cassiopeia's Chair as furniture or Orion as the hunter or Hercules as the son of Zeus.

He dropped the stars as apotheoses of heroes and came to understand them in their own right. They were great balls of gas whose life had a term. Dead dwarfs, vestiges of giants, drifted in the heavens. If not even the stars were immortal, what chance did Jake Gottlieb have? How could our pa maintain his zeal in the shadow of dead stars? One day, a few billion years hence, the sun would become engorged, swallow its own planets as Saturn swallowed his young; then it would cannibalize itself, devouring its own substance. Was justice possible then? Wasn't Jake Gottlieb a fool for dreaming that he could forge an eternal brotherhood that would be forever a testament to himself? Wasn't that bullshit? He risked getting killed when he challenged Happy Weinberg and Hy Kravitz; yet he seemed to have the illusion that after death he would be apotheosized like the sailors of the Argos. But already, at fifteen, Ernie feared that after death there was nothing, absolutely nothing.

III

———◄◆►———

When Fred Emerson learned of the encounter at The Cream of Michigan, he offered his support without being commanded. No one had to force Fred Emerson to swear; his heart spoke. "When they tackle you," he told Jake, "they'll have to take on your whole gang. You got tough boys on your side, too." There was McIntyre, for instance, who might not be naturally belligerent, but in support of Jake he would become a tiger. And, of course, it was Emerson who introduced O'Brien and touted him as a union man equal to any of the Cream of Michigan hoods. Many of Emerson's claims were exaggerated, but he never made inflated estimates of O'Brien.

Fred Emerson was a skimpy man, with an extraordinary voice appropriate to a heavyweight. He said, "Whenever you give the word, Jake, you can rely on us. We'll go all the way. You're the boss."

"No more bosses," Jake told him. "Live for yourself. Consider your own self-interest."

I heard Emerson confess in our living room, "You saved my life, Jake, and I'll never forget it."

"You just had bad luck."

"I was finished," Emerson said, "done for."

We had met Emerson through his wife, who had been a significant element of his bad luck. She occupied the only single dwelling on our block, a white clapboard bungalow directly across the street from us, trimmed with flowers and evergreen bushes. At first there was no man in view, so we had imagined she was unmarried. We observed her in her garden with shears and a trowel, wearing heavy gloves, shaded by a straw hat, an aloof, sour lady whom we avoided when she refused to acknowledge greetings. But it was close living on Richton Street, and we were bound to become acquainted.

I'll have occasion to speak of our Detroit weather. Summer days can transform this city on the Canadian border into a steamy, southern place. The Richton Street elms stretch toward each other across the narrow roadway to join twigs. The elm tree in front of our house soared three stories high. Our view of the neighborhood from the upper flat was strained through leaves. We could spy on Mrs. Emerson without her knowing. There was little to see, however. She snipped at bushes, tidied borders. On Sundays she would put on a white hat and veil, white gloves, and voyage by bus to a distant neighborhood, where there was a church of her choice.

This was the lady to whom Fred Emerson returned one stifling summer night.

It was a week of doldrums; our Richton Street neighborhood seemed as becalmed as a ship at sea, a tedious time. We had no air conditioning to help us bear it. Even at night there was little relief. All the porches along Richton were occupied. Cigarettes pulsed like stars. Kids gathered under street lamps. We could see card games on screen porches. We heard the drone of voices spiked by laughter, and we picked up familiar histories from wisps of sounds that drifted our way. Everyone's pleasures and resentments were exposed for a public airing. Richton Street was still relaxed, despite the tightening of screws in Europe.

We crowded our porch. Ernie and I sat on the stone rail beneath the awning. Jake and Evka rocked in the glider, a grinding of springs as they reared back, a squealing release as they moved forward. We slugged ourselves in pursuit of mosquitoes. No laughter from our porch, because Jake concentrated on the daily news, bending close because of the dim, yellow light, a newspaper fanatic who wasn't eased by reports from Europe. Hitler had claimed the Sudetenland. England and France had said at Munich, "All right, but this is the last straw. This and no more." We had come to believe that the supply of straw was inexhaustible. Hitler would pick the bones of every Jew in Europe without the Allies interceding.

It was at this quiet moment of our Detroit summer that we made the acquaintance of Fred Emerson. The gentile house across the street was dark, no evidence it was inhabited, the blinds down, an aloof house that belonged to a different history and refused to participate in ours. Then the house erupted. A lady yelled, "Help me! Help!"

Her yell froze gliders and petrified kids in puddles of light. Only Jake moved. He rocked the house as he pounded downstairs.

The porch light went on across the street. The lady staggered from her house, dragging a skinny man anchored to her wrist. He was trying to haul her back. She almost jerked free, when he hit her with his fist and knocked her down. Then he kicked her. She wrapped her arms around her head. This man kicked her once, twice, but not again. Jake was on him, and then, of course, it was no contest. One squeeze from my pa, and Emerson, still convalescent from the TB, was helpless.

The lady, noticing the audience she had attracted, clasped her face and rushed back inside, leaving Jake to meet Fred Emerson without any introduction.

"You hit a lady," Jake bellowed, "with your fist?"

"She's my wife," Emerson croaked, that immense voice a shock coming from its frail source. "That bitch is my wife."

"So you kick her because she's your wife?" The neighbors advised Jake to call the police, but he was no lover of cops, having suffered Cossacks in the land of his birth. He led Fred Emerson into our flat, and there Fred Emerson covered his face and released sobs like whooping cough.

"Take it easy," Jake said. "I got no intention to call the police. Get a grip on yourself."

"Christ," Emerson said. "I never let go like this. Never." And he let go some more. Jake waved us out of the room. We listened behind the kitchen door. "Ruined," Emerson said. "I'm finished. She killed me."

He had returned home after a long stint in a TB sanatorium. His wife had received his pension check each month, but another gentleman from the church of her choice received all the profit. So Fred Emerson claimed. He had arrived from California the preceding week, where he had been hunting for work in a congenial climate, but no use. He had returned home jobless and broke. He had endured everything because there had been a prospect of a lovely reunion. Then what a greeting! Ruined! Finished!

Who knows what in fact he had discovered? I afterward had enough experience of Fred Emerson to know he could invent a world of conspiracy and betrayal. He understood his own possibilities, so he trusted no one. That plain lady a whore? It's more likely that Emerson was crazy at the time.

"I never let go like this," he assured Jake. "Never again. Never." Within a few weeks the Emersons sold their bungalow and moved from Richton to be among their own. However, that wasn't the last of Fred Emerson; only the beginning.

The Emersons were reconciled. Perhaps she proved his suspicions were wrong. Or maybe she waited until he ran out of gas and overwhelmed him with her own madness. Who knows what he might have been with different luck? He had once fancied himself promising in the political line. Jake restored his hope and got him a job at Atlas.

Hyman Kravitz said, "A load of wet wash would break him in two. What kind of cripples do you bring me, Gottlieb?"

"Give him a chance," Jake urged. "I know you're looking for a driver, and he's a tough little guy, even if he don't seem to be. Hire him, Kravitz; he'll work like a slave."

Kravitz didn't know at the time that Jake was organizing Atlas. He had a soft spot for Jake. When he later found out what Jake was plotting, he wouldn't have hired Atlas himself if he had come with Jake's recommendation.

Fred Emerson said in our living room, "You saved my life, Gottlieb. I won't forget."

I won't forget, either.

When I first saw Emerson in his Atlas uniform he seemed ridiculous. Sallow, cadaverous, his face eroded by acne scars, he couldn't even support his emblem. The pleated shirt billowed; the globe sagged to the small of his back.

Though I deny Fred Emerson a great deal, I give him credit for tenacity. I saw him stagger under weights that bent him double, but he hung on. Despite his load of troubles, he refused to sink.

"He loves me," Jake said. "In this world of finks I know I can rely on Fred Emerson. I forgive him his bad character."

Fred Emerson came to our house and didn't expect us to return the favor. He never made reference to that summer night.

"He's my right arm," Jake said. But neither Ernie nor I had Jake's sunny view of Emerson. We felt that, if he were ever in a position to get revenge for humiliation, Jake had better watch his step.

"He's a lion," Jake said. "I got to hold him back. He wants a strike now before we even have a place to wash." Jake advised Emerson not to take chances. "Slow down. Time is on our side. The union grows stronger every day. We got to be ready for a long, tough struggle."

25

"Hit him in the pocket, Jake. That's all we need to do. Hit him in the pocket and he'll fold, believe me. I know the type."

Emerson went all out for Jake. I put that in the scales to balance his other actions.

"With a dozen like him," Jake told ma, "I could organize the industry in two weeks."

He told Jake not to fear Happy Weinberg. "We're behind you, Jake. They'll have to take us all on."

Ernie warned pa, "You humiliated him; he won't forgive you."

"Fifteen years old and already you're so wise?"

When Emerson came to visit us, he ignored the house he had lived in for twenty years. His wife had spent her childhood on Richton Street. He turned his back on that bungalow. He parked his car in front of it, but didn't look. He wasn't curious about the Jewish family that occupied his home. He discarded his own history, and I always wondered, what couldn't Emerson forget?

He told Jake, "I owe you my life. You can count on me forever."

IV

SAMMY PERSKY was the main target of Emerson's spite. There were many, like Emerson, who adored Jake Gottlieb. But only Sammy was his pal, and that was a mystery to everyone.

Sammy was an Atlas driver. He was a little guy with a flourishing mustache tipped in wax. He had the biggest route at Atlas. He had sports talk for barbershops, politics for Jewish delicatessens, either a leer or boyish sincerity for Jewish housewives, depending on age and temperament. Though he was Jake's old pal, he was an intimate of Hyman Kravitz as well. He shamelessly enlisted in every camp, sucking up to power like a bee nosing honey.

"How can you trust him?" Fred Emerson asked Jake. "He leaks everything."

Emerson kept his eyes on Sammy. He knew how many trips Sammy made up front to see the boss. "They're arm-squeezing buddies." Was it an accident that Sammy had the best route at Atlas, big stops close to the plant?

"When it comes to selling, he's a genius," Jake said in defense of Sammy. "Customers are crazy about him."

Emerson considered it a bitter irony when he heard someone refer to Sammy at a union meeting as Brother Persky. "That fink is no one's brother. He'd leak on himself if there was an advantage."

Jake told him to stop hounding Sammy. "You got an obsession with the subject. Save your spite for Kravitz."

Emerson didn't have to hoard his spite. It wasn't in scarce supply. He was loaded with spite. Spite seemed to have exploded his acne-scarred face. In profile there was a serenity that vanished when you met him head on and saw the ravage of a handsome man.

"Don't put us in the same class," he told Jake. "It's not me who has a love affair going with the boss."

"It's an old story to me that you don't care for Sammy Persky. Put on a new record."

"Don't think I just don't care for him, Jake; I *hate* the little bastard." When he heard that we planned to spend our summer vacation with Mr. and Mrs. Persky, he was shocked. Close quarters with that fink? Didn't Jake have obligations to the union? What if Kravitz learned about the organizing campaign and the strike plans? "Half the working day Persky is up front with Kravitz. He don't even bother to hide it any more."

"I don't worry about Sammy Persky," Jake said.

"I worry. Kravitz knows every move we make."

"How do you know what Kravitz knows? Are you also on speaking terms with Kravitz?"

"One of these days," Emerson said, "you'll learn the truth about Persky and you'll have to do something about him."

"What suggestions do you have?"

"Teach him a lesson."

"What can I teach a smart aleck like Sammy?"

"Teach him a big mouth is a big target."

"For what is it a target?"

28

"For this." Emerson held up a meager fist. His frame didn't grow muscle with exercise, but became even more brittle. He knew where there were fists available for the instruction of Sammy Persky.

"You're his size," Jake said. "Do it yourself."

Emerson couldn't bear the thought of Jake setting up house with Sammy Persky. He begged Jake to reconsider. He was continually in our living room and kitchen, pressing Jake to alter his summer plans.

"How can you believe Persky's a union man?"

"He signed up, didn't he?"

"What for? What's he after?"

"Maybe he wants the affection of his brothers. How's that for an explanation?"

"Don't give me that bullshit. You're talking about Sammy Persky, the ass-grabber."

There had been many complaints about Sammy's behavior with the ladies. Jake had warned Sammy, who apologized for his weakness but continued to indulge it. Almost a hundred ladies worked on the inside of the Atlas Laundry and Linen Supply Service, which covered a block of a Negro slum, a grimy plant filled with vats and presses, steam hissing when presses clamped down. In summer you could see sweat stains grow from armpits and spread down backs. By the end of the day the ladies were drenched. They operated irons, folded shirts, wrapped bundles, stirred the vats. It was hot on the inside, and business was informal. The ladies wore fashions that anticipated modern dress. Breasts were on view and no girdles. When Sammy Persky walked behind a line of working ladies, yells followed in his wake.

He was vulgar and lightheaded in serious times. I heard Jake say to my mother, "From where comes such a Jew, a rump-pincher, a crotch-grabber, a taste for the ladies? His pa was a religious man."

Yet Jake arranged to spend our summer with the Perskys. Emerson wanted to know why.

"I appreciate that you're a nice guy, Jake. You won't convict Persky till the evidence is in. But that don't mean you need to move in with him. A tent is God-damn' close living."

Emerson dropped in to visit without calling. He was rudely indifferent to Ernie and me. He was barely civil to Ma, not even waiting for greetings to be exchanged before he started in on Sammy.

"Maybe you don't trust my word," Emerson told Jake. "But I know someone who is going to convince you to stay clear of Persky." He mentioned McIntyre.

"What does McIntyre have against Sammy?"

"That he's a fink who masquerades as a brother. That's what he has against Sammy Persky."

V

---·◆·---

EMERSON PICKED on the right man to present the case against
Persky. McIntyre impressed everyone as the model of a ju-
dicial temperament. The size of him argued against any malice.
He didn't need recourse to petty means to see that justice
was done. He could lean on you, and his goal would be accomplished.

He was another union stalwart, another powerful right arm.
His arms had their own monumental status apart from the
rest of him. You were directed toward his arms as if naked
ladies hung from his shoulders. While Jake put forty-seven
years into cultivating an arm like the one on the baking-soda
box, McIntyre made no effort to establish a presence that was
a gift of nature. When he sat wedged into our plush armchair, his knees were pointed in different directions. All his
parts were monumental. His feet were huge; if his shoes
survived him, they could do service as monuments. He had
foot trouble and wore high shoes with hooks instead of eyelets.

A heart, penetrated by an arrow, tattooed on his left forearm, was the only sign of anything dissorderly in McIntyre. His trouble was, perhaps, a too vulnerable heart, lying right there beneath his sleeve, an easy target. Yet, until rough times bowled him over, he impressed me as absolutely solid and reliable, the type of American we encountered in movies conducting wagon trains west.

Why did he join our cause? I viewed him as one of the beefy, stately kind who don't need to make a dent in the world, since they only have to claim their birthright in order to have everything. When McIntyre visited us, I felt that I was the guest and he was the host. He had a long face with a heavy chin, a large nose without any of the coarse swerves we scorned as flesh out of control. He had sandy hair and blue eyes, a fair complexion we found exotic and superior to our own.

In those days McIntyre was another one down on his luck, a hopeless plodder with a low opinion of himself. He treated Ernie and me as if he considered us princelings and himself merely a common soldier. I feared that if he discovered his error in judgment and remembered how he'd toadied, he would make us pay for his shame.

Jake inspired this plodder. "You do the selling. You do the driving. You sort the laundry. You carry the bundles. So haven't you earned a fair share of the profits?" Jake bullied and coaxed. The depression still lingered to remind workers that a job meant life or death. McIntyre had three kids. The littlest—a five-year-old retarded girl—spent her days howling. Nonetheless, McIntyre risked his job out of devotion to Jake. He had a connection with Jake that he never forged with others. He was the tight-lipped sort I never expected would utter his private griefs, yet he spilled everything to Jake. He saw no limit to his grief and he had to talk, and Jake was the man. He held nothing back. He told all.

McIntyre's wife refused to surrender the retarded child to an asylum. She insisted the girl would recover. But what was there to recover, since the girl was witless from the beginning? McIntyre's wife believed the child would never speak until appropriate sacrifices were made for unknown sins. At the right moment the child would deliver the gift of her wits. She would awaken like Sleeping Beauty. It might happen the next minute or the next year. The mother was prepared to wait a lifetime.

The girl had long, blond hair, placid eyes, a sweet mouth. McIntyre saw his own features there, but glorified. She would look at you so calmly, so trustingly—so knowingly—that you weren't prepared for what happened. She stretched her mouth wide and howled. She kept it up till her breath was exhausted. Then she wound up for more. She shrieked, but her eyes didn't change, still that serene look. She couldn't be pacified. You made faces, did tricks, begged, made clucking sounds, hugged her, kissed her, comforted her. The eyes followed with mild interest but the shrieks continued, an hour at a time, then suddenly stopped. After you were adjusted to silence she started again. At night they gave her sedatives.

Emerson advised McIntyre to give the girl up. "What can you do for the poor kid? Kravitz could be her pa for all the difference it makes. She'll be better off with nurses who make a profession out of kids like that. Meanwhile you got to worry you might lose a wife; she looks bad."

The wife no longer took care of herself. She wore baggy dresses that had fitted properly when she'd been twenty pounds heavier. She was beginning to crack. "How can you eat?" she asked McIntyre when he urged her to eat.

For a year now the wife wouldn't let McIntyre fool around with love. At first she'd made an effort, lying rigid beneath him when he was determined to have some pleasure. She'd begun imitating the daughter's lunatic serenity, perhaps trying to discover what her daughter felt, by assuming her expression. She shrieked, too. She practiced little moans under her breath. McIntyre knew what she was doing and gave up any attempt at love. His work was bad enough, but his home was a horror.

There were the other children, and McIntyre didn't have the heart to consider what sort of life it was for them.

Jake told McIntyre to take his problems to a preacher.

McIntyre blurted out the rest of the story. He couldn't go to his preacher, because there was a complication—Kate Russo, one hundred and fifty pounds of voluptuous woman. She had a marvelous shape. Kate knew where you were when you were on top of her. For almost six months he'd been doing business with Kate Russo.

It was amazing to Jake how this Presbyterian opened up. All the details.

He met Kate one night at the plant when he was late bringing in a load of dirty linen. McIntyre had been kidding her for some time. She invited him to share her pasta. He called home; a lot his wife cared. Kate had a small kitchen, and, while she was at the stove, he passed behind her to get wine from the icebox, and they bumped.

"We burned the God-damn' pasta" this Presbyterian told Jake, leering like a satyr. She fought. She slugged him. She packed a wallop. He wrenched off her blouse, tore her brassiere, kissed her breasts. (It's incredible to me that anyone would tell such things to Jake, who was a prude. But, though shocked, he repeated the story to Ma.) Kate clawed his face. He let her rip. All this in the kitchen. He hauled her, kicking, into the bedroom. She fought, but no yells. She didn't wear a girdle. Oh, McIntyre was proud of his conquest. He wanted Jake to hear how every round had gone. Don't think Ernie and I didn't drink it in, too. He pulled down her pants and clutched. Then she quit fighting. She pitched and rolled like a ship in a storm. And so on. For six months she was in his blood, the whore, letting everyone grab, going up front into Kravitz' office, denying that anything passed between her and Boss Kravitz.

"What's it matter to you, anyway?" she asked, a tough lady, with coarse black hair that came down to her waist when she released the coils. She had great eyes. "Expect me to wait around till an idea comes into your head? Do you think you're the Prince of Wales?" The possession of a mistress was a royal prerogative, not a laundry driver's. The preacher would tell him to give her up. He couldn't. What should he do?

"You have a daughter," Jake advised him in a prophetic bass, "what requires your attention." Then, leaning forward, his outrage apparent, "You think you can play around like a Rockefeller when you're only a laundryman? Any day you might lose your job. You got responsibilities to a family. You got responsibilities to your fellow workers."

Once I knew the story, I was embarrassed to be in McIntyre's presence. He had signified to me something that was enviably American. Afterward he seemed like a fool, sitting in our armchair, his meaty, freckled hands in his lap, not enough room for his knees, grinning like a silly kid while Jake bawled him out.

I have good reason to remember these men, the McIntyres, the Emersons, the Perskys, the Kravitzes, the whole Atlas crowd. They came to our house, and no one chased us when there was strong talk. I woke up at night hearing sounds from the kitchen. Ernie was also awake. We went to the kitchen and saw them seated at the table. Tea for Jake, beer for Emerson and McIntyre.

Emerson and McIntyre always seemed to me an unlikely pair. In Emerson's face the disappointed hopes and wasted talent were apparent. His strength had turned sour, and he was incapable of any impartial estimate of Sammy Persky. McIntyre, on the other hand, was magisterial, a man of size, the form of dignity still intact. He was greatly influenced by Emerson, who beguiled him with rumors of conspiracies.

He shared Emerson's contempt for Persky. "He blabs, Jake. Maybe he don't mean to fink, but he blabs." Kate Russo had called him in to complain. That smart aleck Sammy had passed behind her; she'd whipped around and shaken her fist.

"What you grabbing, creep?"

Sammy made a shape with his hands, "I was trying the fit, honey."

She showed him her fist. "This fits, too, you bastard."

He grabbed his crotch. "This, too, darling," and scrammed when she hoisted a flatiron.

Kate Russo had told McIntyre, "Make that wise guy keep his hands to himself."

McIntyre asked her how come she needed help. She could handle Sammy if she wanted to.

"He don't think I can make trouble," she said. "He keeps on grabbing hold. He thinks he's so thick with the big boy."

"Kravitz?"

"Just keep your ears open when Sammy's around," Kate had advised. "I hear them talking."

"What do they say?"

"Watch yourself, Mac."

After such evidence McIntyre wondered how Jake could resist taking measures. How could he share a summer tent with Persky?

"And that's the evidence you expect will hang Sammy Persky? Do you think I'm a fool? Do you imagine that I'll give serious attention to what your Italian lady says? Lay off Persky," Jake ordered them. "You got Persky on the brain. So what if he's a wise guy? Is that a hanging offense? He's Brother Persky. Don't sneer at the idea; get used to it. It's Brother McIntyre and Brother Emerson and Brother Gottlieb. Let it also be Brother Persky. It's not impossible to say. Remember that we're involved in serious business. Don't underestimate Kravitz. He won't go under without making war. We need to stick together like brothers. Otherwise we got no chance. The other side has all the guns and ammunition, while we only got each other."

I've heard the sermons of Jake Gottlieb. I could always be moved by his rhetoric because I believed in his vision. He knew that Emerson was malicious. He knew that McIntyre was ready to explode after steady humiliations. He knew that Sammy Persky was an irresponsible ass-grabber. He knew that almost every one of the fifty drivers at Atlas Laundry and Linen was in some way a damaged man. He wanted to make them whole again through the strike. Through the strike, men would be reconciled to each other. They would become brothers. He urged us to admire the artist in Fred Emerson, whom he had seen shape a boat into being, a marvelous carpenter. That was a man who could be redeemed by the union. The old song advised, ". . . the union makes you strong." They would strike Atlas. They would undergo siege together. They would hold the fort together. They would bleed together, and in the mingling of blood become kin. His object was to form a brotherhood, and he didn't want us to refuse Emerson, just as he didn't want Emerson and McIntyre to deny Sammy Persky.

Well, Hyman Kravitz had other ideas.

VI

ONE MORNING, while the drivers were in the shed loading up,
Kravitz entered on the hunt for a target. You didn't need sharp
eyes to spot McIntyre, who was a lovely target for a nag like
Kravitz. Kravitz worked in a white shirt and tie, his sleeves
rolled, exhibiting pudgy arms. He was a little guy, tight-lipped,
with sarcastic eyes. He got very close to you when he talked.
He stared so openly you felt that you had caught him peeping,
and still he refused to turn away.

He was sole owner of the Atlas Laundry and Linen Supply
Service. He had designed the blue uniform the men wore.
Kravitz dreamed of empire, and if he had owned legions he
would have realized his dream. He had an imperial manner.
He was older than Jake, perhaps fifty.

Despite his paunch and double chin, Kravitz was intimidating. A tone in his voice suggested that you, too, but for the
grace of his close watching, would be a thief. He stood in front
of you, peering into your face, his hands on his hips, and if you

didn't hit him you were reduced to slavishness. You dropped your eyes. You squirmed. You were flustered. He had green eyes and looked like an Irishman, but he came from our neighborhood, a Dexter boy, who lived three blocks from us.

"You got a big load, McIntyre?"

"It's Monday, Boss."

"Come five o'clock and you're finished; correct, McIntyre?"

"That's right."

"You wouldn't happen to know where the clock is located, McIntyre?"

Loading laundry at six in the morning is not a joyful beginning to a day. Those bundles might weigh over fifty pounds. McIntyre, whose mornings were guaranteed to have a miserable beginning before he even left the house, was hard pressed to endure anything.

"The clock over there. Which I pay you by. Where you stick your card into. The clock. You got your eye on the clock, McIntyre. Right?"

"No, sir! I do not!"

"Let me give you a new thought for a new week, McIntyre." Kravitz spoke loudly, and the other drivers in the shed stopped loading. What a dreary place that shed was! It smelled of engine exhaust, of grease and oil, of gasoline fumes, of wet wash. From the doors of the loading platform steam issued. You could hear the long exhalation of the presses, the chugging of boilers. On a hot summer day you felt as if you were in a swamp. But, still, it was a job. And not a bad job. Yet even if it were a bad job, a job. Someone in McIntyre's fix couldn't afford to be touchy. What could you do when you were faced by this Mussolini of the Atlas Laundry and Linen Empire? Lower your eyes and look stupid. "I want you to think about this, McIntyre. When you're out on the road selling, delivering, making pickups, then you're worth something to me. Right here in the garage you do me no good. I don't make a cent till your truck is moving. Isn't that right, McIntyre?"

McIntyre was forced to agree.

39

"You're not alone in watching the clock. It has interest for me, too. And it's right we should be interested. Time is money. My money, eh, McIntyre? You only do me good until five o'clock. Do you see what I'm getting at? Does it penetrate?"

Kravitz probed your eyes, searching for what? Thieves and malingerers? Conspirators? I know how that man could needle. You see him with his fists on his hips, and in his face a merciless, exuberant malice that burned brighter when stoked by a plea for pity. Don't imagine I haven't a good word for Kravitz. I do. But let's face it. He was a ferocious and cruel nag.

"I'll spell it out in simple language, so you can understand. The way you shuffle cards, I see you're an expert. Now I ask you a favor, please. No card tricks on my time. You get what I mean? You want I should be more clear? All right. Don't—DON'T—Don't the minute you show up in the garage start thinking about cards. Think instead that time is money. Wait until the truck is loaded. Wait until you're ready to go on the road. Then, McIntyre—THEN—then you can do your fancy business with cards. Then you can say, hello, to the time clock. That's the thought I give you for the new week. Does it penetrate, McIntyre? EH?"

McIntyre tried holding off until Kravitz was gone. The provocation was too great, and before Kravitz was out of the shed he groaned, "Bastard!" Kravitz waved McIntyre over to him.

"You got three kids, no?"

"That's right."

"The little one's sick, correct?"

"Yes."

"I take an interest in you, McIntyre. Are you nervous?"

"No."

"Your trouble is, you don't get enough sleep. I checked up."

"I sleep okay."

"No, McIntyre. You should get a full eight hours. That's a tough job, driving a truck. I'm worried that you don't take care of yourself. Why do you stay up till one o'clock Sunday nights drinking beer? You should confine your social activities to Sat-

40

urdays. Your health is your capital. I know you got exciting things to communicate to Jake Gottlieb. All you revolutionaries. But on a Sunday night, till one in the morning—you risk your health. Look at you. Irritable. Maybe you'll talk back to a customer. Maybe you'll lose a stop. That puts me in a tough position, McIntyre. Don't do like Jake Gottlieb, who got no sick girl to trouble him. Maybe he can afford to hold social evenings on Sunday night, but you, McIntyre—you better worry about your health."

It had been a secret meeting. All the union members in the shop had been present. They had discussed organization strategy at that meeting. Now Kravitz knew something. Perhaps everything. Someone among them was a fink. McIntyre and Emerson again nominated Sammy Persky for the role.

"It's Persky, all right, Jake. You can bet your life on it."

This was a couple of days before we began our summer vacation with the Perskys.

McIntyre was a different man in the wake of humiliation. He roamed our kitchen, his face very red, pounding his fist into his palm, not humble any more.

"I don't have to take that shit from a little fat-ass." For a moment, listening in the hallway outside the kitchen, I feared something else would come after the "fat." "They're pouring it on. Do I have to take it any more?" he demanded of Jake. "That son of a bitch, Persky. Messing around with the girls. Who says Persky is a union man? How come you trust that runt? Smart-aleck little bastard with his filthy mustache." I've mentioned Persky's mustache. It resembled the elegant bush you expect to find on Rumanians who claim to be royalty. Too elegant for a laundry driver. I can understand that McIntyre would consider any man with such a mustache a potential fink. With a mustache like that, Sammy Persky must have had ambitions no truck driver could support.

Even before Kate Russo had complained about Sammy's pinching, McIntyre had despised him for the usual reasons— Sammy was a loudmouth and a wise guy and joked about

41

serious matters. And besides, he had reached for parts of Kate Russo which McIntyre knew to be accessible and responsive. McIntyre was ordinarily a sensible man; he probably had good reason to suspect Sammy Persky. There clearly was a fink, and Sammy was a friend of Kravitz.

VII

—◆—

JAKE SPOKE to Sammy a few days later and told him to stay away from Kravitz. "How is it that a common truck driver like you associates with such royalty as Kravitz? What do you find to talk about?"

They spoke while in the boat, with Sammy rowing. They arrived at the lake each Saturday night and left early Monday morning. Sammy in a bathing suit exhibited spindly legs, slightly bowed, with hard knots in the thighs and calves. He had narrow shoulders, a soft, pallid torso. He didn't bulge with muscles as Jake did. Yet he made that boat fly. Though he showed little evidence of strength, he was a good athlete. You could see from the way he danced that he had fine control of his body. After some schnapps or wine he turned on the radio and danced with his wife. Minnie Persky was a blimp-shaped woman, but dainty. Sammy's taste for big ladies was well noted. Mrs. Persky adored her husband. She was so tickled by Sammy that she didn't bother to see the blemishes in his character. She was of good cheer and a pleasure to have around, and I could only have wished her better luck in a husband. She had a moon face, which after several days of sun turned an uneven pink, white showing whenever the creases in her neck and chins straightened out. When Sammy commanded her to dance, she stood up like a good sport and wiggled. He kazatskied around her, kicking his legs way out, his rump almost hitting the floor. He caught her hands and whirled her across the room. She quaked with laughter.

"What do you talk to Kravitz about?" Jake asked him.

"He likes me. We talk." When, later, Jake told Ma about the conversation, he imitated Sammy's wink and elbowed her side. "Me and him got the same taste in girls."

Jake reminded Sammy that he was a union man with all the responsibilities.

"Absolutely," Sammy agreed. "First and last. A union man. Still, I got no hard feelings."

An irresponsible fool! Yet who could deny the goodness of his heart? Jake warned him, nonetheless.

"We got a fink. I'd give no insurance on his head if they find out who it is. The boys are nervous. Don't be so friendly with Kravitz."

Sammy protested. Did he have to be a fink? What was in it for him? He didn't have to be a fink. He didn't have to be a union man. He had no gripes. He was making sixty bucks a week, the largest route in the company, all because of his salesmanship. Kravitz needed Sammy more than Sammy needed Kravitz. Kravitz liked Sammy. "But because I'm Jake Gottlieb's bosom pal I put everything on the line. When Gottlieb says, 'Join the union,' I sign my name at the head of the list even though I have everything to lose. So what's all this fink bullshit?"

"I'm just telling you, Sammy—be careful. Because if anything should happen to you, I'd suffer. You matter to me, so I'd suffer. Yet if it was my own son who was the fink—if it was my Ernie—I'd smash his mouth myself. I'd tear out his tongue with my own hands. Be careful, Sammy. Give no one grounds for suspicion. Watch yourself."

You could trust Sammy's heart. But could you trust Sammy's mouth? Kravitz had a line of charm that appealed to Sammy. Kravitz was so resolute, so fierce-willed, that it seemed especially rewarding to a clown like Sammy to be responsible for loosening him up. To see Kravitz smile—even though the smile was sardonic and his good word delivered with contempt—was compensation enough. Kravitz made you feel that, if you wanted a battle, he'd stop short of nothing. He was a match for Jake in that regard, and it was one reason they weren't eager to tangle unless there was a life-or-death occasion. When you got Kravitz to smile, you felt that it was a considerable achievement and that you had been spared a dreadful time.

Jake knew all along that Kravitz wouldn't easily loosen his grip on Atlas. Jake wanted to hold off the strike till it would do the most damage. He aimed for the Christmas season.

"What are we waiting for?" Emerson wanted to know. "He's not so tough. Hit him in the pocket."

"What do you eat to develop such heart?" Jake asked him. "You go around hitting pockets and you could blow yourself up. How do you know what a man's got in his pockets?"

He praised Emerson's spirit, but where was his good sense? Most of the drivers didn't own a truck. Did Emerson expect them to use wheelbarrows? And if they pulled their routes from Atlas, where would they wash? Did Emerson think the wives could do the job at home in their tubs? "Is your lady ready to do the Metropole's linen, Emerson? Will she starch uniforms, fold napkins? Until we find a place to wash, we're stuck with Hy Kravitz."

"So we'll find a place," Emerson said.

"You think it's easy to find someone willing to risk war with Hy Kravitz? Not everyone is a lion like you, Emerson. The entire industry is on the side of Kravitz and will see to it that anyone who co-operates with us has troubles. Whoever washes for us can expect to have his business raided. You got no idea

45

the tricks Hy Kravitz has up his sleeve. We can expect Weinberg and Spiegelman. And what can we offer for such favors? What payment for such a sacrifice? Our good will? We'll call the victim Brother? I appreciate your fine sentiments, Emerson. If you can show me a place to wash, you'll find I'm as ready as you to hit Kravitz in the pocket."

Emerson continued visiting us during the summer even though we shared a tent with Sammy Persky.

We had a site on a hilly campground that overlooked Walled Lake. We had a squad-sized pyramidal tent with low side walls. We were planted among umbrella tents, cabin tents, trailers, makeshift wooden frames covered by tarpaulins. We enlarged our tent by stretching a tarp over two-by-fours and putting screens on the sides. Here we set up our kitchen—an icebox, a kerosene stove, two card tables, folding chairs.

Inside, there was an earthy, mushroom odor that is still the atmosphere of my good dreams.

Emerson arrived on a brilliant, hot Sunday. The lake below was populated with boats. The beaches were crowded. We were all in bathing suits, even Minnie Persky. A slight breeze rippled the cheesecloth that screened the raised tent-sides—a roomy tent, a ridgepole, green canvas hoisted on two center poles, the sides anchored by ropes and pegs. We plugged into an outlet that provided electricity for two bulbs and our Philco radio. The baseball season was under way and the voice of Ty Tyson droned every afternoon like a buzzing fly as he chronicled the Detroit Tigers and the mighty Greenberg at first base.

Emerson refused our efforts to make his visit cordial. We had a fine vista but he wouldn't look. He came on union business, and to make that clear he wore his Atlas uniform. He sat in a folding chair, his back turned to the lake.

Sammy asked him how come the uniform on a Sunday. "You're some go-getter, Freddy, a real American boy."

"You're damn' right."

"Relax. Put on a swimsuit; I'll lend you one of mine. I bet

46

you got some physique under that shirt. You wiry little guys are always a surprise."

"Talk, talk," Emerson said. "I'll tell you one thing for sure, Persky. You won't have the last word."

After the Perskys left for the beach, Emerson told Jake he had found a plant that would wash for the Atlas drivers if there was a strike.

Jake asked me and Ernie to take a walk, even though we were tuned in to the ball game.

They were still talking when we returned, but they ignored us.

"You think I don't know about White Swan? You think I haven't been to Oswego? I know all about it. It's not news to me. You come here like you're Christopher Columbus and have found a new country, but I been there already. I know Sal Fiori. To trust Sal Fiori of White Swan is to invite your executioner into the house. He's a big talker with the heart of a chicken. What will happen when Kravitz finds out Fiori is washing for us?"

"You're the boss, Jake. I been working my ass off, taking long trips on my own time, asking questions which can bring me nothing but trouble. I didn't realize I was stepping on your toes."

Jake was responsible for fifty men and wanted to move carefully. "Don't be impatient," he told Emerson. "The days of Kravitz are numbered."

Jake visited Fiori in Oswego, a town about fifty miles from Detroit. Fiori, glittering with suspicion, denied that he feared retaliation from the industry.

"What they gonna do? I'll tell you what they gonna do. They gonna cry a little; then they gonna say, 'Sal, why do you want to fuck your pals?' An' I'll tell 'em, 'For money, pals. This ain't Russia. I ain't stealin'. I'm workin' honest. We still got free competition in America.'" He could provide trucks if the men struck, but he didn't want the trucks marked. He didn't want the industry to find out he was doing the wash. He wasn't afraid, but what business was it of theirs? "What they don't know, can't hurt me." He insisted that every precaution be taken to keep his part secret. Trips made at night. Care taken to avoid being followed.

Jake had no confidence in Fiori. "What happens to his nerve when the industry finds out he's washing for us? You have never been in a war like Kravitz will make."

Emerson was convinced the strike would be short. "I guarantee you, Jake. He loves the green."

"I know. Hit him in the pocket. Don't be surprised, Emerson, when Kravitz hits back and he don't aim just for pockets. You got a wrong impression of Kravitz."

Jake didn't have Emerson's simple view of the boss. When he was summoned to the front office, he was ready for trouble.

I knew the office, a small cubicle between the loading shed and the plant. It was a cluttered, grubby place, crammed with desks, the only amenity a mildewed sofa that was squeezed between file cabinets. The sofa was a lumpy business that couldn't have been much fun for the girls. There was an autographed photo of Herbert Hoover on the wall to establish that Kravitz was a private-enterprise man.

He invited Jake to sit down, relax, be comfortable. He wanted a friendly talk. Kravitz despised athletics and exercise. He appeared to be soft, except for his face, which was as hard as a convict's. The Atlas Laundry and Linen Supply Service was his single preoccupation.

"I know you're tough, Gottlieb. But do I hold it against you that you want to screw me? Listen. In your shoes I would do the same. A man like you—an educated man who knows the classics—you shouldn't be lifting bundles. With such talents, why waste your time? You think these jerks will be grateful? If you believe such a thing, your condition hasn't improved since the day you were born. I'll tell you one thing, for sure, Gottlieb. There is not a single man of them I couldn't put in my pocket. You think I'm not such a nice guy, okay. At least I got something above the neck besides a lot of bone. I'm your pal,

Gottlieb; when will you know it? There are guys in this business who got no heart, and if they find someone playing footsie with the union, they won't stop with scaring you a little. They might think, 'What's a bump on the head to Gottlieb? He's a stubborn man.' There'd be threats against the wife and the kiddies. Right now you're lucky to be dealing with Hy Kravitz, who's got a heart. But I'm the exception, remember that. I take an interest in you. I know it's only a question of time till you get smart and realize what really gripes you is that you are on the bottom, and until there's an adjustment you'll stir up the world. Who blames you? Move up! There's room. I'm even ready to give a boost."

When Jake asked what kind of a boost, Kravitz checked both doors, then perched on the desk above Jake. "You and me can talk. When I say a boost, sonny boy, I mean I want you to get away from lifting bundles. Think big, Gottlieb. Think in terms of a business of your own."

Kravitz, like Jake, was a passionate man. He was on the job fourteen hours a day. He'd started with a hand laundry and a garage and ended with a plant that sprawled over a city block. Save for him the Atlas Laundry and Linen Supply Service would not have existed. One hundred and fifty employees would have had a different mode of being. Kravitz considered this one block of the automobile capital of the world to be a monument to himself. I'm sure he believed that his employees—the girls inside, the boilermen, the office help, the drivers outside—should have offered grace to Kravitz every time they put food in their mouths.

Kravitz said to Jake in the first interview, "Watch yourself, Gottlieb. Don't count on an old softy like me. You know what a tender son of a bitch I am. If it were only up to me, I'd say, make a revolution. Run me out of business and starve in the streets. Don't imagine I'll suffer. You won't trouble me with strikes. So go ahead and ruin yourselves. That's the kind of easy touch I am. But there are others involved who aren't good-natured guys like me. The whole industry is annoyed by your

49

union. You'll find there are men so cold hearted that before they let you have a penny they will dump you like garbage into Lake St. Clair. And you wouldn't be the only one those no-good bastards would go after. They wouldn't spare the kiddies, either. Not you, not your wife, not your two boys. You risk everyone's neck, not just your own. And why? Tell me: why, Gottlieb? Because you're STUPID. I could puke with all that commie bullshit. The workers? Who are the workers?" He pointed toward the laundry room. "But for me—Kravitz—one hundred and fifty corpses."

VIII

———◆———

WE TRIED to keep city troubles from damaging country pleasures. Sammy Persky may not have been a man you'd want in
your squad if you were in combat, but he was perfect for a
vacation. Better him than Emerson any day.

One afternoon he challenged Jake and Ernie to a swimming
contest.

"Let's make it a real contest," Jake said. "All the way across
the lake."

"You'll sink, Gottlieb. You pack too much *shmalts*."

It was decided that I would follow the swimmers in a row-
boat and pick up dropouts.

They waded out chest deep before they started to swim
through the heavy traffic. The lake was cluttered with boats.
A diagonal channel was left open for the Chris-Craft that
streaked across the lake from the amusement-park pier twice
hourly with paying passengers. Our skimpy beach was at the
base of a shaggy knoll, and there Ma and Minnie were planted

on a bedspread among thermos jugs and sandwich bags. I didn't see a vacant spot on the knoll. The entire camp was out in force; dads were in from Detroit, accompanied by aunts and uncles and cousins. Our beach was bounded by boat docks. Reed patches extended into the shallows beyond the docks, and we had to maneuver through a narrow channel.

Twenty yards from shore the bottom dropped away and the traffic thinned out. Ernie and Sammy took the lead. Jake lagged behind. Ernie started with a fine crawl, but there was effort in his stroke. He was nervous and wasn't breathing properly. It must have been disconcerting to have such good form, such a fine body, and to find Sammy effortlessly alongside, using a breast stroke, his chin stretched high to avoid dunking his mustache. Jake was the least promising of the swimmers. I didn't think he had a chance of reaching the other side. He made progress by dint of painful effort. He lurched from the water with every stroke. He flung himself after his arms, first heaving to the left, then to the right, his body jerking from one side to the other as if he struggled to stay afloat. Surprisingly, his stroke never faltered.

The crossing was a considerable distance, and, when we were halfway across, our ladies had already diminished to dots of color on the hillside.

Ernie abandoned the crawl and switched to the side stroke. As we passed between files of fishermen, posted every few yards in the deep water, he turned on his back to rest, and Sammy pulled far ahead. We crossed the trail of the Chris-Craft, an oily wake that sent out iridescent pods. Jake moved at the same labored pace—still no sign of fatigue. Ernie resumed the crawl and spurted ahead a few yards, but Jake closed in. His glistening arms were so massive they looked as if they would sink him rather than keep him afloat. "Want to rest?" he asked when he caught Ernie. "Grab hold of the boat." Ernie launched into a frantic crawl that gained him a few yards, but he couldn't keep it up. Jake passed him and closed in on Sammy, who also lagged. Before Jake caught up, Sammy touched bottom with his toes, stretching to keep his mouth above water. He raised his hands high to claim victory. Jake swam past him.

"It's only a little way," I told Ernie. "You're almost there." We approached a more elegant shore, private beaches, boathouses, barbecue pits, green lawns. Mansions were set in groves of cypress and birch. Jake swam all the way to shore. By the time Ernie was able to touch bottom, Jake had started the swim back. His great arms never altered their labored beat.

"You're crazy, Gottlieb!" Sammy yelled. "A nut!" With Sammy and Ernie aboard, I rowed behind Jake all the way back. He maintained his outrageous form up to our beach.

"If I knew you planned a round trip, I'd have paced myself," Sammy said. "Under the terms of the contest I claim first prize."

Ma dispensed food and drink, but Ernie, stretched out on his belly declined to eat.

Jake promenaded in the shallow water in front of our bedspread, mincing over stones. His drum major's strut made it seem as if he were performing for the entire beach, inviting admiration for his chunky power. In those binding trunks he was a spectacle. His weight centered on bulging thighs clamped together by heavy buttocks. Sammy, walking alongside Jake, illustrated another extreme. He was meager, save for a paunch. His hips barely supported the Hawaiian-print trunks that hung almost to his knees.

Later, Sammy, reclining on the bedspread, his pasty body blotched by the sun, reared up on an elbow and said to my pa in an overflow of companionship, "If Kravitz takes you on, he's got double trouble. I'm right there, Jake. At your side. We'll screw him together."

Jake told him to forget about screwing. "Just be serious. It's no joke any more. Pay attention for once. You never learn. It goes in one ear and out the other. Again and again I tell you, 'Stay away from Kravitz.'"

I don't know why Ernie took the defeat so hard. Did he

53

really expect to compete with our pa, whose one arm was greater than his two? Nonetheless he brooded, and I could see that Jake was annoyed by the long face and the sullen responses. That evening we finished dinner and sat in our kitchen, crickets chirping, locusts humming, bugs flailing our cheesecloth. We smelled barbecue from other kitchens. Our tent smelled of kerosene. We turned on the radio and listened to Hitler speak, a rebroadcast from Nuremberg.

Hitler wanted Germany restored. He wanted Germans under German rule. He wanted to possess Danzig and the Polish Corridor. And who stood in the way of his noble purpose? Bolshevik Jews. He meant to clear out the vermin and purify Germany—and the rest of the world, too, for that matter.

A hushed baritone translated the shriek of Hitler. I made a trip to the privy across the campground in the middle of Hitler's speech. I heard the same gabble from every tent. I heard rumbling *Sieg Heils* as I squatted in the dark privy among spiders and crickets and bleeping frogs. Canvas sprouted all over the hill, billowing with electric light. Through tent walls I saw card players silhouetted, ladies clearing tables. Portable radios echoed our Philco. Some families sat under the stars, relaxing after dinner, papas sprawled in lounge chairs. Who else in the camp feared Hitler? To them he was merely another entertainer. He preceded Chandu the Magician, Ernie's favorite program.

"A magician?" Jake asked. "You want to hear from a magician? At your age? You're too old for that stuff. Forget about magicians. Pay attention to Hitler. He got a message you better listen to."

When Hitler spoke, our Philco seemed to resemble the head of some brutal, fat man, vent slits for eyes, knobs for nostrils, the station indicator for a mouth—like the parabolic head of a wrestler or a storm trooper, broad at the base, inclining toward a point. It broadcast a terrible message from Hitler, proclaiming all of us, Ernie, Jake, my ma, the Perskys, all of us, vermin to be exterminated. It didn't spoil the digestion of the other camp-

54

ers, who enjoyed the country sky with its extraordinary spread of stars.

Jake roamed in front of our Philco, hammering the air with his fist. "What do you expect from magicians? Will they change your name, make you invisible when Hitler comes? So open your eyes; open up your ears. Pay attention to Hitler."

"I've heard it before," Ernie said.

"Hear it again."

"What good will it do?"

Jake said to Ernie, "You aren't entirely in this world, and it worries me."

That night, when we were almost ready for bed, Fred Emerson showed up, driving his Atlas truck.

"Are you still working, Freddy?" Sammy asked him. "Are you trying to put us out of business?"

Emerson brought a visitor he wanted Jake to meet.

"Bring him in," Jake said.

"What do you say we go for a ride? I don't want to interrupt your party."

Emerson put everyone in the position of being less devoted to the union cause than he. It was almost eleven o'clock, Saturday night, and he still wore his Atlas markings. He entered our tent and broached his business without offering greetings. He ignored everyone but Jake.

"Bring in your friend," Sammy urged. "We're not in quarantine, Freddy."

"This doesn't concern anybody but Jake."

"Don't I smell good, Freddy?"

"I never come close enough to find out, and I don't intend to."

Sammy was irritated that he received no support from Jake. "This Emerson abuses me, and Jake don't say a word."

Ma told him that Emerson faced a crazy woman at home, and we had to make allowances for his behavior.

"He's been trying to do me damage ever since he joined Atlas. What did I do to deserve his interest?"

We stood on the hill and looked down into the dark lake. The sky reflected light from the amusement park. The Chris-Craft scooted along its course, yellow sparks from its running lights. On the far shore, where we had briefly touched that afternoon, I saw what appeared to be a string of Chinese lanterns. Our own campers sat around a bonfire and sang "Roll Out the Barrel."

When they returned, Jake hopped out and Emerson drove off without any farewell.

Jake told us that there was no reason for mystery. He had been introduced to a new driver named O'Brien. "A tough customer; Emerson didn't exaggerate." Kravitz had hired him without knowing that the brawny young man favored the union. "It's a break for us. This guy has seen a lot of action. He knows the ropes. You can tell your friend Kravitz," Jake advised Sammy, "that if he wants to exchange threats, we got men on our side who are in the same line of business."

He spoke as if Sammy were an enemy. Sammy had a right to be worried. Emerson was squeezing him out.

IX

———◆●◆———

My ma was named evelyn, and she was called Evka. In her last days I tried to fix her in my mind. I sized her up as if I were the mortician measuring her for a shroud. She asked me, "What's the matter, sonny?" I put my arm alongside hers and discovered what a slight arm she had. "Don't worry, sonny," she said to me, "you'll be all right." Her head tipped my shoulder. Her waist was an armful. Her hips were spread. That was partly the effect of the clothes she wore, partly the lack of exercise; she didn't eat much. Her shoulders were delicate. When she walked, she carried her hands high, her elbows pulled in. She had small hands eroded by housework.

Gentle Evka pushed a tough point of view. She marched on picket lines with vigorous, short strides, the upper part of her swaying. She held her arms in that peculiarly feminine way, adapted, I suppose, for carrying purses. She had her own political commitments among the local bourgeoisie, some of whom were godless and radical. We attended meetings at

57

Joshua Temple on Joy Road off Dexter—a joyless road and a shabby temple, an ordinary brick box that resembled a market place. There was a hall on the main floor for weddings and funerals and other major functions. There were meeting-rooms downstairs. When Ernie and I were little boys and she was still active, we accompanied her to Joshua Temple. She sat on the platform with other speakers and functionaries, a bare platform save for a podium and folding chairs.

She was introduced by Berle Dresden, a close friend. Jake referred to him as "your ma's love-sick poet." Ernie and I were impressed by Berle. He was a delicate man who didn't look Jewish. He was a serious fisherman with superb equipment. When he came out to the lake, he instructed Ernie and me in the art of casting. He knew how fish matured, what they ate, when they were sluggish, when lively. He didn't have much luck at Walled Lake.

At the meetings he would introduce my mother as "our beautiful Evka," an embarrassment to Ernie and me. She would come to the podium, dressed in a brown suit with black velvet trim and a fine hat with a lace collar, rouged and powdered. She teased Berle in a flirty way that pleased her audience, although I was embarrassed. She had a story-teller's voice, musical when under control, but screechy when she lost her confidence. Ernie and I didn't believe she could hold her audience. We expected her to fail. However, she always received strong applause as she urged bloody war against the bosses.

Her radical crowd used to come to our house and sing and dance and drink schnapps. Berle hugged her in friendship. Who took him seriously? Infidelity was out of the question among that older generation. Besides, her children were present, not to mention a jealous husband. Under the rule of Jake, our house was dominated by the sense of enemies gathered outside, waiting to assault us. We drew behind the barricade of blinds. The radicals, celebrating Evka, relieved that mood of oppression. Jake drank at these parties, even though he wasn't a drinking man. He had a derisive laugh that overwhelmed arguments. He didn't stop laughing until the opposition surrendered, a bullying tactic that demeaned him.

Once he grabbed Berle, a sensitive man with an affection for poetry—not the T. S. Eliot sort, more in the Eddie Guest line; but, still, Berle was to be distinguished from the locker-room type. Jake asked Berle if he knew the story of Abie's monkey. Berle glumly confessed he hadn't heard. Jake forced everyone to listen to the story.

After twenty-five years of marriage Becky leaves home for a two-week vacation. She and Abie have never been separated before. It's a big house; Abie is lonely. He needs a companion. So he gets a monkey. By the time Becky returns the ape is sleeping with him and eating with him. Becky is of course upset.

"Abie, a monkey in the house?"

"I got used to it, you'll get used to it."

"But, Abie, he eats at the table with us."

"I got used to it, you'll get used to it."

"But, Abie, he sleeps in our bed!"

"I got used to it, you'll get used to it."

"But, Abie, the stink!"

"I got used to it, HE'll get used to it."

Jake smacks Berle on the shoulder, laughing so hard at his own joke that Berle is forced to smile. Jake repeats the punch line until everyone is required to acknowledge the joke. "The STINK. I got used to it, HE'll get used to it. HE'll get used to it. The MONKEY will get used to it." Though everyone laughed, they found his performance unpleasant and bullying. Ernie and I understood that he was jealous of Berle. Once Jake began as a fool, he went all the way, out of defiance.

Even I, who forgave Jake almost everything, thought his bullying was outrageous. He ruined parties. He made Evka miserable. He represented himself as a truck-driver proletarian among the soft bourgeoisie. It's true that they were soft in contrast to him. Evka urged them not to be provoked. "Ignore him," she advised. "He talks like a truck driver." But he strained their good will, and there came a time when Evka didn't bother to extend invitations.

Jake said to her, "Hy Kravitz, who threatens to dump me into Lake St. Clair, is ten times the man that your poet is. I prefer the poetry of Hy Kravitz to the poetry of Berle Dresden." Jake meant the judgment to offend her, but it reflected his true feeling. He was more at ease with Kravitz, his enemy, than with Berle Dresden. He prized Kravitz for the blunt language, the shrewd eyes, the ironic tone, the brutal insistence on the priority of his own interests. Kravitz was a man to contend with. Kravitz made service to his interests a worthy life's occupation for one hundred and fifty-odd employees. He could gobble up Berle Dresdens by the dozen. Dresden was all manner, no substance. His hair was too carefully done, his eyes too soft; his voice trembled with feeling when he read poetry. What did Evka know that Jake hadn't taught her? The very word "boss" had meaning to her because he, Jake, had tangled with the breed and brought home scars and sat in the kitchen with her and revealed his wisdom. He considered it intolerable arrogance for her to stand up in Joshua Temple and denounce Kravitzism. What did she know about such men as Kravitz?

Ma said to him, "You go too far. You spoil your case. You give me the impression you're jealous."

"Of you, old lady? Jealous?"

She was thirty-eight that summer at Walled Lake. How can I recover her at thirty-eight? When I turn away from the photos, I can only remember what she was at the end.

Jake was too extreme for ordinary friendship. Emerson and McIntyre were subordinates. Sammy Persky was a clown. She was the only one to whom he confided. She was the only historian he had. She had known him from his Russian days. He didn't intend sharing her with Berle Dresden.

Berle was at the lake toward the end of summer, when we heard H. V. Kaltenborn announce the Russo-German non-aggression pact. It was stunning news. We had believed the Russians were our bulwark against Nazi Germany. Now

Hitler's path through Eastern Europe was cleared. Stalin withdrew Minister Litvinov from public view so that German sensibilities wouldn't be offended by the presence of a Jew.

Our future seemed bleak. What power could restrain Hitler, now that Russia had stepped aside? Berle finally spoke up, having found the good side of the news: a shrewd maneuver on Stalin's part. He needed time to build his defenses. Could you blame Stalin for mistrusting the Allies? Didn't Russia, represented by Litvinov, stand before the League of Nations and urge embargoes against Japan during the Manchurian War and against Italy during the Ethiopian War? The Soviet Union was alone in coming to the aid of the Spanish Loyalists. Didn't the Soviets appeal for a united front in defense of Czechoslovakia? Who were the appeasers? Chamberlain of England and Daladier of France. They favored Hitler over Stalin. They believed Hitler wanted merely to readjust the structure of power and had no revolutionary goal. The Soviet Union, on the other hand, was a threat to their mode of existence, so the Allies were prepared to sell her down the river. Stalin had no choice but to rely on his own defenses. When the Soviet Union finally opposed Nazi Germany, it would do so fully armed. Berle asked if Jake would strike an employer when it was clear he would be crushed.

No such appeal could reach Jake, who stared at Berle Dresden as if he spoke obscenity. Jake said, "I hear 'death to the Jews' from our radio; the rest is only noise." He said he had but one guideline, and it wasn't a line handed down by Moscow for the instruction of bootlickers. His guideline, pared down to its essentials, was simply this: is it good for the Jews? His conclusion, "To hell with Joe Stalin."

Berle wisely shut up while Jake let off steam, and Jake apologized after he calmed down. "I could sometimes drink your blood, Dresden; but, since we're all in the same boat, I'll ignore what you say. You'll croak, too, if Hitler comes."

X

―――――◄◆●◆►―――――

OUR SUMMER at Walled Lake continued beyond the decent weather. The last two weeks we had dull skies and blustery winds. The lake turned steely gray. Its surface was pocked and rippled. We rolled down the tent sides and kept the kerosene stove burning. Ernie and I wore sweaters and corduroy trousers. School days were ahead. New clothes were ahead. We recalled our city friends. The summer people assumed a new appearance when they put on fall clothes. Die-hard fishermen tried for the unattainable big ones. The beaches were empty. A few homes along the lakefront had fireplaces, and we could smell tangy wood smoke.

Though we had the use of our tent site till the end of the season, we didn't care to prolong a summer that was already dead. No more swimming. Dull fishing, with an occasional perch or sunfish—small reward for hours of freezing effort. We read magazines: *Collier's*, the *Reader's Digest*, *The Saturday Evening Post*. By the end of the day we felt degraded, and detested one another. We listened to the ball games, but Detroit was clearly out of the race, and to listen was only to remind ourselves of a sad defeat.

Our boredom was intensified, because the period of our terrible waiting had begun in earnest.

The French and the British said to Hitler: no more. This is it. Pleading, didn't we let you get away with Memel? How about the Sudetenland? Not to mention the rest of Czechoslovakia? Please, Hitler, don't press your luck. Don't ask for Danzig and the Polish Corridor. Did we complain about the Jews? Or the Anschluss? Did we interfere in Spain? Did we prevent the occupation of the Rhineland? Agreed that you're a great man who has restored Germany. All we ask is that you don't push us any more, Adolf. Digest what you already have. Don't be greedy.

What he already had were the Jews of Middle Europe. And he was digesting them. That snack only whetted his appetite.

On the east side of Walled Lake, where the established residential area was located, the road was lined with For Rent signs that put our status bluntly: GENTILES ONLY. RESTRICTED. To what? To anything not Jewish. Negroes, of course, weren't even a possibility. It would have been a shock to see a black child go wading. Perhaps a Negro nurse, if she were hand in hand with her white charge. Their contempt for us was publicized, and we couldn't defend our honor. Our eyes were assaulted by those signs. Our ears were assaulted by Hitler, who was loud and clear over the airwaves.

Thank god for Sammy Persky, who lacked a world view, who didn't even have a city view or a Richton view, but only a Sammy Persky view. He showed up alone the last weekend before Labor Day. Jake was busy with trouble. The glum weather persisted. Most of the tents were already dismantled. The bare rectangles of abandoned tent sites were surrounded by crab grass and weeds and newly filled gutters.

Sammy Persky didn't listen to the radio. As for newspapers, he skipped the headline articles and picked up the filler information about freaky accidents, statistical horrors, believe-it-

or-not happenings. For the evenings, he enjoyed poker or pinochle, or a movie—preferably slapstick comedy. It still surprises me that Jake was so fond of him.

The Russians being neutralized, the Germans were free to take Danzig and invade Poland if they so wished. The French and English armies were a thousand miles away. We spent our nights crucified by the radio, expecting as before—even hopefully—that disaster would be averted by a last-minute compromise that yielded everything to Hitler.

During the greater part of our youth we were required to wait for disaster. We waited each night for Jake to come home. We waited for news of Hitler's next assault. We waited for justice to be done. And we discovered finally that we had been corrupted by that posture of waiting. We lost our nerve listening to H. V. Kaltenborn and Murrow and all the other radio commentators with story-telling voices, skilled in making your heart step up its performance, implying further disasters just ahead; don't turn off the radio. We were stuck to the radio till we went to bed.

Finally we heard the big news on our Philco. The Germans had invaded Poland. England and France were expected to declare war within the week. We thought our waiting was finally over. Now the cataclysm. But it was six years before the war ended. As for Ernie and me, our vigil still isn't finished.

Sammy took his pleasure here and now, which was his power and his weakness. The invasion of Poland didn't trouble his appetite; he didn't share our fears. We had a foreboding of German power that history had justified; the Nazis had poured through Austria and Czechoslovakia; German armor and air power had crushed Spain. Our side didn't stand a chance. The French and English were bumblers, the Poles too primitive. We were accustomed to the defeat of our hopes; our enemy seemed invincible.

We stayed near the radio hoping for news of miracles, but miracles took place only during Chandu's time, not Hitler's. We were told that the Junkers despised the miserable Austrian paper hanger. Would they dump Hitler? Would the good people of Germany take their stand in behalf of justice?

Ernie wanted to lie on his cot and dream of miracles.

Sammy urged us to get out of the cottage. "The summer is still here. Enjoy yourself." He made us stop listening and steered us toward the amusement park. Our camp site was the only one still occupied. Rowboats lay on docks, keeled over. Summer cottages were shuttered and padlocked. The chill had already caused maple leaves to turn.

It was a wearisome moment of transition, with nothing to do but hang on. Anything for diversion! Sammy promised us a Tarzan movie before he left for Detroit, and meanwhile the amusement park. The ladies wanted us out of their hair while they packed.

There was a tricky intersection at the entrance to the amusement park. The main road—a washboard macadam leading to Detroit—tilted into the lane that circled the lake. Visibility was poor. We went out for fun and saw a man die at our feet. An old-time roadster, its rumble seat loaded with kids, squealed around the curve onto the Detroit road. I heard a thud and whipped around to look. The car swerved toward the entrance to the amusement park and was yanked back, weaving from one side of the road to the other, going very fast, the kids in the rumble seat ducked down. A man sailed toward us like a bundle of newspapers heaved from a delivery truck. There was a shoe a few yards away. There was another shoe in the center of the intersection. Ragged clothes, gray hair, a bald spot. The hair needed cutting, the curls thick and tight around the neck, heavy sideburns, a ruddy cheek with gray stubble. The rest of the face, not visible, lay in blood.

The victim was probably a bum. None of the villagers claimed him. There were holes in the shoes he had been knocked out of. A motorcycle cop raced to the scene with siren going, dismounted, and, with a cowboy's rolling gait, strolled first to the rags, then over to the shoes. He marked the position of the shoes with chalk.

The bum had passed through the air as if shot from a gun; he was still alive when they took him away. But how could he survive such a flight? The event guaranteed my recollection of the beginning of World War II.

That accident took the wind out of Sammy; by evening he was ready to make jokes again. "A drunk," he speculated. "A bum. What good luck to end up in a soft bed."

Sammy noticed Ernie's disgust. "How come the long face? You're disappointed we missed the Tarzan movie? Some animal, this Tarzan. Think about him sometime. He has a feeling for apes; he thinks of himself as an ape; he's no baby—a bruiser in a leopard-skin diaper. He's got feelings even you kids have some idea of; don't tell me no. He only associates with apes. Think about it. I don't have to put thoughts in your head. A nice spring night in the jungle. He lies next to a girl ape and her fuzzy bottom gives him nudges. Think about it. Do you know what I'm talking about? Think about this Tarzan, this lover of apes."

Ernie was still shocked by the accident. "There were holes in his socks," he grieved.

"In his socks? You pity him for his socks? A pair of brand-new, expensive socks and you'd have no pity?"

"If there are holes in his socks he's alone in the world."

"You know what holes in the socks mean? No wife, no kids, no obligations. The price you pay is holes in the socks. A small price. The rest is all fun. You can swing from the trees like Tarzan. You can find yourself an ape girl. Holes in the socks mean that bum was a happy man." We knew that Sammy fled from his own shock.

Yet Sammy was irrepressible. By that I mean, push him down and he bounced back. Squeeze him out of shape, and, when you eased up, the original form returned. He surrendered every other quality to preserve his bounce. It didn't matter whether he was shoved by Jake or Kravitz. He yielded, then bounced back, as innocent of disloyalty as any rubber man. Can you appreciate the charm a rubber man has?

XI

McINTYRE had no bounce. He was as rigid as glass. Perhaps that's why Kravitz was tempted to push.

Detroit autumns are unreliable. Sunny days, so soft, so poignant, you mourn for the marvelous world that's dying out. Then bleak, dreary days that foreclose the possibility of a world beyond Detroit. You feel condemned to a flat city with streets that lead to no vistas but simply peter out in weedy countryside. The city begins at a grubby waterfront heaped with the debris of old barges and tugs. The waterfront is bounded by a railroad that adds soot to air already fouled by the chimneys of Dearborn. Of course, Detroit is now a different place; I report the city of my youth. On a blustery day smoke travels horizontally, and you get whiffs of sulfurous air. The sky above is the color of the concrete roadway. The streets are filled with debris herded by the wind—all the air-borne things that have escaped the household. Rotten days on which to suffer despotic bosses, depressed wives, daughters that howl, flirty sweethearts. You grab a bundle of wet wash by the throat, and the dampness works into your hands till they are chapped and raw. You sort filthy linens and shake out roaches.

The Atlas Laundry and Linen Supply Service was an ordeal under the best conditions. It wasn't designed for soft living. You worked with the clear understanding that this was a wasted part of the globe. Not a show place, the Atlas! Jerry-built, its growth was the only sign that it thrived. The Atlas grew. Cancers also grow. The grimy red brick was defaced by chalk messages scribbled by a decade of neighborhood children. Chimneys dumped a black load on the black neighborhood. Soot drifted into houses, soured your mouth, gave density to your spit. The Atlas plant was a makeshift that had become permanent. Partitions were made of beaverboard and unpainted wooden frames. Work was conducted at a driving pace. The bundle wrappers made the operations of wrapping and tying into a continuous motion. It needed blasts from the steam whistle to alter the rhythm. That pace made for bad smells. Who bathed on those chill days? Smelling others, you knew your own smell. Despising others, you despised yourself. The place was ready to explode. Kravitz and his foreman, Red Wilson, sat on the lid in order to prevent murder.

Red Wilson went around in zero weather with his sheepskin unbuttoned, his collar open, clumps of red hair at his throat, a ruddy, burly man who stood in heavy boots as if he dared the ground to rise up and throw him. He had carrot hair and a bitchy tone that reminded you of Kravitz. He was tougher and dumber and less sensitive to conspiracy. He was the tool of Kravitz at a salary of seventy-five dollars a week.

Wilson dealt with rebels in the cowboy way. He took you into the alley, and if you had the nerve to raise a fist he knocked you down. He kicked your ass and gave you a warning. For most, this treatment was preferable to being fired.

McIntyre wasn't, however, a man to be kicked. Though at times he seemed like a buffoon, he was, after all, a proud man.

The trouble came on one of those gray days. He thought he heard his daughter howling and jerked awake. The noise came from his wife, who had perfected her imitation of the idiot daughter. Still asleep, she howled, and McIntyre climbed out of bed. A cold morning, a cold house. It was dark outside. He looked down at the woman who shared his bed, and he had no sense of her grief, no feeling for the injury she suffered. He only saw intolerable self-preoccupation. She possessed his bed and his house and his life, and offered nothing in return. His impulse was murderous. He tiptoed out, gathering up his clothes. He had fantasies of gassing his misbegotten family. He knew he would later suffer from lack of sleep but he wanted Kate. His business with her was no longer simple. It was no longer a case of shoving her down and grabbing her bottom and forcing entry. He once thought of her as gross. He dragged the heavy weight of a Presbyterian disposition. He accepted his station and its duties without any Hebrew inclination to shake his fist at a whimsical lord. Kate opened him up. She discovered possibilities he never dared to consider. He wanted to confess to deep feelings. He wanted to tell her that she was the lucky girl who had tapped his passion and uncovered a new man.

She was only nineteen. He was twice her age. And yet she made him feel as if he were less experienced. He wondered how this splendid woman could be gratified by a menial job at the Atlas Laundry and Linen Supply Service. Kate said this was her slack time and that she expected changes. She was sure someone would show up.

What did she mean, "someone?" Wasn't he someone?

As he turned the corner near Kate's apartment, he saw her lights go out. A man emerged from the apartment house and crossed to a car. The street was poorly lighted. It was a bleak morning. McIntyre tried catching a look, but he didn't see who it was. It might have been Kravitz or Persky, or Red Wilson, who was also hot for Kate and didn't have the handicap of a wife or an idiot daughter.

McIntyre had murderous impulses that morning. He turned back, afraid to discover the work of another man in her sleepy ease. He feared he might sniff the sourness of afterlove. He told Jake how she sweated when she made love. At first this had bothered McIntyre, who was well scrubbed himself. But the ripe odor of Kate had become the aroma of his sweet dreams.

When he returned home and entered his house and sniffed the cabbagey air, he was stunned by the recognition of his clownishness: a jerk who piddled away, supporting a depressed wife and ungrateful kids. Meanwhile some Persky or some Kravitz was in the sack with his sweetheart.

What a morning! When Kravitz started needling again, McIntyre blew up. He apologized to Jake. "It was too much. The bastard poured it on."

He fell asleep in his living room after returning from Kate's. The other drivers were on the road by the time he reached the plant. Kravitz waiting in the shed.

"Where you been?"

"I had trouble at home."

"You can't afford trouble at home. You got enough trouble here at Atlas."

"I'm a little late. Don't blow up a storm."

"You object to my tone of voice, McIntyre? My apologies to your Royal Highness."

"Don't push me, Mr. Kravitz."

"That's an order, McIntyre? Some bank account you must have, that you can afford to give orders to the boss."

"I'll make up the lost time, Kravitz."

"So now it's Kravitz, eh?"

"Okay, Mr. Kravitz. I know how to eat shit."

"You *think* you know how, McIntyre. You still got a lot to learn."

So McIntyre said, "You son of a bitch." When Kravitz asked him to repeat himself, he did so with enthusiasm.

Kravitz was satisfied that he understood the message. He summoned Red Wilson.

"Mr. McIntyre is no longer an employee of Atlas Linen. Pay him through the week and see that he clears my premises."

McIntyre couldn't afford a bad temper, and tried to apologize, but Kravitz wouldn't listen. McIntyre grabbed for his arm, but he jerked away and Red Wilson laid hold. McIntyre didn't want to fight. He was responsible for an idiot daughter and a sick wife and two growing boys. He shook Wilson loose and pursued Kravitz. Wilson clutched him again and McIntyre shoved him into a loading bin. It was ludicrous. He fended Wilson off, trying to explain he only wished to apologize. Wilson bulled him into the street, and the onlookers, who included Kate, must have had the impression he had been hustled out. So it ended with his humiliation.

He and Emerson waited at our house for Jake's return. "It was too much," he told Jake.

Emerson agreed. "You're damn' right, too much. Hit him in the pocket. It's the only lesson that will teach him anything. What are we waiting for? This is it. Tell Fiori to get White Swan ready for us. We strike."

Jake called a meeting in Emerson's garage. The men knew what was up, and there wasn't a single defection. It was a tribute to their loyalty to Jake, since most of them had hoped it wouldn't come to strike action.

"Boys," Jake said, "Brothers, the time has come for us to declare ourselves free men. We'll no longer be the slaves of Boss Kravitz. We refuse to accept our chains. Each of us knows we got a world to win. Isn't it about time, Brothers? We worked like dogs all our lives, and what has it won for us? Nothing. We got nothing to lose. We got no security after putting our lives into Atlas. Tomorrow the boss can fire us, and we're paupers who will starve in the street. So the time has come when we say to Boss Kravitz, 'We are free men. You can't divide us.' We stand as one family of brothers. We tell Boss Kravitz, unless you treat us like men, your plant stops. We take away all your business. We operate our routes for our own profit. We declare you unfit to be a boss of men, because you deal with us like we are animals."

Jake told them that there would be no defections. Any man

who broke union discipline imperiled his brothers. "Our lives are at stake. We're not playing games. We are pressed to the wall and we got no more choices." He listed the demands —union recognition, minimum wages, commission, hours, overtime, holidays. "And the first order of business is, if they want to deal with us, they take back Brother McIntyre." For the next two days, they were to remove all their customers' laundry from the plant. No one was to spill anything to Kravitz. They were to approach all their customers and tell them that they were taking over their routes. If necessary, they were to offer deals. They had an advantage since the customer felt loyalty to the driver, not to Atlas.

Emerson moved for a strike vote and, of course, they unanimously went along with Jake. They gave him a cheer. They sang, "Gottlieb is our leader, we shall not be moved." They sang "Solidarity Forever." They hugged each other as though they'd discovered kinship for the first time. They crowded around Jake, touching him, getting squeezed in return. It was a perfect moment for him, everything he'd dreamed it would be.

Emerson shouted, "We're going to win!"

McIntyre yelled, "We'll take on the world. All we need is each other."

"Hit him in the pocket and he'll fold!"

They sang "Hold the Fort." Emerson passed a bottle around, and they toasted Jake Gottlieb, their leader.

Two mornings later, Kravitz approached Jake in the shed. "You're done for, Gottlieb. You'll starve in the street like a dog after I'm through with you."

Jake said, "Before we can exchange such friendly talk, give McIntyre back his job. That's the precondition for doing business together."

"No one owns his job. Not you, Gottlieb. Not McIntyre. Nobody."

Jake agreed. "In this world it's not only our jobs we don't own. We don't own ourselves. We belong to our graves."

"You bet your life. I'm no philosopher. I don't read the classics like you. But I give you warning now. I been nice to you and it went to your head. Next time you won't hear from someone so nice."

So the war with Atlas began. The men pulled their routes and shut down the plant. They took their business to Fiori in Oswego. For two weeks the strike made surprisingly little difference in our lives. I mean that no one felt the pinch; we quickly adjusted to the new routine. Our pa worked days, nights, weekends, but spirits were high. There was still some vestige of a normal pattern. Then Kravitz brought in scabs, who began competing for stops. Almost from the beginning there was rough stuff.

Waiting for Jake became our entire preoccupation. The terror that ravaged Europe sneaked into our house. Every night we received ominous phone calls. We were awakened by that nagging phone. A muffled voice asked for Jake Gottlieb. We asked who wanted him, but the only response was heavy breathing.

We sat in the living room, the shades down because we feared snipers and brick-throwers. We put ourselves in Jake's shoes, experiencing the dread he avoided by acting.

Evka sometimes forced us to give up the vigil, and we lay in bed trying to stay awake until he arrived. What a relief to hear the key in the lock, his shoulder against the door, his heavy, slow step on the stairs, the fall of his rubbers. Then her timid voice. His bass grumble. The swinging of the kitchen door. Dishes clatter. The refrigerator opens. We hear the slight explosion as the gas stove is ignited. Chairs scrape. Then his voice comes through loud and clear, abusing her. He ridicules her for waiting. Why does she burden him with her anxiety? He tells her he has enough on his mind without having to worry about phoning.

He messed up our expectations. We were ready to celebrate his return, and he spoiled the occasion. We knew the pressure under which he operated. He was responsible for fifty drivers, who risked everything for him.

73

XII

---◄●►---

THE GERMANS carved up Poland fast. They bowled over the
Polish horse cavalry in a few hours. We had listened to flattering estimates of the Polish army. We were told that, while it
was archaic with respect to matériel, when it came to élan it
could more than hold its own against the Germans. We saw
pictures of Polish behemoths, steel-helmeted, belted, rigid with
spirit, moving in disciplined ranks. The Poles loved their land;
their hatred of Germans was rooted in history. When such
imposing men were driven by a passionate hatred for Germans,
how could they be dominated? Very easily. In two weeks. The
Poles hated Germans and yet were defeated; they loved their
land, but the sentiment was no defense against panzers and
Stukas. It was explained to us—after the fact—by the commentators who had based their optimism on the admirable
character of the Poles, that, first, matériel was everything, and,
secondly, Polish generalship was bad. If these commentators
had been generals, they wouldn't have fixed their power in

rigid positions at the frontier. They would have yielded to pressure, allowed the panzers to infiltrate, have arranged a defense in depth. What notions! The newsreels showed us blasted cities. We saw fields of tanks crowding boulevards. We saw German self-propelled guns pass overturned artillery wagons. We saw plane after plane peel off for screaming dives. We saw bombs blossom all over the Polish map. We saw low-level strafing explode gas tanks, vehicles, ships, men. We finally saw pictures of our Polish giants after two weeks of terror: drab, disheveled, resembling Bowery bums.

The power that had leveled Poland was focused on a grand objective: the purification of the world by the extermination of its vermin Jews. I felt this to be a personal threat, as did Ernie. We were students of that marvelous progress of Germany through the world: a jackbooted trampling of Czechs and Austrians and Yugoslavs and Frenchmen, patriots all, but no match for the krauts. Those krauts were admirable. If they had been willing to settle down for a time to absorb what they had already secured, the grateful world would have deferred to them. All were ready to sacrifice the Jews—it wasn't much of a sacrifice—they were loathsome to the world.

We dreamed of almighty power. We dreamed of a God willing and able to undertake miraculous intercession. If there were miracles, then we could dispense with troops and tanks and air power and the rifle range. Still, I was never deluded by such apocalyptic dreams. It was the voice of Hitler I listened to, not the voice of Chandu the magician. Begin with your own body; make a weapon of it. Begin with your own will; make it a fortress for your objective.

Ernie was of the messianic persuasion. He did exercises and his body was strong, but he did it for the sake of mirrors. It was rarely the case that he made proper use of his muscles. He wanted a body that would facilitate his dreams.

There was a game we played which allowed us to dream together. We had played it for years. We continued with the game even after we were shamefully mature. The game re-

75

quired privacy. Intruders ruined our concentration. We used toy soldiers we had owned from infancy. Over the years each soldier had accumulated a personal history that limited the roles he could assume. For instance, Ernie had a lead marine, originally posed while marching, his rifle at the ready position. The rifle barrel was broken off and the marine now seemed poised to throw a baseball or a grenade or a football, depending on the drama we improvised. His stance required us to regard him as left-handed; so, when Ernie maneuvered this little man, he would allow him to behave only as a lefty. This marine was tall and lean, with a hard-bitten face. We cast him in roles that would fit Gary Cooper. Probably all kids provide their toy soldiers with such histories, but I believe our game was different: we didn't place our drama on a miniature stage and imagine ourselves in our marine's shoes. We closed our eyes and dreamed of a stage the size of the world. We gripped the lead soldiers like talismans, and they entered the territory of our dreams; we forgot that we held them in our hands. Our stage might be the bed; the tufts and ridges of the chenille spread became battlefield terrain. When the battle was under way we retained a lax hold on our pieces and spoke dreamily, almost asleep, both in touch with a visionary battlefield. The game could be managed without the lead soldiers. We could use any material. We could invest twigs with character. A short twig of fair-sized diameter became the staunch non-com, lacking the grace we expected from officers, but obstinate and loyal; that was my role. Ernie was the young prince of our games. We saw body types in every kind of material. We saw character in textures of wood, cloth, metal. We gripped our objects, established their character in a preliminary briefing, set our stage; then we'd be off on our common dream. Ernie refused to be distracted by meals or company. He wanted the game to continue at night beneath the covers. He hid the soldiers under his pillow. Evka once found the soldiers and was puzzled.

"You're still playing with these?" She thought it peculiar. She said no more, but we were shamed.

I remember that once, perhaps after listening to Hitler, Ernie began by saying, "I am God; I have the power of invisibility." Ernie made the rules; he provided the script. We put the world in order by means of heroes who, in fact, resembled the krauts butchering our people. I felt degraded by the game, didn't want to play, and did so only as a favor to Ernie. When I came into the bedroom, I saw him sprawled on his back, dreamy, relaxed, his lips moving slightly, as if he were busy with dream dialogue. I'd see this kid who ought to have been on the football field lying there, stripped to his shorts, as languorous as a girl. It embarrassed me. He had sweet looks on his face as if he were taking the part of a woman. You saw in his smiles, his lip motions, his winks and blinks, evidence that characters were performing on an internal stage.

He was fifteen years old, a student of cosmology who speculated on the formation of the universe and on its antiquity. He read popularizations of Einstein. Yet that same kid—rational, skeptical, detached—who insisted the stars were gas and relished the insignificance of man in universal history, dreamed of Olympian gods. He closed his eyes and heard the thunder bolts of Zeus. CRRRACKKK! Adolf Hitler, you're dead.

There were times when I thought he could hate me more than an enemy. I knew facts he loathed himself for. He despised the dreamy boy he was. He dreamed of violent action while pinned to his bed. He was reluctant to leave the house. He moved beyond our Richton boundaries with great caution. He feared monsters who closely resembled his heroes. Their names were Saxon and Celtic. Their color was fair. Their shape was lean. Their eyes were blue. They were the blond enemy who, with a reversal of allegiances, became the blond heroes. Ernie was prepared to worship this kind. Back in Detroit there was Leonard Mitchell, sandy-colored, fine-featured, already powerful at sixteen years of age, and, besides, a Jew. No bookish Jew, though. A thief and hood. When Leonard beckoned, Ernie stopped dreaming. I watched them raid shops on Twelfth Street. Ernie walked out of a grocery store with an economy-sized box of marshmallows, while the grocer closely observed Leonard Mitchell, a more likely candidate for thief. Ernie stole a fountain pen at the dime store. He stole candy from a delicatessen. He became bolder after each theft. They traveled several blocks between Clairmont and Euclid, rifling shops. They stashed the loot in someone's back yard. I refused to participate. I kept an eye on Ernie. I had no desire to serve Leonard Mitchell, who accepted the loot as a free gift from his admiring disciple.

This same Ernie was regarded by his teachers as a model other kids were urged to emulate. He had a foot in each camp, a double-dealer from the beginning. He received top grades in school. He was a buddy of Moshe Bodkin, who was a precocious mathematician and astronomer. On weekends he and Leonard Mitchell robbed Twelfth Street stores.

Leonard Mitchell, at sixteen, already knew his way across the river to Windsor whorehouses. He had no father, and his mother took no part in our community. A dark, burly woman with tangled black hair, she always seemed to be scowling. She had a coarse voice. She focused on you with a squint. She was a scrubwoman—the only Jewish mother I knew who had such an occupation. Her rage was powerful. She was periodically flattened by ferocious headaches. There was a possibility she was an epileptic. Leonard wasn't perturbed by his irascible mother; he refused to be distracted. I heard his mother once howl at him —no coherent anger—just a formless bellow. Leonard remained cool and studied baseball scores while his mother howled. Her fists came within inches of his face. Ernie and I were embarrassed to be spectators of the scene. When she finally smacked the newspaper from his hands, he said coolly as others might say, "Down, Fido," "Don't screw with my paper or I'll chop your hands off."

Did we hear, she screamed, what he said to his ma?

When she kept on, he led us from the apartment, still not troubled.

He didn't piss his life away in dreams. He thought of a woman, and he took the tunnel or the bridge to Windsor. Ernie hoped to convert Leonard Mitchell to our game. What a project—to fire the uninflammable stuff of that hood's mind, transforming him from a violent kid whose thought immediately became action into a passive dreamer. That was a radical project. What did Ernie hope for? Did he expect to mold out of flesh and blood a creature of his will resembling our lead marine? Some magician! Presto! The villain is a hero. He yearned for magic powers so that he could transform the dull stuff of this world into the shape of his dreams. Leonard tried to understand. He sat in our bedroom, considering a troop of lead soldiers while Ernie assured him that our game wasn't childish. The soldiers were merely props. They got you started on remarkable trips. Once you were off you could range the world, unlimited by time and space.

Leonard, not wanting to discourage his own disciple, tried to distract him.

"Let's go to Windsor and get laid."

For two bucks he could mount Mrs. Frances Regina, whatever the time. He didn't need to play games in order to be free of temporal and spatial limitations. Leonard's power was the result of appetite and desire: he liked to play; he liked to fight. He didn't have to do push-ups; no effort was involved in his power.

Ernie informed him of Hitler's intentions; he shrugged. What he didn't experience, he didn't consider. Ernie described horrors already available to us in 1939. Leonard thought the castor-oil treatment some torture indeed. He speculated about the sort of threats that would most likely cause the victim to break. He wouldn't fool around with preliminaries if he were the torturer. He'd go right for the balls. That would make them talk. He couldn't understand that the tortures were senseless and that Jews had no secrets. What could they reveal, the plots of the Elders of Zion? Leonard assumed that in a

79

world divided between torturers and their victims, he would be a torturer.

Ernie tried to enlist his sympathy in behalf of the Atlas strikers. "Alone they're helpless. Together they can beat this man Kravitz." Our pa united them and gave them power. But Leonard Mitchell didn't want union with others. He had no sentiment for brotherhood. He despised the creeps who slaved for Kravitz. His sympathy was with the boss, clearly the role he would have assumed.

Ernie preferred the ladies of his dreams to the real ladies of Windsor. Even now, after thirty years, I am depressed by the recollection of that sizable boy flat on his back like a convalescent. Better Leonard Mitchell. I knew that this was also Ernie's judgment. His admiration for Leonard was rooted in self-disgust.

I said to Leonard Mitchell, "All right, I'll go to Windsor." That forced Ernie's decision, and the three of us set out in a borrowed car.

We crossed the Ambassador Bridge on a cold night, high above the traffic of the Detroit River. It was early evening and already dark. Detroit sparkled below us. On such crisp nights —almost wintry—the city is lucid, precisely detailed. The cluster of skyscrapers around the Penobscot Building have a fine thrust to them, capped by lights, as a school child's excellent performance is capped by a star. The illuminated signs from the factories along the Windsor shore advertise Canada to Detroit, and the Detroit signs beckon Canada.

The customs officer might have been curious about three kids in a car if he hadn't been so cold. Our papers were in order and Leonard was self-assured. Customs waved us on to Frances Regina. So there we were, for the first time on foreign shores, being steered by a knowing pilot. Our nighttime view of Windsor was disappointing. We passed a street of taverns and some modest hotels and shops, and entered flat blocks of residences. The house of Frances Regina was indistinguishable from its neighbors. A lawn, a box, perfectly respectable, no red lights, no fancy curtains.

The host resembled our gym teacher. He was a stocky man with close-cropped red hair and a military mustache. He came to the door in his shirt sleeves, carrying the sports section of the Detroit News.

"Howdy, Creighton, boy," he said to Leonard, who then introduced us via pseudonyms. I was surprised by Leonard's imagination. How did he come up with a name like Creighton? He settled for commonplace pseudonyms for us: Artie and Joe. I knew I couldn't proceed with the action, not in the presence of this man who looked like our gym teacher. And, when I saw Frances Regina, a good-looking Windsor matron in a housecoat, a mature woman of our mother's generation, I didn't try to pretend.

"I'm just here with them," I said. "I'll wait."

Leonard was generous. "Take the kid first. Handle him easy, Frances; he's a cherry."

I never doubted that Ernie had a certain type of courage. He was capable of dogged resistance. He wouldn't run from pain. To follow a nice lady like Frances Regina into the bedroom while critical spectators watched, that was an act of courage of the suffering kind. Perhaps not for some, but certainly for Ernie. Our host, Ray, peeked from behind the sports page to complain of the Detroit Tigers' failure, despite the record-breaking performance of Rudy York. It wasn't an issue that could interest me. I trembled for my brother, who was now discovering what was beneath Frances Regina's housecoat.

It was a cozy parlor, just like someone's home. I wasn't then used to the idea of the place. You entered another man's house, and, after a few polite words, followed his wife into the bedroom while he settled into the armchair behind the sports section of the Detroit News. There was a fireplace to warm us, a mirror above the hearth, and on the hearth arrangements of glass figurines and gimcracks produced for the New York World's Fair, the one represented by the Trylon and Perisphere. I sank deep into a plush chair. There were lamps with beaded shades, now stylish, but which I associate with the overheated living room of Frances and Ray Regina. The blinds were drawn. The windows were draped in lace. Radiators clanked. I itched; I felt sleepy. Ernie wasn't gone long and returned with a swagger. One look and I knew he'd suffered a disaster.

"Great stuff, huh, Artie?" Leonard slugged his shoulder, passing him on the way to the bedroom.

I could never figure out what they saw in each other. Why was this hood fond of my brother? Or, rather, why did he pretend to be fond of him? I always felt that something nasty was working under those sandy curls of Leonard Mitchell. As for Ernie—granted he was charmed by physical grace—how could he bear the vulgarity of that son of a bitch?

Ray squirmed in his armchair, hidden by the front page that reported the Soviet occupation of East Poland.

Leonard emerged from the bedroom with Frances Regina's summary of Ernie's performance. He delivered it to us in the car while we were on the way back to Detroit. "Her grandpa, ninety-five years old, screws better." Told with a guffaw. The bridge lights drummed on the car windows as we sped through light traffic, the windshield steamed up. Ernie was up front; I was in back. Leonard managed the wheel with one hand, his other arm on the back rest behind Ernie. No apparent malice, a Homeric face, tranquil, unblemished, precisely sculpted, the lips turned down in a suggestion of petulance, the look of a pampered athlete. It was a joking matter to Leonard. Ernie's flop was no more serious to him than Ernie's success would have been. "Her grandpa, ninety-five." He laughed at Ernie's disaster, and Ernie laughed, too. I didn't laugh.

When we got home I told Ernie, "Do yourself a favor and get rid of him."

"Get rid of who?"

"You're like his slave."

It pained me to see him servile. He didn't have to sell himself short. He had alternatives. Much excited him. The stars above. Literature. He breathed political air. He began his study of Franco's progress through Spain when he was twelve years old. The fall of Madrid concluded the study three years later. He yearned for victory. He hunted newspapers and listened to radios for auguries of Hitler's defeat. There were frequent optimistic forecasts, all of them lies.

The strike developed its own routine, and Kravitz seemed in no hurry to restore old habits. It was scant pay from pared-down routes with Fiori absorbing most of the take. Kravitz let it be known that he didn't mean to negotiate. He intended to rub out the union, obliterate any vestige of the infection, stop the blight at its source before it could spread throughout the industry. The industry gave him support. They eased the pain of his losses. They guaranteed the restoration of Atlas as it once had been. Kravitz regularly issued final warnings, last chances for amnesty. The drivers received chilling letters from a law firm, threatening fines and jail sentences for stealing the Atlas business. The men received informal offers to be let off the hook if they immediately returned their routes. They would get their old routes back. They would only be docked their salaries. There would be no hard feelings. But it was getting late for them, not only at Atlas, but everywhere. The curse of Kravitz would pursue them to every corner of the world. Only Soviet Russia would be left. All employers would be informed of their irresponsible and criminal actions.

Jake told them, "Forget the lawyers. Forget the black lists. Expect no favors from Kravitz. After we win, he'll eat all his words; there will be no retribution. We gain everything—back pay, union recognition, job security, and, more important, dignity and pride. The boss is hurt. He's yelling. Don't be alarmed by the sound. Rejoice."

Sammy asked, "And if we lose?"

"I tolerate no defeatist attitude. If I have to shut your mouth with dirty laundry, I'll stop that kind of talk."

Jake arranged a solidarity party at Union Hall for the strikers and their wives. Song sheets were distributed at the door. Ernie and I were with Leonard that night and didn't attend, but we heard about the affair, a wonderful flowering of good will and brotherhood. Men discovered that they were suddenly wide open to each other. Evka told us how they adored Jake. They sang several choruses of "Gottlieb Is Our Leader." There was a Polish band which stimulated lively dancing. There were kegs of beer and plenty of goodies prepared by the wives.

And yet a sour note from Sammy Persky, who somehow couldn't lose himself in brotherhood. He danced with Kate Russo, who had linked her fate to the strike, a dance that commanded attention and forced other dancers to become inactive and watch. Kate Russo seemed to have forgotten how Sammy's hands had once strayed. She enjoyed him now, becoming the object of his comic, lascivious deftness. He whipped her around and surprised her with unexpected collisions. McIntyre, a clumsy dancer, stood on the side and watched.

Jake advised Sammy to dance with Minnie.

"I got her all my life. Tonight let me forget my troubles."

He was the life of the party, incessantly talking, occupying center stage. He was so exuberant he couldn't turn himself off. After a few beers he adored everybody, especially Jake. He was under the illusion that his sentiment was generally shared.

When Jake addressed the crowd at the end of the evening, Sammy heckled as if he were at a family dinner, puncturing his buddy's pomposity.

Jake described his vision of a grand world with all men brothers, no man servile, no man boss, class warfare ended, the bounty of life finally available to all—good music, good books . . .

Sammy interrupted. "Good ladies!"

No more intolerance, Jake told them. No more injustice, no more humiliation. The payoff would be in pride and dignity.

"And plenty mazuma!"

Emerson roared, "Shut him up! Get that creep out of here!"

84

McIntyre lunged for Sammy. "You fink bastard!"

He was stopped by the man O'Brien. Evka was formally introduced to him for the first time, and she was impressed. A powerful redhead with a shrill voice you paid attention to. He hugged McIntyre, who immediately became calm. He led him over to Jake and wrapped his other arm around Jake. "Okay," he said, "all together: 'Gottlieb Is Our Leader.' Any son of a bitch brother who doesn't put his heart into it is going to lose his ass." He led chorus after chorus until the song became comic and they were broken up with good will. A hundred men and women stood around Jake, adoring him.

Sammy, of course, was left out. Their ill will surprised him; he was out of touch.

That was the second week of the strike, and perhaps the high point of brotherly feeling.

XIII

———◄•◆•►———

By Thanksgiving 1939, Germans and Russians shared a common border in Poland. And where were the legions of Justice? Crouched behind the Maginot line, securely entrenched, peeping over the top only after the firing ceased. The Allies still hoped Germany might see reason and yield up Poland and restore the peace. Who knows? If Germany had accepted the free port of Danzig and some Polish titbits, there might have been further accommodations. But the krauts refused to disgorge anything. They meant to swallow the whole store. The Allies begged them to be reasonable, but they proceeded to make a meal of Poland. They devoured Poles, Czechs, Austrians, gypsies, Jews—even their own, those cannibals. We had a sense of a brute predator, squatting on the battlefield, gnawing bones while the next victim pleaded for reason to prevail.

War is a catastrophe. Anything but war. That was the line we heard from socialists and communists and fascists and America Firsters. Even the Germans urged an end to war. Why fight? they asked. Submit to us. We'll tidy up the world. Who, after all, desired war? The scavenger Jews who fed on corpses. I suppose the Nazis and their friends were honest in claiming Jews support the war; it was only good sense to resist your exterminator.

That surely was Jake's line. He wanted the exterminators exterminated. He didn't mute his bloody wishes. On the other hand, Berle Dresden refused to be knocked off balance by stories of German horrors. He denied that there were monsters. All phenomena were natural and therefore available to science. Berle Dresden argued in behalf of sanity from the podium of Joshua Temple. He opposed Jake's bloodthirsty sentiment and denied that bloodletting would cure the German disease. That was old-time medicine. Hitler was merely an effect. To remove the effect would not eliminate the possibility of recurrence. Berle Dresden knew precisely what the nature of this effect, Hitler, was. He was the consequence of imperial rivalries for world markets, the lobbying of death merchants. Hitler was the result of the terrible wound inflicted on German pride by the Versailles Treaty. Take your pick as to cause. Berle Dresden kept his ease and sanity and understood Hitler.

He didn't like to think ill of any man. He didn't want to believe in an unappeasable beast, scrounging around battlefields. He denied that there were bad Germans; there were bad treaties. He didn't believe in an appetite for war. However, he accepted the existence of the profit motive. He considered Hitler to be the symptom of an irrational economy. Anti-Semitism was another symptom. Once the way in which men lived was transformed, these symptoms would disappear.

"I agree," Jake said with a sneer. "Transform the way they live; kill the sons of bitches."

Berle refused to be provoked. Was Jake prepared to believe in devils? Did he admit a power for evil beyond human understanding? Was that the attitude of scientific socialism? Berle charged that in denying God Jake pulled the rug from under the devil. Jake had to be consistent: no God, then no devils.

He had to face the consequence: there was no incalculable evil. The Nazis could be explained. Even the slaughter of Jews could be viewed as a human act if sufficient information were at hand. The facts were there to be discovered—in the world, not out of it. If you had the facts, you would find that what passed as German evil was only human possibility operating under the special conditions of a defeated imperial Germany. Germany had been stripped of her African colonies, right? Deprived of the Saar industrial basin, correct? But nothing had been done to harness the power of the great cartels. The imperial giant was humbled, but his expectations were unchanged. The Allies weren't fit doctors for a diseased imperialism. The Germans were the result of a historical necessity. You see? They were understandable and, therefore, not beasts.

Dresden deeply felt world events and studied them closely, using, for the most part, the same sources available to us all, the Detroit newspapers and the radio. He had a special slant via the Daily Worker. Listening to him address the crowd from the podium at Joshua Temple I found him convincing. It was an academic manner. His accent was Germanic rather than Yiddish. He had a tweedy appearance and smoked a pipe.

Berle was no provincial. For instance, in the matter of diet he was by no means restricted to ghetto fare. He sampled the foods of the world. He was an ardent fan of yogurt and wheat germ, and enjoyed strong-smelling cheeses. I remember the rabbit-like sniffing of his fine nose as he hovered over a round of camembert.

Dresden wasn't at his best with Jake, who went all out to win an argument.

Jake said, "What a tolerant guy you are! You even got a big heart for Nazis. Just remember this, Dresden: if thirty years ago you missed the boat leaving Poland, you'd really have a story to tell; you could inform me firsthand about historical necessity. You would have the information about historical necessity a pig learns when he enters the slaughterhouse."

Dresden countered Jake's rudeness with an academic vocabulary he had picked up from his platform experience. He accused Jake of attacking the man and appealing to authority. "With you, Gottlieb, it is always the ad hominem and the ipse dixit. The appeal to authority, Gottlieb. A fallacy known to philosophers for almost two thousand five hundred years. Do you hear me bringing in personalities, Gottlieb? Never. I stick to logic. I pay no attention to your bad habits."

"Don't give me logic. It's blood I want. German blood— not logic—interests me."

"You think German blood is different from any other kind of blood?"

Jake had no reservations about attacking the man. "Why should I listen to your logic? Who are you, Dresden, to talk to me of logic? You couldn't even manage a thirteen-year-old girl. Why should I pay attention to your bullshit about Nazis?"

Dresden was flustered by this reference to his personal history. "That was unkind of you, Gottlieb. How can you expect me to carry on a rational discussion when you got such a malicious attitude?"

Jake was savage-tempered in those days. The first weeks of the strike were a stalemate. The drivers pulled their routes from Atlas; scabs whittled away their business. The strike lapsed into routine, and Kravitz showed no sign of breaking.

It was a dwindling income for the drivers. Fiori took all the profit. Emerson believed the impasse was only temporary and that Kravitz would finally yield to the commands of his pockets. At any rate, something would soon have to give. Neither side could afford such costly operations. Only Fiori thrived.

"You're an old friend," Jake told Dresden. "I got a warm heart for you. But again and again you make the same mistakes like a damn' fool. You let everyone step on you. If you don't yet know my opinion of your affair with the little girl, I'll tell you now: right away you should have gotten rid of her. How can I take you seriously, a grown man letting a child trample you?"

We all knew Dresden's story, since he often told it; it was a dramatic account that established his proper grievance against life and released him from all domestic obligations.

As a young man, living in Warsaw, he was once called upon to rescue his aunt and cousins from a Polish village where Jews had been assaulted by peasants. Among his cousins there was one named Rifke, only thirteen years old, an amazing child, as lean as a knife when the style was to be voluptuous. Hawk-nosed, very dark, with cascading hair and eyes which, as Dresden put it, "entered your heart like fire." A fearless person.

"When I arrived in the village, my uncle was dead. The family watched from the house while the peasants caught him outside. They hauled him by the beard. They beat on him. They hit him with clubs. They knocked him down to his knees. My aunt and the children screamed. 'Moshe! Tate!' It broke my heart to imagine what they had seen. It was said I resembled my Uncle Moshe, a cultured man. We were a progressive family. My father was among the few Jews permitted to live in Warsaw. He managed estates and was in charge of a timber business. My Uncle Moshe was an overseer on one of the estates. He was the sort of man you would seek out when you were in need of help, whether or not you were Jewish. He was loved by the peasants. He was a father to the peasants. He operated the most liberal estate in the countryside. But when the pogrom came, it was straight to Uncle Moshe's house the peasants went. Of course they were drunk. Of course they were egged on by provocateurs. There was resentment of Uncle Moshe, I know. They marched to his house, down the middle of the street, a crowd armed with clubs and pitchforks. Moshe was told to flee, but he didn't fear his peasants. When they stopped at the gate and yelled, "Uncle Moshe, come out, we want to deal with you," he didn't hesitate. He recognized men who regarded him as a relative. He came out and stood among them, and he seemed so tiny beside these behemoths that maybe they were overcome by their own size. Someone grabbed his beard and pulled. He lost all dignity; they laughed. And then it was all over for Uncle Moshe. A peasant, shorter than Moshe, but like an ox, hauled him around in front of the house while my cousins and aunt screamed. The whole crowd jumped on him. Afterward they raided the house, and, when I arrived, my relatives sat among ruins.

"I was twenty years old, a big-city boy. What I saw terrified me. There, but for five miles to Warsaw, lay my own father. There were eight cousins, and they were divided among the three remaining brothers. Rifke and Aunt Bessie came to our house. Does it sound to you like madness that a thirteen-year-old girl could win my heart? If you saw Rifke you would understand. She didn't face me like a little girl. It was at first an outrage. She had no sense of what was fitting. I was already a respected member of the community, sought after by ladies twice her age, more even. Yet she mocked me. She had a sharp tongue and no fear of punishment. I told her, 'So long as you live in my house, you'll know your place. You'll remember who I am and that you're still a nobody.' I told Mamma, 'She needs a beating—she's got a fresh mouth.' My mother defended her at first. 'Remember she has had troubles, Berle.'"

It seemed to me that Berle was surprisingly innocent of what his story revealed. Rifke finally tempted him into beating her. I'm sure he had no idea of how provocative that business sounded. He took her down to the basement, pulled out his belt and tried to force her over his knee. She kicked and flailed. He became truly angry and lashed out with the belt. It wrapped around a pole and barely grazed her. He dropped the belt and tried to use his hand. Suddenly she pushed away. "Such a man," she said. "Is it so much trouble hitting a girl? I'll help you." She drew off her dress and hoisted up her petticoat. "Hit me," she said. She turned around and exposed her rump. "Now it's easy for you. What's wrong, you're so quiet all of a sudden?" She handed him the belt. Dresden said, "I couldn't hit. She defeated me. She was always ready to go to any extreme. I didn't know how to fight her. I could never think of her as a child, and it troubled me." He denied that he had been aroused by her nakedness. Such an immature body, chicken wings for shoulders. Small breasts. A little girl—how could he get excited? He tried to avoid her after that.

There was a crackdown on Warsaw Jews. Berle's father lost his timber concession. The handwriting on the wall was plain to see. It was decided that Berle should go to America and prepare a haven for the family. He was given money and the names of countrymen in Detroit. Rifke came to him and said, "Take me with you."

"I don't even take my brothers; why should I take you?"

"I won't stay in Poland any more. So take me."

Berle refused. She continued pressing him. "Take me. I'll be nice to you. You need somebody in America. I'll keep your place. I'll be your friend. I won't make fun of you any more."

"You're a baby."

"'I'll go with someone else then."

She dressed up and went into the street and paraded in front of the house with a Polack she'd met. Who could have disciplined her? Berle had no influence. Her own mother hadn't been able to control her. There were tears and threats but to no avail. Rifke said to them, "Send me to America with Berle. If not, I'll make everybody regret it. I won't stay in Poland."

Dressed up, she looked seven years older. Berle couldn't bear seeing her with the Polack.

"Take me with you," she told him. "Then you'll know where I am. If you don't take me, I'll go with the Polack."

Finally he went to his aunt and said, "Maybe Rifke should come to America with me."

"She's a child, Berle. How can you think of such a thing?" He promised he wouldn't think of her as a woman.

"So how will you think of her, Berle? You know what a headstrong person she is."

Berle's mother cursed herself for allowing the girl into her house. A monster, she said. She never heard of a Jewish girl who was so bold. No one could manage her. What kind of a wife would she be?

He told them he wasn't thinking of her as a wife. He would take her to America, period.

"How can you know what you are thinking?" his mother asked. "She twists you around her finger."

Berle saw her with the Polack—a big peasant, a blond—walking in front of the house. Berle's aunt yelled at them. They were shameless. The Polack laughed; Rifke paid no attention.

"I came to understand that this monster owned my heart. I took her to the basement and told her I didn't want her to go any more with the Polack. 'So, what will you do? You'll spank me again? You want me to get ready for a spanking?' She saw that I trembled, and she touched my face. I burned where she touched me. 'Take me to America, Berle. You'll never regret it. You can't dream how good I'll be to you.'

"So I told the family I would take her. I promised that for two years—till she was fifteen—I would treat her as a sister. Then in two years, if all went well, she would be my wife. No one wanted it except Rifke. She was stronger than any of us. She beat us down, and I took her to America."

He got a job as a room clerk in a Detroit hotel and studied the hotel business. For two years he spoiled Rifke. He bought her candy. He took her to theaters. She learned English. It was through her that he was introduced to the Party. She met a Polish comrade and they persuaded Berle to attend a Communist encampment outside Detroit. He enjoyed the clear logic of the Marxist line. Monsters disappeared. All was explained. She enjoyed dancing on the open-air stage. She sprouted under his tender handling and acquired a voluptuous shape. She wore her hair piled high. At night, when she lowered her hair and brushed away, he knelt beside her and kissed the locks that hung to her waist. He was ready to kiss her feet. At the Communist camp she danced with big Polish men and lithe Negroes. Almost immediately after arriving in America she had entered his bed, indifferent to the promises he had made.

She left him when she was fifteen years old. She went to California with an American boy from the Midwest, a farmer's Party-member son.

It was the tragedy of Dresden's life. He never married. Yet Berle didn't regret his cousin Rifke. He believed in the education process and felt that he had learned much from her. She had long since disappeared from view, but he retained his Party affiliation.

Evka was moved by the story. Did Rifke's mother know of her fate? How could a mother not be grieved by such a tragedy?

Why didn't Berle try to find Rifke?

There was too much grief, Berle answered. She was unmanageable. Believe it or not, she had scared him. He discovered after some time elapsed that he was even relieved that she had vanished. Nonetheless, it was the tragedy of his life. He could never forget her.

"You don't have the nerve to hit," Jake said. "You got no guts, Dresden. With me it's a different case. I let nobody—not a man, not a woman, not a child—nobody steps on me. Those who step on me will bleed. I want to see German blood. I want to see German blood flowing in German streets. After I wash in German blood I'll be clean of my shame. They degrade our people, and only when I see Germans grovel will I consider that maybe they're human. Only when they grovel will they have had the experience of Jews. Then maybe they'll understand Jews. Bleeding and groveling—that's a German education. Let them suffer what Jews suffered. Then, maybe, Dresden, I myself will no longer be a monster crying for blood.

94

Then, maybe, German and Jew, we'll both be human. But first let them bleed."

Dresden threw up his hands. "What a way to argue!"

"Do you want me to make nice sounds for Joshua Temple? I won't allow it. I'm a truck driver, Dresden. What do I care for pretty sounds?"

Jake ridiculed Berle with deep, nasty laughs that were contagious. Despite your will, you found yourself laughing with him and completing Berle's humiliation.

XIV

———◆●◆———

ERNIE, too, wanted to believe that monsters were explicable. Like Dresden, he felt that if they could be understood, they could be manipulated, a position shared both by scientist and magician.

I walked into the bedroom one day and caught him with a pearl-handled jacknife we had both admired in the window of a jewelry store. He heard me enter too late. He grabbed the knife to his chest. He lay on the bed, reclining on his elbow. Then he brought the knife into the open, as if there were no secret.

"They'll catch you," I warned. "You think you won't be caught, but they'll catch you. Then you'll know how stupid you are."

He told me to shut up. I nagged and he said, "Shut up, shut up." He shoved the knife under his pillow.

"You're afraid to admit that he's a bum. You don't like to steal; you do it to please him."

"Shut up."

"You're almost as strong as he is."

"I'll knock your head off."

"You're a hundred times as smart. You're the only one who doesn't know he's stupid. Everyone thinks it's peculiar that you hang around with that bum. I lie. I tell them it's the other way—he hangs around you, and you pity him."

"Let him hear someone pities him. Do you know what will happen?"

"I'm ashamed of you. That's why I lie."

"Do you know what happens if he hears you're spreading rumors? Do you know what a mean temper he has? When he hits, you'll feel it."

I feared no one. I would tell Mitchell myself. I'd be delighted to tell Mitchell what I thought of him.

"Don't do it." The tone was half threatening, half pleading. "Don't you do it."

I didn't hide my dislike of Mitchell, who didn't seem to notice or care. He waited for us near the drugstore across the street from the school, his hands thrust into his pockets, thumbs hooked in his belt, his corduroys sagging, rocking on his heels, forcing sidewalk traffic to move around him, a sandy-haired visionary: he dreamed of goodies to be looted and Windsor ladies to be purchased. He was a sleepy-looking, handsome boy with dimples in his cheeks and a little mouth and pale eyes. When he came out of his fantasy, he was all motion, ready to execute actions transcribed from his dreams. He was strong and vicious in whatever he undertook. Perhaps that dreamy appearance was only vacancy. I don't know what occupies such heads. Maybe it's a mistake to presume that he had thoughts and feelings like our own. I have always been attracted to the monster theory. Who knows? Like the bullheads we used to catch, Leonard Mitchell may have lacked capacity for pain. Our humanity is defined by that capacity. If Berle Dresden could deny that we hurt bullheads when we ripped out their guts in pursuit of a hook, why not draw a similar conclusion about Leonard Mitchell? He could throw himself into a tackle, get up with spike wounds, receive clouts on his jaw and belly, and a few minutes later swagger off with his hands in his pockets. His performance wasn't affected by nerves. I have often come across serene brutes like Leonard Mitchell.

Leonard Mitchell sought out Ernie. He wooed Ernie with auto rides to Windsor. He wanted Ernie to be a thief, so there would be grounds for kinship. He taught Ernie to value the way a pearl-handled pocketknife is flung open when a button is pressed.

I remember Leonard Mitchell in our bedroom, sitting on the edge of Ernie's bed, holding a soldier in his hand, trying to understand the game. Ernie had worked his magic to the extent that he could get Leonard to participate. He listened to the instructions, received the briefing for the specific action, launched himself into the take-off, but he couldn't fly. There he was, still on the bed, with lead soldiers in his hands, embarrassed by my presence. Ernie couldn't get him to soar to the dream battlefield where the real action took place. I was the only one who could join Ernie there.

A glimpse of Leonard was all Jake needed. "A smart aleck. A bum," he told Ernie. "You got a bad habit of associating with bums."

Jake and Evka were more concerned for Ernie than for me. Perhaps they had greater hopes for Ernie. If his dreams could be translated into action, then what actions, because what dreams! His moroseness, his contempt, his need for solitude impressed us all as by-products of great ambition. Who could predict how he would survive disappointment? On the other hand, they knew I wouldn't fall under the spell of heroes and serve men lesser than myself. After all, did I have a single dream I hadn't received secondhand from Ernie?

XV

———◄◆►———

THE ROAD TO OSWEGO passed through farm country. It was
an alternate route to Chicago and heavily traveled. Past Ann
Arbor the four lanes dwindled to three. In the heart of farm
country it was reduced to two lanes, divided by a white strip
sometimes edged in yellow. It was flatland, an easy country
for roads, but the highway took abrupt turns to accommodate
all farms en route. It was a road we often traveled. It led
to the lake country as well as to Chicago. We bought fresh
corn, tomatoes, and eggs at wholesale prices from the farms
beyond Ann Arbor. In late fall we bought apples by the
bushel, tart Winesaps and pippins. In the summertime the
road was dappled by groves of oak and elm. In the wintertime
the trees were gaunt, the fields covered with snow, scabby
stalks poking through. When we surveyed the barren countryside, we didn't envy the drab lives of farmers whose houses
were set in stubble fields and stale snow. The midday sun
turned snow to slush. The evening gusts turned slush to ice.

At night the driver hunched over the wheel and scanned the road for icy glimmers picked up by his headlights.

Jake was getting only three or four hours' sleep a night. We were safe at home, but we took that ride in imagination. He drove one of Fiori's salvaged wrecks, a van with the motor on the side, its muffler shot, and the constant noise worked on his nerves. It was a strain to stay awake. You swam in darkness, oriented by reflectors on trees, guided by the centerline, which was often blotted out by drifting snow. The approach of another car was heralded by headlights reflected against the sky. The lights sailed into view, then disappeared. You had to guess why. Dip in the road? A curve? Was it an industry car pulled up by the roadside in ambush? The approaching lights returned to view. You pumped your brights to force him to dim his approach. For a moment you were drenched in light, then darkness again, and the encounter left you slightly out of focus.

Weeks of such driving with no Sundays off and no prospect of victory. It was a tedious trip—over the same ground each night, the truck shuddering at high speeds, the bundles on top betraying his objective. A black truck with blacker streaks covering the former designation: WHITE SWAN INDUSTRIAL LAUNDERERS, OSWEGO, MICHIGAN. Rough times in Oswego, and Sal Fiori was ready to try anything. He figured he had nothing to lose. If he kept faith with the industry, he'd be bankrupt.

"The industry got this agreement," he told Jake. "We all keep faith. We don't wash for strikers. I ask myself, 'What's this keeping faith, Sal?' A kid in diapers knows the answer. It's another way to say, 'Let's everybody screw Sal and, Sal, don't you screw nobody back.' I bid my life's blood on the GM plant. They force me to operate there on a profit wouldn't feed a sparrow. GM slows down, do I get any sympathy? They offer to take my plant, but how about a little credit? 'Sal, buddy,' they tell me, 'you're too stupid to stay alive. Do everybody a favor and drop dead.' Not me. Not old Sal. I'm gonna stay breathing, whoever I got to screw."

Still, he was worried by Kravitz and insisted that unmarked trucks bring the wash from Detroit. He worked out an elaborate plan to misdirect anyone following the trucks. Deliveries were at night. Even his own employees didn't know they were washing for the Atlas strikers.

Three trucks left Detroit from Emerson's garage, which was the pickup point. They used the main highway out of town. They left at night when they could easily spot anyone tailing them. All trucks were loaded, and, if any was followed, it turned back. It was a wearying procedure. In order to protect Fiori the drivers spent hours maneuvering on the highway.

And they were followed everywhere. Kravitz' men pursued each driver on his route, offering deals to customers. Kravitz did business at bargain rates.

"What kind of business is that?" Sammy Persky complained after losing several stops. "Isn't anybody interested in making a buck? Verducci, my big restaurant, tells me they made him deals, and he answers, 'No deals. Persky is my boy. I love the little kike.' But this week he says, 'Sorry, pal. I can't turn down a fifty-per-cent discount.' Fifty per cent! Kravitz is paying the customer for the privilege of washing his dirty shorts. What can I do with such competition?"

Jake consulted with Fiori. "Okay," said Fiori. "Fifty per cent. Next it will be nothing. I got one half his business and one half his costs. He pays those scabs a fortune. Two more weeks, and he won't be in business. Anything he offers, match him." Fiori was confident and cheerful.

But Sammy couldn't regain the Verducci stop. He offered a seventy-five-per-cent discount.

"Not even if you pay me, Sammy. I got no choice. It's nothing personal. Personally I like you. You're my boy. But you work for the wrong people." Verducci indicated that the pressure was on him to drop the union.

"What pressure, Joe?"

"Take my advice, kid. Kravitz is your friend."

Verducci warned him that the strike would become rough.

"He says, when the hoods start shoving, he likes me, but not that much. He says, 'Wear a steel helmet, Sammy; the head-hunters are out.'"

All this we heard from Jake when we saw him on weekends. He was home early on Saturday and Sunday nights. He sat at the kitchen table, walleyed and grimy. He entered the house already stripping. He dumped his leather jacket on the newel post, flung his cap on the closet shelf, left his shirt in the bathroom. He washed his hands and face and approached the kitchen table in his undershirt, the hairs glued over his bald spot, gray in his beard, red-nosed from frost, blank-eyed when we asked him questions. After fourteen hours on the road he smelled like a truck engine.

He wolfed down his soup, going at it greedily. He raised a big chunk of soup meat to his mouth, turned it on his fork till he could manage a proper fit, then crammed it in. He forgot to eat during the day, living off his nerve, not recognizing his hunger till he was settled in front of his meal. He lunged at whatever was served. He was in no mood for questions when Evka inquired what his day was like.

"I come home to relax, not talk. Don't worry what my day is like."

He told us to keep the blinds drawn. He told us to avoid giving information to callers.

Evka wanted to know why the need for such precautions.

"Life and death is involved. Kravitz offers to wash free."

"That's legal?"

"By the time a judge tells him no, we'll be dead from starvation."

"How can he afford it?"

"On his side are millionaires. On our side is what? Fiori wants to know if we expect him to buck the whole industry. A hero? Not him. He's willing for us to take our business someplace else."

"What will you do if he won't wash?"

"If he won't wash, you and your boys will beg in the streets, old lady."

"So what can be done, Jake?"

"Don't worry what can be done. I'll do the worrying. Don't stick your nose into my worries. One thing I'll promise you. No one pushes Jake Gottlieb into the street. I have men with me who want to blow up the world if they don't get their place in it."

McIntyre was one of these. What a change in the man in a few weeks! He wore a lumber jacket and a deer hunter's cap with the flaps down. He worked without gloves; I remember the redness of his hands. They were cracked in the way that marble cracks. The beef that had made him seem magisterial had been trimmed down by hard times. His awkwardness, too, had been pared away. He was no longer the bumpkin disciple of Jake. I now saw in him what I had once had a foreboding of, a disillusioned man, suspicious of Jake. He wore the uniform of fatigue that identified all strikers with the exception of Persky. Unshaven, red-eyed, frost marks on the face. His big hunk of nose—a beefy, Celtic nose without any fancy curves, a simple structure, outsized like the rest of him—was always red. The rest of his face was ashen. His blue eyes were out of focus from fatigue. And because of fatigue he had to boom out his speech in order to blast through the incoherence. That was my impression, at any rate. This man whom I once thought of as temperate and modest made every utterance a threat.

His wife was in the state hospital—a temporary condition, he had been told. She was out of touch, but he could expect her back. He was stuck for life with a frail vessel. He was trying to nerve himself to commit his daughter. He had always claimed his wife was the obstacle. Yet, now, when she was out of the way and it was truly difficult for him to keep the child, he couldn't bring himself to let go of her.

His mother, who was almost seventy and didn't need more trouble, stayed with the girl. She, too, pleaded that the loony

103

be spared. The grandmother—like the mother—couldn't accept the paradox of lunacy entrenched in that angelic setting. When the daughter was placid, the howling idiot seemed incredible. However, the shrieks always arrived to confirm the idiocy.

McIntyre said that he was grateful for one thing. He had so many wounds he couldn't feel the goad of love. Between his family trouble and the Atlas strike he had no resources left for grieving over the fickleness of Kate Russo. The bitch! There would come a time when he'd be revenged for that humiliation, too.

"We won't lose this one, Jake. Kravitz got no idea how rough it's going to be."

The thought of scabs living like royalty while he made that tedious journey to Oswego infuriated him. He wanted to make it tough on the scabs. He wanted to break heads. He didn't intend to allow anyone to evade their debts to him. He had put in too much time suffering, and he wanted compensation. "Those scab bastards are cozy while I got to be on the Oswego road."

Jake warned him not to mention any names. He announced for the benefit of all who might have overheard that there was to be no mention of a place called Oswego.

"Just warn your boy Persky to keep his lip buttoned. He's the one to worry about."

You could see in the manner in which he moved around our kitchen—no sense of its being another man's place—that McIntyre was eased by rage. He moved with a cowboy's swagger, a stiff-legged lurching, the chin in advance, the elbows wide as if he didn't care what he bumped.

"Is there a God in heaven, Jake, who's up there screwing me?"

"That question isn't in my line."

"Job is in your bible, Jake. You know Job. He had troubles. But one thing he didn't suffer from was a wop bitch." He remembered Evka was there and apologized. "I'm under a strain," he said.

"We all are," Jake said.

McIntyre turned on him with those intense blue eyes, rimmed in red. "What problems you got, Jake?"

"It's worse for you."

" 'An eye for an eye . . .' That's in your bible, too, isn't it, Jake?"

"Mine? Why mine?"

"I've run out of cheeks. I've run out of eyes. Now I want action. I want to see Kravitz bleed."

Jake wanted Germans to bleed. McIntyre wanted Kravitz to bleed. And there was more chance that we'd see Kravitz' blood than that we'd see German blood.

XVI

———◄◆►———

HEAVY SNOWS came before Christmas. I looked into the alley
from the bedroom and saw lacy skies. The hard turf of
the yard was covered. There were tracks on the lid of the
garbage pail. We had busy rats in our alley. The garage
roof had a dome that curled around the eaves. The garage
windows were narrowed by bulges of snow on the panes and
sills. Our bedroom windows was frosted with starry crystals.
The radiator knocked. Jake tended the furnace before he left
in the morning. Then it was my job or Ernie's to stoke up
before school. I reached in with the iron claw and hauled
out clinkers. I rattled the grate and shook down ashes. I
shoveled clinkers and ashes into bushel baskets. Once a week
Ernie and I hauled out ashes. We banked the coal so it would
last, careful not to bury the fire. We checked the water level
and filled the well in the belly of the furnace. It was a job
I didn't like doing at night. I stumbled down the last flight
of cellar stairs in the dark. I opened the cellar door and passed

the latticed storage bins, batting my hands in the air until I connected with the overhead light chain, dreading something else my hands might encounter. I feared something furry that could see in the dark while I was blind. Whenever it was my turn for the night trip, I nerved myself to go, but I never became used to it.

The hissing of the shovel as it slipped between concrete and coal relieved me. First a hiss, then a grating, then a tumbling of coal. I balanced the load to the open furnace, inserted the shovel, and placed the coal where the fire needed it— not at the most intense point of the fire, or the coal would be too quickly consumed; not in the cooling, ashy part of the fire, where the new coal might smother the remaining embers, but in that intermediate area where the new coal would ignite and provide an even bed.

Jake warned us to keep all doors locked. He made sure the house was buttoned up before he went to bed. He provided inside latches for all the doors. He dropped venetian blinds, then pulled drapes. He warned against snipers who might aim at silhouettes. He knew of men who could slip through tiny openings, who could jimmy windows, cut through glass. They moved without sound. They materialized in the dark; they used knives. Throat-cutters, head breakers, snipers. That was the penalty for having Jake Gottlieb as a pa.

Evka begged him not to frighten us.

"Let them be frightened. That's an education. Let them find out what kind of a world it is."

The ringing of the phone woke us regularly. I saw Ernie rise to his elbows in the bed across from mine. We heard Evka's bare feet on the floor of the neighboring bedroom. Jake wasn't yet home. She shook the house as she ran down the corridor. We heard her ask in a sleep-rusted voice for the caller's name. I heard the tone of mournful pleading as she begged to know, "Who is this?" She repeated the request but received no answer. "Tell me who you are," she said, "or I hang up." She hung up and went to the living room. We heard the snap of the light switch. The crack under our door was ignited.

When I arose, Ernie told me to go back to bed.

I knew what Evka suffered and didn't want her to be alone. She sat in Jake's Morris chair across from the Philco. She wore a flannel nightgown, her bare feet planted among the flowers of the rug.

She urged us to go back to sleep, but I knew she was relieved that we were up.

"Who called?"

"They wouldn't tell."

"What did they want?" We had an entire crew tormenting us by phone, so we referred to each caller as "they."

"They ask, 'Is Jake in?' I ask, 'Who's calling?' They laugh at me for not being able to tell where Jake is. Like they know something I don't."

When Jake arrived, we ran for bed, Evka commanding us, "Quick! Quick!" In bed we listened to the sounds of his approach. Evka closed the kitchen door and the rest was muffled.

Sometimes he didn't arrive till morning, and Evka, grateful for our company, prepared snacks—Ovaltine and cookies—and entertained us. Though I wanted to sleep, I refused her command to go to bed. She wanted us there. Ernie stayed because I did.

Sometimes she got a deck of cards. We sat on the carpet and played gin and casino. Once she produced a song sheet, and we learned "Blue Moon," and "The Isle of Capri." At two or three in the morning we sometimes forgot the occasion for our being there. Evka tried to distract us and became absorbed by her singing. Her hands clapped a different tune. They didn't squeeze misery from the air. They struck an exuberant beat. This mingling of joy and despair resembled effects I've seen in Chekhov plays: each character acknowledges he's come to the end of his rope. Misery accumulates. Then a few drinks. An accordion pumps a tune. An old man does a jig. Suddenly the stage erupts. The mood becomes brilliant. It can't, however be sustained. Enthusiasm peters out; silence weighs even more heavily. Evka's songs had that effect; for a moment we were illuminated, and then her anxiety returned and she went to kitchen and sighed and rocked.

In those early-morning hours you could hear Dexter Avenue traffic from two blocks away. Buses made bleating sounds. Dexter was salted down on snowy nights, and we heard cars throw up waves of slush. The side streets weren't salted, and snow was piled high along the gutters. Wheel ruts were packed with hard snow. The slushy sound ended when a car turned up a side street. We heard tires whine as drivers tried to spin from snowy moorings. Jake's van was unmistakable because of a faulty muffler. It entered Richton in the morning silence as if it were revving up for a take-off.

Often, when the tension was greatest, we'd receive another phone call. Evka leaped for the phone, so awkward in her panic she appeared foolish. She was a perfect sucker for the sadist on the other end of the line.

The same thing. "Who is it? Tell me who it is or I'll hang up."

Ernie yelled at her one night. "Hang up! Just hang up! Don't be so nice to them!"

The next time the phone rang she asked him to answer. "What's your name?" he demanded. The answer startled him. He hung up.

"He wouldn't tell you?"

"He said something dirty."

A moment later the phone rang again. Ernie rushed for it and yelled, "You son of a bitch." He hung up and it rang again. "Let it ring," he ordered. It rang for several minutes. We were quiet and didn't move. The phone pumped its clamor into every room in the house.

"Maybe it's Jake," Ma suggested.

"It's that bastard. Pa wouldn't call this late."

"What if something happened?"

Finally Ernie answered. He spoke politely. "I can't give any information unless I have your name." The voice on the other end made threats. I could see that Ernie was nervous.

Afterward we arranged a signal with Jake. We answered the phone only when it resumed after a three-ring warning. But what if something should happen to Jake and a friend called to inform us and didn't know the signal? As we waited for the phone to exhaust itself during those long nights, we were never sure that a desperate Jake wasn't vainly signaling us.

It was the Christmas season, a fine time for a Messiah to arrive; we were willing to settle for Jake Gottlieb. The trees down the center of Chicago Boulevard were skeletons for snow mounds. A bitter winter. I walked down Chicago Boulevard with Ernie, scarves inside padded jackets, fists bunched inside furry gloves. Snow powder whipped my eyes, chewing my nose and lips. A rotten night to be out. But worse to be in, waiting for Jake. We walked the Boulevard on our way to Leonard Mitchell (and viewed the Christmas spectacle). Christmas trees sprouted on the boulevards off Dexter, where our rich were established in fine English manors with steep-pitched slate roofs. The houses were decked with lights; long driveways were loaded with Lincolns and Chryslers and Cadillacs. Party time. Spectacular trees burned in snowflakes. The Boulevard narrowed to a snow-padded corridor the width of a car. Snow banks were piled high. Snow was fluffy on bushes, new-fallen, still coming down. What a scene from indoors! How lovely! Vacation time, and there were parties up and down the length of Chicago Boulevard. We looked into casement windows where chandeliers picked up the flame of fireplaces. We saw a party moving through a parlor—champagne glasses, food on a buffet, a silver tree in the window—drifting beyond the scope of our vision, reappearing in the next parlor. We saw lovely girls home from school, with fine bosoms and womanly tricks that put them beyond our reach. Our grubby hands would never dare to grasp. Their scent alone put them in a different class. Such sweet-smelling ladies would enter only the dreams of Gottliebs, not their lives. Gottliebs didn't smell so hot. Ernie and I were kin to that Jake Gottlieb who returned home with that special stink produced by Fiori's defective van. We walked down Chicago, not speaking, nostrils burning, cartoon puffs marking every breath. No trees for us. No lovely girls for us. On behalf of the God we denied, we turned our backs on Christmas trees. We enjoyed the spectacle of those who were rich enough to assume any manner that pleased them. Jews flaunted Christmas trees. We froze and watched. We crunched the hard crust of snow and broke through to the fluffy base, snow swelling over the edges of our rubbers, leaking into our socks. Numb feet on Chicago Boulevard. We saw boys our age warmed by pretty girls. Didn't I know Ernie's dream? He dreamed of a different father and a different mother, able to secure a house on Chicago Boulevard and accept the glory of Christmas trees.

Who wanted to return to the morbid home where all we could do was wait for Jake?

We turned on Linwood, past the schoolyard. Snow covered the playing fields. The shadowy buildings in clouds of snow were the size of castles. We turned toward the seedy neighborhood where Leonard Mitchell lived.

A squat, yellow apartment house, snow improved it; it was best seen on snowy nights. On summer days you could take the full measure of that grubby place—a fetid cabbage odor. Did we expect to find Christmas cheer at Leonard's? The window shades were cracked, with ragged fringes and no tension to the roller springs. Some shades were down forever. Those that were raised allowed a view of broken windows. Craters of paint erupted on the ceiling; peels curled back from the center. The wallpaper had pissy stains. The furniture was in crippled condition, chairs with bad legs and backs, a living-room table with a leaf buttressed by a section of broomstick.

Leonard Mitchell was worse off than we were. A lot he cared: he returned home to eat and sleep. The rest of the time he prowled. His orientation was less toward Dexter, the bourgeois heart of our neighborhood, than toward proletarian Twelfth Street, where Connie's Pool Hall was located. At fifteen he was already a talented snooker player. Weinberg and Spiegelman were the reigning lords at Connie's. Leonard was respectful to these men and willing to be of service. He brought them coffee from The Cream of Michigan across the street. He had other ways of serving them that he didn't reveal to us. They provided him with money for his Windsor trips.

Leonard wanted Ernie to enter Connie's Pool Hall while Ernie wanted Leonard to enter the battlefields of our lead soldiers. Pool at Connie's was the riskier game. I accompanied Ernie to make sure he remembered that there were limits. Yet, for me, too, it was a relief to know that Leonard Mitchell was at the end of our walk that winter night. What did he have in mind for us? Windsor again, where I might also take that terrible chance with Frances Regina? He took us to Connie's, with its green-shaded lamps centered above green felt tables, the place alive with colliding balls thudding off hard cushions, clicking beads racking up scores. The cozy smell of cigar smoke. Freezing outside. The spectators on the benches along the walls circulated Twelfth Street legends. They told, for instance, about an Italian—Joe Somebody—who had a special glove fitted so that it could support an ice pick. Joe was a wicked man in a fight. We listened to stories about Spiegelman, who stalked snooker balls in a feverish rhythm at the center table. Spiegelman, they said, moved as though he were disembodied—and not only around pool tables. He could enter any place. Locks couldn't stop him. Nor walls. Not windows or doors. Neither size nor muscle intimidated him. Nor reputation nor charm. He seeped through cracks. He drifted through holes. He materialized in the room of the marked man. There was no way to keep him out when he wished to enter. Spiegelman with those clever hands had a natural affinity for tools and machinery. He was expert with knife, gun, knuckles, blackjack. He was said to be surer than cholera. And the cholera, they knew, was sure indeed. What was alarming about Spiegelman was that he was opaque, no clarity in his mind, so radical in his empiricism he wanted to confirm everything, human and otherwise, with a Johnsonian boot. Liable to furies. He lived alone with his mother; the fellows on the benches took this as a sign that there was a core of tenderness beneath that impenetrable exterior. Wasn't it further evidence of humanity that Spiegelman was so attached to Happy Weinberg? Weinberg, though he might commit horrors, was at least in touch. He recognized you. He remembered your name. He liked kids. You told him a joke and he squeezed your arm and left bruises. Only Weinberg could tease Spiegelman, no one else. Only when he listened to Weinberg did Spiegelman ease up on his ferocious concentration. He never smiled. You had to be careful with Spiegelman. If he thought you ridiculed him, he'd be at your throat. You had to be clear and simple when you approached Spiegelman, no vagueness or ambiguity. The fellows on the benches sought evidence that he was human and were willing to settle for that.

It was a strange crowd at Connie's. Men older than Jake, kids Leonard's age, and yet no hierarchy of age. The good storyteller ruled the benches. The one with the sharpest eye, cleverest hands and steadiest nerves bossed the tables. Charmers like Happy Weinberg were lords of the place. Merit determined rank at Connie's Pool Hall, that yeshiva for our toughs. Age was ordinarily considered to be a virtue in itself in our neighborhood. One presumed practical wisdom in the elderly; a man a generation ahead of you was probably no more foolish than your own father. We respected even fools if they were of an age. Not at Connie's, though, where old men were ridiculed if they were old fools. That troubled me. If they didn't spare old fools, how rough might they be with young ones? Fortunately we had Leonard Mitchell to sponsor us.

We ventured into the center area, where men operated, and I felt as exposed as if I were in Windsor following Frances Regina. Leonard gathered balls within the wooden triangle, swirled them into position on the spot, and lifted away the

frame. He chalked his cue, considered the phalanx of beautifully enameled balls, bent swiftly, darted the cue stick at the
cue ball; then, with a long stroke, drove hard into the crowd
and sent balls flying toward pockets. He explained by doing;
he called his shots and dropped them, keeping his eye on the
table even while giving us instructions. He made his decisions
quickly. He walked to the right, then to the left, bent, darted
at the ball, followed with a sure stroke, sometimes delicately
performed, sometimes with force. You could see that he would
do well in Frances Regina's bedroom.

He was a patient teacher. He didn't embarrass us by making
a show of our incompetence. When language failed him, he
bent down and illustrated. His skill proved to the spectators
that our table was in the possession of someone who rightfully
belonged.

Happy Weinberg showed up with his camel's-hair coat unbuttoned, the collar up, a fedora pushed back so that we had a
good view of that globe of a face, red shiny cheeks, green eyes,
a tiny nose, a small chin, a face so open, so simple, so genial
you could never mistake him for an adult. However, there were
the two hundred and fifty pounds beneath that face, and the
freckled, bulging hands were tools of murder. He was as well
decorated as a Christmas tree. His suit coat, I recall, had lively
checks, and, when the stiff padding was added to the enormous
spread of his true shoulders, he occupied a considerable space.
A hand-painted tie was held by a jeweled clip. He was as
bountiful as Santa Claus.

"How's the pa?" Some pa these boys had, he announced to
the men at Connie's. Gottlieb, the union man. What nerve
that Gottlieb had! "Your pa is crazy, know that, kiddies?" He
said it in so admiring a tone that we realized there was a kind
of madness Weinberg respected. "He got no worries about his
head. He's a baldy, right? What a target. Crazy. He opens his
big mouth. And what for? Not for Lincoln and Washington.
He don't like George Washington or Abraham Lincoln. No

respect for the presidents of the USA." Weinberg reached into his back pocket and produced a wallet crammed with pictures of presidents. Weinberg learned the history of the United States from currency. He was no wise guy like Gottlieb. He learned his arithmetic and his presidents through cash transactions. "Tell me the truth, kiddies: is your pa some kind of a Red?" Ernie reassured him that our pa was no Red. "We're all Americans, right? Like my buddy, Leonard. Right? You know what a buck can do, right, kids? You aren't the ones to knock the presidents of the US, isn't that so? I offer you, for instance, five bucks, you'd have an idea it's not just to wipe your ass with, right? Don't knock it, kiddies; you know what money can buy. You been out to Windsor with my buddy, Leonard. Your pa is something else. What's he, stupid?" He spoke to Ernie so genially, with real puzzlement, that Ernie wasn't offended. After all, Ernie had no contempt for money; he was no Red.

"My pa believes in the working class . . ." Ernie struggled for a vocabulary that would establish him in Happy's eyes as an intellectual, able to make neutral statements about his pa, since his interest was entirely academic. I remember how he spoke about Jake to Happy Weinberg: "He's an idealist. He believes the workingman has a right to the fruits of his labor." Which was no more than Jake had said about himself and therefore no betrayal, but an ingratiating smile informed Happy that Ernie was no fool like his pa.

"The what?"

"The workingman."

"Screw the son of a bitch. Right, kid?"

While Jake was on the highway maneuvering through snow to escape hoodlums, Weinberg mocked him at Connie's Pool Hall.

"I like these kids," Happy said to Spiegelman. He invited us to accompany him and Spiegelman for a drive in his new Hudson.

Leonard accepted for us.

Weinberg's Hudson was better-equipped than home. The dashboard gleamed with chrome fittings. Ernie and I sat in back with Leonard. Whitey Spiegelman drove. He moved the car through slushy avenues and icy side streets with the same confidence he exhibited at the pool table. Spiegelman had a comfortable connection with things. He knew the geography of a pool table or a city as lovers know bodies. He slid through yellow lights, passed traffic in lanes made risky by packed snow. He accelerated on clear stretches, guiding us over patches of ice that could have snapped the car off the road. We headed into the countryside along the Oswego road.

We drove past a darkened amusement park at the end of the city. I saw coils of roller-coaster track loom up in the snowy night. Detroit abruptly ended in snow-covered farms. The sky cleared, and we observed a dazzling moon, not blurred by city lights. I recognized the constellations I had learned from sessions with Ernie and Moshe Bodkin—Orion, the Dippers, Cassiopeia's Chair, the Seven Sisters.

We stopped at the BRIGHTON INN AND STEAK HOUSE, a colonial building with fluted columns in front, gables covered by dark shingles, with dark, louvered shutters, the rest white, a gravel lot in front and back, the windows covered by venetian blinds. There were neon advertisements for Goebels and Strohs beer in the windows.

Spiegelman parked in the back lot.

"Hold it here, pals," Weinberg told us. "Me and Whitey need a few seconds for some business. Don't worry about the battery; use the radio."

We listened to the Eddie Cantor program signing off, a singing farewell that was enthusiastically applauded.

> If they feel like a war
> On some foreign shore
> Let them keep it over there   (*Applause*)
> If some fools want to fight
> And think might makes right
> Let them keep it over there. . . .

Applause drowned out the rest of his anti-Hobbesian message. Who wanted to fight? Fools! The Poles, for instance? The
gypsies? The Jews? Why were they so eager to tangle with
the Nazis? Two years later, when America was blasted at
Pearl Harbor, our comic sage changed his tune. He beckoned
us to war. The cheers went the other way. He reversed his
field with aplomb, lapping up every speck of good will en
route.

When Spiegelman and Weinberg hadn't returned after half
an hour, Leonard went to find them. Ernie and I were left
alone in the car, the motor running, the snow speckled by the
exhaust, the radio competing with the heater.

The car was aimed toward the plowed fields behind the inn.
We saw the tepee shapes of abandoned hayricks crusted with
snow. We saw Detroit reflected in the sky beyond.

We waited for three quarters of an hour. I wanted to go
after them, but Ernie refused. We had our orders from Weinberg, and Ernie was a good soldier.

"What are we waiting for? They're inside having fun, and
we're stuck in the car."

I stepped out to pee. Steam rose from the glittering snow
as I carved through. A lucid night, the whole spread of stars
visible. We were numb in seconds.

"You wait," I told Ernie. "I'm going inside." He followed me.

We entered a bar that was almost totally dark. We could see
an array of faces reflected in the bar mirror. We entered a
dining room with a red carpet and star-shaped chandeliers made
of tinselly material. Light seeped around walls and ceilings.
There were other dining rooms beyond and then a dance floor
with a juke box, where we found Leonard watching the ladies.
He didn't know where Weinberg had gone. He led us back
to the car to continue waiting.

More than an hour passed before they rejoined us. They
arrived all steamed up. Had they been drinking? Happy was
flushed. He smelled of snow when he entered the car. I ob-

served snow on the skirts of his overcoat. His galoshes were covered with snow almost to the top buckle.

"Everybody happy?" He commandeered our assent with his bullying enthusiasm. What good temper! I attributed it to drink. Even Spiegelman seemed amiable. No smile, but the hat was shoved back and his balding top exposed. The slight exposure made him seem relaxed.

Our destination was The Cream of Michigan. We sat up front, at a table reserved for hoodlum royalty. Neckless giants dismounted from their stools and trundled over to greet Weinberg. We were introduced as the sons of Gottlieb. I knew that we compromised Jake by appearing in such company. Still, we were intimate with the heroes of Twelfth Street. The night had brought us unexpected profit. Returning via Chicago Boulevard for a last glimpse of the good life, we were no longer envious. All those party-goers were cozy beneath their chandeliers, but we had rubbed against monsters and emerged intact. We agreed not to inform Jake about the company we kept.

It wasn't a night to be out. The chill had deepened. Our radiators were open to full steam, and they hissed and cracked. The chill leaked through all the seams of our wooden house. Jake was still out there. We heard no traffic. We could barely see the blurred halos of street lamps through the iced windows. A strong wind. The porch glider groaned. Radio reception was bad on all channels save one, which fed us a steady diet of Christmas carols.

It was a relatively dead time for news. The Germans were engorged and quiescent. There didn't seem any likelihood that the war would become serious for anyone but Poles and Jews. On this night we listened to a maverick commentator who defied history and justice and used the airwaves to degrade whatever provoked his malice. His meaning was clear despite his awkward circumlocutions. Who, after all, made a fuss about Hitler? Who, really, had reason to fear the Nazis? Christians?

No. Americans? No. Was Hitler our enemy? No, said this commentator. He was rather the consequence of coddling our real enemies. These he identified as John L. Lewis, F. D. Roosevelt, Earl Browder, and unnamed international financiers. They were the ailment; Hitler was the cure. Admittedly a savage cure. The war demonstrated that France and England were corrupted by socialism. Rotten moral fiber.

We had to listen to this flatulent, sneering, derisive voice deliver its venom in a contemptuous monotone that seemed always on the brink of a belch. Why didn't we turn him off? Why did we suffer? I suppose we wanted to hear what damage was being done to us. Anyone who found Hitler supportable also had a stomach for the slaughter of Jews. The popularity of the man indicated we had powerful enemies in the world, and not only in Germany.

The phone calls started early that night. None were prefaced by the proper signal so we didn't answer. We were asleep when Jake returned.

I came out of a bad dream to hear the wind shake our house. That house could be shaken. It was a big yellow box that was weak in all its joints and visibly lopsided. I remember how it used to grind against itself in a strong wind. On bitter nights it grieved like an old bum caught in the cold, shuddering and groaning. Ernie was on his elbows, a reluctant riser. I heard a thundering bass, a croaking powerful voice that I could make out through both bedroom and kitchen doors. I recognized Emerson. There was another voice that I'd never heard, shrill and buoyant.

Emerson cursed the boss. He cursed Karl Marx. To the idea of class consciousness he said, "Fuck you." He cursed all intellectuals. "I don't need a god-damn' education." Evidently Jake had been urging caution on theoretical grounds. Emerson didn't want theory. Like everyone else, he wanted blood. Blood would ease him. Drink it, bathe in it, what did it matter? Let it pour. That was also his idea of justice.

"No son of a bitch is going to push us around, Gottlieb. If

we get pushed, we push back. That's our way, Gottlieb. Maybe it's not yours. To hell with Karl Marx. Now we got an idea of how Kravitz wants it. Fine. Okay. We can play that game, too. If he wants to get rough, we'll take off our gloves with pleasure."

We went into the hallway and saw Evka there, in her bathrobe, pressed against the wall near the kitchen door. She motioned us to return to bed but we ignored her. The kitchen door swung free on hinges, stirring in the draft that came down the corridor. When the crack widened, we saw McIntyre slumped at the kitchen table, his head covered by a bandage, his face buried in his arms. We could see dried blood on his ears, a stain on the bandage.

Jake asked him, "What happened, Mac? I still don't know."

Emerson answered. "Someone was laying for him on the Oswego road. Guess who, Gottlieb?"

"That's what I want to find out from his own lips. You know my feelings about police. But if necessary, we'll bring them in. We don't live in a jungle."

"The hell we don't. Go to the police? What good will that do? Kravitz got the police in his pocket."

"Where and when did it happen?"

"On the Oswego road, that's where. About nine o'clock. With cars driving by."

"Let Mac tell it, Emerson. I want to hear the story from him."

McIntyre straightened up. Whoever had clobbered him had knocked him free of rage. But, then, he was still dazed. He asked if someone had called his home. Emerson assured him that his mother had been told he was at a meeting and would be home late.

The shrill voice spoke. Its origin was beyond our line of sight. "That's a honey of a beating. It wasn't done with just bare hands. You're lucky to get off with only a headache."

McIntyre told the story. He was on the Oswego road, returning with a load. He saw no lights behind him. The road was icy. He was driving carefully. An old Chevy pulled out of a lane in front of his truck. He had to swerve, and they almost collided. He passed on the left and slowed his truck down and drove hub to hub with the Chevy, keeping it pinned in the right lane. He cursed the driver, a skinny, swarthy man with a doughy nose and not much of a chin. The fellow wore a fedora. McIntyre was in a mood to kill. He threatened to run the guy off the road. The driver stared so insolently that McIntyre was ready to smash him. Oncoming traffic forced him to pull ahead into the proper lane. A moment later the Chevy gunned past and cut so suddenly that he was forced onto the shoulder, so McIntyre chased the Chevy. It turned down a farm lane, and he followed. The farm house was set back from the highway and the Chevy stopped halfway there, its motor running. McIntyre parked the truck directly in back, athwart the lane, so the Chevy couldn't escape. He took a wrench with him. The guy just sat there, grinning, and McIntyre grabbed for the door. That's as far as he got. He saw the giant behind him wearing a blue and gold athletic jacket. McIntyre knew immediately from the power of the grip that he was in trouble. He hauled back with the wrench, and, the next he knew he was on his hands and knees, staring at rubber galoshes. He heard the car door open and someone laugh. He was hit in the ribs and was unable to breathe. He'd come to with his face in the snow and two pairs of galoshes around him. He tried to look up and was hit in the back of the head. He tried to tell them he couldn't breathe. Again he came to with his face in the snow, saliva thick in his throat, unable to smell, breathing through his mouth, his ears plugged. On his knees again, staring at trousers, massive thighs, a huge belly, and then down once more. The next time, he kept his head bent and braced himself on his hands. Someone had his shoulders. These galoshes buckled almost to the knees. It was the farmer. The truck was backed off the road into a ditch, the bundles toppled into the snow.

He lurched up, refusing the farmer's support. At that moment he wanted to be able to swoop through the air and get them in his grip and smash them as they had smashed him, even the score with the lousy fate that pursued him. How could he face his mother and kids, looking as he did?

The shrill voice intruded. "You got your lumps, all right. No use crying about it. They suckered you into going up that lane. Whoever was laying for you knows our route to Oswego. That's what we got to worry about."

McIntyre recalled that his assailants used a Jewish expression: shmuck.

"Whoever did it," Jake said, "Kravitz will pay."

"That's the ticket," said the shrill voice. "Kravitz is the one we go for."

McIntyre wanted to know how come they were waiting for him on the Oswego road. He hadn't been followed.

"There's a fink," said Emerson.

Jake said that Kravitz was in for a disappointment if he thought he could dent the spirit of the union by violence. Violence would only strengthen their spirit.

"How are you going to make it clear to him, Jake?" asked the shrill voice. "You going to preach him a sermon?" For the first time he came into view, with his sailor's walk, a chunky powerhouse with red hair, his axe-shaped chin marked by a dimple. It was the first time I saw O'Brien. He moved with a jerky motion, as though braced against the weather. His movements were always definitive. He was in his late twenties then, just beginning after a false start. He had served a long hitch in the navy; he got out before the war. He emerged from the depression on the make. I can be fair to O'Brien. The others had provincial ambitions, while O'Brien imagined himself in the company of kings. I never heard anyone deny his courage or his intelligence. When I say his voice was shrill, I don't mean to suggest that it was strained or unmanly; it was a commanding voice.

"How will you make it clear, Jake? If all Kravitz has to worry about when he tells the hoods to operate is that you'll preach a sermon, he's not going to worry much. Talk don't worry Kravitz. Kravitz got a big mouth himself."

"He's worrying already," said Jake. "Otherwise he wouldn't turn to violence. When he permits such things, his back is to the wall."

"You ain't the only one who knows him," said Emerson. "We got a fink who knows him."

"What fink?" Jake asked.

Fiori had insisted that the role of White Swan be kept secret. "Now, what if he won't wash?" Emerson asked. "What if he quits on us because some rotten fink has squealed to Kravitz?"

Jake said Fiori couldn't be allowed to quit.

O'Brien wasn't concerned about Fiori. Fiori could be handled, but the fink was another matter.

McIntyre said, "It's Sammy Persky. We all know that."

Jake denied that Persky knew anything. "We kept him out of it because you and Emerson were suspicious. He knows nothing about Oswego."

O'Brien said, "Someone is going to crack. We better make up our minds that it's going to be Kravitz. It's getting rough, and some of our boys don't have a stomach for rough business."

Jake said, "Stomachs weren't made for such business."

"Our boys got to stay in line. They got to know that if they break discipline it'll cost them. That's the only way to run this business."

"What will they pay? They're broke. They got absolutely nothing. They live off their own lean meat."

"They got blood in their veins and brains in their heads. They got something, Jake."

"If you know how to make payments with blood, you're a magician."

"If they step out of line, we knock out their brains. That's how they'll pay."

"In my union we don't practice such magic."

O'Brien reminded Jake of his obligations to fifty drivers who had put everything on the line because of him.

"We don't even know if there's a fink," Jake said. "Why make problems?"

"Sammy's our boy," McIntyre said. "We all know it."

"Forget Sammy. You got Sammy on the brain."

"No, sir. I don't forget him. I don't forget that little fanny-grabber."

"Because he grabs fannies doesn't mean he betrays his brothers."

"Brothers, shit!"

"You're upset, McIntyre, for which I don't blame you. You've had terrible luck."

Evka shoved us toward the bedroom when she heard someone rise from the table.

I told Ernie, "The two who beat up McIntyre are your friends."

"What friends?"

"We were near the Oswego road. The inn is a few minutes away."

"What are you talking about?"

"How come they were gone so long? Where were they?"

"Inside. Where else could they be?"

"How do you know they didn't go out the front and climb into another car? They were covered with snow."

"Why do you think up such things? To make everyone miserable? Are you so jealous?"

"Me, jealous?"

"You want to spoil it for everyone, don't you? You pretend to be such a sweetheart of a kid. You'd love being a friend of Leonard for your own sake, not just because you're my kid brother."

"What can he do for me—take me to a whorehouse?"

Ernie asked, "If it weren't for me, who would know your name? What friends would you have?"

"Just pray that the police don't call Weinberg and Spiegelman," I said, "because they got a great alibi. They spent the time of the beating with Gottlieb's sons."

Two Jewish hoodlums, one doughy-nosed, swarthy, chinless, the other a giant. I had good reason to be suspicious.

We were in the bedroom. The men were still in the kitchen. McIntyre wanted blood, and Emerson egged him on. There was an insult from McIntyre. A pause. Jake spoke softly. We could tell from the rhythm of his speech that he was near an explosion.

Meanwhile, Ernie and I continued to quarrel.

—Jealous, he charged.

—Anything Leonard orders you to do, you'll do.

—Got any friends of your own? Who?

—Frances Regina.

—Don't you wish . . .

—Don't *you* wish, Grandpa?

He jumped into my bed and grabbed me in a headlock and started squeezing. I flailed at his ribs but I could do nothing. He commanded my apologies while I choked. He released me long enough to hear, "Never, Grandpa," and I jammed him with my elbow and provoked fierce twisting. I couldn't yell. He was murderous. I saw his face. Teeth showing, a little growl as he put on the pressure. My eyes bugged, and I managed to wiggle off the bed. Evka heard the flop and came in and broke it up.

"You hear what's going on in the kitchen! Are you insane? What gets into you at such a time?"

Jake blew up, and we stopped fighting in order to listen. "This time I'll let you get away with it. You been hit on the head. I'll assume you're cuckoo from hits on the head. But don't say one word more. Just shut up. Head or no head, one more word will be too much."

"Don't you worry about my head, Gottlieb. All Jerusalem can bang on my head and it won't do no damage."

O'Brien intervened to prevent a fight. He warned McIntyre to watch his tongue when he addressed the president of the union. "You must be scrambled," he said. "Keep it up and I'll take you on myself."

"I'll give him the benefit," Jake said.

"I don't need no benefit."

"Don't be too proud to call the police. We support them with our taxes."

"I'll handle my own problems. I don't need police when it comes to them sons of bitches."

"Take care, McIntyre. Don't say it again. I heard enough from you."

O'Brien told Emerson to get him home, and finally they left. Jake called Evka. "Come out already. I know you been listening. Don't be shy all of a sudden."

Jake remembered what McIntyre risked out of loyalty to him and regretted the argument. He refused to repeat what McIntyre had said. "I feel sorry for him. Do you know how strong he is? I once saw him for a joke lift Emerson on his shoulder and run with him like he carried a baby. A goodhearted man. Trouble has got him down. With such a wife, who wouldn't blow up? And the little girl besides." He took it as grounds for personal shame that Jews had contributed to the degradation of this proud man.

"It's the Cream of Michigan crowd."

XVII

―――――◆●◆―――――

JAKE LIVED in the shadow of Hitler. Even the war against Atlas didn't distract him from the main campaign. No matter what shape he was in he ended his day listening to commentators who broadcast around the clock. He fell asleep in his Morris chair with the daily news in his lap. Years passed before we heard good news. Jake would have benefited more than any of us, but he wasn't around.

We went to Connie's the following night, and Ernie asked Leonard what happened at the inn.

"I don't mean to pry, but could they have left by the front way while we were waiting?"

"Why would they do that?"

"A man in my pa's union got beat up on the Oswego road last night."

"We were in the back lot of the Brighton Inn. Just remember that."

"But we were close to the Oswego road."

"So what? So is Chicago, Illinois."

"I don't want to believe that any of us was involved."

"You weren't involved. I'll swear to that. You were with me and Happy and Whitey."

Though Ernie pressed the questions very lamely, Leonard became irritated. "Just tell me what you're getting at. Quit hinting around and say it straight. Are you trying to say I'd double-cross my pal?"

"I know you wouldn't."

"You're damn' right I wouldn't."

I studied that crew—Mitchell, Weinberg, Spiegelman—and decided that the look of innocence proved nothing. They would remain innocent whatever they did. They focused on the simple responses of billiard balls in collision. Europe wasn't part of their miseries. They listened to every sound of the radio except the news. They even listened to advertisements and considered the merits of competing brands whatever the product—cigarettes, razor blades, automobiles. Even if they had assaulted McIntyre, they would feel neither remorse nor guilt. The loony wife didn't matter to them, nor the idiot girl. They couldn't be touched. They had no shame and they had no fear. They didn't worry about Hitler operating in Europe like a plague. They could slip out of the inn, exchange coats for jackets, step into a Chevy, wait for McIntyre, entice him into a farm lane, beat him into the snow, then retire to The Cream of Michigan and eat with good appetite. In Ernie's eyes such coolness made the world manageable. They were established as heroes. They could operate with zest while Jews burned elsewhere. There was no evidence they remembered their crime: they studied rebounds.

Ernie's most urgent desire from the time of childhood was to evade history by losing his memory. He envied the brutes. I know my brother. He wanted to become a brute so he might be spared the catastrophe we all waited for. Brutes don't anticipate events or remember. They have a brief, interminable journey through life which they accept moment by moment, all preceding moments being dismissed.

And why should we be obliged to our history? Why not Christmas? A time for joy. Parties, gifts. Something wonderful happens. The bitterest days of the year are transformed by bells, chimes, songs. Despite your inclination to hole up until decent weather, you're forced into the world. Your capacity for joy is tested. They say it's a time for suicide. Yet without the winter holiday, how many more might die? Though we refused to carol and acknowledge Christmas, it was imposed on us by displays of trees and lights, rotogravure pictures of brown turkeys belly up in roasting pans, and forced holidays. Jake and I were stained by memory. History was inside our skins. Let them celebrate on Chicago Boulevard and elsewhere. On Christmas Eve we went to the Perskys', where we were offered wine and schnapps.

"I drink to the baby Jesus." Sammy raised his glass.

Jake said, "I drink to a half day off."

"When we heard you were coming, I told Minnie, 'Stick the Christmas tree in the closet. Shove Santa up the chimney. Remove the stockings from the fireplace. Gottlieb's coming.'"

"Some joke."

"'Stand the reindeer on their hind legs so they'll be hat racks. Gottlieb's coming.'"

"If I didn't show up, who knows about you, Persky?"

"You think I'll risk a Christmas tree when Gottlieb would knock my head off?"

"Is that what keeps you honest, Sammy? The fear of damage?"

McIntyre may have encouraged Jake's suspicion of Sammy, but the idea was already there. He knew that Sammy's loyalties had shallow roots. Sammy's talent was for good times. He didn't piddle around with Christmas trees. He had more radical ideas of fun. Minnie, loops of imitation pearls dangling over the deeps of her bosom, honked her nose and sighed.

"A fine night," Sammy complained. "Peace on earth we can

have later. Right now I'll settle for peace in my own house."
Minnie had also been receiving anonymous phone calls, and she was upset. "At her age, a boy friend? Not my old Minnie. She got more than enough in her little Sammy here."

"That's what worries me," she sighed. "I'm not enough for him."

"Look at the size of her. Not enough? I got a surplus. What gets into her head all of a sudden?"

The anonymous caller offered details of a love nest Sammy shared with Kate Russo.

Sammy ridiculed the idea. "I told her that some bastard scab was trying to make trouble for the union."

"I believe you," Minnie said. "Because of the strike they want to torture me. Only why should such ideas come into their heads?"

"They got dirty minds is why. What a thing to tell a man's wife for Christmas!"

Minnie assured us she had complete faith in Sammy. Yet why should the man who phoned go into such detail? What good did it do anyone to torment her?

"Don't listen," Sammy told her. "You hold the phone in your hand, right? So who's boss, you or your hand? Did you think to hang up?"

A giggle bubbled through her sighs. "To tell you the truth, I'm interested to hear."

Later that night Jake gave Sammy another warning.

"Stay away from the Italian girl. She wants nothing better than to cause you trouble. She works for Kravitz."

Sammy didn't want any advice. "About my personal business I'm my own boss."

"I speak for your own good, Sammy."

"Every time somebody speaks for my own good I'm screwed. Next week we're broke. Not a cent in the bank. I begin starving for my own good."

"We're all in the same boat."

"It gives me no pleasure I got such company."

"It bothers me that you're such a wise guy, Sammy."

"You ask me to make sacrifices, but do you trust me when it comes to union business? You act like I'm a spy. I'm not even supposed to know you wash in Oswego."

"Where did you hear such a thing? It's a lie."

"Sure it's a lie. Some secret. Even the Italian girl knows."

"What does she tell you?"

"She asks, 'Are you poor slobs still driving to Oswego every night?'"

"Pay no attention. She doesn't know a thing."

"Quit kidding me, Jake. It's your old pal, Sammy. Is it right that I sacrifice my income and yet you don't trust me? You can trust that ox McIntyre, but your old pal, who loves you, you can't trust?"

"I trust you, Sammy. I'm just sorry you hear things. Keep it to yourself and don't believe everything the Italian says. She's not so accurate."

A blizzard drove all traffic off the road on Christmas. That night there was an explosion at the Oswego plant. Jake was informed after dinner that White Swan had been dynamited.

"I got to leave for Oswego."

"In this weather, Jake?"

"Without a place to wash we can cut our throats."

He phoned Oswego before leaving. Fiori moaned that it was a mess. Ruined. The whole plant gutted. Nothing worth saving.

"How bad is it?"

"Bad enough even for you, Gottlieb."

"You're insured. It's my drivers I worry about."

"You got plenty to worry about, okay. You better worry about a place to wash. You're finished washing at the White Swan."

"I'm coming to look at the damage."

"Don't bother. There's no more wash from Detroit. I resign, Gottlieb."

"I'll be there in one hour."

131

Jake took O'Brien along. O'Brien is the man you'd think of for rough times. He had the nerve to undertake radical actions. Jake relied on him as he didn't on any of the others.

Jake didn't return till early morning. I never saw him so whipped. He sat at the table in his leather jacket.

Ma asked him, "You all right, Jake?"

"What a life!" He said this as if it were a life to surrender rather than cling to.

"Do you want to talk?"

"Why do we go on?"

She asked timidly, "Can you still wash at the White Swan? Was it a bad explosion?"

The plant had suffered only minor damage. A snow bank had served as a buffer against the dynamite charge which had cracked the wall. There was a mess of clothes inside but only minor damage to the equipment. But Fiori had lost his enthusiasm for the union. He refused to continue washing.

"What's here we'll finish, but no more. I'm cutting my losses."

"You're cutting our throats," Jake said.

"That's tough luck. But what more do you expect? My only shirt belongs to someone else in the wash. I'm broke, pal. You're all nice guys. Only I wish I never made your acquaintance. I still got my plant. Next time I won't be so lucky."

"You agreed to stay till the end."

"So the end is here. I'm saying right now is the end. I'm through."

"But we're not through, Fiori. For us it's life or death. We can't resign."

"Then go to Kravitz and make a deal. Maybe he'll take you back."

It was then that O'Brien intervened. The rest of the negotiations belonged to him. "Christ," he said, "why do we have to listen while he flaps his stupid mouth?"

Jake told O'Brien to calm down. He was sure Fiori would see reason.

O'Brien disregarded Jake. "I'm going to wash that smart-ass

look off your face, Fiori. I'll teach you something about washing."

Jake was shocked when O'Brien—without any further provocation or warning—slapped Fiori, a hard slap that made a fist of each finger. Fiori stumbled against a washing machine and fell down.

"Say," he said, "say, what is this?"

Jake told us he'd been stupefied while O'Brien undertook the beating of the little Italian. He protested weakly, "I don't go in for that stuff, O'Brien. Let him alone."

O'Brien twisted a soaked sheet into a braid and folded it over; aimed for the torso. Fiori crouched against the machine. He made no effort to defend himself. He covered his face.

"Ain't you got any pity?" O'Brien asked him, slamming him with the sheet to teach him pity. He grunted as he slammed the sheet sidearm, pulling Fiori's arms away from the place he chose to hit. "You give us a nice present for Christmas, don't you, Fiori? You son of a bitch welsher." He laid in with considerable muscle, and Jake let it happen. He felt womanish. He could take a beating, but he'd never been on the side of the torturers. He didn't intervene until Fiori was thoroughly clobbered. Perhaps the beating wasn't as prolonged or severe as he wished us to believe. He despised himself for having allowed the torture of Fiori.

Finally he grabbed O'Brien's arm. "That's enough. I don't like it."

"He can take it, Jake. Don't worry about him."

"I won't permit it any more."

"If we got no place to wash, the strike is finished. We lose."

"Ours is a long battle, O'Brien."

"If he puts us out of the plant, it's over tomorrow."

"We got a lifetime."

"You're kidding."

"You'll make terrible enemies for us, O'Brien."

"Fiori? An enemy? Naw, Jake. You'll see. There's no hard feelings. We won't have a better friend."

"I don't need such friends."

"You still playing games, Jake? Or don't you know a war when you're in one?"

"I've been in more wars than you, O'Brien."

"That's why you'll see it my way, Jake. You got no choice."

Did Jake fear O'Brien? His argument was lame. Both he and O'Brien had understood that he'd protested for form's sake and that O'Brien would be allowed to continue the education of Fiori. The fact was that Fiori and O'Brien did later become very close.

Jake wasn't easy on himself when he described the night's business to Evka. He'd waited outside in the blizzard while O'Brien had finished up, all sound deadened by an abrasive wind that sculpted a snowy world. It hadn't taken O'Brien long.

"He'll be glad to wash for us. He loves the union."

"They got tough guys working for them, too."

"We're tougher, Jake. When they believe that, they'll quit."

Jake understood that O'Brien was exceptional, not another McIntyre or Emerson. At twenty-seven he was in a rush to advance his ambition. He was prepared to excel at any cost. Nothing the Cream of Michigan crowd could dream of was beyond his imagination. He aimed sky-high, and he was ready to put his own life on the block; his life was his only capital.

Jake asked what would happen if Fiori went to the police.

"It's us against him. Our story is, he came at us and we defended ourselves. Fiori don't want publicity. What's he got to gain? He's our friend."

Evka was silent when she heard the story.

"So you finally got nothing to say?"

"What can I say?"

"Say you don't like it."

"I don't like it, Jake."

"Do you think that in this life we're free to do what we like?"

"We're not free. I know."

"I can hit a man, too. It's happened."

"You never could do like O'Brien, Jake."

"What gives you that idea, old lady?"

"O'Brien is a different type."

"My type loses. Maybe what we need is O'Brien."

"A fine world this would be."

"Who's talking about the world? I'm talking about Atlas Laundry and Linen. Unless we make Kravitz bleed, he'll put fifty men out of work, and all because I made big speeches. It's in none of your books; it's not in Karl Marx, but it's the way of the world. If we refuse to accept it, there will be no mention of us in history."

"Can you like this man and what he does, Jake?"

Jake said again that in this life a man wasn't free to do what he liked. Jake was in his late forties, and, while his ambition was high, his station was low. There is always the possibility that O'Brien was the man for the job, not Jake Gottlieb. I've said that Jake was tenacious, but maybe another quality was needed.

When he and O'Brien arrived at the plant, the firemen and the police had already left. The electricity was out. Someone had provided a kerosene lantern. Fiori wanted to be rid of the union since the power of Kravitz had become clear to him. He had gambled on the wrong team and wanted to cut his losses if possible. He had at first been abusive and truculent. Then O'Brien decked him. This was the kind of argument Fiori found convincing.

Jake despised Fiori, who dealt with men as if they represented only cash value. Fiori had a knack of saying what you loathed to hear. His manners were terrible. He was greedy and mean. Nonetheless, when Jake had seen him gray with shock, gagging from the belly punishment, trying to heave but only expelling air, his eyes pleading for help, he'd understood the price of victory and hadn't wanted to pay.

The route to Oswego was known. There was no longer any

135

need for subterfuge. The strike had reached the point when someone had to crack.

Emerson had his bundles dumped in slush while he was making a delivery. Others had their tires slashed.

Another driver was beaten while delivering to a barbershop on skid row, one bundle on his shoulder, another under his arm. Two men had started quarreling near the barbershop. A crowd gathered. There were bummy loiterers all around. The driver stood at the edge of the crowd and watched. He was hit from behind. He blacked out for a few seconds and came to with blood running down his cheek from a cut on his head. The bundles were broken open, sheets soaked in a puddle. His wallet was gone.

The police called it an old con. They didn't think it had anything to do with the strike. The strike was nothing but trouble to the police. Their lack of enthusiasm made it clear that the union couldn't rely on them to safeguard heads.

"Either we do it or no one will," O'Brien told the drivers assembled in Emerson's garage to consider the Oswego situation. "If it don't trouble us when we get knocked around, no one else will be troubled."

"Hit him in the pocket," said Emerson.

O'Brien doubted that Kravitz could be intimidated; he was no Fiori.

"Hit the plant," said Emerson. "He'll feel it. Give him a taste of the White Swan medicine."

"We are none of us here going to suggest anything illegal," O'Brien said. Do you see how he was taking over? He didn't intend taking a back seat to Jake. He ran that meeting. "For all we know, someone here is a fink."

McIntyre wanted to speak about the fink question. "How did they know about Oswego?" He turned around and studied Sammy. "Got any ideas, Persky?"

"Why should I have ideas?"

"We know Kravitz is your buddy. Why don't you ask him for us who is the fink?"

Little Sammy, always the wise guy, answered, "I admire you, McIntyre. You're not only beautiful, you got some brain; like a dinosaur you got a brain."

McIntyre, on the edge of an explosion for weeks, needed only this provocation. He grabbed Sammy by the pants and jacket and flung him out of the garage into the snow. He threw Sammy as if he wished they were at the top of the Penobscot Tower with forty-seven flights down. No damage was done. The snow was piled high near the garage. Sammy arose stiff-legged, his arms spread out, snow in his shoes, up his legs, covering his mustache and eyebrows. A ludicrous sight, and it got a laugh from some of the drivers.

Jake helped brush him off. "No more trouble. Just don't talk. Just don't open your big mouth."

He couldn't shut up Sammy. "Ask McIntyre who is the fink. Tell him to check his own mouth which is always yakking to his girl friends. Ask Kate Russo who is the fink. She'll tell you where to look."

McIntyre rushed at him. Jake spread his arms and blocked the way. "Let him alone, McIntyre."

"I'll tear his mouth off."

It was slippery footing in the center of the alley, where the snow was packed tight. McIntyre tried to evade Jake and get at Sammy. Jake pressed against him and wouldn't let him pass.

"Let me go, Jake."

"You'll kill him."

"You bastard, Jake. Let go of me."

"Don't push, McIntyre; I'm getting sore." Jake wasn't easily pushed, and they slipped and staggered in the snow. Sammy waited on the other side, his arms folded.

"Out of my way, Jew bastard."

That did it. Jake launched a haymaker. He wound up for a great swing. McIntyre ducked and received a clout in the back of his head. It sent him off balance into the snow. Jake regretted the punch immediately. McIntyre still bore the marks of his beating.

O'Brien restored order. He called McIntyre a jerk. "You're lucky he don't tear your head off."

He got McIntyre to apologize.

The damage was done, however. The following day Sammy Persky returned his route to Atlas, the first driver to defect. Emerson said, "All he wanted was the excuse. He's been waiting for the chance ever since the strike began."

"We can't let him get away with it," O'Brien said. "We can't allow anyone to break ranks. We got to demonstrate once and for all that any deserter is going to pay."

Sammy was all wrong for the union. They shouldn't have demanded such dedication from him. There were enough volunteers willing to sacrifice themselves. Sammy participated out of love for Jake, but he was no man for hard times. He couldn't take miserable weather and poor compensation.

Kravitz restored Sammy to his original route with a raise in pay.

"It's no use talking," Sammy told Jake, who immediately went to see him. "I got nothing in common with my 'brothers,' those sons of bitches. That ape McIntyre has been circulating rumors. You think I don't guess it's him who's been phoning Minnie? He outweighs me by fifty pounds. He's a half foot taller. But he's got reason to be jealous when it comes to the girls."

"You can't resign from us, Sammy. If we let you go, then there will be others; we'll be finished."

"Be finished, Jake. Hy Kravitz admires you. Come back to Atlas."

"Do you know what you're saying? Do you know the mood of your enemies?"

"Screw McIntyre. Save your own neck."

"Do you understand, Sammy, that I can't let you abandon us?"

"How are you going to stop me, Jake?"

Jake told Evka afterwards, "I tried to hit him; I couldn't even make a fist."

"Of course you couldn't! Hit little Sammy? Never! Our little Sammy? How could you even think of it?"

"I thought of it plenty, I assure you. I'm not the only one who has thought of it. In fact, better he should be hit by someone who loves him."

"You mustn't allow it, Jake. They mustn't touch him. Nothing deserves such a thing. Absolutely nothing, Jake. You mustn't think of it."

Evka didn't defer to Jake on this issue. She was never really confused about her allegiances, which were only superficially to doctrine, and essentially to those she loved.

"He's weak," Evka said. "Does that surprise anyone? Who said that he was Patrick Henry? No one expects that of Sammy."

"I can't afford sentiment; I'm responsible for fifty men."

"Sammy must not be hurt, Jake. Nobody's job is worth it."

Jake didn't want to hear any more. "It's not in my power," he said, "so why talk?"

"What's not in your power?"

"I can't hit him; it's not in my power."

XVIII

---◆◆◆▶---

WE KNEW that to successfully resist tyranny you had to be nerved to kill. This was a lesson we mastered each Saturday afternoon at the Dexter Theater, where we were instructed by Hollywood cowboys. As long as Cooper and Scott and Mc-Crea abstained from shooting, they were humiliated. Everyone kicked our hero. Drinks were splashed in his face. The girls despised him. Only when he could no longer bear his disgrace and pulled his gun and slaughtered his enemies was his dignity restored. He won the sexy ladies by shooting. The Saturday communion with Gary Cooper et al. was an experience shared coast to coast. It was perhaps the definitive American experience. We were made one people by attending Saturday afternoon movies. We lined up to undergo the same ritual, confess to the same creed, hear the same sermon, soft drinks and pop corn serving as wine and wafer.

Until you're ready to shoot, you'll merit no respect.

I suppose it's a message that in one form or another has been transmitted since long before Homer.

Even Leonard Mitchell affirmed it.

We assembled within the cavernous interior at noon Saturday in cliques that were determined by age, reputation, sex, social standing, synagogue affiliation, if any. There was much visiting up and down the aisles and between rows. With the notorious Leonard Mitchell as our companion, we attracted considerable attention. The steady bedlam made me drowsy. In the half hour before the lights dimmed and a cheer greeted the Fox Movietone News, I had fantasies—I presume Ernie did as well—of achievements that might win this crowd. As the lights went out and brass flourishes summoned us to attend the news, we eased into our caves, undergoing an experience at once common and private. There was a thrilling unanimity at the appearance of Hitler. Raspberries, cackles, loud ridicule. That monster seemed manageable when we all laughed. Cheers and applause for Roosevelt. Then scenes of war. French generals in stiff, visored caps sprinkled with stars walked the wooded rear of the Maginot line. Our position was impregnable. Hitler would never break through. Between Detroit and Hitler was the Maginot line, a mighty barrier. The British navy escorted convoys across the Atlantic. Destroyers dropped depth charges. Finally we were through the solemn events and viewed Florida bathing beauties in the Cypress Gardens. By the time we reached the event with which we had enticed Leonard Mitchell —a cowboy extravaganza—we had been weaned away from Hitler's time into a more desirable world, where magic worked.

We killed time by means of a double feature, a cartoon, a travelogue, a newsreel. When we emerged, night approaching, we found that the world was unaltered despite the triumph of cowboy justice. Three and a half hours of powerful feeling to no effect! Jews were still hounded in Europe. Jake still hadn't resolved the dilemma of Sammy Persky.

A clear day at the end of the year, deep shadows closing in at five in the afternoon. A slight warming earlier in the day, but now the freeze intensified. Streets were glazed. Elm twigs were enameled with ice.

Leonard was reluctant, I suppose, to return to the dump he lived in, and suggested that we prolong the day by stopping at Perlman's for something to eat.

"We got no money," Ernie told him.

"We don't need money."

We entered Perlman's on Dexter, and I whispered to Ernie, "Don't do it. Let him do it, but don't you do it."

He shoved me with his elbow. To spite me he grabbed a package of halvah. He did it brazenly, but he wasn't noticed. However, Perlman saw Leonard take candy bars.

Perlman wiped his hands on his apron and leaned over the counter, his meaty, freckled arms ready should Leonard try to run. "Okay, smart aleck. What's in the pockets?"

"Who you calling 'smart aleck'?"

"I said, 'What's in the pockets?'"

"Candy bars is in the pockets. That's what's in the pockets. What do you think is in the pockets?"

"On the counter. Empty it on the counter."

Leonard stared at Perlman. "What shitty nerve," he said bitterly.

"Hold your tongue or I'll call the police. Empty the pockets."

"Okay. That does it. You lost yourself a sale, buddy."

Perlman, surprised by the possibility he might have made a mistake, muttered, "I don't want your business."

"You ain't got it!" Leonard flung a candy bar on the counter and swaggered out.

"Hey! The pockets." Perlman went to the door scratching his head. "A wise guy," he told his other customers. He didn't realize that we were with Leonard and made no effort to search us. When we joined Leonard around the corner, he was eating a candy bar.

Afterward I said to Ernie, "Perlman is a friend of Jake's."

"Don't be a creep. Get some fun out of life."

"A lot of fun you get out of life. You spend most of your life in the bedroom on your back."

He stopped walking and faced me. "Look," he said. "Why don't you find friends of your own? It may surprise you, but I can get along without you. Honest." He motioned me to pass him. "Walk by yourself. You're always knocking. You'd think if someone was so damn' critical he wouldn't hang around. Why do you stay? Why don't you go with kids your own age? Why don't you associate with other creeps."

I remember vividly how it hurt. There was real dislike in his tone. "I don't want you walking with me," he said. "Get moving." I stayed because I was numb. "I've been stuck with you all my life. You drag me like an anchor."

He started walking and I followed and he stopped again. "I mean it. I'm not kidding."

"I know," I told him.

Leonard Mitchell was the proper brother for him. I was a handicap, an undersized kid who had to be protected when trouble came, and was, besides, a kibitzer. Who needed such connections?

He refused to walk with me. He crossed the street. We walked down Richton on opposite sides of the street. He headed away from home, and I followed.

"You're a sheep," he yelled at me, not caring who heard. We were both too stirred to care about the weather. A bitter day, thick ice in the gutters, hard snow in the streets. The sidewalks were scraped, but patches of ice made walking tricky. A street of yellow brick flats, each flat with its porch, each porch with its denuded glider.

He yelled sheep sounds at me. "Baaaa. Baaaaaaaa. Sheep!"

The Perskys lived near the intersection, a fine house, brick, not wood like ours. A single home, not a flat. A porch with a triangular roof, a picture window framed by evergreens and a border of bushes. The Perskys' door was wide open, a yelling offense in this weather. I went to shut it. There were cinders on the stairs to cut the ice. I heard Minnie wail—what a sound

—a swooning Oiiii! Oioioioiii! I entered the living room and saw my pa embracing Minnie. Ernie followed me in.

The house had been a pleasure for us because of Sammy. Thick wall-to-wall carpeting. Over the mantle a reproduction of a country scene—a girl in a wide-brimmed hat walking down a wooded lane. The radio continued grinding out the "Beer Barrel Polka" while Minnie Persky wailed. "Roll out the barrel, we'll have a barrel of fun. Roll out the barrel, we've got the blues on the run."

Jake hugged Minnie. "It's all right," he said, trying to soothe her. "It's all right, Minnie. It's going to be all right."

She made sharp, yelping moans, "Oh, oh, oh."

"My Sammy," she said. "Oh, my Sammy. Oh, oh, oh."

"It's all right," Jake said. "Try to calm yourself, Minnie. We need you in sound condition."

"Where's my Sammy?"

"He's in Receiving Hospital."

She screamed her "oh, oh" again and Jake comforted her. "Be strong, Minnie. Get hold of yourself."

"It's a mistake," Minnie cried. "It's not him. His route is downtown. They got the wrong person."

"It's him, Minnie. I already been to see."

"A truck? He was hit by a truck? On the highway? How could he be on the highway? His route is downtown."

"Minnie, darling. He's in bad shape."

I can still hear her scream.

They got Sammy Persky on the Oswego road. He was hit while running across the highway. His truck was parked in a tourist court. We heard the whole story later.

O'Brien and McIntyre were the ones responsible. Emerson may have been an observer. They had witnesses prepared to assure cops and judges that Persky had started the trouble. They had only meant to teach Sammy a lesson. We knew that O'Brien was a stern teacher. He had wanted to make an impression on Sammy, and he had succeeded too well.

Kate Russo lured Sammy to a tourist court near Ann Arbor.

O'Brien promised her that Sammy wouldn't be hurt. He only wanted to put a scare in Sammy, which wasn't difficult. Sammy hadn't even made a gesture toward heroism. It wasn't his style. He gladly relinquished war and gallantry to big men like Jake and McIntyre and O'Brien. He wasn't even embarrassed by cowardice. He used to say, "If trouble comes, I'll whistle for a big guy." But all the big guys were on the other side.

We heard the story from Kate Russo and McIntyre, who both confessed to Jake.

Why had they staged the scene on the Oswego road? To make it clear to all potential defectors that they were punishing a fink. The tourist court was shut down for the winter. It consisted of frail cabins on the edge of a plowed field. I remember once awakening in such a cabin and stepping out into a night sky whose stars were as sharply defined as the fake stars in the ceiling of the Fisher Theater.

The circular drive was blocked by snow. Sammy parked his truck behind a clump of oaks near the office. The cabins were boarded up. He went to meet Kate in number seven at the far end of the court. She had told him the proprietor was a friend. She must have suggested to Sammy how cozy they could make their little cabin. Sammy may have been a coward in all other things, but he was a bold adventurer on the terrain of love. It must have seemed like a great idea to redeem a drab afternoon with McIntyre's lady.

He followed Kate's footsteps through the snow. The others had come the back way, so there was no evidence of their passage. Kate opened the door, and, when Sammy stepped in, McIntyre grabbed him and smothered his jaunty greeting. Kate left immediately, just a glance back. McIntyre's arm covered Sammy's face, but she'd seen his eyes. She felt terrible. Why had she agreed to participate? To scare a fink. O'Brien said no harm would be done. He waved her out with a tightly rolled copy of the Sunday newspaper.

"The poor son of a bitch," she said to Jake. "I once complained about his grabbing just to needle Mac. I wanted to tell O'Brien not to hurt him, but I kept my mouth shut."

I've never seen Jake as he was in those days. He wasn't interested in the news of the world.

"I knew what they were thinking about," he told Evka. "I let them do it anyhow."

Evka said that O'Brien was to blame.

"I blame no one but Jake Gottlieb. Jake Gottlieb takes full credit."

Did they expect to frighten Sammy back into the union? That was a foolish calculation. He might have promised anything to escape a beating, but he had no memory and wouldn't have kept his promise.

O'Brien clubbed him on the arms and shoulders with the rolled newspaper. He jabbed him in the belly with the butt of the newspaper. He flailed Sammy with the news. McIntyre covered Sammy's mouth so no one would hear any screams from number seven. Kate waited in McIntyre's car, and she didn't hear a thing.

O'Brien talked to Sammy while he hit. This we learned from McIntyre, who—though shocked—participated to the end.

"You like to TALK, Sammy." In the mouth with the newspaper. "Talk to us, Sammy. We're your buddies, you little shit. Would you fink on your buddies, Sammy?" He landed with short, measured strokes, letting Sammy see the blow coming. O'Brien was evidently a close observer of the body, who recognized what part you wanted withheld, what part you didn't want touched, and he touched you there. There was no need to torture Sammy in order to scare him. He hung in McIntyre's arms, a dead weight until struck, then he shriveled. McIntyre tried to hold him rigid. They turned him around and bent him over so that O'Brien could work on his back.

McIntyre told this to Jake. He wanted to talk, and we have all the details of the death of Sammy Persky.

You can injure a man with a rolled newspaper. You can bruise him with the news of German victories in the headlines, especially when the newspaper is wrapped around a length of pipe. O'Brien had wanted Sammy to learn a lesson. O'Brien didn't need a charge of rage in order to be a torturer. He didn't need to hate. He figured that it made good sense to punish defectors, and he was able to do what reason commanded. We're told by Socrates that such is true courage.

He beat the newspaper into shreds, exposing the core of pipe. Sammy collapsed in McIntyre's arms. McIntyre was himself in such a condition of shock that he was barely able to sustain the slight weight of Sammy. He pleaded with O'Brien, "Enough! Please. Enough. You're killing him."

"We'll let him get his breath."

"No more. Look what we already done."

"We got to make sure he's convinced. Wait till he comes to."

McIntyre by this time had dropped all grievances against Sammy. No injury he might have suffered justified the punishment. Sammy was out cold, and McIntyre was frightened.

"You hit him too hard."

"With a newspaper. It won't kill him."

"I saw what was inside the newspaper."

"Put snow on his face; that'll bring him around."

McIntyre opened the door and went outside for snow.

I wasn't there, but I've spent much time considering what happened to Sammy Persky. I know those who were involved, and it's easy to fill in the gaps. Besides, McIntyre told everything in the hope that Jake would forgive him.

"I was crazy," he told Jake. "That bitch made me crazy." She had refused to see him. She had said he was a bore. He had spied and seen enough to stoke up his jealousy. He had twice observed men leave her apartment. He hadn't had the heart to discover who they were. Terrifying fantasies had focused on Sammy Persky. The thought of Sammy with Kate dizzied him. Still, he had tried not to let that affect his judgment. He had clear evidence of Sammy's treachery. He had been convinced the union would benefit if Sammy were taught a lesson. Any other potential defector would have second thoughts.

O'Brien supported this argument, and Kate agreed to cooperate.

Only when Sammy lay on the cabin floor had McIntyre understood how he had deceived himself. He came to Jake for punishment. "Beat the shit out of me. I got it coming. I can't tell you how sorry I am for that little guy."

They had dragged Sammy outside and rubbed snow in his face, and despite his condition O'Brien seemed resolved to continue with the lesson. "We go all the way. He isn't hurt. Don't let the son of a bitch con you, Mac. I didn't hit him hard. He's faking."

While they argued, Sammy—the sly fake—got up and ran for the road. He moved into the open and there was so much traffic on the Oswego road they couldn't pursue him without attracting attention. Before they could reach him he ran into the side of an eight-wheeler. He flew through the air.

I remember how that Walled Lake bum had sailed through the air and landed at our feet. I remember how terrified Sammy had been by this preview of his own death.

XIX

So THE TROUBLE started with O'Brien.

Jake said, "I don't want you in the union. I don't want you at Atlas. You get a job somewhere else. If you can't get a job somewhere else, starve to death. Better you starve to death than stay here. You can't stay here. Kravitz doesn't want you. You're finished in Detroit. Go where I'll never see you. The sight of you stirs murder in my heart. You're a young man. With your talents you'll rise to the top, wherever you are. You'll stand on bones and reach the top. You'll be a big success. I predict it, O'Brien. Away from me, you'll have a good life. But stay far away. Near me you stand no chance."

"Who are you to say, Jake?"

"Find your destiny in another place. Near me you'll get squashed."

"I don't run, Jake. This is my town. I got friends here."

"You got no friends. I refuse to let you have friends."

"It's me who won this strike; the boys know that. Kravitz

broke down when he saw we meant business. I proved to him we meant business. You didn't have the guts."

"The business you meant is not my business. It's not union business. It's O'Brien business. You got no future in my union."

"You're real tough, I know."

"Oh, yes. You'll see."

Jake made the firing of O'Brien part of the agreement that ended the strike.

"That suits me," Kravitz said. "I'd like to see you all go."

Kravitz finally surrendered. He must have been convinced that the lunatic Gottlieb and his crowd would destroy themselves rather than yield. He had watched the business of a lifetime vanish, and he couldn't bear to see it go. He called in Jake and put up minor resistance before surrendering at every point.

"You screwed me," he told Jake. "I gave you a job and you screwed me. I don't ever forgive you, Gottlieb."

"I don't want forgiveness; I want a contract."

"I knew you were a troublemaker but anyhow I took you in. I liked you, Gottlieb. I thought after you learned the business we could talk and I'd make something of you. So you screwed me."

"I carried bundles for you. I worked like a slave. You gave me no handouts."

"You screwed me, you son of a bitch."

"No more son of a bitch, Kravitz. Speak to me with respect."

"Respect is in the contract, eh? I'll even give you respect. But what a fine cause you represent! And what nice people! With O'Brien at least I could do business. He's not so stiff-necked."

And Jake said to him, "O'Brien got to go."

"That's in the contract?"

"We don't want O'Brien."

It wasn't easy to get rid of O'Brien, but Jake was persistent. There was a meeting in Emerson's garage to ratify the agreement. McIntyre said, "This strike isn't finished yet, boys. One of our brothers, O'Brien, has been let go. He stuck by us; now we stick by him. He was one for all; now we got to be all for one." McIntyre pushed O'Brien's case. Though he had assured Jake he was through with O'Brien, he stood in the doorway of Emerson's garage and demanded that the drivers hold out for O'Brien. Fifty men crammed into the oversized garage that Emerson used for his carpentry. He had considerable talent. He'd built a motor boat for Lake St. Clair, a beautiful boat. When I saw this garage, I was impressed by its neatness: there was a pegboard on the wall for hanging tools; there was a neat coil of hose. There was a handsomely equipped workbench. Instead of grease there was the smell of wood-shavings.

Why did McIntyre support O'Brien? O'Brien wasn't an easy man to oppose. To stand against him was to stand in the path of a flood. He rushed toward his glory like a river out of control.

Jake told the drivers to accept the contract without qualifications. What existed between O'Brien and Kravitz, he said, wasn't a union affair.

McIntyre pleaded the case of O'Brien as if he didn't recall what had happened in cabin number seven.

But these were Jake's men. He had freed them from bondage to the tyrant Kravitz, and, when he told them to affirm the Atlas contract, they did. O'Brien was finished at Atlas. So also were Emerson and McIntyre. When the drivers returned to work the following day, Red Wilson told McIntyre not to load his truck; he was fired. The strike began and ended with the firing of McIntyre.

McIntyre wore a clean uniform the first day of work. His Atlas cap was perched on his dome. He appealed to Jake but was cut off. "I got to get loaded," Jake said. "This is a big day for me."

McIntyre begged my pa to remember his sacrifices. He had risked everything for the union. Because of Jake, he'd put his fortune on the line.

"I don't work with the murderers of Sammy Persky. They can starve. It doesn't trouble me."

"What will happen to my girl, Jake? And my wife's in the hospital."

Jake couldn't be budged. He had no pity for McIntyre.

"After what I've been through, Jake? Because you talked me into it, Jake? Now you throw me out? I'll kill you for this, Jake!"

This was said. Jake told us so. And who could ignore the possibility? The wolves had tasted blood and were still famished.

After the funeral of Sammy Persky he made us swear again.

"Remember your father. If something should happen to your father, remember O'Brien."

And what should we do when we remembered O'Brien? Jake meant business. One hand on my shoulder, one hand on Ernie's. "Remember O'Brien. He will be the man."

I said, "Yes, pa." And Ernie—reluctantly, it's true—also swore to remember O'Brien.

Jake didn't spare Emerson. He faced him in the garage after the union meeting. "I once saved your life," he said. "I regret it. I let a wolf into my house. I can't wish you any worse luck than to spend your life with your missus. Stay home and enjoy her. Don't come to Atlas."

Emerson didn't whimper or beg. "It's no surprise; I figured as much."

"You hounded Sammy Persky. You convinced me to turn my back on him."

"I should have known you people stick together."

"From now on," Jake told him, "stay out of my sight. If you come to where I can see you, I'll see nothing; I no longer hear you or see you."

Emerson smiled. That smile took Jake by surprise. Perhaps Emerson was relieved to have his sense of conspiracy confirmed. At any rate, the ambiguity of his connection with my pa was clarified. And a spiteful man like Emerson would always rather settle for war.

Sammy died on Saturday and was buried on Sunday. His death was the least imaginable. The possibility had never occurred to Sammy, who had dreaded solemn thoughts. The death of a Sammy Persky is a danger to us all. He was still brimming with plots; his appetite was undiminished.

The ceremony at Joshua Temple transformed that place of conspirators into a pious setting. The lectern I'd seen clutched by those wild radicals, Evka and Berle, now supported a bearded rabbi who was orthodox and obstinately Yiddish. At the foot of the platform was the plain black casket, the head end unscrewed, Sammy available for a last viewing.

Jake sat with Minnie, up front. Afterward they studied Sammy Persky. The morticians had made him something to remember. Enviable wife, able to look on husband and fix him forever in leisure of that last view. He doesn't stir. You don't have to drop your eyes from his. No embarrassment. You can study him, and learn his face for the first time. Glory to the cosmeticians, that they can hide bruises and present to you, not the actual Sammy, but the Sammy who might have been, a mature Sammy, a dignified Sammy, a Sammy in repose. For the sake of our children we all deserve such artists. She howled. Her face was squeezed like a rubber doll's. Red and drenched, hands clasped beneath shaking chins, the passion was as unstagey as an infant's. I wondered how they could bear to look. How could they step up to the casket and face that horror? Not me. Not Ernie. Never. We missed the chance.

Jake stood in the front rank at graveside as they lowered the coffin into the frozen ground. A raw site, a ruddy brown, the only interruption in the snowy field. The snow glittered fiercely. My eyes teared from the glitter. There were forty-seven drivers present, Jake's men, his partisans. No one could wean them away, not O'Brien, not McIntyre. They honored Jake. They might ridicule his integrity, which was too fanatic to be American, but they trusted Jake; he was daddy to them all. That was the bond that couldn't be broken. He secured men's hearts. It was surprising that he had made no greater progress, but at forty-eight years of age Jake Gottlieb began to move.

He publicly vowed to remember Samuel Persky. He sometimes was embarrassingly stagey, as at the time he commanded our oath. I learned at the funeral the seriousness of the drama he played. He stood ankle-deep in snow, in a black coat and a level-brimmed black fedora, his face burnished from all the driving, his thick, square hands in black leather gloves, and he promised Minnie that he would never forget Samuel Persky. I'm sure that the performance was to some extent for our benefit. He wished to impress us all—me, Ernie, Evka, Berle, his drivers—that he was the star, front and center. Yet no one ever doubted he would keep faith, whatever his motives. He would be there at the unveiling of the stone. You could rely on Jake to keep faith and to mark the grave.

He was forty-eight years old before he had a purchase on power. But he moved fast, that year of the phony war. Within a few months he took on the entire industry, and they folded up, one by one, and Jake was their master.

XX

---◄•●•►---

WE MIGHT have endured phoniness indefinitely. We might have atrophied in that tension of waiting while Hitler flourished. He was swollen from his diet of horrors. Nowhere in the world was there a resolve as strong as his. Though there were boasts of developing Allied prowess—boasts we wanted to believe —the little forays across the Maginot line, involving a few men, hardly seemed an adequate response to the great leaps which monster Germany had made. And, when the Nazis finally moved again, how admirably!

All those timid advances, computed in yards, casualties in tens, were countered by the liberating German imagination. Great strokes! Denmark in days! Norway in weeks! A plunge through Belgium, and the krauts were on their way, headed by panzers. It was a language that fitted the terms of our fantasies. Blitzkrieg! Panzer! Storm troopers! These weren't constipated notions. The Germans moved in fact as we moved in fantasy. Ernie in his games had summoned the thunderbolts of Zeus; Hitler launched panzers. The animated maps that detailed his progress in the Movietone News plotted the itinerary of our dreams—but in reverse motion. Our dreams would have had the arrows perform great flanking movements across the Rhine. We'd have spotlighted Berlin. It was a dreadful time. The Nazis made all our dreams come true. They showed us that our fantasies of power were in the realm of possibility, but all directed against us. It was as though our fantasies—those irresponsible dramas which took the edge off horrors—bred their opposites, which were no longer confined to an interior stage but were projected onto the world.

The Maginot line was plucked off the body of France as though it were a scab.

The heroic French poilus, led by fierce martinets who had once humbled the Germans at Verdun, were rounded up in armies. Their weapons were antiquated, their strategies pedestrian. They hollowed out mountains to build the Maginot line. They buried themselves in steel and concrete. They huddled in their bunkers, peering through slots at the teeth of the dragon. They swiveled their giant guns to survey the German landscape. They should have had another Maginot line for the rear. They had unprotected rears. And that's where they got shoved. They hunched over, peering at Germany, and were assaulted from behind. They were anchored in their underground fortifications, which had taken them years to develop, and couldn't move. The French commander was named Camelin, the executor of that constipated strategy. He had a vacant, seamed face. Yessir, wait till the old French seventy-fives get a crack at those Boche panzers—an all-purpose artillery piece, mobile, and powerful enough to shatter any armor.

How wormlike to burrow into the ground in the face of an attack!

How much grander, how much nobler, was the predatory lunge of the Germans, that breakneck rush toward the rump of the enemy in disregard of defense! It was a liberation—no more debilitating dreams. Here was the horror down on us.

Now we had to move or perish. And what little hope we salvaged from our debacle was the result of the English successfully scrambling for their lives, racing from Europe as a lover might race from a bedroom when the husband approaches. Out the window—forget the pants! Nothing saved but lives! France down the drain in weeks, the rough beast balanced on the edge of the Channel for one more fatal leap.

Can we ever forget the lesson of the Maginot line? You dig in. You wait. Your life is governed by the moves of the enemy, who lounges insolently in front of your fortifications. His muscles are exercised. He is out in the air. He has no dread. And you have only the vision you can eke out of a steel slot, every part of you immobilized except the eyes. And what do the eyes see? Very little. You infer all. Out of tedium and ignorance you spin fantasies.

We had the fantasy of Allied power. Though the Nazis had tumbled the small boys—the Czechs, the Poles, the Danes, the Norwegians—once they took on the big fellows their time would be up. What in fact happened was that within weeks France was gone and England scurried back to its island. All that talk of English tenacity and French élan was delusion. Savages with bows and arrows would have resisted better. What a shock to discover how deluded we'd been! Hitler danced a jig outside the railroad car where the French surrender was negotiated. It was nice to see the ogre in good humor.

He was now in a position to plunder France of its Jews and other resources.

Europe's done for, said the America Firsters and the ambassador to England; let's not get into it. The socialists, too! The Bolsheviks weren't saddened by the downfall of the capitalist heartland; they foresaw a revolutionary future; they were far-seeing and claimed a hard vision which a year later turned mushy.

So, who wanted American involvement? The Jews. There was a myth, widely circulated, that Roosevelt was a Jew named Rosenfeld.

Congress approved the draft by only a single vote.

And why shouldn't the Jews have wanted Hitler crushed? What a job he did in his soap factories!

How grateful we are for small things. A Pope says, "Spiritually we are all Semites," and we applaud. We suspect he may feel unhappy about the campaign to make the world *judenrein.* The men of good will concede that Jews are a Christ-killing, cowardly, unpatriotic, money-changing, usurious bunch. Still, you shouldn't go so far as to exterminate them. Thank you, Christian Brothers, for small favors. How marvelous your equanimity to bear with us! What a pain in the ass, the Jews! Maybe if you could surrender them, the nutty genius Adolf would be appeased. The Jews are getting you into it.

Can we ever forget the craven idiots who agreed to consider us as less than human?

It marks our lives.

What can any death mean after the Nazis made the whole business so monotonous? Persky was a lucky one. He died before the great flood of death made no death noteworthy, no life memorable.

Still, that spring and summer of 1940 had something to recommend them. The Tigers, led by Hank Greenberg, won the pennant after four years of Yankee victories. And, when balmy days reached Dexter Avenue and elms sprang into leaf, you couldn't spot grieving Jews.

Even a street like Richton, which on our side of Dexter was grubby in wintertime, was splendid in the spring. The clay yards, which leaked yellow mud onto sidewalks during thaws, sprouted crab grass. The elms in full leaf made our narrow Richton seem like a country lane. We turned off Dexter and saw trees bend toward each other, upper branches almost touching, a lacy pattern against a soft sky. On these fine days no grief reached us, no death intruded.

Minnie's good nature entirely deserted her; she stayed behind drawn blinds and wept. But with spring arrived, the baseball season under way, the juices running everywhere, sweet rain, soft days that had a bouquet I haven't sniffed in twenty years, who wanted to bother with sufferers?

Ernie played the outfield on his class softball team. He wore a T shirt, gym shorts, sneakers. I saw him crouch in readiness, left foot slightly forward, on his toes, black hair in a tangle, a tall, husky boy. My brother had sprouted. At sixteen he had suddenly taken off, and the man he would be had become apparent. I saw him race for a deeply hit ball and snatch it in stride. Later I saw him at the plate, his concentration ferocious, nervous because of the heckling, but professional in the way he wiggled the bat, his closed stance, his crouch. He slugged the ball and took off. It was a man-sized clout beyond the outfield, and he came all the way around. I saw him round third, his eyes blazing, accepting congratulatory wallops from his teammates with a relish that tickled me.

One day Leonard Mitchell came to the field at Ernie's invitation. Leonard, too, had soared. In his case, though, there wasn't a transitional phase of stripling. There he was, seventeen years old, three inches taller than Ernie, twenty pounds heavier, a full-sized man in any league. He grabbed a bat, knocked the plate, told the pitcher to send one over. The pitcher lobbed it in. Leonard took a big swipe and missed. Powerful, but surprisingly awkward at this game. He was deft at the pool table. He missed another, then slammed a ball over the fence. He insisted on taking a major position. They didn't dare exile him to right field. They sent him to first base. He had large, quick hands, but he didn't know the game. He disregarded his position. He raced for every ball. He ran across the diamond and dropped a pop fly that the third baseman circled under. He fumbled a grounder the second baseman was reaching for. He struck out twice and hit a home run. Somehow he spoiled the game. The team, which had previously done well, was plastered with Leonard in there. Afterward they told Ernie to get rid of him. Ernie refused.

"He's my buddy."

"We'll let him play right field. That's all."

Ernie didn't have the nerve to tell Leonard to play right field. Leonard showed up for the next game and resumed his position at first. He must have guessed that he was responsible for the gloom. He turned the game into a farce. He shoved base runners off the sack, blocked the path, tried for trick plays. He got rough. When finally the opposing first sacker objected to being pushed and shoved back, Leonard knocked him down and hurt the boy.

"What boy scouts," he said to Ernie.

Ernie quit the team.

Why did he stay with Leonard Mitchell?

I was convinced Leonard entered the game only to derange it and pry Ernie loose. He was intractable. He faced in a direction and moved, and couldn't be dissuaded. He flunked his courses and didn't care. It was silly for him to be in high school. He was ready for the extreme business of men. He didn't even have to bother with Windsor any more. He had a nice girl whom he laid at will. She lived in his apartment building, and her name was Sherry. She was fifteen, a lovely blonde girl. My first impression was of a cheerleader type, a supple, firm body dressed in an angora sweater, pleated skirt, saddle shoes. Leonard gave her hard pinches; he tweaked her breasts; she smiled. He showed us by his rough handling that he could dispose of his property as he wished. I felt that Leonard understood the effect of his bullying: he meant to disrupt the game; he meant to humble Sherry. I had failed to give him credit for enough intelligence to operate with a guiding vision, but he had one. He was no ordinary hoodlum like Weinberg or Spiegelman.

The heart of his vision was this: men are contemptible. I don't know how he came to this conviction. Men are contemptible and they will try to saddle you with their pieties, and you have to marshal all the force of your being to resist. I heard him tell Ernie, "You're okay, you're no creep, but you never learned not to take shit." He wanted it made clear that he was invulnerable to benevolent feelings.

Live dangerously, said the fascist.

His mother no longer fought him. They rarely spoke. She was an exhausted, fierce woman; Leonard didn't much resemble her. She was chunky, her face coarse, her forehead seamed. She grimaced as if she had a bad stomach. She had a heavy walk, planting her feet as though she wanted to kill with every tread. Leonard was a new generation of hoodlum and showed little sentiment favoring Mom. She wore heavy shoes with thick heels. Her legs were powerful and slightly bowed. You could see hair matted beneath her stockings.

I heard her once say to him, "What a surprise! He's home." The sarcastic effect was lessened because she uttered it so gloomily.

Leonard was about finished with home, as he was with school. He was ready to abandon his ma. He needed some anchorage, and I suppose that's how Ernie served him. Ernie was like a brother to him. I surely wasn't.

Two years separated Leonard and me, and yet the difference in size and self-conception was more like a generation. Besides, I couldn't ignore what Ernie seemed indifferent to; we had been used by Leonard to establish an alibi for Weinberg and Spiegelman the night McIntyre was beaten. Ernie didn't care to be reminded.

Have I conveyed to you Ernie's intelligence? He sucked up libraries. At sixteen he was reading Plato and Nietzsche and Dostoievski and Karl Marx. When he wasn't with Leonard Mitchell, he located stars in Moshe Bodkin's back yard.

Delicious nights! Plum trees in the Bodkin yard, flowers along the fences, earth newly hoed and fertilized! The Bodkins had a large house facing Russell Woods Park, a chic neighborhood in our Dexter community. We entered Russell Woods Park and settled down as far from street lights as we could get. We pointed flashlights at our star map, turned them off, and considered the sky.

I've told you how Ernie was preoccupied with the evolution of stars. He wanted to believe that the universe was gas, that it began with an unthinkable compression, then a cosmic explosion, after which the fleeing heavens precipitated stars. The distances thrilled him. Light traveled the lifetime of a man to ignite our vision. The beginning had receded billions of years from us. He relished the inevitable deterioration of our sun and world. There would be an end to everything, to Jew and Nazi alike. Germans burned Jews as though they were a cosmic evil. Another day would come, prescribed by law, when we'd all burn. Eventually the cosmos would fry, star by star, everyone and everything expunged, justice done by an impartial natural law that was its own executioner.

If that distant end of the world saddened us, we were also soothed by the prospect. Our butchers would not prevail. Whatever myths they invented, whatever gods they improvised, they couldn't evade their mortality. There were times when we could hardly wait for the whole thing to burn. Earth nourished Adolf Hitler, so let it burn. We sniffed the grass of Russell Woods Park. We listened to crickets. We dreamed of the sweet girls that lay ahead of us. And we were ready to see it all consumed.

However, it was a great season for the Detroit Tigers, and we couldn't stay fixed on cosmic possibilities in the light of that event. We went to Briggs Stadium and watched the giant Greenberg loft one into the left-field bleachers, almost into our hands. Fifty thousand cheered for Greenberg.

Fifty thousand fools, in Jake's opinion.

"You mean they'll admit Jews are human because one of them hits a ball?"

"Each land has its customs," Berle Dresden argued. "Accept the way of the land."

Our Marxist was an ardent fan. He sometimes took us to the stadium. His enthusiasm for the game annoyed me, since his reasons were political and esthetic and had nothing to do with a proper appreciation. He was really there to hear praise of Greenberg, a name more prominent in the Detroit headlines than even Hitler's.

Leonard Mitchell had no interest in our heroes. He concentrated on his own advancement. His face already had the solid, bearded maturity of a man who was regularly laid. Sherry wasn't the only one. He told us of other achievements. He was one shy of being an ace. He had punctured four virgins. He ticked them off for us by name, shape, age, color, creed, nationality. He was the pleasure of ladies. His stories made me shiver. One girl had taken him in her mouth. He'd been drunk at a party. He'd gone with Sherry. He woke up in a bed on top of coats, and someone was mouthing him down there. He thought it was Sherry and took a swing and cracked her. It turned out to be someone else, a redhead. A beautiful girl, he assured us. He patted her cheek and encouraged her to resume. To give him credit, he was very handsome. As his beard darkened and his face lengthened and his shoulders broadened, his direction emerged. He would be very tall, well over six feet, lean-hipped, long-legged, broad-chested. Hair sprouted on his chest. His arms were hairy. Though his hair was light brown and he was blue-eyed, there came into being a slight resemblance to his mother. His features were bunched together in a frown that reminded me of his black mother.

He was sometimes bored with Ernie, who couldn't easily discard childish ways.

I wanted to tell my brother: watch the stars. Remember that the cosmos will be consumed. Don't be fretful. Stay away from Leonard Mitchell.

One by one we peeled off and became men. Or failed and remained sixteen. Leonard suddenly spurted. Girls flocked to him despite his contempt. He had no capacity for tenderness. His proposals were put to nice girls as bluntly as to whores. He didn't plead and he didn't say thank you, and he acknowledged no obligations.

Weinberg no longer treated him as an errand boy. He was a respected peer. Happy, chalking up a cue, his sleeves rolled, his tie loosened, his tiepin flashing, his hat perched back on his ruddy head, said to Sherry, "Sharpies like the kid are bad for

163

your reputation, sweetie. He got funny-shaped hands from handling cue balls."

Leonard said, "It makes the right fit for her."

"Nice cue balls, eh? What you been dropping in her pocket, kid?"

"It's one shot I never miss, Happy."

Lovely Sherry, among the dummies at our high school, but still beyond the hopes of Ernie or me, let the pool-hall gang pinch and squeeze. She looked to Leonard for support, but he didn't mind his friends handling the goods.

She wasn't a hard case in the beginning. Leonard made it rough when he was resisted, so she didn't resist.

"You got strange friends," Jake said to Ernie after hearing gossip. "People tell me Gottlieb's boys are in strange places with strange friends. With Whatshisname—the bum—whose ma scrubs floors."

"Is that any way for you to talk, who represents the proletariat?"

"Your pa is a snob. He thinks it beneath your social standing to associate with hoodlums who are a disgrace to the Jewish nation."

"What nation is that?"

"Your nation—the Jewish nation."

"Next time I look at the stars I'll look for the Jewish nation."

"Look in your heart, you fool."

A good part of the Jewish nation would soon be located in the stars. Jews burned before the rest of us did. Up they went toward Orion and Cassiopeia's Chair.

How could Ernie tolerate the humiliation of Sherry?

Leonard asked her, mocking us all, "Why don't you show my buddy a good time? It's all in the family."

Sherry became wise fast in the school of his hard knocks. She was a lovely girl. Now I'm used to such loveliness and avoid it. It's rooted in a simplicity that I once cherished but could never understand; it no longer interests me. She paid no attention to the news of the world. She never sat on the turf of Russell Woods Park, waiting for the millennium, when stars would blossom and we'd all be incinerated. Her father was a cabinetmaker, her mother a saleslady at Kern's. The father, absorbed by the news from Germany, ignored us to huddle by his radio. We saw his skinny neck, bent for some executioner's axe, his bald head cocked to receive the distant sounds of holocaust, his eyes blurred behind thick spectacles, a meager man with sinewy arms and calloused hands who twirled the dial from station to station in the hope that good news would come to focus. His wife ordered him out of the main line of action. "Give Leonard a chair, Lieberman." He surrendered the armchair and moved to a leather hassock, close to the radio.

When I asked for the news he seemed surprised that I might be concerned with what he had come to regard as his private grief. "It looks bad for the Jews," he said. He wasn't used to transmitting complicated messages. He may have participated in ardent and dramatic interior dialogues. Only banality issued. He tiptoed around his own living room, unwilling to disturb anyone. He wanted to be left alone with the bad news. He shriveled from Leonard Mitchell's boisterous contempt.

Sherry couldn't deny a will as powerful as Leonard's. He laid her two weeks after she moved into the building. She was a virgin but he had no trouble. It was their second date. In her own apartment, in the middle of the day, the couch bloodied. She was fifteen years old. Leonard gave us all the details.

There was no weeping around Leonard nor any holding back. He wanted no extreme of sorrow or reserve. He wanted her tailored for his moods. He used her as a master uses a slave. She wasn't slavish to others, certainly not to me or Ernie.

Despite everything it was a lovely spring. We used Russell Woods Park for the stars. We went with Sherry to Belle Isle Park on Saturdays. She was given in trust to Ernie because Leonard did business with Happy Weinberg on Saturdays. She was grateful for small favors. She showed her pleasure openly as neither of us could. Her only problem was Leonard Mitchell and she accepted him as a catastrophe of nature there was no use complaining about. She was the sort who could live on the edge of an abyss and continue her daily business without teetering. She led us to the botanical gardens, where we sniffed flowers. We went to the aquarium. We rode a pony cart. We waded in the Detroit River and studied the Canadian shore. We walked across the Belle Isle Bridge and caught the Grand Boulevard bus and sat pressed together, nosing the open window to escape the fumes and recover the spicy spring air. She sat between us, a warm girl with a rosy color, a creamy skin, a sweet smile, her hair falling across her cheek. She brushed her hair back with slender fingers that had bitten nails. She rolled against us without timidity, more experienced than we were in the use of bodies.

So Ernie loved her. What a word! He was sixteen years old. He had feelings.

See? Wasn't it a good spring and summer with all sorts of proper beginnings despite the news from our Philco, despite the smoke of Jews in the air? This was the spring we awakened —me, too, yes—to the possibility of a lithe girl whose breasts had sprouted, who smelled of wood smoke from huddling over a park grill on which we burned hot dogs and marshmallows.

She had moist, near-sighted eyes, and until you came into focus she stared in your direction, frowning, her forehead wrinkled; then, when she spotted you, a great smile. Her hair was long, and she sometimes wound it in coils which she pinned over her ears, a lopsided effect that made her neck seem fragile. She had Evka's manner of holding her hands.

Our attitude toward her changed. At first we resented her for being Leonard's whore. Her slavishness was contemptible. She spread herself beneath that obscene, savage kid, allowed him to climb on top and pound her. She revered him for it. We considered her to be brutalized by this self-sacrifice. Her continued good nature was outrageous. A few Saturdays at Belle Isle and the thought of what she did with Leonard—on her couch and in his cousin's car—was painful.

She admired Ernie's brains. She stared at him when he

spouted the news of the world, as if his brains were visible and made good viewing. She wasn't herself fluent, and was placed among the dumb section of her class, where girls concentrated on home economics and the boys on shop. It was a mistake of classification, though. She was far less stupid than we were.

Ernie read Browning to her—*Porphyria's Lover* and *Andrea del Sarto*—a stagey reading that embarrassed me because it revealed more than he intended. His emotion was in his own behalf rather than the poet's.

Sherry sat on the grass listening, hugging her knees. The wind stirred her light dress, exposing smooth thighs. "That's nice," she said. "That's very nice."

. . . a man's reach should exceed his grasp, / Or what's a heaven for?

Ernie didn't even have the nerve to grasp for her reachable thighs.

She often sang to us. She had a good memory for lyrics, though she didn't do well with academic bards. She had a clear, sweet voice for such ballads as "Deep Purple" and "My Reverie." Later in the summer we took her to the night concerts at the Belle Isle shell. The memorial fountain spurted rainbows. Buzzing nights, safe for anyone with a blanket. We went to the casino for hot dogs and rented a canoe. We paddled down lagoons, Ernie and I rowing, Sherry reclining on cushions. I looked back and saw Ernie staring down at her with a face so naked it embarrassed me.

Afterward we joined Leonard at Boesky's for sandwiches. She pressed her face against her master's shoulder, her eyes closed. He offered her the back of his hand, and she kissed his knuckles.

They made Ernie grovel.

Leonard gave details of their love-making, and Ernie offered polite observations. "She's the sweetest person I know," he told Leonard. "She worships you."

"After she comes," said Leonard, "she flutters. It's the best part."

167

Ernie, a student of magicians, was impressed by the power of Leonard Mitchell, who had reduced Sherry to slavery. Ernie tried poetry readings, nighttime concerts on Belle Isle, canoe rides in the lagoon, gentleness on the park green, domesticity in front of an outdoor grill. He treated Sherry with respect. Leonard casually offered his hand, which she kissed. There was no justice, only magic.

One day I told Ernie, "She could be your girl if you wanted her."

Some advice from a fifteen-year-old who had never been kissed.

"She's Leonard's," he said. "Are you crazy?"

"Does he have a receipt? Did he buy her at Hudson's?"

I felt that if the world was bound to blow up, why shouldn't Ernie find out how Sherry fluttered? What was there to lose?

"He's my friend."

"He treats her like a pig."

"She doesn't care for me that way."

"Did you ask?"

"Leonard would murder me."

"Don't tell him."

"I wouldn't even know how."

"How are you going to learn?"

He listened to me as if he were the younger brother. He was obsessed by Sherry. I could see him tremble when he sat next to her on the bus to Belle Isle.

He listened while I spoke on the subject of himself. He was eager for information that would ease his pain.

"You're a hero-worshipper," I told him. "You live with your ear to the radio to find out what Greenberg is doing. But how about you, Ernie? You stopped playing on the team because Leonard sneered. You were batting cleanup. You do push-ups and you got big muscles on your arms. You, too, can make the news. Why should someone as strong and as smart as you only dream? Very few are stronger. How many are smarter? This Leonard Mitchell, your pal, is nobody, as pa says. Your pa, who is a great man, you pay no attention to. But Leonard Mitchell—because he has fornicated, because he is respected by hoodlums—you admire. Listen. Twenty years from now you'll be something. He'll be nothing. And this Sherry. Who is she? You see what her mother looks like? In twenty years that will be Sherry. What's wrong with you, Ernie? Do you have no idea of someone's true worth? She can flutter, but she flutters for Leonard Mitchell. So what good is she?"

I was hard on Sherry for his sake. I denied the sweetness that I also recognized. My brother was my obsession; I would have sacrificed any number of Sherrys for him.

"We're young," I said to Ernie. "We're not men yet. We got a lifetime to do what Leonard Mitchell can do. But he'll need more than his lifetime to do what someday we'll be able to do."

He had a moment of brotherly feeling and, I'll admit, I glowed. "I appreciate your support, Vic, even if I don't always let you see how I feel. I know I can always count on you. But you should have more confidence in me. Don't always imagine I'll make a fool of myself."

I thought he was a giant next to that bum, Mitchell. I felt that he could have anything he wanted. "You can have Sherry," I told him. "Do you want her? Take her."

He defended Sherry. He said I was too hard on her, as I was on everybody save Jake. "You accept everyone's name for her. But you miss something if you don't see that she is a remarkable person."

"He pulls her tits like she's a cow, and she lets him get away with it. What's so remarkable?"

He said that it was easy for me, who disliked Leonard Mitchell, to slight his power. "He's a generous person who has taught me a lot. You refuse to admit that side of him."

"You've learned how to steal, is that it?"

"He's my friend, and he offers me what he can."

XXI

IN RETROSPECT, I ask who was the wiser, Ernie or I? I remember his summation of Leonard: "He offers me what he can." Ernie had great talent as a fantasist. He was able to put himself in Leonard Mitchell's shoes and understand the poverty of that point of view. He spoke as though Leonard were a moral cripple, unable to accept the full range of obligations we impose on healthy human beings. Impressive, such sympathy! Except Ernie didn't extend the same forbearance to me or to Jake. I didn't feel that it was Leonard's weakness that secured Ernie's compassion and loyalty, but rather Leonard's power.

"He'll teach you a few lessons about loyalty," I told him. "Get in his way and he'll break every bone in your body. He won't have to think twice. Don't mistake fear for friendship."

"Who says I'm afraid?"

"Why should you be? Didn't he offer you Sherry? As far as he's concerned, she's only a mattress that flutters. You make gods of those two. You offer flattering judgments. Naturally they're your friends."

He didn't want to hear any more, but I knew I'd expressed what he had already considered.

The following Saturday he and Sherry went to Belle Isle without me.

"What if Leonard should find out?" he said.

"What's to find out? Anyhow, she's not so stupid she'd tell. Enjoy yourself."

He gave her deep kisses that night. That was dull business to Leonard Mitchell, who despised any kind of foreplay and never delayed entering the heart of matters. But Ernie kissed the girl of his dreams. She gave him instructions. She taught him to use his tongue. She illustrated the delights of nibbling and ear-licking. His passion was appeased, his pain was relieved, until the following afternoon when he watched Leonard lead her upstairs to be couched.

"Take her away from him," I urged.

"I can't."

"Why would you want to, the little whore? But if you want to, you can. Don't treat her so nice."

He had no alternative.

So as the spring turned into summer we had an interesting season under way. Who was I to give instructions? For my brother's sake, I would have written a Machiavellian handbook.

"What do you think of my babe?" Leonard asked Ernie.

"She's a wonderful person."

"She screws, too."

"It pleases me as a friend that you got someone as intelligent and sensitive as Sherry."

"Her brains are in her ass."

"You don't appreciate her."

"I got pals for that."

"I like her," Ernie admitted.

"I bet you do. You read her poetry, she says. She don't care for that crap."

171

"She has talents you don't realize, Leonard. You should understand your own friends."

"Do me a favor, yeah? Lay off the bullshit."

Ernie had tried to convert Leonard to a poetic vision. Now he stood before us in a natty, two-tone polo shirt and pegged pants, thick sandy hair, heavy brows. A ruddy flush in his skin was evidence of the vital sap. He didn't want any poets intruding. Whatever childish diversions had once tempted him no longer had any force. He made it clear in blunt language.

"Lay off my girl," he told Ernie.

A week previously he had offered Sherry as though she were a free commodity. Now he didn't want her touched or recited to.

Ernie wondered why.

"He's jealous of you," I said.

"He only has to say what he wants, and I wouldn't cross him up."

"That's right. You'll jump for him."

"I wouldn't let her come between us."

"Leonard won't share a single nibble with you. Not one ear-lick."

"How did you come to be so wise?" Ernie asked.

Leonard blossomed into a sharp dresser, Weinberg serving as his model. His pants ballooned at the knees and thighs and hugged the ankles. He wore long, pointed collars, and we saw him absorbed in perfecting a Windsor knot.

He asked Ernie, "Why don't you take care of yourself? What kind of crappy shirt is that?"

Weinberg got him a job driving a delivery truck for a cleaner's. He lied about his age and got a chauffeur's license. He was good at shop work but refused that kind of job.

"You think I'm going to piss away like Sherry's old man?"

He bought a car with his first paycheck.

A vulgar kid, and yet Ernie was his disciple.

Ernie had surrendered his dream of being Almighty God or an intimate thereof in order to cling to Leonard Mitchell.

"Why is he sore at me? I did nothing except in friendship."

He was relieved when Leonard gave no indication of being angry the next time they met.

Leonard told him, "I'm quitting school. I'm not going back in the fall. How about that?"

We sat on a bench at Connie's and studied the action. "What are they going to teach me," he asked, "them farty old ladies? I don't need a god-damn' diploma."

I saw how he hooked my brother by being hot and cold, controlling him as he would a girl.

Jake was too busy for a vacation that summer. He suggested a nearby cottage in Canada, where he could join us each night. I'm sure he wanted to avoid Walled Lake because of Sammy. He knew of a place on the Canadian side of Lake Huron.

Ernie refused to go. "My friends are here," he said. "What kind of vacation would it be for me?"

Jake reminded him of the summer heat, the cold Huron waters, the good life in the piney woods of Canada.

Ernie wouldn't be forced. He didn't have the heart to leave Sherry. His agony was visible to anyone who cared to look. He imagined, I suppose, that he disguised his feelings. The fall of France was of less concern to him than her cheerfulness in plain view of his misery. Leonard delighted in crucifying him.

"You hung up on Sherry?"

"She's your girl. How could I be?"

"I'd love to help you, buddy; I keep telling her to give you a tumble."

Ernie tried staying away. We spent some nights with Moshe Bodkin in Russell Woods Park.

Moshe had heavy sideburns and a phlegmatic heart and no conception of Ernie's misery. His emotional resources were expended in behalf of the Old Testament God and in fathoming celestial designs. We met him at night to locate the constellations. He wasn't confused by Greek myths. He uttered the names of Greek heroes, knowing them only as celestial locations. He didn't need to visualize the hero before he could spot the design in the sky. He consulted the co-ordinates of his star map. It was an admirable mind, arrogant, precise, not subject to distraction.

So it was all the more remarkable to me that Moshe was a religious zealot. He came from a pious family that ate only kosher fare. He donned his prayer shawl and phylacteries each morning and prayed. No work was allowed on the Sabbath, and he refused to carry money in his pockets then.

He proselytized Ernie, hoping perhaps to recover him for Israel. There was a time when I thought he would manage the trick, even though we were the children of Jake Gottlieb, who had instructed us to ignore gods and magicians and keep our eyes on Hitler.

Moshe Bodkin once invited us to attend Yom Kippur services at his synagogue. He urged us to come for the sake of a cantor who had a magnificent voice and could make the occasion impressive even if we lacked piety.

I entered a synagogue for the first time. We did as Moshe Bodkin did. We held prayer books. We rose with Moshe and sat when he did. We turned pages when he did. We rocked as he did. But the effect he hoped for didn't take place. I felt uncomfortable with the skullcap on my head. The service didn't make sense, despite Moshe's briefing. There was no awe in the synagogue to worry me. There were no dark places for mysteries to lurk. There were no silences. It wasn't a particularly impressive congregation. I thought they were a shabby bunch, beards at a time when beards weren't stylish. The plaster walls were streaked, the wooden floor unvarnished. The attitude of the congregation seemed to me social and familial and without reverence. There was informal visiting among the men downstairs and the women above. Some finished prayer ahead of others and sat down. There was no unity, and the ceremony became a bore and we suffered the endless ritual. The dreadful house of God was a tedious place with stale air and a soporific drone. I became relaxed and irreverent and no longer pretended to follow the text. I must have been dreaming because suddenly everything was changed. I came awake to hear the cantor singing and was hit by a grief so unexpected that I had no defense against it. Everyone was at the same point of feeling. I heard chants like wailing. There was one bass groaner who put me in touch with every martyred Jew. I tried to hold out against him but the groans bowled me over, and finally I let go with a sob I vainly tried to stifle.

"Shut up," Ernie hissed at me. "Shut up, you fool."

Who was I, a fifteen-year-old punk who had never set foot in a synagogue, to compete with these pros? Yet Ernie was himself in trouble. I saw his eyes redden. He clenched his teeth to keep control. If I'd kept my mouth shut and my eyes dry, I'd have no memory of that encounter in the synagogue. Ernie paid for his dignity with the loss of his memory.

After Pearl Harbor, Moshe Bodkin enlisted as a paratrooper. I don't know what broke him down; perhaps it was unkosher food or the severe military routine, which left no room for ritual, or maybe, like so many others, he was a Dexter boy, lost in the wide world, one of the kind who ought never to cross the boundary.

He came home on a furlough, crew-cut, skinny, bug-eyed. A crazy laugh at inappropriate moments. Stared while you talked, as though he were feeding on your words. Then said, "I can kill a man ten different ways in ten seconds."

I don't know what the time limit referred to. Whether he could kill in ten seconds or it would take him ten seconds to recite the ten ways. But if you were polite and expressed an interest he'd have an arm around your throat demonstrating. The second time he came home on furlough (something had happened and instead of being a killer they'd made him a clerk) he never returned to his outfit. It was not clear to me exactly what happened. I understand there was violence. The neighbors heard him weeping. An ambulance was sent for. And Moshe passed out of sight. I hear that he's showed up again recently. Not in the old neighborhood, since our Dexter is gone. He has a beard, is thin and red-eyed. There were lessons to be learned in synagogue. You pay a price if you remember your fathers. That's the theme, you see, that I come back to.

"If there was first the word," Moshe asked, "why couldn't it have been 'gas?' Why not, if first there was gas?"

He didn't really care to reconcile God and the stars. He just didn't want them to be in each other's way. He described a universe ruled by cosmic repulsion. Everything fled from everything else, as if there were a loathsome stench that permeated all and that all found unendurable. Yet it was the same world made purposeful by the work of God.

He had fuzz on his solid cheeks and a smudge on his upper lip, and on hot summer nights he sweated through his T shirt. He gushed sweat, an ugly boy with imperturbable dignity. Moshe Bodkin would never have been seduced by Leonard Mitchell. He would know his mind about Leonard Mitchell at first sight and cast him from thought. He wore thick spectacles. He squatted on the thick grass of Russell Woods Park, resembling a near-sighted buddha, and watched the stars.

"Do you know Sherry Lieberman?" Ernie asked Moshe, hoping, I suppose, that this scholarly Bodkin had a formula for easing lovesickness. Moshe didn't know her or any other girl.

"She's a fine person," Ernie said. "Her father is Lieberman the cabinetmaker. They live on Tuxedo near Twelfth Street, where Leonard Mitchell lives. How can you not know Leonard Mitchell? He's the toughest boy in school."

Ernie told Moshe his problem. "He describes how she flutters, and I want to cut my throat."

"What do you mean, 'she flutters'?"

Ernie explained.

Moshe said, "You're crazy," and changed the subject. In the beginning, he said, there was an almost incalculably dense cloud of free hydrogen, and the work of creation needed no other starting place. From so simple a beginning one could trace all subsequent development, but what before the beginning? Was it impossible to speculate? Was the very notion of a time before the beginning meaningless? Wasn't that the point at which one leaped toward faith?

Ernie was more concerned with the flutter of Sherry than with the pulsing of stars. The small enclosure where Leonard Mitchell performed his magic contained greater mysteries for Ernie than did the universe.

He asked Moshe, "How can you believe that the stars run away from each other and still pray every morning?"

"What's one thing to do with the other?"

"You pray to Almighty God, Who made everything in a week and spoke from a burning bush and gave us the Torah. Where is He in the universe? Expanding, too?"

"One thing has nothing to do with the other, is my answer. There is first Israel . . ."

"First there is gas."

"First there is gas for a few billion years, then comes Israel. For me, that's the important beginning."

Moshe, like Leonard Mitchell, was uninterested in current events. He was absorbed by stellar happenings and the ceremonial recollection of a history. He didn't read the newspapers. He didn't tremble at the fall of France. He couldn't begin to conceive of Ernie's problems with Sherry.

Leonard Mitchell had advice to offer, "Learn to talk straight. I see you jump when I say, for instance, 'cunt.' What's it there for, Genius? You think it has ears to listen to poetry? Don't you know that Sherry is a cunt? I'll tell you something. If you don't know how to handle your cock, give it to her and she'll recognize what it is. It won't surprise her. Believe me, it won't. She won't ask, What's that, a baby dirigible? Hand it to her and she'll learn you something."

Ernie told him, "It embarrasses me to talk like this."

"Read her poetry. Who gives a shit? But what's poetry for 'cunt'?"

"My feeling is not just physical."

"I can't stand the way you drag around. Get it out of your system."

He spoke with such contempt that Ernie asked him, "Are you sore, Leonard?"

"It's no skin off my ass."

"It's in my nature to treat all people, men and women, with respect. Believe me, I wish I could get over it."

I intruded then. "What's wrong with respect? Is respect dirty all of a sudden?"

"Just don't bullshit," Leonard said. "Don't give me excuses. If you say you want something, show me some action."

Ernie confessed to being inadequate; he didn't know the score. He admitted that Leonard was wiser than he, and more courageous and more skillful.

"Act like a man," Leonard said. "You don't have to do everything your pa says."

"My pa's all right."

"He hates my guts," Leonard said.

"He doesn't even know you."

"It's all right with me; the feeling is mutual."

Ernie made a lame defense of Jake. "He's no ordinary man, my pa. He's not like Sherry's father."

"What's so special?"

"You know about my pa. Everyone knows about Jake Gottlieb; he is respected even by Weinberg and Spiegelman. You heard the flattering things Happy says about my pa."

"He's kidding you. Happy thinks your pa is a creep."

Again I intruded. "Let him express that opinion to my pa's face; he won't have the nerve."

"Happy won't have the nerve? What the shit do you know about Happy? If he didn't get laughs out of your old man, he'd knock him over."

"My pa," I said, "is no laughing matter. Weinberg is a laughing matter. A big man like that—two hundred and fifty pounds —who plays with kids all day long, is a clown."

"What a big mouth on the shrimp."

Ernie told me to stay out of it. "Who asked your opinion?"

"I give it to you free of charge."

"One of these days, when he's not funny any more, your pa will get creamed."

"If something happens to my pa," I said, "we know where to go, Ernie and me. We know who to look for."

Sherry worked days at Cunningham's Drugstore. She wore a white smock, and might have passed as virginal while she dispensed Kleenex and nose drops and candy bars. She wasn't the type you'd ask to sell you rubbers. Dexter was drenched in sun, and dazzling. It was pleasant inside the fragrant, soapy store, where everything was hawked from aspirin to window fans. A radio behind the soda fountain was tuned to the ball game. The counter was packed. When her lunch break came, I took her to the ice-cream parlor across the street from Cunningham's.

A brief passage through the heat, and we were refrigerated again. We had a tiny corner table, pressed up against the display window. She yawned wide to take the end off a hot dog, and I told her to quit making a fool of my brother.

She stopped eating. "Are you sore about something, Vic?"

I told her to yield to him or to release him, but to let him off the hook.

"What happened, Vic? You talk like you're sore."

"You got such bad taste," I told her. "You think Leonard's something and my brother is just a flunky."

She said that wasn't true. Not at all. Why was I sore? Then, as if the possibility surprised her, she asked, "Didn't we have great times at Belle Isle, Vic? Remember the concerts? The picnics?"

"That's not important."

She wanted to know what she had done to suddenly make me dislike her. I told her to let Ernie alone.

Radios were going all over town, because the Tigers, led by Greenberg and Gehringer and Tommy Bridges, were ahead of the pack, and it was already midseason. Whenever Greenberg

179

came to bat, you sensed he might fulfill your dreams. And this
announcer, Ty Tyson, with the bored voice, would become excited. It's GOING, he'd say. It's GOING, it's GOING, it's
GOING. IT'S GONE! Peace followed that rhythm of orgasm.
All over town men clapped each other's backs, hammered shoulders. On Dexter we took personal credit for Greenberg. Passersby nodded to each other. A Greenberg home run was an
occasion. I listened to every discussion of the day's game, hoping
to hear Greenberg celebrated.

It was also that time of radio when we listened to other
dramatic voices summon us to wake up and worry.

"We interrupt this program to bring you a news bulletin."
Then some grim disaster from Murrow or Kaltenborn or a direct
report from Shirer in Berlin, crackling with static, reporting
Nazi jubilation. I sat with Sherry in the ice-cream parlor, my
pity barely suppressed as she bit her lips to keep down sobs,
her head ducked. The ball game was interrupted and we were
given the summary of a Churchill speech delivered to the British nation. Dunkirk had been evacuated. Churchill promised to
fight the Germans everywhere, on the beaches, from Australia
if necessary. He would never surrender. I wasn't so much inspired by the message as made miserable that our fortunes had
come to such a pass. It was a relief when the bulletin was
over and we were returned to Greenberg and the Tigers and
some chance of victory, however trifling.

"Why don't you get rid of Leonard Mitchell? It's disgusting
the way you're his slave."

"Didn't you mean it when we were at Belle Isle and we were
such pals?"

"Well, don't cry or I'll leave."

"My gosh, you hurt my feelings. You know how I feel about
Leonard."

"You kiss his hand in public, that's what I know."

"You shouldn't call me a slave. That's not fair, Vic."

"He humiliates you, and you love him for it."

"If you felt like I do, you wouldn't be ashamed, either, to kiss somebody's hand."

"Kiss whatever you want; just stay away from Ernie."

I was at Moshe Bodkin's that night, playing chess. Beetles flung themselves at the screen. Moths fluttered in the yellow light meant to repel them. Though I never could beat Moshe, he wasn't concerned with the lack of competition. He hunched over the board, his head as solid as a bowling ball, pulling at his thick underlip, bothering his pimples. He nudged a chessman with a stubby finger. His T shirt molded his fat belly.

Ernie broke in on us, breathing hard from running. He came through the back yard to the porch door. He wanted me to come outside with him. We walked into Russell Woods Park, but not to see stars.

"What did you say to her?"

"I said, 'Leave my brother alone.'"

"You finished me with them. They were my best friends."

I wanted Ernie to respect his own power. I didn't want to see him submit to Leonard Mitchell. I took it on myself to shake him loose.

"It turns my stomach when she kisses his hand," I told him.

"Did anyone ask your stomach for an opinion?"

Leonard had been virulently insulting. "It had to happen," Ernie admitted glumly. "They're in a different league."

He met Leonard several times in the next few days, hoping for a reconciliation. I could have told him that it was useless. Leonard simply wanted a pretext to end a relationship that bored him.

I saw Leonard Mitchell in the evenings outside The Cream of Michigan, dolled up in a silk shirt, a wide-brimmed hat, billowing trousers that hugged the ankles. He encouraged Sherry to wear tight sweaters that showed her nipples. Whenever Ernie disappeared, I knew that he'd gone to put himself in the path of an indifferent Leonard Mitchell. He humbled himself to that vulgar jerk.

XXII

JAKE FLOURISHED that summer. His name entered the pages of history via the Detroit newspapers—the *News,* the *Times,* and the *Free Press.* A blurred photo appeared. There was a small place for him. He was crowded into filler space, since big news ruled the columns. England survived, though clobbered from the air. Anti-Semites and villains governed at Vichy. Meanwhile, Jake carved out his own empire.

One by one, each laundry and linen establishment, the diaper suppliers, the industrial suppliers, fell under Jake's sovereignty. At the end they fell to him in clusters. You might think, Small potatoes! An insignificant duchy! A puny Luxemburg compared to the great powers in the labor world! But Jake's star was ascendant. He was intelligent. He had courage. He was revered by his men. He had perfect integrity. How could he fail? Who was of his stature? O'Brien? O'Brien was, perhaps, closer to the men. Jake had no simple, comradely connections with the rank and file. He could be resented for his imperial manner. There were some—for instance, McIntyre and Emerson —who wished to bring him down.

O'Brien was a man you could talk to sensibly. He understood your point of view. You could negotiate with O'Brien. Of course, it was dangerous to oppose him. But there was no reason to fight O'Brien, who was a reasonable man and didn't represent a foreign ideology. He believed in a natural aristocracy established by the facts of power.

Because of Jake Gottlieb, O'Brien was finished as a union man. He and McIntyre and Emerson pulled their routes and started their own business. They had a firm base of operations in Oswego with Fiori. O'Brien had been right about Fiori. He had made a friend; there were no hard feelings. Fiori offered him a partnership in White Swan, and with that base O'Brien began to accumulate a fortune. He operated like a buccaneer, raiding businesses throughout southern Michigan, offering substantial discounts for stops. He also had more-violent inducements.

"I got no hard feelings," he told Jake when they bumped trays at the Greenwich Cafeteria on Woodward Avenue. "You did me a favor."

Jake told him, "You didn't move far enough away."

"I have good will for you, Jake."

"When you come into Detroit, your business becomes my business."

"Don't interest yourself in my business, Jake. You already got away with murder."

Jake dropped a loaded tray and grabbed for O'Brien. They were immediately separated by friends, fore and aft, who were braced for the encounter. O'Brien was stained red with borsht. He dried himself and ignored Jake, who struggled to get at him.

"You see, Jake. No grudges."

"Bum! Killer!"

"That's libel, you son of a bitch." O'Brien refused to be provoked. Everyone knew he wasn't a man to tolerate insult, but he didn't want trouble with the union. The weather being hot, he could endure cold borsht.

When McIntyre came to the union office to seek a reconciliation, Jake advised him, "Stay out of Detroit. I don't yet have the power to touch you in Oswego. But come into Detroit and I'll cut your business off."

"I didn't come here to talk business, Jake. Once we were friends. I came to say I got a lot to be sorry for and I apologize."

"Tell it to your preacher."

"We put away my little girl, Jake. Peggy is all broke up about it."

"I don't want to hear the details. I no longer have to listen. I hear your Italian girl friend is now a business associate. Talk to her."

"That's all in the past and forgotten, Jake. We're friends, that's all."

"I got a good memory. Don't worry. You can rely on me to remember."

Jake brought home a bundle of newspapers. All three dailies carried the same photo of Jake being released from the Highland Park jail. He had chosen to violate an injunction against picketing and had been arrested five times, returning to the picket line after each arrest. He harangued the cops on the way to jail. They asked him, What's your name? What's your nationality? He asked them, "What's *your* name? What's *your* nationality? I'm a citizen who pays your salary. You're here to serve me, so I'll ask the questions. What's my nationality got to do with my picketing Stay Clean Overall?"

The photo showed him coming down the jail stairs, his chin high, his chest out, his arms stiff at his sides. He resembled a Frankenstein monster. Jake distributed that issue of the newspaper gratis to all takers. He carried the clipping in his wallet. His name was misspelled. The reporters had accumulated the facts in an abusive sequence. They didn't like Jake, who had the manner of greatness without the reputation, and so appeared absurd to them. They were further put off by his accent and his brash tone. But Jake was on record, his power proclaimed. He was the notorious Jake Gottlieb, arrested five times in one day. He was on the phone for hours one Sunday receiving congratulations. I heard him say to one caller, "I'm ready to spend my life in jail. We'll flood the streets. Let them use clubs against us."

He had an office at the Labor Temple, a building that resembled a warehouse, located at the terminus of skid row, near the river. The corridors were bleak, the windows grimy. The meeting hall was a dusty room with rows of folding chairs. The dust of old Detroit was in its seams. A photograph of Franklin Delano Roosevelt, draped in an American flag, was on the office wall. There was also a signed photograph of Governor Frank Murphy extending personal regards to his buddy Jake and, on the desk, a framed triptych of Ernie, Evka, and me.

Roosevelt was big and solid. He had large teeth, and distinctly resembled McIntyre. FDR spoke to us often via Philco, a chipper man who took offense at Hitler. He communicated to the nation his optimism that, since he was now involved, the process of history would take a turn for the better.

The Labor Temple was near the location of the original village of Fort Detroit, founded by the Chevalier Cadillac to fend off the British. Not far from the site of the Labor Temple Chief Pontiac had initiated his conspiracy. He'd entered the fort with his braves, presumably to smoke for peace. But the Commandant had been forewarned that beneath their blankets the treacherous Indians carried arms. Pontiac had been caught red-handed and so had had to pretend he was in earnest about peace and was offended that the palefaces didn't trust him. The tactic had since become a standard maneuver in labor negotiations.

There were strange acolytes in this temple, paunchy, genial men who ruled the crafts. They were of the breed of McIntyre, sweetened by affluence. Black limousines were the sign of their status, and Jake, too, became the operator of a Buick Roadmaster with dual carburetors and twin exhausts, a considerable improvement in our station. These good-natured men, risen from the ranks, didn't seek revolution. They were willing to settle for a Buick, a summer cottage, a brick house in a good neighborhood and the same for the members of their local crafts. For men at large they had small aspirations. Jake was a different kind of fish, an ideologue. However, they were impressed by the size of his shoulders and his touchy insistence on respect.

The big chief was Charley Hammer, the council chairman. He had an elegant, senatorial presence with waves of silver hair. Even in shirt sleeves he appeared well tailored. He smoked long cigars and raised his little finger when he tapped off the ash.

He invited the Gottliebs into his office and complimented the sons on their father. "You boys have any idea what a problem this old dad of yours is? If the phone rings, I don't say, 'Hello,' any more. I ask straight off, 'Okay, what is it with Gottlieb now?' In fact," he said, turning to Jake, "I just hung up on an old pal of yours, Hy Kravitz. You seem to have stirred them up, Jake. You're in a great bargaining position. They want clear sailing for the Christmas season. They want to know why the delay in negotiations for the new contract."

"How come he calls you? What good can you do for him?"

Hammer clapped him on the back. "Exactly my question, Jake. I explained to him that Gottlieb's his own man and not even God Almighty himself has any influence with Jake Gottlieb. I sure don't."

"That's right," Jake said. "I'm only responsible to my membership."

"I told him I'd speak to you. Consider yourself spoken to."

"What have you got to say?"

"It's your baby, Jake. Shove it in him and break it off for all I care. Things are going to be hot around here in a few months with the elections coming up. We're advising all locals to go slow on any strike action. We don't want a bad press."

Jake didn't mind a bad press. "The newspapers are the organs of vested interests. Why should they love me?"

Hammer tried to give hugs, which Jake resisted. "I love this bastard," he told us, getting an awkward grip on Jake, who inflated his muscles so that Hammer's arm slipped. "Jake Gottlieb won't kiss anybody's ass."

Jake said to us afterward, "I trust him like I would a snake. Do you see how soft he is? He socializes with the mayor. He gives speeches on Labor Day. He keeps a woman on Euclid Avenue, a married man with grown children."

Jake wasn't eased by success. He was an edgy, difficult man after the death of Sammy Persky. Not many of Evka's friends were able to take him, and only Berle continued to visit regularly.

I heard Berle ask, "How come I don't see you any more Gottlieb? Are you forgetting your old friends?"

"I never forget a friend."

"You're a big man now. Your picture is in the papers."

"Receive a knock on the head and you, too, can have your picture in the paper."

"I come by, but you're never in."

"Better for you. You can visit your girl friend without me interrupting."

Berle protested, but Jake paid no attention. "What do you hear from your Uncle Joe, the Red butcher?"

"Let's not have arguments, Jake. I'm also upset by the way the Soviet Union behaves."

"The two butchers do business together. They put on bloody aprons and carve up Jews."

"You don't mean to compare Stalin to Hitler? You're not surely making such a comparison?"

"Did Uncle Joe sign a pact with Chaim Weizmann or Norman Thomas? No. He shook the hand of Adolf Hitler, and now the blood of our people is on his hands."

"You push me, Gottlieb, but I don't want to argue. I tell you again, I'm sorry about the pact. I wish it didn't happen. But as you know from personal experience, Gottlieb, it's an imperfect world."

"Who says I know? Why should I know?"

"We all got to do terrible things when we keep faith with our principles. You as a labor leader know that."

"Who says I know that? Why should I know that?"

"It's common knowledge, Gottlieb, that you had to break a couple eggs to make your omelette."

"I broke eggs? What eggs did I break?"

"You push me into an argument when I don't want to argue. Let's for once not speak on controversial subjects."

"What is this common knowledge? Name an egg that Gottlieb has broken. Think of one egg."

"I got no names."

"Then why do you open your mouth?"

"I was speaking in the abstract. It's common sense that if you're in a rough business, you sometimes are forced to employ rough methods."

"Then you were speaking about abstract eggs? And abstract omelettes? And you compare me to the butcher Stalin on such an abstract basis? Does Stalin, too, break abstract eggs?"

"I don't compare you to Stalin. Who are you to be compared to Stalin? You're only . . ." He clamped down at the last moment, then completed his statement under tight control, ". . . an ordinary mortal like the rest of us. Don't imagine you're a god."

"Is Stalin a god? Do you go on your knees to Stalin?"

Dresden finally broke down and yelled, "And how about Sammy Persky! Sammy Persky, Gottlieb! There's your egg! And some omelette! Some omelette!"

He didn't show up for weeks afterward.

Jake approached the bargaining table with the resolve to go all the way, whatever the cost. He couldn't be diverted by lawyers or accountants. He didn't permit debate to follow rules of order. He refused to give up the floor. He heckled the opposition. He operated at full blast and forced them to yell back.

He deliberately outraged. Others were shamed by the performance he required of them. He exhausted the opposition, which finally yielded.

He no longer drove an Atlas truck. When he now confronted Kravitz, it was not as a subordinate to a master.

"Didn't I say, Gottlieb, you don't belong on a truck? Look at you. A fine desk. American flags. A secretary. A silk suit. A year ago you'd be wearing a uniform this time of day. I never grudged you, Gottlieb. Not for a second. Even when you screwed me I said to myself, 'Wouldn't you do the same thing if you had to start over again with no capital?'"

"You would never do the same," Jake said. "It's not in you to be on my side of the fence."

"You're on one side; I'm on the other. Yet we both got the health of the industry in our hearts. We don't want to see this industry go on the rocks, Gottlieb."

"We got different ideas about health."

"You'd be surprised; they're not so different. Didn't I come to your office out of interest in your ideas? I listen with respect."

He felt that it was time Jake learned that he was dealing with men, not beasts. Kravitz asked him to join the bosses in their annual retreat at Lake Charlevoix.

"No families. Fishing. Cards. No business. Business is out. Absolutely. You talk business and you're fined. You'll breathe good air. Maybe a few drinks. Friendly games—poker, pinochle. No one's obligated to anyone else. Each one chips in. We get to know each other like human beings, Gottlieb. You got some funny ideas about us."

Evka watched Jake assemble camping and fishing equipment. "I'm tickled you're going," she said. "I'm a little surprised."

"Is there a law I shouldn't play poker?"

"To begin at forty-eight is a little unusual."

"I still got life in me, old lady; I'm not dead yet."

"I thought you had such strong feelings about Hyman Kravitz."

He knew that she favored gloomy poets, effeminate hotel

owners, but he intended to experience a full life before he was finished.

"Be careful when you gamble," she warned him.

"You expect me to lose, eh?"

"They're experienced gamblers. They play together every week."

"They could play till the world ends and they wouldn't be such a gambler as I am. Enough of your knocking, old lady."

Evka explained to us later, "I'm delighted he's going on a vacation. But I wish he had some restraint. He'll play till every penny is gone. I don't even expect him to catch minnows."

I can only speculate about the dreams of that boy from Siberia. He went into the land of Hemingway, among the great hemlock trees, along the dune beaches of Lake Michigan, and spent two nights in a cottage with four other men. He came out winners in poker—a modest sum—and brought home several smoked whitefish.

It was at this time that we got to know Kravitz.

Kravitz made use of the world. He didn't listen when you talked unless you were on the subject of his business. He was all ears with respect to Atlas, but when you spoke of other affairs his eyes became vacant. He interrupted before you finished. We once stopped at his home and met his mousey wife. She seemed uncomfortable in our presence, and after a few moments excused herself. Kravitz' daughter, home from college, was an entirely different case. She considered you so arrogantly you wanted to take arms against her at first sight. She had the same knack as her pa of provoking you to resist before she had even assaulted. On this occasion, she was angry with her father and barged into the living room, completely ignoring us. Kravitz had refused to lend her boy friend the family car.

"That's a hell of a note," she said, a powerful voice for a lady. "He's from out of town, so how about a little hospitality?"

"Tell him to speak to his own pa in regard to a car."

"His pa is eight hundred miles away in Newark."

"I'll give him an airmail stamp. He can drop a note."

"You miser!"

"Do I need to let him smash up my Chrysler for hospitality? I'll give you bus fare to get to the movie just to show you I'm a nice guy."

She stared at him and shook her head. "You are champ," she said. "You take the cake. You just don't have any competition in the miser contest. You stand all by yourself."

Kravitz was unperturbed. "You have an accident," he said blandly, "it's on my head."

She turned to Jake. "Take him for every cent he has, Mr. Gottlieb; make him yell."

She had an athletic, muscular shape. Her breasts made large, fuzzy mounds in her angora sweater. She carried on the family squabble as if it didn't matter that we overheard.

Jake told us afterward that we should see the Kravitz son. "He goes to school in New York. He takes after his ma. He weighs a hundred and forty pounds and is already bald. You speak loud to him and he pisses. They got the sexes mixed up when they made the children of Kravitz."

Kravitz, whose name had signified something monstrous a few months before, appeared now entirely within the human range. His ferocity seemed on closer look to be only the symptom of an eccentric nature. How could a man with such a daughter be the tyrant Kravitz who had humiliated McIntyre? The old monsters were humanized, while our onetime allies, McIntyre and Emerson, became our new monsters. Who took any of them seriously? It all seemed the by-product of Jake's histrionic manner.

"They're nice to me," Jake explained, "sure. They think because we catch fish together I'll do them favors. Don't kid yourself. That nice man Kravitz with the loud-mouth daughter would have me ripped to pieces like an old sheet if he knew what plans I had for him."

Still, he preferred Kravitz to Charley Hammer, although anyone else would have picked Charley, who had started as a printer for the Detroit *News* and reached the top of the labor game on the strength of his charm.

His ease was the product of a long cocktail hour. He also took a couple of belts at lunch. To see him at Fred's Steak House—a napkin tucked into his collar in order to save the white tie and the gold clip—settled in front of Fred's specialty, prime ribs rare, you saw a man with a gift for pleasure that others were inclined to indulge. Nothing could go too far wrong in a world that served up such fine dishes for Charlie Hammer. He wanted you along to share his pleasure. He insisted that you order the same cut of rib, the salad with chef's dressing, afterward the cheese cake. He pressed you to drink with him, at least a beer. Why deny yourself pleasure because it was only the middle of the day? Why should we only accept ease when the day was finished? He enjoyed his work. He enjoyed the process of negotiation, and arbitration, even war. He urged a good war on a full stomach, panic quelled by sour mash. As for the larger war that occupied the world, he didn't believe in it. Out of sight, out of mind. He spoke one language, Midwestern American. For all he knew, the world came to an end beyond New York on one side and Los Angeles on the other. He wouldn't have found it much of a wrench to return to a Ptolemaic point of view and a pancake world. The sphericity of our globe must have been mildly disconcerting when he thought about it, but global events didn't have much interest for Charley Hammer.

He was born in Chicago, Illinois. His grandparents fled the demise of the Irish potato. He believed in the existence of Ireland and consequently in Britain. The Irish legend stirred him; yet he wasn't one of your passionate Irishmen when it came to that affair. Charley loved any man with a vote, whether he was Irish, Italian, Pole or Jew. He demonstrated his love by telling ethnic jokes.

Did Jake know the one about the Italian who made a pilgrimage to Rome to meet Il Papa—which means pope in Guinea? His buddy, Angelo the barber, says "Whatta ya mean, see

Il Papa? He no see a punka lika you. A tousanda milliona peopola wanta see Il Papa. Why he see you?" So the wop goes to Rome and he comes back, and Angelo says, "Well, smarta guy. They letta you in to see Il Papa?" Giovanni says to him, "Sure I see Il Papa." "You see Il Papa?" "I see Il Papa." "Whadda Il Papa say?" "I bend down to kiss his ring. He look at my hair. He say, where do ya getta sucha lousy haircuts?"

He prefaced his jokes by advertising the subject matter. Did you hear the one about the Polack who just came across on steerage? Or about the nigger-eating crocodiles?

He asked Jake, "How come I don't get a laugh out of you, Gottlieb? Do you know the one about Abie and Becky?"

Jake said, "I don't want to hear. I don't have a sense of humor."

Charley never interfered with the tribal powers of subordinate chieftains. He represented a consensus. His good nature was his strength. But Jake made serious inroads on Charley's good nature. Jake didn't go in for heavy drinking, didn't like his meat rare, and was touchy about ethnic jokes.

"You got a lifetime," Hammer told him. "You don't have to solve the world's problems this year. You'll put these boys out of business. It's your own people will suffer."

"I pay no attention when Kravitz cries. I heard him cry before. I'm no longer impressed."

Charley told Catholic jokes to indicate he wasn't so serious as to lose his sense of humor. He never argued matters of religion.

"I may not be a credit to my church and I may not be a credit to my race, but I sure have done a job for the distilleries. I'm one Irishman whose wake is going to disappoint the liquor industry, because they got so much invested in me."

Still, Charley wasn't so indifferent a Catholic as to have any sympathy for bolsheviks. He vaguely identified the breed: their land was Russia; their creed was socialism. "I'm a free-enterprise man myself," Charley Hammer said.

"You can't push for a raise that size two years in a row, Jake.

Kravitz has a point. They're willing to show their books to an agreed third party."

Jake said, "I don't want to see their books. I can't read their books. It's their business, not mine. My business is to see that the working man receives the fruits of his labor."

"You got to be reasonable, Jake. If the books show there is no profit, what choice have you got but to negotiate? Ask for the moon, but negotiate."

"When they accept my terms, I'll negotiate."

Charley was everybody's pal. His wife Irene was a great favorite. Her corset buttressed a hefty chest. Her once-red hair had been restored to an orange hue. Charley was proud of Irene's great laugh. "You know you got your punch line delivered when you hear old Irene cut loose." She didn't kill fun with her piety. Though she was a church lady, she didn't force religion down your throat. Her big heart had nourished five children. She had a mink jacket, a house near Grosse Pointe Farms, drove to church in a Cadillac that was black in order to avoid ostentation. She had a deep voice and a temper whose ferocity Charley proudly advertised. Her temper was in his behalf. She was a great soldier to have in your army. Better than a whole troop. He was glad to acknowledge that Irene was boss. It pleased him that she was. He considered it a credit to himself that he had a wife who could manage him like a mother. There was a great deal of the little boy in Charley, who—as everyone but his own family knew—had a Polish girl friend on Euclid Avenue, much younger than Irene, with no need of a corset, and very docile. I'm sure the Polish girl no more existed for Charley than did the world beyond Long Island and Catalina Island. He advocated rotarian pieties as though he in fact were living a boy-scout life.

"Run your own affairs," Jake told Charley. "Do I tell you how to live? I keep my nose to myself and advise you to do the same. When I need your help don't worry, I'll ask."

Jake imagined that Charley's affability had no limits. He was mistaken.

"Defy me, Jake, and you lose your charter."

"Losing my charter is about as serious, Hammer, as you losing your virtue. You have it back by Sunday afternoon."

Irene Hammer disliked Jake; I know from personal experience. We were entertained at the Labor Temple after the Labor Day parade. Union executives and their families gathered in the assembly hall, which had been cleared of chairs. A long table was set up and covered with a linen cloth. Mrs. Hammer sat at one end behind a coffee urn and a tea service. There were cookies and sandwiches and soft drinks for the kids. Irene wore a wide-brimmed hat and elbow-length gloves, though it was a hot September day. Other ladies participated in the festivities. I remember that Evka wore her brown suit with velvet trim and a hat with a veil and a sprig of cherries. Evka managed to charm despite her anxieties. She sensed what worked with you and what didn't. She didn't want to offend, so she was an ardent listener. She joked with the ladies and flirted with the men. She allowed them to give her big hugs, and she squeezed back.

Irene Hammer said, "Golly, honey! What a shame you aren't president of the laundry drivers! You and us would get along fine. Jake is a porkypine when it comes to getting along with him. Why don't you do something about that man of yours, honey? I'll be darned if I'd ever let Charley get away with what Jake gets away with. He should learn to be one of the boys like you're one of the girls."

Jake overheard. "Some girls," he said. "Twenty years ago it was already too late for that title."

"Jake Gottlieb," said Irene Hammer, summoning him in a voice like God's, "you don't scare me; I'm not fooled a bit. I happen to know you've got a heart as soft as a Teddy bear no matter how tough you speak."

"What do *you* know?" Jake asked. He spoke to her in a surly manner; he wasn't kidding. "What you learn in a bedroom or a kitchen you know. About me you know nothing." There was no way for her to misinterpret his contempt.

"You do have a problem," she told Evka.

"Jake," Charley said, "don't plan on a strike. We won't support it."

"I don't ask for your support."

Kravitz urged Jake to look at the books. He was willing to forget the stipulation that a person agreeable to both parties do the looking. Jake could use his own accountant. Jake could look at profit and loss, asset and debit, and whatever he decided upon as a basis for negotiation the employers would seriously consider. Kravitz spoke for the entire industry in extending the offer.

"I don't want to look," Jake said.

Kravitz urged him to be reasonable. He had talked his head off to get the others to co-operate. It was a revolutionary move. Never before had a group of employers offered to show their books to employees, the results to be used as a basis for bargaining. He was Jake's pal. He knew how stubborn Jake was and how costly it would be to war against Jake. He didn't want war. The industry didn't want war. The men were better off than they had ever been. Did Jake want another disastrous, bloody battle like the year before that had cost the life of a man they both loved? Who could tell what would happen if Jake drove the industry to the wall? Did he figure on the backing of Charley Hammer? He wouldn't get it. The picket line wouldn't be respected by the other unions. Jake didn't have any alternative but to accept such a decent offer.

"O'Brien is on our side, Jake. Don't count on his help."

"I thank God he is on your side. Your side will pay for it."

"We played cards together. We lay on the ground together. We breathed North Michigan together. We caught fish together. Gottlieb, you surprise me. I always thought of you as a man of honor."

"I don't sell out for smoked fish, Kravitz."

Kravitz cried, "Ruin," but Jake answered he had heard that lament before. Let the employers beware. They knew the resolve of the union, which had already proved it could endure bloody violence.

Why did Jake push so hard? He was unreasonable. He wanted war when no one else had the desire.

It was a relief to him that he didn't have the support of O'Brien.

He told Evka, "We can now act with clean hands."

With a month left of the contract, the employers probably figured Jake was bluffing. They expected him to modify his proposals.

But Jake couldn't be swayed. He had fixed on his purpose and he marched toward it, as intractable to reason as a hurricane.

"You're as bad as Hitler!" Kravitz bellowed.

"You dare to make such a comparison?"

"Mussolini, then. Do you feel better?"

There was a resemblance to Il Duce, as a matter of fact. The same baldness. The same massive chin. But Jake didn't have the outthrust jaw that gave Mussolini the absurd petulant appearance of a little kid. When combined with his exaggerated swagger, that look made us giggle when we saw it in the Fox Movietone News. Il Duce minced like a pansy. In a wig and a wide-brimmed hat such as Mrs. Hammer wore, he would have resembled someone's spinster auntie.

Our elm trees shed. Richton, overgrown with weedy lawns, its sidewalks split by seams of clay, shabby and stale in the last days of summer, grew lean with the fall. Skeleton trees emerged through brown leaves. The gutters filled with leaves. The skies darkened. There was thunder. Then hard, chill rains resumed the erosion of front yards.

Jake weathered everything. He refused to acknowledge rainy days or changes in season. He was forty-eight years old and in a hurry. Hitler was only three years older.

Charley Hammer said to him, "You're something, all right, Gottlieb, but you ain't Napoleon—yet. You're still small potatoes. You got a crummy little local, a few hundred men. So quit rocking the boat, Gottlieb. You're only one year off the truck.

Keep that in mind. You might find yourself lifting bundles again."

Jake had his own ideas about who was small potatoes. He read off his credentials for Hammer's benefit. Siberia at sixteen. A soldier boy in France. Fired by Ford. Hit by billies. Threatened by the elite hoodlums of Detroit. "And what are you, Hammer? A printer who don't practice his trade, who lives in Grosse Pointe and drives a Cadillac. You think I'll trust the destiny of my local to you, Hammer, who feeds on raw meat? Who are you to speak to me about small potatoes?" He asked Hammer why he was such a zealous supporter of Kravitz. "What's in it for you, Charley?"

"How do you mean that question, Jake?"

"Take away my charter and I'll picket the Labor Temple."

"You picket the Labor Temple and you'll get your head split."

Now he was talking Jake's language. Jake offered his head to be split. "Be my guest, Charley."

Jake had made so little progress that when he began to move he wanted to fly.

Well, we needed heroes, so why not him? Everyone else was either reluctant or bashful. Jake was willing to climb into the main arena and take on tyrants. He denied that there was any genius to Adolf Hitler. He refused to even designate him an "evil genius." He called Hitler a maniac, criminal, monster, murderer, and attributed his power to the gullibility of foe and degeneracy of friend. Jake Gottlieb wasn't of a size to be noticed. It was an accident of history that others managed the fate of the world. Jake Gottlieb would have done a better job.

He was confident that the industry would find a way to accept his terms. He left them no way out. He insisted upon opposition. He demanded unconditional surrender. He threatened the industry with a ruinous strike or a contract they thought impossible. He compelled Charley Hammer to either fight him or eat crow. It was bullying tactics. What was he after? He could have won a respectable victory with less trouble.

Did he aim for Charley Hammer's job, as Happy Weinberg had once implied? He could have built that job into a solid platform for his next thrust toward fame. Jake was another man in a rush to be glorified. It must have grated on him to see mediocrities like Charley Hammer ranked over himself.

XXIII

———◆———

ERNIE ENTERED the new school year with great resolutions. He would suffer his father. He wouldn't be provoked. He would resume his place on the softball diamond and afterward try for the football team. He'd take another crack at Plato's *Republic* and *Don Quixote*. He figured that, given a steady rate of progress, he could work through the Harvard Classics five-foot shelf in three years. He intended to become a wise man. He intended to enlarge his muscles. He aimed for integrity and courage. He knew without benefit of Aristotle that it would take training and good connections. He would no longer lie in bed and dream. He was finished with Leonard. His crush on Sherry seemed inexplicable.

To all that, I said wonderful.

But, when Leonard phoned, what happened to those great resolutions? Leonard didn't treasure grievances. He didn't even remember hard feelings. He filled Ernie in on recent history. He had his own apartment near Wayne University. He was free of all obligations. He wanted Ernie to drop by for a visit. He said, "Bring the kid along if you want."

I asked Ernie if he was going. He said, "Why not? I'm not afraid I'll be infected. He has no communicable disease. Relax," he told me. "It's an experience. I'm interested."

"And your promises?"

"What did I promise?"

"That you were finished with Leonard Mitchell."

"Did I promise not to look?"

Everyone has the right to look. Otherwise, how get an education?

Home was never anything but a makeshift to Leonard. He used Connie's as his parlor and The Cream of Michigan as his dining room. His new apartment still bore evidence of other transients who had passed through. There were pictures from *Life* magazine tacked to the wall, a reproduction of an elaborately scripted HOME SWEET HOME above a mantelpiece that shaded a phony fireplace. I remember a braided oval rug and a day bed whose iron frame showed beneath a frayed paisley spread. He shared a bath with four others. All the roomers had access to a dank parlor off the vestibule. Sherry made the bed and washed the dishes.

The passage of decades discovers Ernie and me still carrying the same baggage. We hardly change. I await the second coming of Jake Gottlieb, and when I'm ninety years old it will be the same. But Sherry and Leonard are a different case. You don't see them for a couple of weeks and you find there's been a change in appearance and even in character. They learn quickly. They adjust fast. They march toward a definition of themselves. They profit from experience.

It was amazing how quickly that innocent, sweet-tempered Sherry came to accept Leonard Mitchell's terms. She didn't perish in the jungle of appetite into which she'd been thrust. On the contrary, she developed an appetite, and became carnivorous like the other cats. A few weeks previously I could still make her weep. Now she was beyond my reach. She faced down her mother, who foretold the death by grief of Mr. Lieberman and herself. What a rotten life they had submitted to in behalf of their only child! They had slaved for her. Now she was in the hands of Leonard Mitchell. That was mismanagement of valuable property.

Sherry learned how to be tough by practicing on her parents. In drawing blood, she advanced beyond sixteen. She swelled to womanly shape as we watched. Her hips broadened, her bosom increased. There was a thickening that didn't make her seem gross, but substantial. Leonard Mitchell was inclined toward the monumental, and she was still too slight for his taste, but she developed toward his idea of a woman.

We saw the aftermath of their battles, a sullen Sherry, a steaming Leonard, his mark sometimes visible on her. He had no reservations about rapping a woman. He leaped with enthusiasm to the challenge. Her arms were bruised. We once saw her with a swollen lip and a black eye.

He called her a drag and urged her to get off his back. She was willing to get off his back, provided she could first plant knives.

"You're not dumping me so easy," she said. "Maybe you'd love it if I vanished. Fat chance, you bastard."

I hoped Ernie would be repelled by this brazen Sherry. But her new manifestation had even greater charm for him. He was awed by the bitch. She had a marvelous skin, her innocence had no apparent blemishes, and yet obscenity issued. The Belle Isle days were finished. She had gamier tastes. She could handle herself in rough company.

Leonard wanted us to drop by often. "Any night. I'm off at five o'clock. We'll rack up a few at Connie's or drop by Weinberg's for a drink."

Ernie said to me after our first visit, "I feel sorry for Leonard. What a grubby place!"

"Dirt isn't news to him, and you forget he has Sherry."

"It's a mistake for him to quit school."

"You think we lost an Einstein when Leonard Mitchell

dropped out? They better get him into jail fast, is my opinion. Get him off the street and behind bars."

I suppose Leonard needed Ernie for whatever skimpy continuity he could eke out of his past. He was jealous of Ernie's other interests. He knocked the football team. He ridiculed the Harvard Classics. He pressed Ernie to grow up and take real risks. Meaning, I suppose, Windsor whorehouses and nine ball at Connie's. He teased Ernie with Sherry, sometimes urging them to love one another, at other times warning against trespass. "Stay away from that creep, Bodkin," he advised. "What kind of pansies are you? Sitting up at night and watching stars—shit!"

He taunted me. For a man without an inner life, he had a surprising instinct for secret grievances. "Why don't you get a life of your own, shorty? Would you know how to piss if you didn't see your brother do it first?"

He didn't read books. He went to movies in midweek. He hung around Connie's. He made money at snooker and nine ball. Weinberg let him come in on low-stake poker games, but Leonard didn't have the money to operate on Saturday nights, when the games were serious. He smoked the same brand of cigar as Weinberg. His beard arrived in full flower, and he shaved once a day. He got a job driving for Kravitz on the recommendation of Weinberg. It upset me that a boy of our group could do the same work as our pa. Although he joined the union, he had no fraternal feelings. He despised the job. The time clock ruined his day at the very beginning. He wanted to be in business on his own. Like Charley Hammer, he was a free-enterprise man.

We saw his ma arrive at his room with mop, pail, soap, scrub brush. She aired the rug on a clothesline in the back yard. She got down on her knees and scraped the floor with a stiff brush, jets of soapy water hissing ahead of her. The motion resembled an Oriental obeisance, a deep bend forward, then returning to her haunches as she drew in the brush. Leonard sat on the couch and raised his legs so she could rake the floor beneath him. Her wiry black hair veiled her face and almost touched the floor as she bowed forward. She gave us one ferocious glance, then bore down on the floor as if she intended to skin it. I once saw him driving on Dexter, his mother in back like a domestic being delivered to a bus stop.

He never spoke about her, and perhaps his reticence indicated feeling. I remember seeing a gift he bought for her birthday, a framed photo of himself. The tinting made his eyes seem dead, his cheeks fat, his lips womanish. The photo was signed in a childish square hand: TO MA FROM LENNY.

I grant him feeling for his mother. And the ferocity of her look probably didn't mean anything; she may have been nearsighted or frozen-faced or epileptic. She had headaches so severe she passed out. When she rose to her feet after cleaning, her dress caught for a moment above her hairy legs and I saw callouses on her knees.

If I try to exercise my sympathy—and it's an effort—I can see mother and son as isolated and pathetic.

Leonard wanted to travel in the style of Happy Weinberg, who was continually on the move to Miami Beach, New York, Chicago, Cleveland, Toledo, Los Angeles, and, later, Las Vegas. He traveled near and far and without ever putting in an eight-hour day. A phone call from Weinberg, and Leonard had a job with Kravitz.

Whenever we visited Weinberg's apartment we found it loaded with card players, the radio going full blast. Weinberg had a great talent for sleep. His bedroom door was open, and we saw Weinberg flat on his back, heaving snores, unaffected by the living-room noise.

"You got to blast him," Spiegelman said. "He's a corpse." Spiegelman marveled at this capacity for sleep. "I seen him go twenty hours in one shot and you still got to slam him with a cue stick to move his ass."

The card games were sociable during the week, but on Saturday blood flowed. Several games were simultaneously under way and continued until there was a concentration of capital among a few winners, who battled for enormous pots. Weinberg was a plunger: when luck was with him, he'd go all the way. He accumulated everything. When luck was against him, he was wiped out, and he didn't lose graciously. Some of his more vicious moments were at the tail end of Saturday-night poker games. But he usually won. He could operate all night loaded on Four Roses. He was generous in victory, and a night out was always on Happy.

When Happy slept he was close to death. It took him only a second to blank out. He didn't stir till the end of his sleep. No one was eager to wake up Happy. It was an unnerving experience to watch him wake up. There was no evidence of geniality. He seemed just arrived from wars and wanted to go back and finish the battle. When he couldn't resist the nagging prods of his buddies, he made lunging swipes that they easily avoided, since he wasn't all there. He flung whatever was in reach. His buddies recognized that this lurching behemoth wasn't as yet Happy Weinberg, and they got away with indignities they wouldn't otherwise have risked. A practical joker who warmed the bench at Connie's, a bald, stoop-shouldered realtor with enormous ears whom we called "Wingy," went to the bedroom and yelled, "Up and at 'em, Fatso; the wops is coming." Happy didn't budge. They told stories about fights with the Italians during prohibition. Now some of their best friends were Italian.

It was a modern apartment for that time, with refrigerator and range set in an alcove that could be closed off by sliding doors. There was wall-to-wall carpeting, casement windows with venetian blinds, a bed covered with a chenille spread. The décor previewed the motel style that was to become popular a decade later. Happy wanted a place that would be comfortable for his buddies. He kept his radio tuned to a twenty-four-hour music station so he could be sure he wouldn't return to a silent house. He kept the lights on day and night. When I passed his bedroom, the door wide open, I saw him laid out as for the grave, his shirt unbuttoned, his tie loose, tufts of reddish chest hair visible. He couldn't sleep in an empty apartment, so he had the boys over for poker.

There's no doubt that Ernie rejoined this crowd because of Sherry. He wrote a poem in celebration of her: "Ah! sweet, laughing, dancing, nymph of the woods . . ." I begged him not to make the poem public. "Don't read it to her. Just keep it between you and me. What do you mean, 'nymph'? What woods? How do you know she even dances?"

Ernie fell into the groove of suffering worshipper as though there had been no interlude. Sherry preened in the limelight of his eyes. She pulled her shoulders back, thrust out her chest, did considerable bending to give him a flash of the goodies dangling free in the peasant blouse that came down off the shoulders. She was drenched in an odor of jasmine that put the taste of her body in your mouth.

It was old stuff to Leonard, though.

One night Happy took us out on the town. A crowd went along, including Ernie and me, Leonard Mitchell, Spiegelman, and our realtor Wingy. Happy took us to the Olympic Arena to see a bout between Sugar Ray Robinson and Jake LaMotta. Weinberg and his friends were partisans of LaMotta. Having no more strategy than a fireplug, he didn't capture my fancy. He endured Robinson's cunning and allowed his scar-thickened face to be sliced up. He plowed ahead and worked on Robinson's belly and ribs with heavy fists. Robinson was a swift, handsome man, and I wanted his triumph. Hs grace made him seem human, while the other's immunity to pain put him beyond my sympathy. He couldn't be hurt. It seemed like a heroic business when Robinson entered the ring.

Weinberg came to his feet yelling when LaMotta staggered Robinson. "In the face. In the face. Spoil his pretty face." He explained, "The bastard is afraid to get his face marked. LaMotta should go for the face. In the face, Jake baby." Robinson had a trim mustache and fine features and a jaunty air I associated with Douglas Fairbanks, Jr. Weinberg ate steadily through the fight, a heavy intake of popcorn and peanuts and paper cups of beer. Spiegelman concentrated on the fight and didn't eat. He gripped the back rest in front of him. When Robinson was staggered, Spiegelman also came to his feet, punching with LaMotta, more ferocious than either man in the ring. He was out of control, and I saw his capacity for murder.

Robinson won the decision, and Happy took the defeat personally. "All LaMotta got is bone and muscle. You don't move in on Robinson like that. You come in with a weave and crouch. You aim for the gut and then in the face. In the face. Cut him a little and he starts running." Happy demonstrated against Spiegelman. His fists barely stopped short of the mark. The two faced each other, tensed for a scrap, then simultaneously delivered friendly thumps to the shoulder.

"What's your pa's whole name?" Happy asked, "'Jake' for what?"

"For Jacob," Ernie answered.

"He comes from Russia, yeah?"

"From the Ukraine."

"I hear he's a reader. I didn't finish sixth grade myself." He was a big man without benefit of schooling. He had all the money he needed, with prospects of more. A fine apartment, nicely stacked broads. When he heard anything of Culture he wanted to shoot, just like any other storm trooper. All the dealing in bullshit would have seemed laughable to him if it didn't result in reputations. Bullshit dealers ruled the world. Happy Weinberg had to risk life and limb, including his own, for rewards others received just for having a big mouth. What right did Jake Gottlieb have to be in the ring when he was equipped only with blab? Weinberg had more respect for LaMotta, who didn't have any pretensions. The other Jake—our pa—would soon learn that he couldn't operate in the major leagues with no more ammunition than big talk.

Occasionally Happy let you see the truculence that underlay his seeming good nature. He laughed it off. "Don't get me wrong, buddies. That pa of yours is something. He's no average punk out for a dollar. It's just a shame he don't know the score."

Happy was too charged up after the fight to let go of the evening. He was irritated that LaMotta had bungled the job. "You don't stick to the body when you're up against a cutie like Robinson. Go for the face. You can see by his mustache he got big plans for his face. What worries does LaMotta have with that mess he carries around? He can take a half dozen just to deliver one bomb. It won't do him any damage."

We'd seen the great care with which Happy readied his two hundred and fifty pounds for a night's excursion. He worked in front of a mirror, finishing off his tie with a double loop that filled the wide spread collar. The tie was a hand-blocked print, a Miami import. Weinberg criticized Leonard's extreme taste. He now considered creased lapels and pegged pants vulgar. Double breasted suits were for the ignorant. His own lapels were rolled. He went at his thinning red hair with comb and brush, one trailing the other in a crisp rhythm. In straightening his tie he shot his cuffs forward, revealing fourteen-carat gold cuff links. Hound's-tooth check suit, glistening light brown shoes—enormous canoes with sharp prows—a white-on-white shirt, he had a burnished look, an expensively tailored whale of a man, sleek despite his size. He wore rings on his fingers, and on his wrist a calendar wrist watch with a diamond at each compass point. And all this just for the fights.

Afterward he led us to Frank Ricci's club on the East Side. We were sponsored by Happy Weinberg, so there was no question of our age. Ricci himself shepherded us to a ringside table, his arm around Happy. We received great service. We listened to a Sophie Tucker-type lady. A comedian told dirty jokes. A crooner sang the ballads we had learned from Sherry.

Ricci's skin was fertile ground for beards. He shaved closely but you could see the hair ready to burst through. He had a pencil mustache that curved up under his nose like the mustaches of movie gigolos. He asked after the Cream of Michigan hoodlums, and Happy inquired about the Italians. Ricci asked if there was any song Happy wished to hear. "Main' Yidishe Momme." It was done. The comedian knew the song. He consulted the band leader. He readied himself before the mike, clasping his hands to indicate he was about to shift to the tragic muse. He launched into the song. I could see that, whatever joke Happy originally intended, he was moved. He stood up to applaud, and the rest of us arose to support his sentiment. Even Leonard was in sympathy with the tune. Though he used his yidishe momme as a scrub-woman, with the help of orange juice and gin he was softened by filial sentiment and grieved for some imaginary mother without callouses on her knees. Weinberg stripped bills from his wallet, folded them into a pellet, tucked the pellet into the comedian's palm.

The offensively solemn comic, no kid, bald and paunchy, offering jokes with a high-pressure delivery, clung to Happy's paw, pumped it, held on. "It gives me a thrill, Mr. Weinberg, when a man of your reputation appreciates my work. It means more to me than dollars." He didn't count the bills till he reached the stage door. Then I saw him look.

"You got to crowd Robinson. Lean on him. Then get him in the face." Happy made short, chopping motions. "Slice him up. Make him worry that the mustache isn't going to look so hot. Then you give it to him in the gut."

There were still motions he needed to perform. He faced Robinson in a dream arena and committed mayhem. Dreams weren't sufficient. He yearned to unleash the pulled punches.

"I don't like slick customers. I don't like wise guys. I like someone who comes out swinging." He returned to the subject of that other Jake, our pa. "What's he after? About money he is stupid. A guy his age operating for peanuts! Stupid! Is he after Hammer's job? I got it on reliable information your pa won't win any popularity contests. The difference between me and him is I put it on the line, no crap. Anybody who wants to know what Happy Weinberg wants, I'm glad to tell him. I level with him. Anything for a buck is my motto. I'm no Holy Moses. Anything! For a buck!"

Ernie assured Happy Weinberg that our pa was just the sort he had in mind. No bullshit. No guile. He feared no man and led with his chin.

"Your pa thinks because he's a reader he got an advantage. Do you know what that advantage amounts to? Shit, it amounts to!"

You would never find Jake at ringside. I remember, in earlier years when we tuned in on a Joe Louis fight, Jake retired behind the daily news while the issue of Joe's reputation was contested. Joe Louis was celebrated as a credit to his race. He took on Schmeling, the avatar of Hitler Youth. What a match! Finally we had trapped good and evil into a direct confrontation. We expected the Brown Bomber to do the work of our dreams. He came out flat-footed, his shuffling more ominous than Stepin Fetchit's. He was expressionless. Totally concentrated. No butcher. A delight to watch because of the artistry with which he killed. So, at least, we were informed by Philco. His opponents trembled to be in the same ring. And we trembled, too, staring at the mouth of our radio. We shivered with reverence for this dazzling hero. The daily news prepared us for the fight with reports from training camps, estimates by experts, a statement of vital statistics—comparison of biceps, wrists, fists, chests expanded and deflated, lengths of reach. Joe Louis had been often outreached and outweighed and outchested. He had confronted bigger fists. Yet till that Schmeling bout there had been only a single outcome, Louis triumphant. His reach had been equal to his grasp. The voices of fight commentators were shrill with near-hysteria. These sportscasters and sportswriters lived in the prospect of other men's wars. They came to a focus at championship fights, events that defined their lives. They exchanged mawkish sentiments during prefight introductions. It was the kind of sentimentality you expect from soldiers about to enter combat. They may hug each other and say loving things, though afterward they resume their spiteful ways. A kind word for everyone as a prelude to butchery. They called Schmeling a great guy, not to blame if certain people with strange mustaches made political hay of his fighting skill. Schmeling's American manager, Joe Jacobs, was of the Hebrew persuasion.

That first Schmeling fight was among the disasters of our lives. Schmeling hurt Louis in the early rounds and Joe struggled to stay on his feet. Then Schmeling knocked him out in the 12th round.

We slinked through the streets as though we had been personally whipped. Again it was demonstrated that the strength of our wishes had little effect on the course of events. A Hitler favorite had vanquished our man, and Hitler danced his jig. We took our defeat as evidence that we were exterminable.

In the rematch, Joe Louis finished Schmeling in the first two minutes of the fight. It was passionate murder. He penetrated Schmeling everywhere. In the newsreel of the fight Schmeling screamed from kidney punches.

Though we regained hope that justice could prevail Jake scorned our heroes. He saw no moral outcome to prize fights. History wasn't affected by sporting events. He thought we were idiots for becoming so absorbed by another man's career. If Ernie had a talent for idolatry, why didn't he revere his father? Why did Joe Louis receive the honor that ought to have been Jake Gottlieb's?

Happy Weinberg despised slick operators of the Sugar Ray kind. He had no affection for Joe Louis, who was a credit to his race. He admired self-seeking, cocky men who made no pretense of being involved in a chivalric calling. He liked a man who came out winners and didn't balk at means. O'Brien, for instance, was his sort.

"You pa better get out of that Irisher's way. O'Brien comes on like a steam engine."

It was late and we should have gone home after Ricci's, but it was a memorable night for us and we were easily persuaded to remain. Our next stop was the Torch Show Bar, a black-and-tan night club featuring a jazz combo and exotic dancers. There were no boundaries of age when we moved with Happy Weinberg.

It should have been clear to us that he wanted trouble. He was still affected by the fight. He was red-eyed and loaded by the time we reached the Torch Bar.

He found what he was after the minute he spotted the major-domo, a dapper Negro in a black suit with a Sugar Ray mustache, who offered to lead us to a table. Happy stared at the mustache, then elbowed by to find his own place. A black woman in gold lamé pants and tiny sequined cups for a bra performed an exotic dance to a bongo beat. The drummer wore a fez and a cotton shift and sat cross-legged to one side of the small stage. Happy stood in front of the lady and stared, blocking everyone's view. The major-domo and two husky bouncers gathered near the bar and studied us.

The dancer concluded her number by turning her back to Happy. She gave him a close view of her clenching, rolling buttocks. When he had had his fill, he joined us at a table.

I whispered for Ernie's benefit, "There's going to be trouble, so let's go."

Ernie refused.

The waiter wore a tight red jacket with gold buttons. His black pants had velvet stripes down the seams.

"Send me the boss," Happy said. "I give my orders to the boss. Send me the boss with the mustache." When the major-domo appeared, Happy started needling. "What does he remind you of, Spiegelman, with that mustache? What guy in the movies? The English guy?"

Whitey Spiegelman was poised for any action Weinberg might lead him into.

Happy asked Leonard, "Who am I thinking of with the mustache?"

"Who?" Leonard asked.

"The guy with the voice. The English guy. What the hell, we saw him a few weeks ago when we went with Clare. He had a twin, was a king."

"Ronald Colman," Ernie contributed brightly.

"That's the one. Ronald Colman. Did anyone ever mention that you look like Ronald Colman? With the mustache. Without the mustache I got no idea what you look like."

Our host excused himself to get the show under way. "Have fun, boys."

Happy observed one of the bouncers studying us from the back of the room, a stocky man with a heavy, round face and tight hair. Happy beckoned with his finger. The jazz quintet took its place on stage.

"You wouldn't be watching this table, would you, pal?"

"Enjoy the show, Mister."

"Because if you're getting any pleasure watching me, you better know that I charge."

"What charge?"

"A entertainment charge."

"We got some fine music, pal. Enjoy it."

"I had the pleasure of being entertained by Sugar Ray Robinson tonight. He is my idea of a entertainer. They should put him on stage where his mustache won't be damaged."

"A great fight. Yeah."

Happy said, "If LaMotta didn't fight dumb, Robinson wouldn't look so pretty. LaMotta is my idea of a fighter."

"Okay. LaMotta won the fight. Right. He sure did. I believe it. Why don't you settle down and enjoy the show?"

"I got no pleasure with your ugly puss staring at me."

I got up, and Ernie, to give him credit, followed my lead. Leonard asked where we were going; did we want to miss the fun?

I said, "It's no fun for us."

Ernie said to me afterward, "That's the worst side of him. There's something more that you won't let yourself see." This is what happened to Weinberg and Company: they left the bar and waited outside for one of the bouncers. They taunted him into swinging, and Weinberg caught him from behind, grabbed his head, hauled back, and Spiegelman drove his fist into the exposed throat. They left him writhing on the sidewalk.

"Fast," Leonard told us. "You never imagined Happy could move so fast." There had been no provocation, and even Leonard was startled by the gratuitous assault although it didn't much trouble him.

They were drunk, Leonard explained to us. There was no failure of co-ordination, but they were pissed. They'd been drinking steadily from early afternoon in preparation for the Robinson-LaMotta fight, and they'd taken several strong belts at Ricci's, a few more at the Torch Bar. Even after they returned to Happy's apartment he refused to let go of the night. Leonard cleared out when he saw that Happy was out of control.

We searched the newspaper for a report of the bouncer's fate, but there was no news.

Ernie conceded that men like Weinberg should be rubbed out; they were scarcely human.

"Squashed," I said. "Flushed down the toilet like cock-roaches."

Yet Ernie managed to come to terms with them. He argued, Why be a hypocrite? Wasn't it a thrill being around Happy? No place was out of bounds. A night with Happy was a venture into jungles where predators were sovereign. Happy went where he pleased and was at home everywhere. He had buddies in Hamtramck among the Poles, in Hungarian Village, among the Irish. He even walked Hastings Street, the Detroit Harlem. He was a Dexter boy who wasn't confined to his origins. No one could deny his generosity or his courage. You weren't bored around Happy. Was anyone more loyal to pals?

I asked Ernie, "But how about the man who got punched in the throat? Was he a bully, a Nazi, a crook, a murderer, a Ku Klux Klanner? No. A workingman. Happy wanted to hit someone because he was disappointed in the fight. Don't tell me what a fine man he is."

Ernie agreed that he wasn't a fine man. We lived in a brutal world. All we had to do was listen to the news. Instead of running from Happy, we'd better get used to him.

It was an effort to understand Happy Weinberg. There were moments when you imagined you grasped the architecture of his being, and you took pleasure in him as the child of your understanding. Your child and therefore no monster. An abandoned kid. A mere lad of thirty-eight when his mamma died.

Leonard Mitchell received lessons from Happy Weinberg and proceeded along the grain of his possibility to become a brute.

XXIV

A SNOWY NIGHT. Another Christmas approached. Street lamps snow-muffled, telephone lines fringed with ice, eaves and window sills bearded, domes on cars, a first snowfall, a thrilling time, the world radically transformed without benefit of arms. A bus came down Dexter, windows blanked out, wipers plowing the windshield, exhaust blackening snow, an armored, indomitable saurian beast, churning up weather. Under the disguise it was the same old Dexter bus that on summer days bobbed in traffic until I was seasick. Shapeless pedestrians, dressed to fend off weather, shuffled on icy walks, mistrustful of the ground they walked on. It was the first snow, and the weather hadn't yet become a grievance; the snow hadn't been reduced to slush, ice hadn't narrowed streets, forcing new channels in old thoroughfares. I stayed home; Ernie went out. He should have stayed home, too. He had a bad night.

Leonard was in a bullying mood. Abusive jokes, shadow-boxing that verged on assault. He clipped Ernie in jest, a stunning blow that Ernie discounted as horseplay. Sherry was the prime target. She was snuffling and weepy. Ernie supposed it was the aftermath of a blowup. Leonard called her flabby-assed and stupid.

For her sake, Ernie went along when Leonard suggested a walk. It was two in the morning. The storm was at its peak. They drove to the Dexter neighborhood and parked. They began a silent walk, Leonard in the lead, along Wildemere, up Monterey, along Dexter, down Boston, to Wildemere again. They made the long circuit twice, Ernie struggling to keep up, hoping that Leonard would dump his rage in the process of freezing. A miserable walk, his feet wet. He continued without complaint, a loyal friend, a good soldier who didn't ask, "Is this trip necessary?"

Leonard wore a light jacket, gloves, no muffler, his throat exposed, his face ruddy, those blue eyes fixed on a distant target. A dedicated youth about to cross a threshold. Ernie—not directed toward any thresholds—could barely keep up as Leonard plowed through snow.

The third time around, Leonard picked up a board from an alley. When they came to Orlitz' jewelry store he didn't hesitate. He stepped up, poked out the window, stuffed his pockets and began running. What could Ernie do, stand there gaping? He was chased by the alarm. He yanked at his muffler to get air, unbuttoned his overcoat to free his legs. The car was moving when he floundered up to it. Leonard thrust the door open, a leap carried Ernie in; they were off with headlights darkened. Save for the initial whine of tires spinning in snow, their flight was muffled, the alarm also muffled, a Merry Christmasy sound, their wake blotted out by heavy snow. Leonard zigzagged down side streets and alleys, pulled to the curb when they heard sirens. They ducked down. Back in Leonard's apartment they spread the loot on the kitchen table: watches, rings, bracelets, a necklace. Ernie refused any part of it.

His indignation was futile.

When he complained, Leonard said, "Your friend Sherry got herself knocked up. The doc wants two hundreds bucks. Do you have any bright ideas?"

As though Ernie, because he had once licked an ear and probed near her tonsils, was under an obligation.

Leonard handled his problem head on. He went to Weinberg for an abortionist and to Orlitz' jewelry shop for money. He refused to go any farther. The rest he left to Sherry. He was finished with her. What a filthy trick! He told her to visit the doctor and get her belly scraped. If she came whining to him, he'd belt her. What did she mean by getting knocked up? He was only seventeen. He wasn't going to be reduced to the size of Lieberman, the cabinetmaker. What did she mean, trying to have a kid?

Leonard dumped his guilt on the innocent and disclaimed ownership. He remained blameless and righteous. This coolness in real peril counted toward the development of character.

Ernie did his best to comfort Sherry. He told her there was no reason to be afraid. Lopez was celebrated from Dexter to Twelfth Street. If he wasn't an M.D., he was something better, a specialist in abortion, with two decades of experience. Who could expect loyalty or tenderness from Leonard, who, to be fair, had never made any promises? He had no talent for such sentiments.

Ernie offered consoling hugs. She rubbed her wet face against his throat. He gave a hard squeeze and she pressed in response. Unlike Leonard, he was flooded with sentiment. He dived into her mouth, his tongue flailing. She spat him out. She wailed, pounded his chest. What was he doing? At a time like this! The fix she was in!

"Because I love you," my brother said.

She called him a jerk and a bastard, offering obscene attention to a girl whose bosom was enlarged and belly expanded in service to love.

Ernie told Leonard, "She's scared. She needs help. Someone should be with her."

"You go. You're the one with the hots."

Ernie pitied the little girl who would be alone in Lopez' office. He said to Leonard, "For more than a year she's been your girl."

"I'll get another."

Perhaps Leonard quaked in his shoes, and his coolness was merely an act to impress Happy Weinberg and Ernie Gottlieb. Perhaps it took effort to stifle his sympathy. But he got away with it. He got away with the robbery of the jewelry store. What may have been foreign to his character became natural. He spent the night of the abortion at Happy Weinberg's, playing cards with the men. He held winning hands. When Sherry called to let him know she had delivered an embryonic Mitchell and only wished he'd suffered what she had at the hands of Lopez, he told her in a loud voice, so that an apartmentful of card players might hear, that if she wanted to know real trouble she should try to see him again. He'd teach her with both fists.

"You're an idiot," I told Ernie. "Don't you even know when it's not your problem?"

But what if Lopez botched the job? Who would get her to a hospital? Lopez didn't belong to the AMA. For three days a snow-storm had blotted out Detroit. Richton was impassable. There were hills where once there had been cars. Where would she go if she were turned out by Lopez, bleeding and terrified?

The prospect of her loneliness was unbearable. He wanted to wait outside Lopez' office. What could he lose besides his nose, his toes, his fingers? A terrible night, not only snow, but wind. He regarded himself as contemptible for considering his own discomfort. For more than a year he had claimed to love Sherry.

I asked him, "If Leonard has the good sense to get out, why should you jump in?"

He begged me to consider what she was enduring at that very moment. A sixteen-year-old kid, steel in her belly and no ma or pa standing by. How would she get home on a night like this in her condition?

So we went to Twelfth Street and waited in the doorway of The Cream of Michigan and watched Lopez' office. The shades were drawn. We saw nothing. Snow piled up so thickly the salted streets couldn't dispense the load. Buses came sliding into stops, the only things moving that night. We stood in a puddle on the threshold of The Cream of Michigan while snowbanks accumulated around us. Lopez' windows were blanked out.

I find the sweetness of Ernie in the picture of him waiting. Was it merely obligation? I don't believe that. He pitied Sherry. Whatever the case, like all waiting, it was a mistake. Our feet were numb. We had to piss. While Leonard Mitchell played cards at Weinberg's apartment, warmed by whiskey and steam radiators, we suffered. Twelfth Street was abandoned to all traffic other than buses. Buses passed silently, only the spray of wheels and the clacking of wipers audible. They rolled by without stopping. There were no cabs. No private cars. No pedestrians. Telephone wires hummed under a weight of ice. A bitter wind cut through the corner entryway of The Cream of Michigan. We tried Lopez' door and it was locked.

"If she comes out of this," Ernie said, "I don't ask anything more." Some sentiment for a sixteen-year-old kid! He wanted to be able to get home, to his room, under his blankets, and be dreamy again. There was also the jewelry store to worry about.

Should he turn himself in?

No. Turn Leonard in.

Never. That was treason. Besides the police would ask why he waited so long.

Maybe this time you'll learn to stay away from Mitchell and his friends.

As though he could.

We waited till midnight and finally called Happy Weinberg's

place. We learned Sherry had returned home hours before with a bellyache. Leonard was in the middle of a card game and jeered at Ernie's concern. "If it was you," he said, "there'd already be a houseful of bastards."

Ernie didn't mind the insults, just so she was safe.

For weeks Ernie expected the police to come for him. He holed up in his room. He made no effort to contact Leonard or Sherry. He asked me to deny his whereabouts to any callers. He believed he was being watched. He once arrived home in a panic, convinced a burly man had tailed him. He described some heavy-set guy who had followed him from Linwood all the way up Elmhurst. Ernie cut through a lot on Holmur, and sneaked through an alley and back yards. When he reached home, he shut himself in his room. He asked me to go out and check. I didn't see anyone around.

"Who could know," I asked, "unless Leonard squealed?"

"Suppose there was a witness."

"Who could see in a snowstorm at two in the morning?"

His ease came gradually, and he didn't profit from the experience. He couldn't forsake hoodlums despite his promises. Ernie knew the names of the rebel generals of Spain. He had followed the blight of fascism up the Iberian peninsula into Bilbao, Toledo, Barcelona, Madrid. He knew of the castor-oil treatment. He had seen pictures of pious Jews swabbing German streets on hands and knees while brown shirts in jackboots straddled them. How could one shrink from power? Ernie wanted to learn the magic that enabled men to be brutes. He believed, as I did, that one day our turn would come.

XXV

———◄◆►———

McINTYRE MOVED to Six Mile Road in the vicinity of the university, a few blocks from his buddy Emerson. He had a yellow brick house with a large back yard shaded by elm trees. He showed himself to be what I had first imagined, a ponderous, magisterial American. There was no indecision in the drawing of his map. Every feature was sizable and well marked. There was no evidence of treachery, infidelity, cowardice. None of his mean actions marked him. He stood on his front porch and surveyed his snow-covered property with the assurance of a plantation owner. He was O'Brien's Detroit emissary, the manager of Soil Free.

Jake told them to stay out of Detroit, but the money was in Detroit. So long as O'Brien stayed in Oswego he either had to settle for small potatoes or compete for Detroit business at a considerable handicap. O'Brien operated in the American way, in the market place, counting among his resources enthusiasm, intelligence, industriousness, and hoodlum connections. The rumor was that both the Cream of Michigan outfit and the Italians had a stake in O'Brien's highly regarded future.

Jake didn't encourage any bets on O'Brien's future. He refused to offer Soil Free the contract he negotiated with the rest of the industry. After a show of belligerence, the opposition to Jake folded. Kravitz led the parade of bosses in signing contracts. They accepted Jake as an inevitable part of operating expense. They weren't, after all, political zealots, prepared to sink rather than be humbled. They were businessmen, who decided that they could live profitably despite Jake. In fact, Jake normalized the industry, reduced unfair competition in order to protect the drivers' routes. It wasn't only the Atlas drivers now who stood in the ranks of his partisans. He had several hundred men backing him. He was no longer the Siberian exile, dreaming of a new day, when he would rule. The new day was here, and my pa, Jake Gottlieb, was, in a small part of the world, like a Czar, but a good Czar. Wasn't he a wise man? Wasn't he a good man? Wasn't he a fatherly man and a noble warrior? He was in his small domain a philosopher-king.

However, he had his faults. He never forgot an obligation. He never renounced an oath. He had a duty to Sammy Persky. Jake offered Soil Free a special contract, guaranteed to put them at a competitive disadvantage that would have made operations almost impossible.

The Soil Free lawyers said, "Discriminatory!" Jake said, "Between you and me, you bet, discriminatory. I don't allow O'Brien to operate in Detroit."

Did Jake imagine the industry was in his pocket, to be disposed of according to his whim? This was America, and the free-enterprise system. There were anti-trust laws. There were men who could split his head open and were eager to do the job.

McIntyre urged that he let bygones be bygones. Personalities had no place in business. The market place was the sole arbiter of profit and loss, of success and failure. What right had Jake to intrude himself?

McIntyre was a solid burgher, all anxiety dissipated. He imagined that the past he shared with Jake was a common ground for intimacy. He accepted rebuffs with determined amiability.

He didn't believe you could hold a man responsible forever. He had come to terms with his mistakes. His daughter was in an institution. His wife had made a surprising recovery. She had put on weight, and submitted to pleasures. Kate Russo, O'Brien's fiancée, was off limits, and McIntyre had no inclination to trifle. In fact, he had already begun the job of tidying up history so that it would seem umblemished from a distant view. He didn't want Jake or anyone else reminding him of details.

He told Jake that he had considerably exaggerated the affair with Kate. "Maybe I wanted to impress you with what a big shot I was and stretched things a little. I admit I liked her. Do you blame me? She's a splendid lady. A great gal. A good friend. For a couple weeks I felt pretty strong about her. But I wasn't myself those days as you know, Jake. We had us some war, eh? The hoods sure worked me over, didn't they? I was all out for the union. Maybe I represent the other side now, but I never forget my old loyalties. Once a union man, always a union man." He considered what happened to Sammy Persky to have been a terrible accident. Terrible. If only Sammy hadn't panicked.

Jake couldn't be softened. "Do you imagine I'll just listen while you use the name of Sammy Persky and don't bleed? I swore an oath that O'Brien and McIntyre would not live in my shadow. Where my shadow falls there is no place for you. You got no chance in the industry. You better get used to the idea."

The industry yielded to Jake. Despite the threats of Kravitz and Charley Hammer, Jake had his way. The contract was negotiated on his terms. Hammer's threat to put the union into receivership didn't have a chance. Jake was his own man in Detroit.

"There's a lot of people," McIntyre said, "who are in deep in Soil Free. They mean to do business in Detroit. They got the money, they got the plant, and they got the drivers."

Jake said, "Then all they need is a contract and they're in business."

"We want fair treatment, Jake—the same contract as the rest. You know yourself how cutthroat the industry is. We can't give away an advantage like that. We want no trouble with the union. We offer the union every break, but you got to deal square. You can't let personalities enter in."

"Personalities are in. Make up your mind and save yourself from heartache. As far as Jake Gottlieb is concerned, there is no future for yourself or your friend O'Brien."

McIntyre had moved from a working-class neighborhood near Dearborn to Six Mile Road, where he lived among small businessmen and professionals. How sane the world now appeared to him! He remembered bad times as nothing more than the distorted perception of an overwrought father and husband. His new view consisted of snow-covered lawns, a brick house with a linoleum-tiled rec hall downstairs and a finished attic upstairs.

I couldn't imagine O'Brien ever becoming so content. O'Brien hadn't begun to fathom his limitations. When we'd first seen O'Brien, he was a chunky man whose size wasn't apparent until you were beside him and could make comparisons. A reddish man with an open stance. He faced you directly, met your eyes. There was nothing crouched or defensive about him. He gave me the impression of being ready to move quickly, a James Cagney type but with twice the heft. I wouldn't describe him as volatile; rather, as calculating. He sniffed out his chances wherever they might turn up. He pretended to be easygoing, but that was only a political manner. He was no drunk. He made no public display of his relations with the girls. I never understood why he'd served in the navy, especially back in the thirties when a sailor hadn't much of a reputation. He didn't need to join the navy to see the world. He had enough imagination to arrange his own itinerary. Given the virulence of his ambition, I suspect he might have been escaping something more serious.

Kate Russo was the woman for him. She was docile under his hand. If she wanted a man who could raise her from drabness, she had hitched on to the right one. O'Brien wouldn't settle for Six Mile Road. He already had dreams that carried him beyond Soil Free. But Jake wouldn't even let him have Soil Free.

What was Jake after? Why did he push? Enough of Sammy Persky. Sammy Persky's dead. His widow moved to Chicago to be with relatives. There's nothing left of Sammy Persky. O'Brien bears no grudges. He admires Jake. Is he cruel? Is he violent? Don't restrain him, then. Let him rise. He'll become genial when he's pacified by achievement.

I remember Berle Dresden arguing with Jake. "Why is it, Gottlieb, that all the Jews of Dexter Avenue can live in peace while around you there are stormy times?"

Jake wanted to know how Dexter could be peaceful when on the other edge of the ocean the rough beast was poised for more butchery, his slaver already bloody with Jews.

"I don't ask for peace," Jake said. "Within reach there are stormy times, so I hunt them out."

Berle never trusted Jake's claims until they were confirmed by an independent witness. He didn't believe Jake had been arrested five times in one day until he saw the clipping. He didn't believe there was violence until the death of Sammy Persky. When Jake drew the blinds and warned of snipers, Berle was outraged by the performance. "You think maybe you're Trader Horn?"—a reference to a movie about Africa that many years before had caught Berle's fancy. Berle avoided the movies as a bourgeois medium that warped a nation's perception. But, whenever he looked or listened, he was un-critically responsive. He praised each movie he saw as superlative of its kind, an exception to the bourgeois rule. He also spared baseball from the Marxist critique that condemned so many of our pleasures as illicit.

He asked Jake, "What will you change by breaking heads? To tell the truth, Gottlieb, maybe I'm not such a hero, but I have very little respect for a hard fist. What, after all, is accomplished? Whoever applies his energy to an object so insignificant as my gray head will change very little in his lifetime. He wastes his energy. We don't need big shoulders or a bad temper to make a revolution in the way we live. Keep calm. History is on our side. Anyone—even Joe Louis— if he turns his back, can receive a clop on the head. Someone can always be hired for the job. We need to reach men's hearts, not their skulls." He wondered if Jake didn't really exaggerate O'Brien's stature as a despot. Who was O'Brien, after all? He owned a linen supply. "Forgive me, Gottlieb. I'm an iconoclast from long standing. But, for a linen supply, 'tyrant' is too big a word."

Jake called Berle a theoretician, out of touch with the world of affairs.

"What's so bad about a theoretician? I'm flattered you use nice language for a change."

"A theoretician," said Jake, winding up for the insult, "is like the constipated man who offers himself as an expert when the argument is, which is the softest toilet paper."

"I don't get the insult, Gottlieb."

"He never wipes his ass, how would he know?"

"Okay, our discussion is ended. When insults begin, I no longer debate."

"A theoretician knows all the reasons why we shouldn't fight Hitler. The theoretician proves we are involved in a bourgeois war. Once the panzers cross the Soviet border, it's a different matter. Suddenly the theoretician has new arguments to prove that all along we are involved in a proletarian struggle and the whole world should jump in. The theoretician doesn't rec-

ognize tyrants. He sees no tyrants. The tryant is on his own
back, so how can he see? He carries Uncle Joe on his back."
"No discussion. Period. That's the finish."

"Do you think panzers change minds by appealing to the
heart? Do you think nothing is changed by the fist of the
storm trooper? It makes a big change. A revolutionary change.
Somebody's old grandpa is hammered down. He's rubbed out
and burned like trash. The old man disappears. No sign of
him left. That's a big change in the world, Dresden. Big
fists, strong backs, clubs, boots; instruments of revolution.

In his last conversation with Berle Jake said, "Forgive me
if I'm tough on you. You have a good heart; that's the important
thing. It's myself I have a grievance against. I don't have any
friends to spare. When I lost Sammy Persky, I lost the best."

He had no one else around to ridicule the news of the
world. Jake was no good at grieving, and I sometimes forgot
how much he missed Sammy.

Berle agreed that a man's first obligation was to his friends,
not his ideology. "There are real bandits waiting to attack us.
Why should we abuse each other?"

As far as Jake was concerned, O'Brien was the chief bandit
and would have to be confronted. He represented some tough
customers who were heavily invested in Soil Free and who
didn't intend to take a loss.

McIntyre pleaded with Jake. "You think I wanted it this
way? But what can I do? You force me to operate a non-
union shop. Your contract is out of the question. For the sake
of our old friendship, Jake, take my advice: play fair with
us. Don't go out of your way to block our operations. I wish
you were friendly, but I'll settle for neutrality. We just ask
to be let alone. You remember what O'Brien is like. You and
I have reason to know. I got no control over him."

Jake told McIntyre to remember what Jake Gottlieb was
like. "If you think I'll let you enter the industry without a
contract, you don't know your Gottlieb. You're bringing me

scabs from Oswego and you're bringing me scabs from Cleveland. You're bringing me an element I won't allow in Detroit."

"You had experience of O'Brien. I warn you, Jake."

Jake went to Charley Hammer. "Soil Free is operating with no contract. So I say, all deliveries will stop. All coal, oil, all over-the-road haulers delivering to Soil Free, everything stops. The operating engineers stop. The electricians stop. The inside stops."

Charley Hammer said, "Offer them your standard contract, Jake. If they turn it down, you're authorized to strike."

"I got no standard contract. I got a Soil Free contract."

"Soil Free can't meet competition with your contract."

"Since when do you represent Soil Free?"

Nothing stopped at Soil Free. Not the electricians, not the engineers, not the deliveries, not the inside help.

Jake spoke to the drivers in the Soil Free shed. "What kind of men are you that you would screw your brothers who suffered to build a union? Right now O'Brien offers you conditions you can live with, but what will happen if O'Brien breaks the power of the union? I won't tell you, don't be selfish; you're too cynical for such advice. But I'll advise you for your own sakes, don't be foolish; if you abandon your brothers now, there will come a time when they will abandon you."

These men didn't recognize brothers. O'Brien offered good pay. They may have been shamed by Jake, but nonetheless they crossed the picket line. Jake knew, however, that one day they wouldn't cross the picket line. There was no one more tenacious than Jake. He would have hung on till they surrendered to him. He would have brought them into the union. He would have shut O'Brien down.

He went to Kravitz. "Why do you let O'Brien do business? He raids the industry. He takes your stops. He brings in a bad element. Why do you allow him? I offer you the co-operation of the union to keep O'Brien from doing business in Detroit."

Kravitz wasn't interested. "I got twenty more years of good living, Gottlieb, that I don't intend to risk because you have a grudge. Do you have any idea who backs Soil Free? I'll mention no names but I'll offer some good advice. Don't make conspiracies. What's the use anyway? It's all arranged."

The only arrangement Jake would tolerate would be one that eliminated Soil Free.

"I swore an oath to remember Sammy Persky," he told Evka. "I'll never make arrangements with O'Brien. If he stays in Detroit, I'll see that he's buried. I won't let him breathe here."

He increased the pressure on Soil Free. He was prepared to prolong the war indefinitely. He could wait. He knew he'd win.

Ernie asked Evka how she could justify him. Why did he press for conditions that no one else desired? Why did he insist on wars no one else wanted to fight?

"Do you think he could accomplish what he did if he wasn't such a stubborn man? It's his character," she said. "By now you should have learned to accept it."

Whatever McIntyre had done, didn't Jake have some sympathy for him? He had been a friend. He had once put everything on the line for Jake.

"Your pa would love to embrace McIntyre and call him friend. He still loves his old comrade. He has no other close friends. He admits that he misses them. He misses McIntyre and especially Emerson. He tells me this—at night—when he can't sleep. He tells me, They were like brothers. We shared the same battles. I would have died for them like I am ready to die for Sammy Persky.' But he'll never forgive them. Never. He swore an oath to honor the memory of Persky. Whatever it costs him, he'll keep his word. Don't you know by now that he's such a man?"

XXVI

———◆◈◆———

WHAT HAPPENED to us is that one night Jake Gottlieb didn't
come home. That's the big event in our lives.

Evka woke us up. "Kids, it's three o'clock. Pa isn't home."

She had a talent for worry. Why did she oppress us? Hadn't
we served our time waiting for Jake? Why didn't she refuse
to worry for a change? He was probably out with the boys.
He fancied himself an expert poker player after his modest
success in Northern Michigan. Evka said, No, he wasn't with
the boys. He had a meeting of shop stewards and then an ap-
pointment with Kravitz to talk about Soil Free once again.

"Maybe we should phone Kravitz."

The catastrophe of our lives! And yet I'm hard pressed
to recover details. I can hear speeches uttered thirty years
ago. I can recover the smell of a house, the face of a radio.
That night I wanted to go back to sleep after Ma woke us
and announced the end of our world. The news which should
have been unacceptable, which we should have thrown back

in the teeth of the lousy gods who broadcast it, annoyed us because our sleep was interrupted. We stayed awake out of obligation. When I try to recall the events of that time, I confront dead spots. The details have vanished; I guess them only through inference.

We called Berle Dresden at four in the morning, and he thought we should give Jake more time. "I'm sure it's all right. When his enthusiasm gets the best of him, he forgets the time." Berle offered to join us in waiting. But it was a family matter, and Jake would have started a revolution if he'd found Berle when he returned. His absence was irritating. Hadn't we suffered enough? He compelled us to live in the shadow of his adventures.

We concentrated on the sound of traffic, listening to the familiar Dexter noises. This time it wasn't Fiori's van we wanted to hear but the sound of a Buick Roadmaster.

At five-thirty in the morning Evka phoned Kravitz. She apologized for getting him out of the bed.

"The police should be informed," Kravitz said. "Hang up and I'll call for you."

It was Kravitz who summoned the police.

When they arrived at midmorning we had taken the irrevocable step of acknowledging that Jake was missing. Why were we so reluctant to have the police? Perhaps we didn't want to invite a terrible fate by admitting the dreadful possibilities. And we didn't want cops in our living room. They arrived to probe our closets and bedrooms, poke around the basement, behemoths, the shape and size of McIntyre. The distance between chin and crown seemed to measure yards. Not rude, not unsympathetic, and yet their presence made us feel criminal: what kind of queer birds were we to have lost our pa?

They asked for vital statistics. I could have better informed them on Joe Louis or Hank Greenberg. I summarized my pa for the first time—short, husky, bald. The front teeth crowned, casualties of a battle that had brought him home bloody, but home. A scar above the eyebrow. He wore spectacles for reading. Who knew what was relevant? They asked strange questions. Did they want to unravel the mystery of these queer Gottliebs or were they after my pa? They didn't seem to have any idea of how to pursue Jake Gottlieb. They were sidetracked by his Russian birth. They pressed the matter of his Siberian exile as if he might be the victim of a Commie conspiracy. I felt that they wanted to know, "What kind of people are you to let such things happen?"

I told them, "There's a man named O'Brien. Get in touch with him and don't waste time."

They asked blunt questions about Jake. Was he suicidal? Was he under a doctor's care? Recently hospitalized? Any trouble at home? Any debts? Did he gamble? How about trouble at work?

I said, "Find this man O'Brien."

Berle Dresden came to the first interview with the police. The questions asked were devious, our answers incoherent; Berle offered clarifying details that annoyed everyone. He said, "Pardon me, officers. Nobody mentioned that on his back he has a birthmark, unmistakable, the size of a saucer." The detectives didn't care for the poetic manner. "You should know, officers, that lately he enjoys playing cards and he becomes wrapped up in what he's doing." We didn't want these detectives alienated, so Ernie took Berle into the kitchen and told him to shut up.

I hadn't slept the night before, yet I felt wide awake, and, though intermittently pounded by a drum roll of anxiety, I felt at peace. I went out on the porch. We were in April. The old Emerson house was in less tidy shape under the management of new tenants. The evergreen shrubs were rusty, lawn borders ragged, shutters in need of painting. It was a splendid day following a long period of rain. The weather had suddenly cleared and it was unusually hot. I saw pale green lawns on Richton. New blades poked through raked ground. Opening day at Briggs Stadium was only a week off.

Time to unroll awnings, put up the porch canopy, restore the glider pads. Jake had planned to resod our lawn. A few days after he vanished, a truck arrived carrying rolls of turf. We sent it away.

Detroit can steam up before its proper time. One of the detectives removed his jacket, and I was disturbed by his cheap taste in shirts, one of the crinkly, short-sleeved variety, with a heavier fabric running in strands through a transparent material. A reddish man, with blotches on his throat from close shaving. At any other time I'd have ridiculed him. His name was Cassady, and he became a comfort to us all.

Cassady said, "Don't let your imagination get out of control. We had plenty experience with missing persons. It usually turns out there's a secret life the family never guessed. I'm not saying that's the case with Mr. Gottlieb."

"With him it's not the case," Evka said. "We got no secrets."

"It's hard to believe," said Cassady, "but I seen it too often. We got no idea, Mrs. Gottlieb, what goes on in the minds of our own family."

"Nothing goes on in my husband's head which would surprise me." She was worried that they would lose valuable time following the wrong track. The man they were after wasn't an embittered spouse who dreamed of abandoning his family. Cassady had no idea of our pa.

I said to Evka, "Maybe he did have trouble that he didn't want us to worry about."

"You mean he doesn't want us to worry, so he doesn't come home all night?"

For months I clung to the belief in a mysterious Jake. I sometimes was thrilled by the possibility that instead of the transparent father whose motives we easily penetrated there was a different Jake, capable of going underground, emerging in a different guise.

There were these drum rolls. A drummer pounded my heart. But that was only an occasional discomfort. We were calm that first day. The world was brought down around our feet, yet we continued to operate as if it were the old familiar place, on substantial foundations. We went through that first day concerned about detectives, neighbors, friends, schoolmates, unable to realize that Jake was gone.

We stayed home from school and there was a feeling of holiday. Visitors came to support our vigil. Evka brewed coffee. In the afternoon, sandwiches were served by the ladies. When the doorbell rang, everyone braced for Jake. I remember feeling how embarrassed he'd be if he were greeted by a crowd in our living room.

That night there was a flash storm. Lightning hit close around us. Thunder boomed in our ears. The air was black. I felt tornadoes piling up. I wanted to get out immediately and hunt the whole world for Jake and offer him shelter.

It was our second night without sleep.

For months afterward whenever the weather was bad, I imagined his suffering. He'd worn a new suit when we last saw him. He became a dandy in that year of his affluence. Loud ties, double-breasted suits with powerful stripes and broad lapels, snap-brimmed fedoras, monogrammed hankies in the breast pocket, a heavy gold union ring with the insigne marked by diamonds. He'd never broken his habit of early rising. Even after he became a power in the union and no longer needed to hustle, he still got up at six to prepare himself for the new day. He took a cold shower every morning. We heard him gasp and snort and spout and thump himself. His beard was heavy. He shaved with long strokes. I heard his beard crackle as the razor passed through. The bathroom was a steamy, fragrant place when Jake was finished. When he raised his arms, one hand stretching the skin, the other drawing the razor, muscles plowed across his shoulders. Below the left shoulder, I saw his birthmark like a spreading ink blot. His back view was more impressive than the front. There was a swell of belly beneath a heavy, sagging chest. He bore his weight in front. His back was hard and youthful. He wore heavily starched shirts with French cuffs. He came to breakfast fit for a wedding, his eyes sharp, already boisterous, eager for the day.

What could the police do? We craved reassurance. But how could they help us? Jake Gottlieb was no father of theirs. It was not possible to assume our duties or share our grief. Jake was one of thousands who were missing. They had to close their hearts or they'd never sleep. And yet Cassady stretched his imagination to find hope despite the lengthening absence. He knew of men—seemingly good husbands, loving fathers—who suddenly plunged underground and didn't emerge for years.

A new Jake came into existence, one who could vanish. The posture that Ernie had dismissed as histrionic was after all justified. Jake was out in the world somewhere living a secret life. Perhaps he had another wife, other sons, a different job, lived in a strange neighborhood. I had a fantasy that Jake had abandoned us for another family. He lived somewhere in this world, unrecognizable because he had a new shape, a new accent, even a new religion. He abandoned us; I grieved. The fantasy dulled me to more terrible possibilities. I'd be with Ernie and Evka when suddenly these terrible thoughts occurred to us at the same moment. On a sunny day when life quickened for us we had a vision of his awful ripening. On winter days we felt the chill on his flesh.

Cassady said that there was nothing to do but wait. Did Cassady see that we wanted relief from our obligations? I paid no attention to the advice of cops. I hunted for Jake. I went alone, so that no one would call me a lunatic and try to divert me.

I sometimes walked with my eyes shut so that nothing would interfere with an inspiration that might direct me to Jake. I covered every part of the Dexter neighborhood. I ventured beyond to Highland Park. I took a bus to the East Side, walked down Gratiot to the Italian neighborhood. I went to Hamtramck. I had no instinct for these places. I became aware of the size of the world hunting my father in Hamtramck and along the East Side. I walked along the river. I spent days on the beaches of Lake St. Clair. I even rowed into the lake. I had a feeling that he was in water.

For weeks I looked, forcing myself to measure the size of our catastrophe.

They found the car two weeks after his disappearance, located two hundred miles from Detroit on the shores of Walloon Lake. They dragged the lake. I shivered with relief when they gave up looking. I continued to hunt in Detroit.

The Buick had been his delight. The chrome was heavy, the body streamlined, the upholstery red. He argued in favor of that car as if it were a member of the family, defending its virtues against the claims of Cadillac fanciers. A less expensive car than the Cadillac, not so snooty, but swift. Jake had driven a truck for twenty years with no more sense of what was inside than if he had been an African native with animistic faith. But he knew a statistic or two. Dual carburetors, a hundred miles an hour in a matter of seconds, the most potent engine on the road. Built solid. He smacked his car on the fender as though it were the shoulder of a buddy. He took the car to the corner service station for a wash every Sunday. He had been an impetuous driver, and his car had taken a beating. That Buick needed considerable repair in the half year he owned it.

The car was parked in springy turf, its wheels half buried in spongy ground. No one had seen it arrive. It was assumed that it was owned by someone in the neighborhood. Walloon Lake was then not much changed from the days of Hemingway. It was the country of the Potawatomis. A long lake, with fingers stretching toward nearby Lake Charlevoix and Lake Michigan. Traverse City is an hour away to the south, Petosky half an hour away to the north. Standing on the Lake Michigan beach at Charlevoix, the far shore invisible, you feel as if you're at the edge of an ocean.

There were no fingerprints in the car. There was no evidence of a struggle either inside the car or out. We listened to

Detective Cassady as if he were a surgeon bringing us estimates of a cancer condition. He said anything might be the case, but the longer Jake was gone the worse it looked. His frankness was intended to keep us from going off our rockers with vain dreams. On the other hand, he thought it promising that there was no sign of a struggle. Again he insinuated the possibility of a secret life.

Evka didn't leave the house for weeks, because we figured Jake might recover his wits and phone.

The police wanted to know what to do about the car. Evka said, "Give it away. I don't want to see it."

Jake would have been furious at her doing anything that stupid. It was still in mint condition, its dents all straightened. We stored the car for Jake.

XXVII

———◆◆◆———

IN THE SPRING of forty-one the Nazis plunged into Soviet
Russia and met less resistance than a diver entering the family
pool. They raced for Leningrad and Moscow. Through White
Russia, Minsk, Pinsk, the Pripet Marshes, they headed for
Kiev, where the Gottlieb line originated. The Russian soldier
was as helpless as the Pole in the face of the German blitz.

The great events of the world were occurring, and I couldn't
care less. Six weeks to put an end to Russia—that was the general expectation. The Germans could be arrested only by their
own traffic cops. The experts hoped that the fall rains would
turn the steppes into a quagmire and stop the German panzers.
General Mud might achieve what Generalissimo Stalin couldn't.
And after General Mud would come General Winter. Look
what happened to Napoleon. In the meantime, Russian fathers were done in wholesale, by the tens of thousands. What
did one Jake Gottlieb matter?

We shut off the news. I was inclined toward the comics—

Jack Benny, Fred Allen, Bob Hope—but I refused to laugh, out of respect for Jake Gottlieb. Our house was silent. Even when visitors were present there was a hush. Everyone was intimidated in this house, where Jake Gottlieb had been lord. His effects were still hanging in the closet. When I opened the hall closet I saw his winter coat. His suits were in the bedroom closet. His shaving equipment was in the medicine cabinet. The position he'd occupied at the dinner table remained empty. His reading spectacles were on Evka's dressing table. His lotions and powder were unused. No more snorting and thumping in the morning. When we didn't hear those sounds, we remembered he was gone.

We stayed home from school. Ernie didn't care to return. How could we move while waiting for Jake? A discarded leather jacket hung from a nail in the basement. He'd worn the jacket over his Atlas uniform, his visored cap shoved to the back of his head. He rolled like a sailor because of his muscle-bound gait. The jacket was stiff and cracked, the lining ripped, the elastic cuffs frayed. I suppose it stayed on its nail till our Richton house was torn down two decades later.

I hunted for Jake throughout Detroit and environs, but I never had any inclination to explore Walloon Lake. I blocked out that part of Michigan. I ignored it. I wanted Jake near home, quick or dead.

There had been no evidence of a struggle near the Buick. No one could have overcome Jake without a struggle. The absence of a struggle seemed to me sure evidence that Jake had run off for unknown reasons. He owed me an explanation. I'd kept faith with him; why had he betrayed me?

They dragged Walloon Lake in the vicinity of a sand point. Cassady brought us daily reports. We didn't want to hear, but we had no alternative. I was grateful that our pa didn't rise into being as he did in my nightmares, popping out of the water, bloated and dreadful.

He'd been a great swimmer. Back and forth across Walled Lake, lofting his weight with sailing arms, an unsinkable man.

He would rise in the shallows, water streaming down his chest, his fringe of hair flattened, the great thighs coming into view as he trudged toward the beach, the lake yielding him up reluctantly.

I had a recurrent dream I have now forgotten save for its last moment. I hear myself yell, "I can't swim. It's not my fault," and I know that I'm lying and that I can really swim.

Ernie refused to return to school. Evka told him, "It's better that you go." We walked as far as Elmhurst, but Ernie wouldn't continue.

"You go," he said. "I can't."

Jake was headline news. The old photo of Jake descending the stairs of the Highland Park jail was republished. Out of respect for a lost man, they set by its side a more flattering picture, a close-up taken in an amiable moment before he'd had a chance to pose. In two weeks he ended up on page twenty. Afterward he occasionally appeared as filler material, and I tried to give up the newspaper habit.

I was bowled over by the commiseration of students and teachers. In order to measure up to the anguish they expected me to show, I almost wept. Jake seemed more possibly a corpse when I saw our situation reflected in the eyes of others. Still, I managed to finish out the semester. I took the exams and survived. Ernie missed the final month of school but received top grades nonetheless. Such was his reputation as a scholar.

I once surprised Ernie playing with the lefty marine. He was too absorbed to hide it. I could see him sometimes as he appeared to strangers—a good chin, thick lips which gave him a sullen look, tight curls low on his forehead.

Ernie was one of your more passionate endurers. He stopped everything to wait. He rarely left his bedroom. He wanted to be around when the call for action arrived. In the meantime he refused to move.

Jake dwindled away. Everyone seemed to acquiesce in rubbing him out. The union slipped into the hands of the secretary-treasurer. The industry no longer had to submit to Gottlieb's demands. In his own house he went unmentioned.

Detective Cassady uttered the brutal facts that we conspired to suppress. He did it naturally, a solid citizen who insisted that the world be normalized and nightmares not be allowed to be taken for facts. "I'll tell you the truth. It don't look so good for your pa. The picture don't give me grounds for optimism."

So Evka came to terms with fact. "Pa won't return to us," she told me and Ernie after Cassady reported the abandonment of dragging operations on Walloon Lake. "We must bear life without pa."

Cassady didn't contradict her.

She was no longer the submissive liege of Jake Gottlieb. She was a tough lady, prepared to accept any enormity.

I damned their willingness to be reconciled to fact. I knew that my pa was an unsinkable man.

The lakes of Michigan were formed by the retreat of the glacier. There are deep holes in these lakes that have never been fathomed. Grotesque things sometimes rise up. Fishermen have landed sturgeon weighing hundreds of pounds, garfish the length of a man, anachronisms belonging to some Thalean age when all was water. When I swim and remember what's beneath me, I panic. I flail the water, struggle for a footing. My breath goes; I end by sinking. Jake had given up trying to teach me to swim. He had been the unsinkable one. Did they expect me to believe I would only find him in my nightmares, among monster carp and sturgeons, gigantic bullheads and garfish, his flesh swarming with lampreys? I dreamed it night after night, and still I wouldn't surrender him and ease myself.

Life was made easier for a great many. Emerson and McIntyre were better off. O'Brien's path was now clear of roadblocks. And my mother and Ernie? Were they better off?

I asked Cassady early in the investigation if he had seen O'Brien.

"We checked everything out. Don't worry about it."

"Did you see the Cream of Michigan crowd?"

"We touched all the bases, Vic."

"Happy Weinberg? Whitey Spiegelman?"

"Don't you worry, son."

"Frank Ricci?"

"We didn't leave anybody out."

"You should also talk to Emerson."

"Emerson got nothing to tell us."

How could I press matters, when I expected Jake to return? I didn't hold O'Brien or any of the others suspect, because I denied that a crime had been committed.

Jake, whom I imagined to be the cornerstone of the world, disappeared, and yet everything remained standing. There was no sound of the edifice tumbling, though the foundations were gone. How quickly we got used to a world without Jake. There was a hush where once there had been the noise of Gottlieb.

What a classic, fine death had been Sammy Persky's! The remains had been there to be marked and celebrated. We'd wailed for Sammy Persky; but for our own pa?

I blew up at Ernie one evening. "Get off your ass instead of lying there like a woman. Are you afraid someone will remind you of what you'll have to do?"

We had sworn an oath, yet Ernie sprawled on his bed.

I couldn't bear the sight of his vacant eyes, the lips moving in a fantasy dialogue. One leg drawn up, the other extended, one hand flung back, the other hooked in his belt. He lay waiting.

Evka urged me not to press him. "We got to be patient, Vic. It's harder for him."

Did she imagine I lacked his capacity to feel, that I didn't suffer what he suffered? The truth is, Ernie was frozen to the heart. I have the opposite frailty. My sentiment gets out of hand. A few years ago I was in a hotel room in a strange city, and I turned on television to kill time and saw Shirley Temple. There she was as she had existed more than thirty years before, complete with blond ringlets and dimples, a fine hoofer for a six-year-old, the tunes discovering grooves in memory and setting off other tunes that moved my heart. What does it matter if it wasn't a fit experience for a grown man? The little girl is at a boarding school. She lives in the prospect of her daddy's return from the war. He's reported missing. She refuses to believe it. She hunts him in a hospital that receives battle casualties. In the absence of her father she has no place in the world. She's victimized by everyone. It's as simple as a cartoon. And yet—I'll let you know the worst about myself—I burst into tears. I wept. I despised myself for it and wanted to stop. I sniveled, I croaked, I gushed, I bit my knuckles. For Shirley Temple. Twenty-five years after Jake had disappeared, I recognized that my pa was gone and that I was alone in the world. It's said of some that they have the gift of tears, as though it were an advantage. And I believe it is a gift. You need only consider Ernie to appreciate the advantage of tears.

Evka said, "Maybe it will be harder for him than for us to admit that pa is gone."

I promised Evka, "Pa will come back. Don't be so quick to draw the curtains on Jake Gottlieb. He might return any minute."

"If it was possible, he would already have come back." Jake was three months gone when she came to this conclusion.

I told her that she didn't know everything. There were mysteries she had no idea of.

"What's to know about Jake Gottlieb that I don't know?"

I accepted Cassady's suggestion of a secret life. I cherished the dream of a mysterious father. Was it so absurd? Did we have any conception of the true shape of the world? Did Evka, for instance, have any real idea of her own son Ernie?

"What's to know," she asked, "that I don't already know?"

"Everything's to know. You're absolutely ignorant."

"What is it that I don't know?"

"Do you know that Ernie is a thief? He steals from delicatessens and jewelry stores. Did you know?"

She dismissed the charge as further evidence of my ill will. Only three months after Jake's disappearance, and Evka wanted everyone to concede he was gone forever.

She urged me and Ernie to find some distraction. One night she told us to go to a downtown theater and see a movie. It was time that we began to recover. Three months after Jake vanished we took a step toward normalcy and went to see a movie.

I asked Ernie what we should see. He didn't care. Anything I chose. I didn't want violence. Even extras toppling from horses could trigger my pity. The anonymity of the movie death, its casual impact on both killer and victim, seemed to me absolutely convincing. Should we go see a story of love? I found the idea of a man and woman pretending to be seriously affected by trivialities repugnant. So Ernie suggested a Bob Hope movie. We looked at the familiar face on the screen, and we laughed. I saw Ernie laugh and I laughed. But halfway through I couldn't take it any more. I went into the alley behind the movie theater and rolled my face on the stone foundation and wept. Ernie stood behind me, his hands in his pockets, frozen-faced, waiting for me to finish.

We walked as far as Wayne University and took a bus.

"It was a stupid idea," Ernie said. "Neither of us wanted to go. We did it for Ma. She's had a rough time. We should try for her sake."

I knew something had changed the minute we stepped into the house. There was no evidence of Jake in the hall closet, in the toilet, in the bedroom. The kitchen table was moved. There was no place that remained clearly his. She had cleared him out.

When later I hunted for some effects, all I could find was the jacket in the basement.

"What happened to pa's things?"

"They're gone," she said. "Pa is gone. Accept it. We got to continue living."

"Who said we got to? Did Berle Dresden tell you we got to keep on living? No one forces us to."

She wouldn't tell me how she had disposed of Jake's things. Jake had emulated the flashy style of the bosses with whom he negotiated. He'd had his suits tailored to fit his difficult shape. Even when we were poor he'd been careful in his grooming.

I let him slip out of my life. He made no shout and I didn't yell, but I've dreamed of his fall. I address him in my dreams. I blame him for not answering.

His salary continued to arrive. His union boys checked to make sure we were well fixed. Even Charley Hammer asked if he could help. "We're all right, Mr. Hammer. It's kind of you to show an interest."

"Don't thank him," I told her. "He was no friend of Jake's."

She said people only wanted to help. "We can't hurt their feelings."

Charley Hammer was no friend of Jake's. Jake stood in his path. We owed nothing to Charley Hammer. That softy from Grosse Pointe had much to answer for. Yet even when my plans were barely conceived, O'Brien was the target.

I never doubted that my oath was a valid contract.

Evka suggested that we take a long trip. She had in mind blue water and tropical skies.

"Go with Berle Dresden," I told her. "Ernie and I have business in Detroit."

She begged me not to be hard on her. She tried her best not to impose her grief on us. "You suffer enough," she told me.

"Impose," I said. "Show me the hurt. Let me see a few tears. You cried for Sammy Persky, who was only a third-rate man. Now when you lose the best in the world, tears are in order."

"I try to return from the dead," she told me. "Sometimes the effort is too much. I try for your sake."

"For my sake you can spend the summer in Detroit."

So we stayed in Detroit that summer.

Berle Dresden offered her a job as a receptionist in his hotel.

She thought it was a good idea. "When the salary stops coming, we'll have trouble."

I refused to allow it. Berle Dresden was already too involved in our affairs.

I was still a shrimp at sixteen. There was no evidence that I was going to mushroom. It was some years before I began to stretch and put on weight. But from the beginning I made sure that no one dismissed me lightly. All I needed was a sign from Jake and I was ready to explode. None arrived. I studied all sights and sounds as possible heralds of Jake. A change in climate? It would stir Jake's memory; he'd recall other seasons and the family he had abandoned, and he'd return to us. When the Germans started rounding up Russians by armies and it looked black for the world, I expected Jake to impose himself between us and our fate. When we heard the news that Kiev was occupied, the vestige of Gottliebs in Europe exterminated, I expected Jake would return to seek our comfort in his bereavement.

Brisk weather before Labor Day, and the parade will begin without Jake Gottlieb. The vacation is over, Jake. It's time to come home. I tried by hard listening to force sounds into being. I wanted to hear the doorknob rattle under Jake's heavy hand; I wanted to hear the stairs tremble under his heavy tread. But there was no Jake. Berle Dresden showed up instead.

"I don't want him around the house so much," I told Evka. "I can't stand his sour face."

"We can't refuse an old friend, Vic."

"He hangs around like a jackal."

"A sweet person like Berle? You're mistaken, Vic."

"The lion is gone, so he moves in for the leavings."

If he really grieved, would his hair be so beautifully combed? He had slender hands, long fingers and polished nails. A manicured radical! I never forgot that he'd been the victim of a thirteen-year-old girl. The fool now tried for someone his own age. Evka, though, was far, far out of his range.

He grieved for Soviet Russia as well as for Jake. Why didn't

America intervene? Why didn't Britain step up the pressure? Soon Moscow would be swamped. Stalin and his crew had already removed the seat of government. Leningrad was under seige. Once the Soviets were defeated, we would lose our only bulwark against nightmare. America was miserably unprepared. The draft bill had passed, the year before, by a single vote. Trainees practiced with broomsticks instead of guns.

I jeered at his alarm. "You didn't want us to be militarists. You argued against the warmongers. Now that you need them you change your tune."

He admitted that the entry of Soviet Russia had transformed the nature of the war, which had become something more than an imperialist competition for markets.

I told him, "They just finished off my pa's home town. The Russian Gottliebs have been rubbed out. I don't care about the fate of nations. It's the Gottliebs who concern me." I blasted his appearance, which was incompatible with his revolutionary claims, a tweedy man with a dreamy manner. It was stupid, since there was no chance of altering Berle. He said to me, "Somehow it happened that I didn't marry and I had no children, though it was always my intention. I have come to consider the Gottliebs like my own family. It's in that spirit I accept your abuse."

I resented his efforts to insinuate himself into a place that wasn't his, yet I can't deny that he was tender to us and always loyal.

During those days, I had the feeling that I was the only one interested in keeping our fortunes afloat. I refused to allow our pa to be jettisoned as if he were merely ballast. He was our treasure, and, if Jake went, everything went.

XXVIII

─◄◆►─

He was found two weeks before Thanksgiving. Our pa emerged from Walloon Lake. None of us had believed he was really gone. Evka never had really believed it. How could you believe it? We used to hear Moshe Bodkin speculate on the death of stars and describe how the sun would finally swell till it incorporated all the planets and then collapse on itself, diminishing to a dwarf. I could easier believe in the death of the sun than in the death of my father.

Washed up on a sandspit, a shredded rope tied to his middle. Anchored to the bottom, at a deep spot of the channel. Tatters of cloth crumbled at a touch. Cassady brought us the news. What witness could identify the bloated remnant of our pa? Cassady didn't want me to look. Did he imagine my nightmares couldn't produce a corpse to match the one that swelled to the surface of Walloon Lake? Berle went to Traverse City in our behalf. He looked at my pa and tried to remain a poet.

Someday the true witness of his dying will tell me all about

Jake's last hours. Till then, my dreams will reproduce the event. They recovered him near the spot where the Buick had been found.

Cassady wanted to spare me horrors, but what did he imagine I'd dream about when he indicated that the thing they had found could only be related to Jake by a deduction? There was no point of resemblance. The union ring was missing. There was no wrist watch or wallet. There were only shreds of clothing. All features were puffed away by the gas that inflated the dead body.

Identification was later made by a dentist, whose imprint on our pa was more durable than any made by God or family. All scars were erased. There was no evidence of a man, no vestige of his ambition, his arrogance, his bad food habits, his concern for his sons. Killed by a bullet that entered the base of his skull. The man with the broken teeth in front and the bridge in back was said to be my father.

When Cassady told us a body had been found, Evka rose on her toes, raised her arms, and fell backward. Cassady eased her fall. She let out a moan that was clearer to me than any funeral oration at Joshua Temple. I knew exactly what vision required that moan. Ernie ran to his bedroom and I followed him. He curled up in his bed, his arms around his knees. He trumpeted grief. He wailed as our grandpa had prayed, rocking back and forth. I knew what vision we all shared. We saw Jake at his last moment, attended only by his executioner, tortured by the prospect of the bullet he was soon to receive.

I listened for the cues that presaged his arrival. The sound of the Buick, the quivering of the house when he forced open the tight door at the bottom of the stairs, his distant bass as he greeted neighbors. I knew how he slammed car doors, how long it took him to reach the front stairs. When cold weather arrived, I woke up hearing his shovel scrape coal from the cellar floor. The ordinary noise of the world advertised Jake.

Berle Dresden didn't recognize whoever it was that had

popped up in Walloon Lake. When he returned from Traverse City we looked at his face and asked no questions. Berle tried to control himself, so that he wouldn't communicate his horror. But one glance—all his mannerisms blasted away, no more stagey eloquence—and we knew what he had seen. He told us in a smothered voice, "I couldn't be sure, but the dentist made it definite. They promise he didn't suffer."

Did Jake suffer? Suppose they had brought him alive to the lake. They rowed him out in a hurry to be done with the job. They dumped him over. He appealed to his murderers and they shoved him down, pressed him under with their oars, jabbed at his eyes. My father implored mercy as they poked him with the oars.

There were times when it was suddenly clear to me that the dead man wasn't Jake.

Jake wouldn't have been so obliging to his murderers. He wouldn't have let himself be docilely anchored in Walloon Lake. An imposter had risen to the surface.

We learned that the body had been anchored some distance from shore. The boat service across the lake accounted for all rentals during the period Jake was reported missing, so it must have been a private boat that had carried the dead man into Walloon.

Emerson owned a boat. He had shaped it, planed it, sanded it, enameled it, lacquered it, named it FAIR LADY after Mrs. Emerson. He had a forty-five horsepower Mercury engine. I had seen the boat in process of construction; I saw it completed. Emerson's good fortune was linked to O'Brien's. The same star. Emerson was another who had graduated from menial labors. He worked up front at Soil Free, an associate of O'Brien's.

"We know he has a boat," Cassady told me. "We checked everything out." The police had scoured the lake vicinity for any witnesses to the events of that cold April morning. Jake disappeared before Easter week. A boat had been seen around the bend. There'd been no tourists and few fishermen at that time of year. A vague report, a nondescript boat, a nondescript boatsman, no motor visible. Not a promising report.

I was able to construct a fully characterized man from the one quality, "nondescript." I saw Spiegelman, among others. He fit perfectly.

The time had come to put an end to Jake and plant the vestige said to be him. I had no alternative. Later we would pin him down with a stone bearing his name.

The matter was decided. The dentist connected Jake with the Walloon corpse.

He sank to the bottom of a deep channel. Bullheads and carp and other scavengers are down there. And, while Jake putrefied, while these limbless, whiskered things wiggled on his flesh, we thrived in his house. When I saw my pa rise from the water, hauling the lake after him, trudging against the pull of the lake with tremendous thighs, I'd believed he was unsinkable; but he'd gone under, devoured by the lake. His eyes were eaten, his tongue eaten, the brain putrefied. Yielded up by the lake, bloated till he burst, bloodless lesions opening to the bone.

How could we eat? I forced everything down. I wasn't accommodated to the death of my father. But I ate in order that my flesh might someday honor his flesh.

I see his death as clearly as if I'd witnessed it. The knowledge comes to me so vividly that I find it difficult to remember that it's only a fantasy. The vision of my father's death is as sharp as a hallucination. I have invented it. In my dreams I've worked out all the details.

Jake is on the Oswego road, answering a summons. Whose call would he answer? Fred Emerson says, I've betrayed you; meet me in Oswego, I'll give up O'Brien.

Jake fears nothing. He meets Emerson in Oswego. Emerson lures him into the country. He's afraid they'll be spotted by O'Brien's people if they stay in Oswego. He has everything to lose, but he can't bear this separation from Jake.

There are deep woods around Oswego. Heavy stands of birch and fir and pine. The road flees through a gothic gloom, broadening for turnoffs where there are picnic tables and rest rooms. Somewhere near Oswego they turn off the road so that Emerson can go to the rest room. There is another car at the turnoff, hauling a boat.

It's a cold day in midweek; the traffic is light. You occasionally hear an axe. There are only a few farms in the vicinity. It's the off season, but target shooting is common here. Jake waits in the car for Emerson. He listens to the bad news from Europe on the radio. He's deaf to all else. And his murderer comes to him, deft, quick, oozing from one car to the next. Was it Spiegelman? Does he use a lead pipe? Does he shoot? All the materials of this world are his weapons. Does he touch my pa with his hands. My pa is grieving for Jews when he is bowled over. A gloved hand pushes him away from the wheel and the murderer enters the Buick. He drives carefully, observing speed limits.

Emerson follows behind, hauling the boat.

Jake can bear punishment without being put out of action. They would risk much trying to punish him. They can't intimidate him with guns. He knows the resolve of O'Brien, and he would fight. They must act quickly and conclusively if they want to deal with my pa.

Jake is murdered outside Oswego. I believe they shot him on a sheltered turn off surrounded by chilly birch woods, the ground mucky from spring rains, Passover three days off.

The vision of his death is intense. I see it again and again. New details come to mind and I feel that it must have happened as I imagine it.

It's dark by the time they reach the lake, and bitter cold. They know the terrain from practice runs. A car backs down to the shores of Walloon Lake and releases a boat into the water. They load Jake aboard. They tie an anchor around his waist. They operate without lights and don't use a motor. They row out. Two men pulling? Emerson cringing in the stern? There are no fishermen on the lake. A patrol boat occasionally surveys the beaches. There are lights from farmhouses. It's a lonely spot in the off season.

When they reach the center of the channel, they drop anchor. They can't risk capsizing. Emerson balances the boat on the opposite side as the weight shifts. He observes the final scene. And isn't O'Brien present? Could he compel even a spiteful man to undertake such risks unless he were there himself to make it seem like a proper act? Was Emerson really there? Hadn't my pa saved his life?

They ease my pa over and he goes down into that cold water, wearing his light spring suit and an anchor around his middle. The Buick has been parked elsewhere in the woods. A tough night. It needs a drink and mutual congratulations. They've become wed to each other through that night's work. By releasing my pa into the water of Walloon Lake they are made kin. They touch each other. They hug each other. I know Emerson. He might kiss O'Brien on the lips. Who was more capable of idolatry?

So, farewell to Jake Gottlieb. Visions of his death convinced me that the pudding in the box was my pa and the time had come to put an end to him and plant this vestige. Later I would honor him, but I wanted that debased version underground without ceremony. No ceremony. Bury him quietly. Sneak him under. Honor him? I dedicated my life to that.

Evka begged for a ceremony. "I can't let him go like this." Let him go? Hadn't she been letting him go for the past seven months? Did she want to cling now? They'd been man and wife for twenty years. She had no real idea of a world without Jake. She had prematurely let go. Now she held fast to Jake.

The body was delivered to the mortuary in a sealed box. There were moments prior to the funeral when I experienced my first relief in months. It was nippy weather, a pleasure after the intense heat. A mild fall. We'd gone into November with no indication that Thanksgiving approached. Good news from the rest of the world. The Russians had slowed the German advance. Bitter weather where it counted. There was after all some basis for trusting the strategies of General Mud. The Russian armies still existed. Moscow held; Leningrad held.

I soared high and sank low. I didn't understand my own feeling. I knew that I was in the shadow of a mountain of grief that was in unstable equilibrium. Someday it would topple and bury me. I woke up from dreams, terrified that the phone might ring.

"We don't want a fuss," I told Berle when he offered to help with the funeral arrangements.

It was between Ernie and me; no one else.

I told Ernie, "No ceremony. I don't want Kravitz there. I don't want Charley Hammer showing up. I don't want any exhibition like there was at Persky's funeral."

He felt we were obligated to undertake a ceremony. However, he took an even stronger stand than I in opposing any ritual observance. He didn't want rabbis around.

Our pa deserved a funeral as magnificent as the one for Hector of Troy. I didn't mean this to be the final ceremony. Jake Gottlieb wasn't ready to be buried.

Visitors arrived to help us shape our plans, a rabbi and his retinue from Jake's home town in Russia. Two little men accompanied the rabbi. They sprouted hair like fur, wearing wide-brimmed hats with derby domes like those you see on Mennonites. The rabbi wore a black gabardine coat that hung to his ankles. I suppose he guessed our irreverence and, being a proud man, addressed us via his intermediaries, who were a shabby contrast to his elegance. They were my size, and I was only a sixteen-year-old shorty. They spoke yiddish, the rabbi with a cultured tone, the others with a saliva-rich speech that I found both incomprehensible and grotesque.

I thought they wanted charity and, having no charity, tried to stop them at the door. They paid no attention, beginning their pitch at the bottom of the stairs. They pushed toward Evka, who recognized them. A famous rabbi from the old country. Our grandpa, Jake's father, had been an esteemed member of his congregation. The rabbi recalled Jake as a wild boy who had created a stir in the old home town. Arrested at sixteen, sent to jail, then to Siberia. A precocious boy, an ardent Talmudist until he'd turned his back on Holy Israel in favor of a secular nation. No one had been able to do anything with Jake. He'd invaded synagogues to preach revolution. Out of esteem for Grandpa Gottlieb, the rabbi wished to reclaim Jake for Israel.

The rabbi's side curls hung down his cheeks almost to his neck. Black hat, black coat, black shoes, black side curls, shaggy eyebrows, he looked as if he were covered by a black pelt. He and his friends were an ugly bunch, big noses with flared nostrils. They looked as if they had emerged from lairs. Their prayer rooms were lairs. I remember the tiny shul where my grandpa prayed, windowless, cinder-block walls, concrete floors, lit by candles, a dank and smelly place crammed with bearded, chanting men. Ernie didn't want any dealings with the rabbi. The sight of these old Jews disturbed him.

We went to the kitchen while our guests remained in the living room. Ernie was vehement. "It's absolutely out of the question. I don't want them."

Evka told us the rabbi had a great reputation in the old country. "People would come from all over the country to receive his blessing. He was a close friend of your Grandpa Gottlieb." She was honored to receive the famous rabbi.

Ernie refused to violate our pa's revolutionary testament. He didn't want rabbis to degrade the ceremony. Jake would never have allowed them.

When I saw these old Jews in their prayer shawls—white silk with blue stripes—fringed at the corners, wearing phylacteries on left arm and forehead, chanting and rocking, I knew they belonged at Jake's funeral. The phylacteries, leather cubes containing instructions for the observance of law, were anchored by thongs to forehead and forearm. The cube resting on the forehead seemed like a device for tapping brain effluence.

"Get them out of the house," Ernie told ma. "Send them back to their holes."

I have in my album a photo of storm troopers gathered around an elderly, bearded Jew. The storm troopers are handsome Germans, long faced, slim, tall, clean-shaven, well tailored. An unusually attractive bunch. They resemble each other as if they were all made from the same mold as Gary Cooper. I see in them the features of our heroes. They smile, and I smile, too. The focus of their smiles is a wretched, ugly bum out of Beckett—barefoot, wearing baggy trousers, a tangled gray-beard with a powerful nose. The nose is baroque with all sorts of flourishes, no economy in the construction. It uses up a considerable part of the face. His shawl drapes from his head over his shoulders and upper arms, the fringes reaching his knees. A jumble of ragged colors. Save for the nose and the beard and the skullcap and phylacteries, he could pass for a gypsy. A ludicrous specimen. The thongs of a phylactery wrap his left arm. Another cube sits on his forehead. He is absorbed in prayer, but he takes an embarrassed peek at the storm troopers, who are amused by the spectacle.

One of them has a baby face. His grin is as malicious as a schoolboy's. It's difficult not smiling with them. And what do we have in the foreground? Legs. Shabbily dressed legs. Women's legs, men's legs, the short legs of children. Heaped up. What's at the other end of this pile? What faces? We read the text. It appears that we have here a pile of freshly butchered Jews on view. Our smiling krauts who resemble our heroes have just slaughtered them with machine guns. The text informs us, "Awaiting his own execution, a Jew prays over the bodies of his brothers." They left him for the last. It's a face I've seen replicated on Dexter. It's a heavy-boned, cavernous face, bags sagging beneath the eyes, thick lips, bushy brows. The face of a fool or a wise man. This fool is the only one left to pray. Is he embarrassed to perform for so critical an audience? I've encountered dead men in my time: I've seen them fill up ditches; I've seen them arranged along highways like railroad ties; I've seen them stacked in trucks like firewood. But I've never seen a face like this Jew's among the dead. The dead men I knew all resembled storm troopers. I look at the krauts in this photo and I see dead men. The ugly Jew lives. It is unthinkable to me that he'll be slaughtered. The Nazis have the anonymous faces of the dead. When dead, they produce no more horror than, say, cut wood. Hollywood has prepared us for their dying. There are only handsome dead men in the movies. Ugly people don't die. The Nazis in this photo are the dead men. To encounter the body of that trampy-looking Jew would be terrifying because I can't believe in the possibility of his death. A glance at his face and you're forced to imagine his life. The dead men will execute him.

I begin by seeing him as loathsome. I finish by grieving.

Another photo. A less savory crew of Nazis. Here the rot shows. Tall and flabby. Fat jowls. Paunchy and sway-backed. No Gary Coopers here. They also have a Jew in their midst. This one is younger, his beard jet black. He is very short. Not a bum like the first. His shawl looks expensive, with rich embroidery. The Nazis are without charm. You suspect evil nights and bad breath. Two of them, well over six feet, their paunches pressed against the prayer shawl of the Jew, stand at the Jew's side, narrow-shouldered men with considerable bellies. They reach out with scissors, beaming maliciously, each gripping a side curl of the Jew. This Jew is also barefoot. His fly is open. His belt has been removed. His trousers sag, the cuffs gathered in folds. We evidently see the last phase of his debasement. Much has preceded. Why is his fly open? But he stands firm. His chin is raised. His hands are rigid at his sides. Eyes steady. No cringing. I want to celebrate that Jew. I want to make a funeral for him. His bones have been rendered into soap and manure. There is no stone to record him, no wisp of him in my memory; only this photograph I own.

I later walk among the German dead and eat my rations and take my rest. They could have been uprooted cabbages for all the impression they made. A handsome folk. No evidence of a life in those dead faces. They're dead already before we empty their veins. Beware of dead men. They have nothing to lose. They undertake anything.

Our rabbi came to snare Jake in the rituals of Israel. He would allow no part of Israel to go unnoticed. I said it was fine with me.

"No lies," Ernie said. "No hypocrisy. These ceremonies have nothing to do with Jake Gottlieb."

I hear those distant sounds of Jake, that familiar noise, the footstep, the door-slam, the car motor. The rabbi, however, brings me news of an unfamiliar Jake, a prize student of the Talmud confined to a grubby part of a Russian city. The first decade of the century. No autos, but there are electric trams. Horses do the work. Jake wears shabby clothes in the style of a European proletarian. Pants unpressed, the jacket doesn't match. A sweater beneath the jacket is buttoned to the throat. He wears a cap with a shiny visor. He owns a prayer shawl and knows the use of phylacteries. Each morning he binds his left arm with seven coils of the leather thong, three times around the hand. He wears a skullcap. He doesn't ever grow a beard within the congregation of Israel. By the time a beard is possible he has set himself against orthodoxy. He discards his shawl and carries a knife. He takes the matter of justice out of God's hands. At my age he was already exiled among the Tartars. A man at sixteen, while I still dawdled. The rabbi regarded him as a promising boy who had lost his way.

What a man you are, Rabbi! Aren't there enough dead Jews in the world that you have to seek out the recalcitrant? No one escapes your net. You're as much an anachronism as a dinosaur, but you're the man for me. You have a nose for the dead. You have received the word and nosed out Jake. He's yours; take him, Rabbi.

The funeral convinced me Jake was gone. He was in a plain box beneath the chapel stage. The box was sealed. The screws were tight in the lid. The lid wasn't tight enough to seal in the smell. I thought I smelled the odor of formaldehyde. I recognized the smell from hospital visits. Maybe the morticians had fixed it so there would be no smell. But I thought there was a smell. So we had our ceremony after all. Dexter was at the funeral. The union was there. The bosses were there. Old-timers from Russia were there, friends of grandpa's. Charley Hammer was there. Hyman Kravitz was there. I'll tell you who wasn't there. O'Brien, McIntyre, Emerson. Happy Weinberg, Whitey Spiegelman, Leonard Mitchell. Sherry wasn't there. But Moshe Bodkin was there and his pa as well. I was as close to my pa as I had been in seven months. At the graveside I sank to my knees and watched the coffin descend.

Jake made us swear. We swore, but we never realized he meant business.

Charley Hammer approached us after the chapel ceremony, staging sorrow on that marvelous face with its bony ridges, its precise furrows, a fine ruddiness admirably framed by waves of silver, capped by a Homburg. "We've had a loss we'll never recover from. We'll miss him. Anything in my power or in the power of the union—anything you might need, Mrs. Gottlieb— you or the boys—say the word. We owe him a debt we'll never be able to pay. They never made a better man." He sang Jake's virtues. He thought it noteworthy that Jake would never take a cigar, as though that were a marvel in a world where everyone grabbed what he could.

Charley Hammer carried off this panegyric to our pa so convincingly that we were buffaloed. I didn't ask him, "What are you doing here? You got plenty of cigars, Charley." I didn't say to him, "If you owe him a debt, turn up his murderer. Who knows what you'd turn up?" Instead we thanked him. Evka did, at any rate. He caught us at a moment when we were too crushed to speak what was fitting. I should have told him, "You smell of lotion, you pig. That black suit is no custom-made job. You're tailored for funerals. Where are your wife and daughters? Why did you come alone?"

It was a couple of weeks before Thanksgiving. The cemetery was near Mt. Clements, a town celebrated for its mineral baths.

A cozy, fecal odor advertised Mt. Clements. Other than the sulfur baths there was an air base, Selfridge Field. Perhaps the air base came later. We weren't then familiar with the nomenclature of airplanes. There were no B-17s, B-26s, P-38s, P-40s, P-51s visible. Clear skies, the end of football season, a chill wind among the tombstones. The weather turned bleak. Red noses at Jake's funeral. Drivers puffed on hands. They wore their Sunday best, unrecognizable out of uniform. We received commiserations from all. Some were eloquent—as in the case of Bodkin, Sr., who spoke to us in yiddish. The orthodox weren't bowled over by death. We stood among tombstones topped by the Star of David, bearing simple inscriptions. So-and-So, Beloved Son, Honored Father. Born and Died. A message in Hebrew. The drivers wore crepe-paper yarmulkes, secured against the blustery wind. The grass had been killed by frost in the past week. It was a sere, brown graveyard, the wind blowing from the north. Snow already on the upper peninsula, on the shores of Lake Superior. Gales whipped up waves on Lake Michigan and Lake Huron. Our state was encompassed by rough seas. In Detroit the elms had shed. Oak and maple were bare. Leaves burned in gutters. Coal deliveries had been arriving for several weeks, wooden ramps laid down over the curb to support wheelbarrows. We heard the thunder of coal poured down chutes and afterward the hiss of coal settling.

Jake had installed an automatic stoker the previous winter and we had to shovel coal only once a day. Jake never profited from that convenience.

We drove to the funeral with Berle Dresden. He stood at Evka's side and shared the condolences we received.

After a year of observance a stone is planted on the grave and the business is over with. For a week following burial, the orthodox sit shiva. They mourn intensely and then back to the Book.

But we had sworn an oath.

I made the same discovery again and again. Jake wasn't coming home. After the funeral it often occurred to me—the thought

261

once had the power to bring me to my knees—that I hadn't made a proper fuss. I missed my chance for a last view. I should have gone to Traverse City with Berle. It was Jake's body; I shouldn't have abominated it. That was cowardice. Men familiar with death—the Greeks of Homer—know how to venerate remains in whatever grotesque form they appear. Featureless? I would have recognized him. The stench? I remember him in his leather jacket, smelling of an unpleasant machine odor following a day and night on the road. That was no dead man; that was my father. Couldn't I penetrate bad smells to reach him? To embrace him? Because I never again had the chance. I see a dead animal flattened by the side of the road, the guts drying in the sun; after a few days it has deteriorated into dirt. The bodies of men have come to be managed like such carcasses. We haven't been fighting Trojan wars lately. The funeral pyre, once meant to celebrate heroes, becomes in our time the incinerator.

At the Graveside Ma offered the Kaddish prayer. Where did she dredge up such memories? She wore black. She wore a veil. Her face was raw. Gusts whipped her skirts. She also fell to her knees. A paper yarmulke went sailing over the grave. Above us flocks of geese bolted south in arrowhead formation. She chanted the prayer. Others who had lost dear ones joined in. Berle, that Commie, also prayed. His silver hair fluttered around his yarmulke. His black overcoat had a velvet collar. A long face with a fine chin, bags under his eyes, but beautiful eyes, a mourner's eyes with a great deal of white beneath the pupil. He prayed with a poet's voice, tremulous, a bit too high-pitched. They celebrated God, our God, whose glory transcends all praises. They asked for abundant peace from heaven for us. And for all Israel. Amen.

I don't remember the details. I reconstruct events.

I kept my eye on Ernie, who was ugly in grief. The lips spread out, thickening even more, the eyes squeezed shut, the body heaved. He ducked behind his hands. Did he imagine his feeling would go unobserved if he covered his face? Pa sank into his grave and I went to my knees. I didn't cover up. I wasn't troubled that my feeling had an audience. I may have surrendered Jake to his grave but I didn't release myself from obligations to him.

I know what it is to be driven to my knees. There was no intention to worship; my knees wouldn't hold me. That sudden instability, my forced humility, the sight of others sinking—even truck drivers—why, I was impressed by that tough little rabbi, who kept his feet. He had survived this moment a thousand times. He had a ceremony that carried him through. I lost myself. I sank down. The orthodox responded to the chant of the rabbi with a chorus of amens.

When you go down, there's an impulse to sink all the way, as Ernie did. What a fall he took! It was clear why he had refused the rabbi. The man bore him down, crushed him, rolled him up like a wounded spider. Ernie folded over his knees and hid his face, a terrible letting go. Evka broke down, and Berle, too. Even the drivers wept.

I resisted what went on at the graveside. One paid for such a humiliating surrender. There was something of my pa I had relinquished, but there was something else I would never let go.

Ernie completely reversed his attitude toward rabbis after the ceremony. He succumbed entirely to the rabbi's appeal. He wanted to rend his lapels and pour ashes on his head and pray for Jake in a synagogue. He wanted a prayer shawl for spiritual warmth. He had no knowledge of Hebrew, no membership in a congregation, no prior history of faith in the God of Israel, but he aimed for full orthodoxy and asked Moshe Bodkin for instruction. Moshe Bodkin was delighted to impress him into the service of that faith to which he had been a lonely adherent. Some switch, eh? A dodge. A great show, but a diversion. Did he imagine I wouldn't summon the pious to war? I'd never allow Ernie Gottlieb to become a conscientious objector.

XXIX

I KEPT O'BRIEN in mind even when he was out of reach.

I started by phoning him. Kate Russo answered, so I hung up. I phoned later, and she again answered. I phoned at two in the morning and finally got O'Brien. I breathed into the phone, trying to make my breath obscene. I stirred up the beast, and when I heard his shrill voice it took courage not to slam down the phone. I imagined that if I hung on he would pursue the sound and find me at the other end. It was a thrill to make him suffer as we once had.

I ruined his sleep. He tried to needle me into responding but I only let him hear my breath. He hung up and I called again. After two weeks his phone was disconnected.

It was a cheap satisfaction; I only irritated him.

I put myself in his shoes and shared his contempt for the obnoxious caller. I shivered, listening to that shrill voice, imagining the heavy face with the thin lips pulled back, exposing a powerful bite.

Ernie said, "It's cowardly and degrading. I want no part of it."

I agreed with him. Guns were better.

XXX

---◆◈◆---

JAKE HAD A SHORT-SNOUTED REVOLVER. He brought it home at the time of the Atlas strike, a secondhand weapon with a tarnished barrel and a chipped handgrip. He never used the gun. He spread his double-breasted suit coat and showed us the weapon tucked into his belt. He aimed at a table lamp and said, "Bang, bang."

Evka grabbed the gun away. "Are you crazy? You'll kill somebody."

What did he know about guns? It was absurd for him to own one. He never went to cowboy movies. The subject bored him. Even as a soldier he had never used a weapon. He'd dug trenches under enemy fire at Château-Thierry. When there was any rough stuff he relied on his heavy chin and bear hugs.

I found the gun hidden in Evka's dresser, wrapped in a girdle.

I stood in front of a mirror and posed with it. I closed my eyes and sighted the target I always kept in mind, imagining the ruddy, weathered face explode, the red hair flapping. POW, POW, POW.

I spun the cylinder, flipped the safety, aimed at myself in the mirror.

Ernie asked where I had found the gun.

"In the dresser."

He told me to get rid of it, throw it away. He grabbed for it but I held tight.

Weren't Gottliebs to bear arms? In a world loaded with killers were we always to be ranged alongside the victims? John Wayne and James Cagney and Whitey Spiegelman and O'Brien could shoot as casually as they pointed a finger. I studied myself in mirrors to make sure I didn't look like a freak with the gun in my hand.

"What are you dreaming of?" Ernie asked me. "What do you know about guns?"

"I'll go into the woods and practice."

"Men have spent their lives practicing. What competition would you be?" He pleaded with me to get rid of it.

I went to a downtown sporting-goods store and bought gun oil and patches, but, when I asked for ammunition, the clerk wanted to know if I had a license for a handgun. I told him the bullets were for my father. He was a bald clerk in a full-length white smock, his name signed on his chest in red yarn, busy with an order.

"No, sir," he said. "No, sir. Tell your dad to come himself."

I later found a hardware store near Walled Lake that served hunters and didn't make a fuss about selling ammunition to minors.

I reamed out the rusty barrel and made the piece glisten. I spent weekends hunting for targets.

I took the bus to the end of the line and hiked across fields into woods. I took a few shots, then moved on so that the owner of the field wouldn't spot me. Once the hunting season began, there was less trouble.

I remembered instructions from cowboy movies. I squeezed my shots and avoided jerking. I held my breath. I pointed the gun as if it were an extension of my hand. It leaped when

I fired, and I couldn't control it. I had to get very close to hit anything. Even at close range I needed big targets.

Berle Dresden supplied us with a prepared turkey for Thanksgiving. He realized that there could be no holiday mood in our house—not for a long time, he acknowledged. Who knew when the memory of so vivid a man would dim? But we were alive; there were turkeys to be eaten and at least small things to be thankful for.

It was a clear day, a winter light; long shadows. The air lucid. Every object had frosty outlines.

I missed my bus and waited almost an hour for the next one. My shoes stiffened with cold. I jumped in place, holding the revolver up the sleeve of my jacket, the cold muzzle under my glove. By the time I reached the end of the line the sun was on the way down. I hiked along a farm road lined with cedars whose shadows stretched across the brown stubble of a hayfield. The wind cut through my corduroys. My cheeks stung; my eyes teared. There was no traffic. I saw smokey wisps from distant chimneys. The stubble cracked underfoot. I headed across the field toward a creek lined with brush and willow. The creek ran through a culvert beneath the roadway into the woods. I ripped a branch from a dead tree and placed it ten yards away, near the stream. My hands were cold and I had trouble inserting bullets into the chambers. I flicked off the safety, aimed, squeezed, shut my eyes. The gun fired and I missed the branch. I fired twice more, troubled by the noise, not caring what I hit. I walked up to the limb and fired point-blank and was struck by splinters. I climbed to the top of the bank to see if anyone had heard. I saw a kid taller than I, in high boots, wearing a hunting cap with flaps down, his hands thrust into the slit pockets of his jacket, a shotgun supported in the crook of his elbow. He veered away when he saw me. I was obviously no hunter. It was nighttime when the bus picked me up. I didn't eat turkey. I had no thanks to offer even for little things.

I had small power in my hands, not much in my arms. I began exercising to eliminate my defects. I awoke at five-thirty every morning. I did push-ups to muscle my arms. I elevated my legs and held them tense to harden my belly. I chinned myself on the molding above the back door. I ran along Richton and Dexter. When the snows arrived, I continued running. I wore sweater and gloves, never a coat. I returned from my morning exercises and took a hot shower, followed by cold. I spouted like Jake. Exercise didn't change me as fast as I wished. I remained scrawny, a frail kid without much of an appetite.

I have since become the hero of my dreams. Once I couldn't shoot, and I dreamed of a hero who could. I was short; I dreamed of a tall man. I was skinny; I dreamed of a substantial man, someone as powerful as O'Brien, but my advocate. Dreams were no gratification for me as they were for Ernie. I used them to scout possibilities. I sketched my hero and proceeded to realize him in myself. There wasn't much material to support my dreams, and I feared that I might stay a shrimp all my life.

Ernie had the right size. A bit lanky, but even at seventeen he had thick forearms and sloping shoulders with heavy muscles. He didn't realize how well equipped he was.

I told him that it was too late to be religious. Someone like Moshe Bodkin acquired the habit early, when he was still in his mother's arms. "But, for us," I told him, "it's unnatural. It's more unnatural than shooting a gun. You've never read the Torah; but you've played with soldiers, so you can imagine being a killer. Even thirteen-year-olds are better informed about religion. Think of yourself in a synagogue when they call you up to read the Torah. You'd make a fool of yourself."

I would have been delighted if he had truly discovered Israel, but it was a dodge that I couldn't take seriously. He gave up his religious studies after a few weeks.

He asked me what I intended doing with the gun. Did I realize I appeared ridiculous?

Practice would change me. Someday I would carry my weapon and would no longer seem ridiculous. We had plenty of time, I told Ernie. It was worth our lives to honor Jake Gottlieb.

XXXI

PEARL HARBOR seemed at first just one in a series of incidents, no more provocative than the shelling of the gunboat Panay. Who could deny the Japs were a nasty bunch? They mounted China like a tiger on a placid ox. There was a newsreel clip of Japanese soldiers using Chinese for bayonet practice. We saw babies launched into the air like clay pigeons and impaled on bayonets. This was on the screen of the Dexter Theater, and, therefore, true. A terrible folk, near-sighted, stocky, bandy-legged, determined to have the largest battleships, the best swimmers, the mightiest empire, the most convincing suicides. Their suicide ritual—a knife thrust into the abdomen and rotated while crouched in ceremonial garb before a Shinto altar—demonstrated they could stomach all excess.

I tried not to read or listen, yet I couldn't resist the habit of a lifetime. I began with the comics and was lured to the more deadly part of the newspaper. I tuned in my Philco. I watched newsreels. And what did I see? What we all saw.

A squat, impassive Jap officer, thick spectacles, thick lips, brush mustache, almost no waist, wearing olive drab from knees to visored cap, his sword raised high, ferocious and fanatic. Down flashes the sword, and a Jap soldier launches a Chinese baby. He tosses the infant as if he were its daddy, a chubby bundle swaddled in a coarse, brown material. And there's our Jap trainee, an ordinary soldier, without epaulets or high boots or samurai sword, his bayonet ready, gazing up at his soaring target, facing the enormity each one of us might have to confront. Did I see the baby impaled or did I complete the action myself? I shut my eyes. Why? Because I didn't want to face what was expected of me? CAPTURED JAPANESE MILI-TARY FILMS. Truth? Propaganda? Did it make any difference? It was someone's fantasy and therefore possible.

Consider this scene, viewed at the Dexter Theater. Another Jap officer with raised sword. He stands beside a row of posts to which blindfolded Chinese civilians are tied. They are dressed in that same coarse brown cloth. Facing them at attention, bayonets poised, a row of Jap soldiers. Nothing moves. A command, the sword flashes, then a precision thrust by the row of Japs, an imprecise straining from the row of Chinese. Then thrust and thrust and thrust till the writhing bodies are eased, become mere dummies for butt strokes and bayonet thrusts.

That's what we had to be prepared to do, or have it done to us. No quarter given, no mercy. Japs don't surrender. If they tried it, we'd make them pay for all those sordid newsreels. We'd repay them thrust for thrust. We saw German prisoners of war in the newsreels, but rarely an Oriental. When he appeared, he was a tiny, skinny fellow, stripped naked. We were told that sometimes they surrendered with grenades inside their torn clothes. They waited till our boys assembled, then pulled the pin, and flayed us with their bursting crotches.

On one side the Germans, a western folk whom we under-stood insofar as they amplified our own impulses to murder, degrade, pervert. On the other side, the uncanny Japs, whose devotion to their god-emperor had stripped them of any love of life. They burrowed into jungle islands. We needed to root them out by flame thrower.

They blasted our fleet, overran our island bases, humbled us in the Philippines. We saw files of American soldiers prodded by fierce little Japs. Our boys had the same shocked appearance we had noted in the faces of Poles, and French, and Russians, and Jews. The same could happen to us as happened to others. We had the same incapacities as the French and the Poles. Later we demonstrated that we had the same capacities as krauts and Japs.

So what were two orphan boys to do, forbidden by their pa to treat men as bugs, sworn by him to take arms only for a just cause, that being himself, Jake Gottlieb?

Ernie left for Ann Arbor to become a college boy. Only forty miles away, but our life together was finished. He could have made the trip home easily enough, despite the weather. There were good train and bus connections. Hitchhikers were posted on the overpass leading to Detroit, and they had no problem getting rides. I made the trip to Ann Arbor often enough, an hour and a half, portal to portal, but Ernie rarely bridged this short distance.

The revolutions in my life never had precise beginnings. Jake slipped away, and his death didn't come to an end. My vision of his dying was the by-product of dreams. I found no witnesses to the event. Ernie also slipped away unceremoniously. One night in our bedroom, sleeping across from me as he had for seventeen years; the following night in an Ann Arbor dormitory.

He fled the only honorable destiny available to us.

Ann Arbor was a kiddish place, out of this world, a Treasure Island for straying Pinocchios. The town focused on the campus. The campus focused on nostalgia. And nostalgia for what? For gridiron heroes. The union basement was a repository of football memories. The walls were hung with photos of all-Americans, beginning with the turn of the century, advancing to our time.

271

Glass-encased trophy bowls were etched with the names of heroes who were the Ann Arbor version of Achilles and Hector and Ajax. The verse of local Homers was carved into oak tables preserved in shellac for future generations. You could read the lists of those who had done battle for Michigan. Drinking songs, in their original published format, were framed on the union walls. It all hinged on nostalgia:

> I wanna go back to Michigan,
> Dear old Ann Arbor town,
> Back to Joe's and the Orient,
> Back to all the money we spent.

Tree-shaded mansions, picturesque boardinghouses inhabited by kids, restaurants doing a land-office business in kid food—fried chicken, hamburgers, chili, milk shakes. The long diagonals of campus intersected at the steps of the library. Boys perched there; girls moved past in display. All these kids of America were tuned to their rhythm. It wasn't ours. Campus life was natural for them. Their music, their heroes, their traditions. When the time came, they even had an easy response to war, as if their roles had been long rehearsed. By the end of the year the diagonals were filled with uniformed students. The university enlisted for the duration, at the service of ASTP, V-12, ROTC, the army language program. The football team was improved by military recruitment. There was an active German-American Bund in Ann Arbor, which became quiescent as pro-German sympathies became unfashionable.

A lovely city before the war. What was Ernie doing there?

The Ann Arbor railroad station was beneath an overpass that carried highway traffic to Detroit, a grimy stone depot in a seedy part of town. I used to wait by the tracks. The approaching light of the engine would sweep a passage down the right of way. At the other end of that passage was the Detroit Central Terminal, already heavily loaded with war traffic. Soldier boys arrived home on leave. Draftees decamped, still in civvies. Wives and kids journeyed south. Lines formed early.

A mob crammed the lobby. There was a good prospect that some would stand all the way to Kentucky, and Alabama, and the Carolinas. Luckier ones slumped on john benches or settled on suitcases in the aisles. Mom and Dad, Grandma and Grandpa, all the kin, were at the station for the send-off. Around the clock. Each group centered around its hill of luggage. Children slept on the long, wooden benches, the varnish rubbed off, everyone begrimed before the trip started. Sandwiches available at the counter, cold cuts soaked in mayonnaise, pasty white bread. Coffee with a metallic taste, served in paper cups. For the next several years we were all transients.

I wanted to get home fast after my Ann Arbor visits.

"I'm not leaving Detroit," I told Evka. "I'm no college boy. My business is here."

I woke up nights, smothering in our empty house. I willed Jake's return. I sharpened my ears for the preliminaries of his homecoming. I made myself feel, Right now, he's at the door, it's going to burst open. I'll hear his overshoes drop. He'll stomp the stairs. "Surprise, everyone! I'm back!" and he'll receive our love and kisses. How he's made us suffer. I forgive him, though; our house is alive again.

When I visited Ernie in Ann Arbor, I warned him, "Don't get too comfortable. Don't pledge yourself to the fraternity boys. I still got business for you. Don't imagine it's left my mind."

Ernie had fastened a bulletin board to the wall of the dorm room and pinned quotes he'd culled from his reading. There was one from Melville: Ahab speaks to the blacksmith, who pounds out dents in metal. "Blacksmith," asks Ahab, "can you straighten any seam?" "All but one, Sir." "Blacksmith," asks Ahab, pointing to his forehead, "can you straighten this seam?" "Aye, that's the one, Sir."

How did that quote serve him? Did he imagine, as I did, the seam in Jake Gottlieb's forehead, mounting the sheer bone wall, arriving at the smooth plane of his dome cut by that deep scar? No blacksmith had straightened that seam. Walloon had erased all lines. It had gulped him down and spewed him back shapeless.

I recall another aphorism on his wall. "When a sword enters your innermost being, look calm, lose no blood, and meet the coldness of steel with the coldness of stone." It offended me. He spent his strength becoming stone. He holed up in his dorm room so that he wouldn't risk the loss of blood.

I hitchhiked to Ann Arbor, sometimes arriving late at night, and even if it were Saturday I could rely on Ernie's being there. I passed the beer parlor and saw college boys emerge arm in arm, singing Ann Arbor songs, not bothered at all by the war. I entered Ernie's silent room, dark save for a circle of light shed by a desk lamp. He hunched over the desk, scouring books, denying his power.

I told him, "You're getting skinny; a kid could take you."

He said to me, "No one can take me where I refuse to go."

I sat in his room while he worked. I tried to read. He wanted me to be excited by the subjects he studied. I couldn't finish more than a few pages without feeling smothered. He had a flair for mathematics. He tried to interest me in problems of infinity. He reminded me of our nights observing stars and tried to convince me that the elegance above was reflected in mathematical structures. He explored the simple notions of arithmetic and rose to the calculus. He led me through a few demonstrations, but I couldn't see the point. I saw no structure emerging. Though we shared an interest in history, our motives were different.

He wanted to demonstrate how ludicrous were the wars of men. He found history loaded with hatchet men and throat cutters and martyrs. All our nightmares were on record, rendered fact by men. I couldn't scare him with current atrocities. He knew that throughout history men had managed to remain as cold and invulnerable as stone, observing all enormities, and surviving to record them. The trick was to be a historian and remain outside of history. The lives of monks and philosophers and historians and academics proved that it was possible.

I observed him slumped over his desk, saintly and serene, trying to find a place for Jake Gottlieb within the framework of an acceptable perspective.

Size, shape, manner—he changed so radically I saw no connection to my familiar brother. I could have knocked at his door and asked him, "Is Ernie Gottlieb there?" All he would have had to do was deny that he was Ernie Gottlieb and he'd be out of sight and untraceable.

This sweet, bookish Ernie scared me; I had always counted on him to lead the way.

I sometimes went shooting around Ann Arbor. I walked along the Huron River into the country and looked for targets. I climbed the ridge above the river. I forced my way uphill, wrestling tree trunks, lashed by twigs. I stood in sere underbrush, among defoliated maple and oak, the skeletons of trees allowing me a broken vista of the Huron. I aimed at targets in the river.

Ernie thought it was absurd.

He said that I was trying to enter O'Brien's house, where I would always be a stranger. Why did I torment myself? Violence was his way, not ours.

I asked him, "Don't you remember what we promised? Were you lying, Ernie?"

"The truth is," he told me, "I didn't take it seriously."

"Then you're stone," I said. "You've made it. Congratulations."

One day he confessed that my visits depressed him.

I told him that it would be easy enough to get rid of me. "Keep your promise to Jake Gottlieb, and I'll vanish. Then, even if you want to fly to the other side of the world, I won't trouble you any more."

But he didn't want me to vanish. He didn't have any brothers to spare.

While he carved out a new life, I got my bearings in the study of O'Brien.

O'Brien was my subject: I didn't choose the continent of Africa; I was no expert on Asian affairs; I had skimpy information about the cosmos; but I was a specialist in O'Brien. I tracked him everywhere, even though he was the hunter.

In the past two years he had become a master of the sport. He went to an island in Lake Michigan and followed an Indian guide through snowy woods. He'd pot deer. He'd knock off coon and fox. In the fall he'd sit behind a duckblind on Lake St. Clair and bag mallards, Canadian geese, whatever else would come into his sights. He had rifles of every caliber in his gun rack, some fitted with telescopic sights. He had shotguns with beautifully tooled stocks. He owned handguns. He lived in a small house near Grand River Avenue and put his money into weapons. He wore cheap suits to work, but he was something to see in his red parka and boot packs, his canvas vest studded with shells.

In the old days he wasn't skilled in the refinements of hunting and used makeshift bludgeons. He hadn't known how to bring down fowl with shotguns made to order by Bavarian smiths, but he'd been able to bag a man with a rolled newspaper. He believed he had a right to everything. Who else could have so thoroughly domesticated Kate Russo?

If you saw him on Manitou Island, moving down a snow-packed trail between hemlock and beech in pursuit of an albino deer, you'd never believe that this sportsman had flailed Sammy Persky with a length of pipe wrapped in the Detroit *News*.

He enjoyed contact sports. He watched the fights. He believed that there was no man alive he couldn't handle, by hook or crook, from the front or the back, alone or with collaborators. He was a sportsman less concerned with the game than the reward. He wanted to be winners. He wouldn't quit his three-day hunting trip without a deer. If it came to a pinch, he climbed into a tree and squatted in a platform above a feeding-trough. He waited for his deer to approach, first the doe, then

276

the cautious buck. He couldn't miss at a range of twenty yards, especially when the target was stationary and off guard. O'Brien's guide didn't mention the violation of the sporting code. I knew his guide, a moon-faced Indian from Shawbeetown named Clarence. He worked at Soil Free and ate at the Rex Diner. Why did O'Brien insist on the kill? Did he need venison? He could buy venison. Was it for the sport? What sport? He sat wrapped in a blanket thirty feet above the ground, sheltered by hemlock branches, zeroed in on the feeding-trough below. The answer is, I think, that O'Brien was an esthete, who found any incompleted action intolerable. He hunted to kill, so kill he would. He was ready to blow up the world to get relief. His hunting parties were great affairs, plenty of booze, marinated venison, delicious morels—the specialty of the island, taken from the freezer and fried in butter. Great food, a gamey, fecal taste that readied you for the primeval Manitou wilderness. Beneath the snow was springy turf made of decomposed hemlocks and firs. There was a tamarack swamp at one end of the island, a network of grotesque roots. Beneath the shallow, brackish water, stained red from tamarack bark, the muck could gulp you down whole.

It was a good life for O'Brien. He was determined on having it, and he wasn't denied. Jake Gottlieb had been the price of his contentment. Jake Gottlieb had been the bottleneck.

XXXII

O'BRIEN REMAINED in his old neighborhood. He lived among the Irish, not far from the ball park. Border incidents preceded what later turned into a full-scale war against encroaching Negroes. O'Brien didn't value brick patios and cookouts. He didn't care for the amenities of Six Mile Road. Doctors and businessmen weren't his cup of tea. He lived in a dumpy box with an obviously faked brick façade. The house was wedged between grimy apartment buildings. The front yard was barren clay, save for weeds. O'Brien didn't trouble with appearances. In the center of the yard, along the paved walk leading to the warped stoop, there was a stunted tree with a fussy top and chunky, short branches, bare of leaves, the twigs growing vertically, an obscene tree, its private parts denuded, as unwholesome a sight as a mangy dog. It was a dark house, the two narrow front windows curtained, blinds down. O'Brien didn't live in the open; he didn't care if appearances deteriorated.

Only a few inches separated the house from the apartment

buildings on either side. The alley behind was paved with a variety of materials: brick, asphalt, concrete. His garage fronted the alley, next to it a cement incinerator and a row of garbage cans. A heavy gate was bolted from the inside. Dusty vines covered gate and fence, obscuring the view of the back yard. I peeked through clotheslines hung with stockings and Kate Russo's panties. He owned the most advanced laundry and linen service in town, and yet Kate Russo did the wash by hand. Did he prefer the simple life? Did he mean to ridicule the impulse to cultivate gardens?

He made no effort to put on a show for the neighbors. He didn't hoe his garden, paint his house, uproot the tree in his front yard which seemed to have come up roots in the air. He aimed for Grosse Pointe, where his acres would be tended by a Japanese gardener. He always found someone else to do his dirty work. He contributed the conception and the will. Even that savage Kate Russo served his needs.

He arrived at the Soil Free office at 7:30 each morning. Soil Free was brand-new, with a milk-white façade. The machinery was new; the linens were more durable than the stuff Kravitz distributed. Drivers didn't steal from O'Brien, who knew all the tricks. He was strong competition for Kravitz. He offered customers streamlined uniforms with the insigne stenciled in fancy colors. He didn't run a one-man operation, as Kravitz did. Kravitz obstinately relied on his own intuitions, which had always been sound, but there had been technical innovations in the linen industry—new machines, new materials, new bookkeeping methods. O'Brien was available to any idea that would bring profit.

He invested in land, backed a trucking firm, financed a bowling alley. He was a plunger, just when boom times hit Detroit. By our standards he was rich, yet he was in no rush to leave his old neighborhood. The drab house suited him fine. It was close to his office, a ten-minute drive to Soil Free. He lunched at twelve, returned to his office at 1:30, left work at 5:30, parked his Buick Roadmaster in his garage at 5:40, the same type of vehicle Jake had used, a later model, of course.

He wore tight suits. A good stretch and the seams would be done for. His bristly red hair crested on either side. He greased his hair but couldn't keep it down. He seemed like a rube with his broad face and strong cheekbones and heavy chin. He wasn't one of your funny Irishmen. No poetry or banter in O'Brien, no playfulness. Until he discovered how you might be used, he ignored you. He had a capacity—obnoxious or intimidating, depending on one's temperament—of looking through the space you occupied as if you had been rubbed out. But, when he discovered how to use you, he made you the target of his sight. I'm convinced this was a factor in the strong loyalty he commanded. He employed men in ways in which they never before been used, and they were delighted. McIntyre became a sales manager. Emerson ran the inside. The Oswego branch under Fiori was expanded to take in a considerable part of central Michigan. O'Brien never expected to be betrayed. He had absolute confidence in his judgment. He trusted his men and didn't nag or otherwise interfere with their work. Do the job for him and you'd never find a vestige of prejudice. He was ready to accept hoodlums, Communists—anybody who could be of use.

He made the law. He bought the cops. He paid the judges. He took in good air and released toxin. Every second he drew breath depleted my air.

It was easy to get information about O'Brien. Every lunch counter on Jefferson Avenue near Soil Free was a source of gossip. He began to appear in the newspapers as a municipal power. Ripples of his destiny radiated to all the boundaries of Detroit and beyond.

The Jefferson Avenue gossip esteemed him as a family man. He didn't drink; he didn't smoke. Cuties worked for O'Brien, but, though he had opportunities with the ladies, he didn't screw around. Kate Russo was lady enough for him. He gambled, which would have been a frailty, except he didn't lose.

They spoke of him as if he were father of them all. Yet he entirely lacked sentiment. If you didn't produce, he got rid of you. In his own behalf, he was ready to undertake massacres. If you worked for O'Brien, you became his tool. That was your only mode of survival within his shelter. I didn't have the inclination of ass-lickers and cowards to glorify tyrants.

Red Wilson came over from Atlas to serve as O'Brien's foreman. While he had done Kravitz' dirty work merely for cash, his labors for O'Brien were acts of reverence. I heard him swear that he would die for O'Brien. Red Wilson offered a tough face to the world, but O'Brien scared him, and he reverenced what he feared. He stuck to O'Brien's heels, serving as watchdog and flunky.

I discovered that O'Brien played handball Monday nights at the Y. I walked down a shabby corridor with half-tiled walls and a linoleum composition floor to the locker room. Metal doors slammed. Naked men stood on benches and sawed themselves with towels. There was a thunder of showers. Basketball players entered from the gym. I heard shouts, racing feet; basket rims vibrated.

A stairway led to a lower floor. The corridor beyond resembled a cell block. Heavy doors guarded the courts. I peered through a slit of glass fortified by wire mesh. I saw gloved players, stripped to the waist, jostling for position, then lunging at the ball. I recognized O'Brien, built square, powerful thighs and arms, the thick neck spotted by freckles, the red thatch parted in the center. He crowded his opponent, jamming with his elbows, working his hip in front, blocking the view of the return shot. His opponent couldn't budge him. O'Brien jumped aside at the last instant and smashed the weak return. He deliberately irritated with hip and elbow, forcing his opponent to concentrate on the abuse. He stood sullen and cool at the serving line, slightly tensed, while the opponent jockeyed in the rear court, trying to guess the serve. A teasing serve along the wall, a weak return, and O'Brien took the point.

I later observed him in other contests. It was never merely

a workout. A padded torso, the color of a ruddy steer. Even when I carried the gun, I felt disarmed in his presence.

He caught me spying. He sniffed me out. He looked over his shoulder as he was about to serve, a tigerish look; he'd caught a whiff of danger. He stared at me through the mesh-covered window slit, and I turned and ran. Up the stairs, through the locker room. He'd read me as easily through that tiny slit as if I had broadcast that I was the telephone heckler who had been hounding him.

I told Ernie I had tracked him to the Y.

"Tracked him!" he said. "To the Y? You're some bloodhound."

XXXIII

———◄◆►———

A Soil Free advertisement appeared in the daily *News*. A laundryman with a ruddy, Celtic face had posed for the ad. Smiling O'Brien. "Take a load off your shoulders. Put it on my back." He wore a Soil Free uniform. The little cap balanced on waves of red hair. He hoisted a white bundle, smiling Irish eyes.

How could I let him continue to smile? His smile wiped out Jake Gottlieb. That smile could kill me, too.

I ran through the summer. I wore shorts and gym shoes, stripped to the waist, the muscles now apparent on my arms and chest, sliding along my legs, swelling my calves. It was the body I dreamed of having, and yet no satisfaction. Was it only for mirrors? I posed with my gun and dreamed of murder. Meanwhile O'Brien took over the world, and Jake Gottlieb continued to diminish. My body was only the mock appearance of myself.

I had to look in mirrors to make sure I wasn't putrescent

flesh. I groped my body to convince myself it was there. I felt my muscles. I inflated my chest. I was something sculpted by me. The artisan inside the statue remained weak and ugly.

Consider the true hero, able to move, reflected by his actions. For instance, Rommel, the Desert Fox. His power lay in movement. He ranged across North Africa. He forced the British Eighth Army back into Egypt. He snatched Tobruk. He cornered our side at El Alamein. Slashing movements. Thousands slaughtered. Panzers raised dust storms in the desert. Messerschmitts and Stukas cleared the Mediterranean of Allied commerce. The murder he intended was immediately translated into the ruin of men and cities. His middle-aged body was made colossal by the machines he commanded. Churchill praised him as an admirable foe, and this in the midst of war, when praise for the enemy is grudging. A worthy foe!

Worthy to whom? To those able to survive his victory. But how about us, Evka, and Ernie, and me, and our Dexter Avenue neighbors? The object of his gallantry and intelligence was our extermination. How were we to admire such heroes?

I ran into the country; dreaming of the murder of heroes, I burst through twigs and underbrush. I dreamed of cornering O'Brien and Rommel and Hitler and destroying them like bugs.

German armies penetrated to the Volga, entered the oil fields of the Caucasus, aimed for Stalingrad. I could exhaust myself in dreams, but the heroes were on the other side—the gods, too, for all I knew.

I stopped in swampy ground, my feet soaked, standing among milkweeds and saplings and reeds, harried by gnats, my ribs abraded by the gun under my sweat shirt. I pressed the muzzle against my temple and squeezed without releasing the safety, hoping to suddenly discover what was in my father's eyes.

Across from his garage there was a run-down tool shed. I crouched in O'Brien's alley and became familiar with the voices of neighbors, the sounds of their car motors. I learned the rhythm of alley life as well as any rat. I knelt on burlap sacking under the window. The shed was abandoned. There were piles of boards so dry I could split them with my hands, rusty garden tools braced against the walls, rolls of tar paper knitted together by dirt and water, bundles of newspapers collected years before. Working in the dark, I arranged an aisle to the window and learned to move through the clutter blind. O'Brien's car stopped at the mouth of the alley. He jolted in low gear over the bad pavement. I dreamed of a natural moment when my aim would be perfect, the decision and the will to act inseparable. But when O'Brien came near I was absolutely numb.

XXXIV

————◆◆◆————

ONE MORNING I ran into Sherry, and for me, too, everything was changed. She was waiting for a bus and called joyfully, "Hi, Vic!" I nodded and continued running and swerved off the sidewalk to pass her. She was no longer a slim girl; in fact, sizable.

I saw her in the same spot the following day, in the morning, alone at the bus stop, wearing the same summer outfit, a lavender suit with a broad white collar, the material almost transparent. I saw the shadow of her body. She offered condolences and asked for the news. How was Ernie? I shrugged. She briefed me on her recent history. She had switched to Commerce High and studied typing and shorthand. She dreamed of a rosy future as secretary to a tycoon. She wished me to take pleasure in her new career.

"I thought you were doing okay with your other career." I resumed running and didn't even say good-bye.

But there she was again the third day. She asked why I

ran every morning. Did I want to be physically fit for the army?

"I want to be tough like your ex-boy friend."

She had no news of Leonard. She didn't bear any grudges. "It's past history. It's over with. Anyhow, what can I do about it? My folks really put their foot down."

Though she was plump, I found her shape still marvelous. I saw staunch hips, a narrow waist, large breasts, and I knew that somewhere there was a flutter. She wasn't marked by her experience of abortion and Leonard Mitchell.

Her afternoons were free. She asked me to drop over. "I never see my old friends any more. I get lonely, Vic."

I was seventeen and it was my turn with Sherry.

The approach already diminished her, a pissy yellow building with blisters of green paint erupting all along the stairwell. The tile was stained yellow. The tarnished mailboxes were sprung open, name plates missing, apartment numbers penciled on the metal. Leonard's mother still lived on the floor below. By the time you made it through mildewed corridors, pressed a buzzer that didn't work, and summoned her by hard rapping, she had lost her right to queenly pretensions.

She asked me the old questions. Didn't I like her? What did I hold against her?

"I got more on my mind than liking and not liking. I don't have time for small feelings."

"What kind of feelings do you have time for?"

I admitted that there was considerable hatred in stock. I was loaded up on hate.

"But there's no cause to hate me, Vic. I was always nice to you."

"We used to wait downstairs while Leonard brought you up here."

"Well, don't you get any smart ideas. No one shoves me around any more."

"Ernie wanted to touched you on the bus to Belle Isle. You let

287

him touch. Then Leonard gave you the real business up here on the couch. He told us all the details."

She wanted to know if that was the way men talked. How could we claim to have any feeling for her and yet allow such things to be said?

"You look so sweet," I told her, "but I learned better from hard experience."

"What experience? You don't know anything about me. You never had any experience of me."

I had my experience that afternoon.

She had coffee cake on the table, nuts, dried fruit. Outside there was a heavy rain, the stuff coming down in buckets. Midafternoon and the street lamps were turned on. She had arranged pillows on the sofa, readied a book for my inspection. It was face down and the title was visible. *Leave Her to Heaven*. Commerce High didn't require *Leave Her to Heaven*. Perhaps she wanted me to bring the news home to Ernie that she wasn't confined to movie magazines and the *Reader's Digest*.

Later, I pushed her down on the sofa. She lay with her arms back. I pulled up her sweater, went under her brassiere, felt her breasts. I pulled down her pants. I had no difficulty discovering her flutter. I didn't kiss her or make vows or in any fashion betray my father's memory.

I left the apartment and started running again. I changed my connection to the world by making love to Sherry on an otherwise dull Summer afternoon. I was surprised by my tender feelings. Sentiment sneaked up on me. When I phoned her again, she wasn't available.

"That was an enjoyable afternoon," I admitted. "I meant to tell you what a great pleasure it was."

She hung up.

Far more than pleasure. In the course of an afternoon I passed from one condition to another. It was a significant event, not to be dismissed as mere fun. There was no evidence that it was significant to her.

That's the power of people like Sherry. They observe no

landmarks. They deal with extraordinary landscapes, but their eyes superimpose the commonplace on what they see. They ignore volcanoes, earthquakes, tidal waves, bombing, artillery, and they remain joyful.

I went to Windsor and hired a cab and asked for a whore. The cabby took me to a place like Frances Regina's. The lady brought me into her bedroom and discarded her housecoat. She had weighty breasts and supplied free rubbers. She lay on her back on top of a chenille bedspread, drew up her legs, flung her arms back. The sight of the tubby belly and mottled thighs depressed me.

I called Sherry and she still refused to see me. I went anyhow and found her in curlers, getting ready for a date.

"Come in for a second. Then you got to leave."

I didn't humble myself. I didn't grapple like a kid. I was prepared to rape if she didn't submit, and it was almost rape. I tore the buttons off her blouse. Her curlers scratched my face. I had difficulty entering her. She wept. She cursed me. It was a fight all the way. But she fluttered before I was finished. Afterward we lay on the sofa without speaking. I didn't apologize. I was tempted to say, "I love you, Sherry," but I kept my mouth shut. I knew from the beginning that words created situations, and silence was my policy.

Was she an ignorant girl, already launched on an ordinary life? She was delighted to be able to write shorthand and type forty-five words a minute. A disaster like Leonard Mitchell left no impression. She had a fine capacity for love, and yet she was unmarked by her talent. She moved through the world as if there were no risks. She didn't acknowledge that we were at war. She paid no attention to Hitler. She'd never heard of the dam on the Dnieper, or Kiev, or the siege of Leningrad. Did she know that Paris had fallen? She was familiar with the war in Britain, after viewing the Greer Garson-Walter Pidgeon reconstruction of Dunkirk. A simple, ordinary girl.

Yet she was bold and lawless when screwing. I oscillated

between the extremes of her character, hunting for some definition so that I could dismiss her, but it was more difficult than I'd imagined. Every time I put her down, the job had to be done over again. She was stupid and intractable. Or perhaps she had the ease of someone divine.

I didn't know what I was getting into when I got into Sherry.

She had once associated with a tough crowd, and a bitchy pose was necessary. Still, there was a flutter to this girl. Her impulse was generous. She could open up. She had a gift for total surrender. She tried to toughen herself, but at the last moment she became joyful and good-natured. I pitied her for having encountered so many cold hearts like myself.

Though I kept a lid on my feelings and didn't speak, whenever we made love we did each other no cruelty. She lay with the sweet flesh of her armpit available. She exposed her throat to nibbles, a chubby chin, buoyant flesh. Her belly was soft, ruddy colored, the odor of baby powder around the navel. I covered the soft, reddish pubic nest with my hand. She responded to all the commands of my hand, drew back her thighs, let me cuddle her bottom. She was gracious and accessible.

She predicted fame for Ernie. She respected his poetic feeling and his generosity of spirit.

"It's news to me. I find my brother a cold fish."

Sherry said she would always have a tender spot for Ernie. She found him in every way a loving person. Some men, she said, enter your bed; others, your heart as well.

"Did he ever get into your heart, Sherry? It's no trick getting into your other place."

Sprawled on top of her, buoyed up by that soft body which was impressed by mine as if it were clay shaped by a sculpting hand, the smell of Sherry became my necessary atmosphere. I was inflated by that smell. I walked through the countryside, lifting my boots high to get free of the muck left by spring rains, trampling clover underfoot, wild flowers intoxicating me.

I soared like a wind-filled balloon suddenly released, chased by its own air.

I had no impulse to shoot. I no longer cared to visit O'Brien. There were times when I came from Sherry thinking, "Who are you to swear oaths and be your father's safeguard? A liar, a hypocrite, more concerned with her than with O'Brien."

I, too, conspired to forget Jake Gottlieb.

So what was I doing as the time drew near to commemorate my father? Making love to Sherry. Who could have guessed that she would have been able to get to me so quickly? Maybe there was a kind of peasant wisdom in her bones, but in most of the ways that counted with me I considered her dumb and boring. Yet I surrendered to her.

I recall a crisp, brilliant October day on a Lake St. Clair beach, lying under a blanket while she spread mayonnaise on Wonder Bread for our sandwiches. A plump, blond girl in dark slacks, the lavender sweater rising. She was framed by an endless Lake St. Clair, a monumental woman. She was as much at ease in the face of a carnivorous history that wanted us for its meat as the Venus de Milo. Not a goddess, only the witless representation of one. The simple mouth, barely complicated by a pout, the straight line of the nose, the skin of marble clarity—not a seam of fear or envy or hunger to spoil the classic line. She prepared her edibles in total disregard of what happened to Jew girls across a different pond. Nothing alarmed her, surely not me. She dealt with me as if I were just another seventeen-year-old who was prone to an early marriage.

I told her horror stories from Europe and it didn't affect her intake of Wonder Bread sandwiches. What happened in Europe could have taken place in some other world among a different species, as far as she was concerned. I told her of the oath we'd sworn and she dismissed it as another of my exaggerations.

I wanted to burrow into her and be safe.

I saw the sweater rise from her slacks as she bent over,

exposing a creamy soft back. I led her behind a sand dune and we made love. Afterward we polished off the picnic lunch. I watched her mouth swallow food and her cunt love and I couldn't see any result. She seemed no more after her intake than before.

I was immensely bored by her.

She asked if we could stop off in Ann Arbor and see Ernie. I said no.

"Doesn't he know about us?"

"Is there anything to know, Sherry?"

She saw my change of mood and begged me not to spoil a beautiful picnic by quarreling. "I don't know what gets into you," she said. "All of a sudden you're someplace else. You're not here any more. You're up in the clouds somewhere."

"Up in the clouds, Sherry? Do you know what it means to be up in the clouds?"

"Well, you're just not here."

"To be up in the clouds is to be a dreamer. Do you imagine I'm a dreamer, Sherry? Are you so stupid as to imagine that?"

"Well, you're just not here. You're somewhere else."

"And where are you, Sherry? Do you know where you are?"

"You're up in the clouds somewhere. I don't know where you are."

"We're on the edge of a lake. Do you know what's under there? Would you be so cool if you knew what rose from deep water?"

She wasn't put off by my contempt or my anger. She wasn't afraid of me. She knew my rhythms as if I were a dumb animal. She made up her mind to swallow me, eccentricities and all. Nothing threw her off balance. And she swallowed me. That was my condition a year after the burial of Jake Gottlieb.

So what did it all come to, his years in Siberia, his union struggles, the conquest of the industry? If any life was memorable, wasn't his? His life was our treasure, and we threw it away.

XXXV

---◆◆◆---

THERE WERE eight mourners at the unveiling of his stone.
Four strangers. Evka, Ernie, me and Berle. It was a different
rabbi, a younger man, with a wiry black beard and horn-
rimmed spectacles. He read the services under an umbrella
held by an old man who leaned over to follow the text.

A rainy day with no horizon. A muddy grave had been
opened next to ours, a raw trench with a reddish clay bottom.
Dirt was piled along the sides, dark loam on the bottom, the
rusty clay on top. The rain turned it into mud. We had to
climb over mud to get to his grave. Evka stepped in mud, and
her shoe was encased in a clay mold. There were flecks of mud
on the rabbi's trousers.

The rabbi had never known Jake. He didn't have an honest
word to say, so who could blame him for wanting to rush
through the ceremony?

The black drape over the stone was soaked. When pulled
aside we saw the bare summary of Jake Gottlieb. 1892–1941.

BELOVED HUSBAND, HONORED FATHER, NOBLE WARRIOR. The last had been my doing.

It was a modest stone. His grave wasn't distinguished from others. I saw glittering monoliths with long biblical texts and encomia.

A steady, chilling November rain that soaked me through. Mud caved into the open grave, where a stranger would soon languish alongside Jake Gottlieb.

Ernie asked, "Didn't anyone know? Were the union people told?"

Evka said that she'd sent out the announcements. "It's the weather."

Ernie said, "He was out in every kind of weather for them." "For us, too." I said.

We were between Thanksgivings. There were two that year. Roosevelt had changed the date of celebration to provide a greater margin between holidays, but some had insisted on keeping the old date. We were at graveside while America sat around turkeys, dead on their backs, legs up in the air, waiting to be cannibalized.

Ernie said, "What a pitiful stone!"

An insignificant stone with one flourish of rhetoric, NOBLE WARRIOR. Passing through the field of stones, I saw monuments to loved ones. To a fourteen-year-old girl: "You passed like a dream, leaving inconsolable parents." To a father, dead like ours at forty-nine: "You were a good worker and a good friend. We shall never forget you." From children to their folks: "To our beloved Mamma and Papa, for whom we shall forever weep, Your mourning children." I stopped at Sammy Persky's grave. There was a sizable stone, in which Minnie had invested everything. "To the love of my life. Here lies Samuel Persky, born May 28, 1905, died by accident January 8, 1940. The years pass, but the memory remains."

Why didn't we promise in marble to remember our father forever? Why didn't ma call him the love of her life? Why didn't we admit we were inconsolable?

We had all found our consolation.

I took a bus to Ann Arbor on a stormy night. Fraternity houses were buttoned up. The streets were empty. Terrible weather brewed, hovering between rain and snow.

Ernie was sitting outside, on the dorm steps, in his raincoat, bushes flailing around him, trees reeling. Darts of rain struck like needles.

I asked him why he was waiting out there.

"I can't stand it in my room."

His hair rose in tufts like a Teddy bear's. There was a Halloween lantern still on view in the window across the street, a proper night for pumpkins, though three weeks after the holiday. I walked fast to keep up with Ernie. While we walked, the street lights flickered, brightened, then were suddenly extinguished.

I had to yell to be heard. "We should have had a bigger stone!"

He led me down State Street, beyond the depot, toward the island park. He didn't speak until we got to the park and huddled under the eaves of a locked recreation building. He said to me, without conviction, that no one had power over his body.

"What?" I yelled.

"Power!" he yelled back.

No one. Not even O'Brien. No. Not even O'Brien. Any madman, lying in ambush, could steal O'Brien's power. STEAL HIS POWER. O'Brien was doomed by his appetite. DOOMED. BY HIS APPETITE. He didn't need to be punished by us.

"WHO, THEN?"

His own desire would do him in. His OWN desire. He was a slave.

"O'BRIEN?"

The worst kind of slave. So desperate for gratification he had to kill. HAD TO KILL. HAD TO.

Ernie bent into the wind with a grimace as if he were about to weep. He said that O'Brien was doomed—DOOMED—to continual disappointment. Didn't that satisfy me? Wasn't that enough?

"HE ADVERTIZES IN THE DAILY NEWSPAPER. I SEE HIS PICTURE THERE. HE'S SMILING."

Every winter O'Brien went hunting. He ate venison and wild mushrooms. He enjoyed good company, and provided excellent whiskey. "WHAT'S HE MISSING? HE HAS EVERYTHING HE WANTS. HE'S IN LUCK." And all his luck come from the death of Jake Gottlieb.

The Huron River rushed all around us. Wires hummed. A merry-go-round turned in the wind, grinding and squealing. The rain penetrated everywhere.

"How do you know it's him? What if you've been haunting the wrong man?"

"HE'S THE ONE, ERNIE. YOU KNOW IT IN YOUR HEART."

How did I know what was in his heart?

"DON'T PRETEND YOU DON'T FEEL ANYTHING. DON'T PRETEND THAT YOU CAN GO ON READING HISTORY."

He wondered why I took such sadistic relish in his feelings. Did I want to see him join the ranks of snivelers and weepers in a charade of grief? He choked in the false air of my melodrama.

He headed back for the dorm, and I couldn't keep up with him.

He called me in Detroit and asked me to come see him again. I went despite the bad weather. We met at the union. We took one look at the cozy atmosphere and headed again into the park, crouching in the same place by the rec building.

"DO YOU REMEMBER THAT DAY?" I asked him. "IN FRONT OF THE CREAM OF MICHIGAN?"

Ernie said, "He quarreled with Happy Weinberg. He was excited."

"You know what we swore."

He hadn't slept since the unveiling. He had given up attending classes. As soon as he lay down to sleep, he was wide awake.

It was such a small stone, he said. That stone was unbearable to him; and finally, defeated, almost weeping, he asked me, "What can we do?"

I woke up one night and found him sitting on his old bed, staring at me. He asked the same question, his voice shaking, "What can we do, Vic? We swore. We can't get out of it."

XXXVI

THE DEATH OF O'BRIEN was unimaginable. When he came to mind, he was always in motion; I could never make him be still.

But wasn't the lesson of our history that the unimaginable furnishes the world? Didn't we accept the death of Jake Gottlieb? We came to believe that the moldering porridge in the sealed box was our pa. We were even grateful to morticians for banning the sight. A dentist did our work for us, considering only the teeth. I accepted his judgment. I accepted everything.

We, too, could become magicians and transform the unimaginable into plain fact. We could do for O'Brien what some other magician had done for Jake Gottlieb.

I gave my brother the chance to join the ranks of magicians.

A great night—I felt that I could soar straight up and be deified like Orion. A clear sky without a moon, everything brittle, leaves crackling underfoot. I wore jacket and gloves. I felt that I could hit any target.

It was almost midnight when we passed Tommy's Irish Bar. The neon sign blinked and exchanged a shamrock for a cocktail glass.

The alley coursed through the block, joined at its mid-point by an intersecting branch. Street lamps at either end, a dull light, a wash of yellow on the pavement. High oaks arched over fences, shutting out the stars. On either side, a wall of garages, incinerators, fences, gates, all entrances secured, garage doors bolted, gates latched, our shed the only break in the defense. A tough neighborhood that expected danger from the rear. The alley heaved with rats.

I can guess Ernie's terror. It would have been different advancing behind a beefy barricade of Weinberg and Spiegelman and Leonard Mitchell. But he approached O'Brien with no other support than me. Beyond the street lamp we entered oblivion. The surface under our feet wasn't stable.

I took him step by step down the alley. I led him to the shed. I guided him to the window and showed him where to kneel. I reassured him. Gunshots would be dismissed as backfire. We could easily make our escape down the alley. We were close to Grand River Avenue. Detroit factories operated around the clock, and Grand River would be jammed. We'd merge with the crowd.

A damp, cold shed that smelled of rat-shit and mildew.

Soon we'd be finished waiting. We'd no longer be kids, released to be ourselves, finished serving a dead man.

"Just a little longer, Ernie; then you're free."

I described what would take place. O'Brien would stop the car and leave the motor idling. We'd hear gravel crunch, the padlock fall open, the garage doors scrape, the hinges groan, shoes echo on concrete. A moment of silence as he grappled for the overhead light. When he returned for the car, framed by the interior light, less than fifteen feet away, he became a perfect target and justice would be done.

"What are we doing here?" he whispered, coming awake in the terrain of his nightmare.

The executioner seems monstrous at the moment of action, but afterward we understand the necessity of what he's done. He transforms the world. His act isn't to be judged at the moment of horror, but later, when we see what it has achieved, a world without O'Brien, a new world. The executioner is the hero of revolution. He attacks when we consider retreating, and he commits us irrevocably. We have to go all the way or be hanged for what he has done.

With all my heart I welcomed—as O'Brien did—the role of executioner.

Ernie was out of tune. Being in that shed violated his feeling.

I squatted on burlap bags, taking deep whiffs of tar and grease and the putrescent stew of the alley. I felt that we were kin to the rats—like them, nocturnal hunters, preying on householders who latched their gates out of fear of us. An open window released the music of "The Lucky Strike Hit Parade." I watched a flashlight move down a back-yard lane toward an incinerator. A trash can squealed along concrete, a brash, noisy trip by someone afraid of the dark.

I recognized the sound of O'Brien's car from blocks away. He stopped to shift before entering the alley. There was a slight squeal of tires slipping on gravel. The familiar flatulence of a powerful engine operating at low speed. O'Brien's headlights swept our windows. The brakes squealed. We were eyed by red taillights.

Ernie whispered, "All right, I won't stop you. Do it."

He held himself aloof from my act.

I saw O'Brien, illuminated by red light, stride heedless as if there were nothing to fear in his alley. Jake Gottlieb never entered his mind. I braced the gun on the window ledge. The garage door opened, scraping on rusty hinges. He entered the garage.

"I won't stop you," he whispered. "Do it."

It would have been wrong to hurry this moment we'd rehearsed. If there was a time to be ourselves it was at the moment we meant death to O'Brien. We'd have gained nothing by doing it unnaturally, obsessed by fear, tranquilized by shock or drink or alibis, withdrawing ourselves from the act. I wanted to consider my duty to Jake Gottlieb, nothing else.

"Do it," he said. "Do it."

He shoved me.

"Do it!" He shoved me again. I lost my balance and scraped the ledge with my gun.

The garage didn't light up.

The car idled; the garage doors remained open.

If there was any disharmony near him, he was alerted. He had the sense of an animal of where each part of his world belonged and what noise it made. To hunt O'Brien we had to be extraordinarily still. We had to be in tune with his alleys and his streets. We had to walk in his steps, enter his shoes, so that we were not two but one. Then we'd become hunters who could stalk O'Brien.

The headlights swept the north end of the alley, illuminating a mushrooming oak, projecting a distorted leaf pattern on the blank side of a frame building.

He'd killed our pa and Sammy Persky. Were we the next candidates?

Ernie whispered, "Let's go."

I told him to go.

Let's go, he said.

Go.

You, too.

He reached over and took my gun away.

The air changes in the presence of O'Brien. I know his sweet-and-sour smell. He bathes sparingly and soaks his face in after-shave lotion like my pa.

"Give me back the gun." I grabbed for the gun and Ernie pulled away from me. I tore the palm of my hand on a nail. I squeezed my wrist and sucked my hand. The pain shot up my arm in fiery spasms. I rolled my face against a beam and swallowed my groans. Ernie tried to pry my hand open so that he could see, but I couldn't open up. He put his arm around my shoulder and led me out of the shed.

O'Brien was there, all right.

He collared us. He grabbed us by our necks and shook us as if we were dogs.

Ernie said, "He's hurt! Please!"

O'Brien lifted us by our belts. He straightened us with his knees. He hustled us into the alley. He bumped us along with his knees.

Ernie said again—still whispering—"He's hurt! Please!"

He dragged us under clotheslines. I collided with wet sheets, pillow slips, socks, panties, undershorts; waves of clothes hit us as we ducked under and bobbed up.

I squealed, a blare of sound from my palate and nose; my tongue rolled. I didn't have the power to block that piggish sound. It was squeezed from me as though he pressed the bellows of an accordion.

He bumped us up the back stairs. No resistance. He could have controlled us with his little finger. I leaked blood on his trousers. He squeezed us in his arms and scraped my cheek with his bristly jaw.

He pressed the buzzer with his elbow, and I heard Kate Russo pad toward us.

I saw Kate Russo in a dazzle of light which penetrated her nightie, outlining bare tits and silken panties, hair showing, a wealth of form exposed by the kitchen light, dressed for the return of an ardent husband.

He pushed us through a large, shabby kitchen with warped tiles, dishes draining on the sink apron. He shoved us down a long corridor and released us in the living room. A last shove wedged us into a worn maroon sofa with stiff springs that tilted toward each other.

"Picked them up in the alley," he told his wife.

"Who are they?"

He was as broad as a boar, unruffled by the excitement, still dressed for a night out, only his tie disarranged. A shrill voice, as though his vocal chords had been filed.

Cheap furniture with garish upholstery, florid rugs and drapes. The wallpaper dragged you into a monotonous repetition of a farmhouse and a barn. A ratty carpet, a plump sofa, furnishings that would have served Okies.

I saw the gun rack in the dining room, glistening weapons arranged one above the other, the heavy-caliber rifle with telescopic sights on the bottom rack. Deer heads were mounted around the entrance to the living room.

And was that the family O'Brien? A tinted photo of a severe old man who looked like Henry Ford, a starched collar, cold eyes, grim mouth. A fat lady with a pleasant smile and O'Brien's face. And a picture of the Soil Free associates. O'Brien behind the others, but still at the focus. There was a wedding photo of O'Brien and Kate in a gilt frame, both of them as unnatural as immigrants in those clothes. Above the sofa there was a dimestore reproduction of a haloed Christ in long robes, beckoning to a bleeding heart.

"Gottlieb's boys?"

He looked at Ernie's wallet and we were identified.

"Well, boys," he said, "here's O'Brien. What's your pleasure?"

He hunted clues to our definition and saw nothing.

"What did you expect to find in my alley?"

"Our pa told us to remember O'Brien."

"The little one's the talker, eh? Say," he said, "could you be the bastards who made the telephone calls?"

"I never called you," Ernie said.

"How about the little one?"

Kate Russo bent to look at my hand, drenched in the same fragrance as Sherry, her heavy breasts showing. O'Brien told her to let me be, that I'd live.

He took off his jacket. He loosened his tie and rolled up his sleeves.

Kate said, "We never had any quarrel with your pa. He was a fine man. Isn't that so, O'Brien?"

He told us to get up.

"What were you doing in my alley?"

"We wanted to see you," Ernie said.

He grabbed our jackets and pulled us from the sofa, moving us easily.

Kate Russo begged him not to hurt us.

He yanked open our jackets and saw the gun in Ernie's belt.

"You see," he told her. "These boys are serious. They got something in mind." He spun the chambers, looked down the barrel. He stuck the gun in his own belt. "I can't let you drop in any time you feel like it. Or make telephone calls whenever you want to say hello."

"They're going to stay out of trouble, O'Brien. They didn't mean you no harm. Isn't that so, kids?"

Ernie said that we never meant to make trouble.

He had freckled arms, thick beef hiding the veins, rough skin over the knuckles, heavy, dumb hands with manicured nails.

"We wanted to meet you," Ernie said. "We didn't feel we could introduce ourselves."

O'Brien tapped the gun. "You sure brought along funny friends."

"That's cops and robbers. That's nothing serious."

"That toy is loaded. What kind of game is that?"

"It's only play acting. Only dreaming."

"What were you dreaming about, kid?"

I said to O'Brien, "We're here to remember our pa."

"How did you mean to remember your pa in my alley?"

"That's for you to worry about."

Kate Russo yelled, "Keep a civil tongue in your head, you smart-ass kid!"

"Why should I worry, shorty? What's on your mind?"

"I'm only seventeen. I got a long life ahead of me."

"I sure hope so."

"We missed this time. Maybe we won't the next."

"Missed what, son?"

I felt no pain in my hand but my hearing and sight were affected. His Jesus trembled on the wall. The room hummed. "We know the story of Sammy Persky. We know what happened to him. And we know who waited for Jake Gottlieb outside of Oswego and took him to Walloon Lake in MY FAIR LADY and dumped him overboard."

Kate yelled, "You crazy kid! Shut your mouth!"

O'Brien asked Ernie, "You were laying for me in that shed, right? You had the gun, right?"

"It was play acting. Nothing would have happened."

"Have you been waiting there before?"

"Me!" I yelled. "Not him. I was there!"

I'd waited long to be hit by O'Brien, and when it happened I felt nothing. He cuffed me. A roar in my ears. I knelt on the floor and heard Ernie plead, "Don't hurt him, please."

I underwent the experience of Sammy Persky. Maybe shock saved him, too, once the torture began.

"I swear," Ernie said, "you won't have any more trouble with us."

I told O'Brien, "You better worry about me, because it will be a different story in ten years. You're as big as you'll ever get, but I'll grow; you can't know what size I'll be in ten years."

Kate got between us, and he shoved her aside. "I bet these kids have been hanging around for days. They knew about that shed. They probably knew this is my night out."

"I swear," Ernie said, "you have nothing to worry about."

O'Brien twisted his arm. "Were you laying for me, you little son of a bitch?"

I lay on the floor and watched O'Brien twist Ernie to his knees. He ignored Kate Russo, who begged him to let us go.

"I swear," Ernie groaned. "I swear."

O'Brien didn't permit us any dignity. He saw that we could do him no harm, yet he still meant to teach us a lesson. He hauled us through the corridor, through the kitchen, out the back door. Kate Russo ran alongside, her night dress open,

and I saw the voluptuous shape that had once obsessed Mc-
Intyre. "The little one's hurt, O'Brien."

He moved us under clotheslines, through the garage. He
returned us to the alley.

"Take it easy," she begged, trying to get between us, but
warded off by his elbow. "They won't give you any trouble."

His car was still poised in front of the garage, the motor
idling, the lights on. He braced us in front of the headlights.

"Okay, boys. Let's get a few things straight. No more phone
calls, right? No more fucking around my alley, right? Now,
just so you'll get the idea—" He aimed us toward the street
and kicked. He shrugged Kate off. He kicked Ernie in the ass.
Then me. We sprawled on the pavement, and he kept kicking. Ernie scrambled up and he kicked him flat. Ernie scrambled
on all fours and he sent him sprawling, five, six kicks.

I lay in the cold alley and watched. I said to him, "I'll come
back."

He raised me up. "Maybe we'll be buddies. I got no hard
feelings." He dusted me off.

"Someday you'll pay for what you did to our pa."

He raised me off the ground and shook me. "What did I
do to your pa?"

"You . . . drowned him . . . in . . . Walloon." The Walloon
came out as a moan.

"Should I let him go," he asked Kate, "so he'll come back
some night and blow out my brains? Don't you see I got to
teach him a lesson?"

He wanted to instruct the whole world to stay clear of
O'Brien. He wanted an open road to glory. Without malice, even
with affection, he slapped a lesson into my head. He embraced
me with an arm that hoisted me clear of the alley, held me
immobile, and with the other hand he rapped my ears until
both sides of my head were on fire and whatever my resolution
I yipped like a dog. OW-OW-OW. No windows opened. No one
interrupted.

I saw Ernie lunge for O'Brien and come away with the gun.

Then O'Brien leaped from my arms, backwards, becoming for an instant what I'd dreamed he might be, hair jolted out, arms spread, smelling sweet and sour. He dived backwards toward the car headlights, his back striking a moment before his head. I saw his chin in the glare of lights, his mouth open, his eyes out of sight, a hole like a scab above the nose. Kate's screams followed us down the alley. Someone yelled, "What's happening out there?" I don't remember the pavement. I remember Ernie's breath as we ran, HUH-HUH-HUH-HUH. We still heard her screams when we came out of the alley near Grand River. A few steps along Grand River and there was no evidence of trouble in O'Brien's alley. There was heavy traffic in both directions bearing shifts back and forth, around the clock, to the River Rouge plant. The city was alive all night long on behalf of war. The bars were crowded. Bus stops were jammed.

"How do I look?"

His hair was mussed.

He ran his hands through his hair. He straightened his trousers, zipped up his jacket. He wrapped a handkerchief around my hand.

"We better not go home."

He began to sob, but clammed up as a crowd moved toward us. "We can go to Ann Arbor. Let them come for us there." I felt no pain. I was absolutely calm, even though I trembled.

We hiked from the Oswego road. We were picked up by a well-dressed fat man, driving a Packard with a Chicago license. He must have imagined that we were shy college boys, so he did the talking. He told us of his experience of women throughout the world. He preferred the English ladies, who, he said, had mastered a technique he called the Cleopatra clutch. His approach was to be frank and funny.

Ernie occasionally mumbled, "Oh, I see. Yes," his voice dreamy. I slumped in back, listening to the fat man tell sex stories at two-thirty in the morning. I remember what he said with great clarity. What happened in O'Brien's alley is out of focus.

He'd discovered the business of the Cleopatra clutch from a redheaded elevator operator in a London hotel. He'd been the only passenger. He stationed himself behind her, and, when she asked, "Floor, please?" he'd goosed her and said, "Basement, honey," even though the elevator was going up. She walloped him, and he said, "Thank you," as chipper as Santa. By the time they reached his floor, he had her laughing. That night she was in his bed getting more laughs, and he discovered the Cleopatra clutch.

We entered the quiet dorm and sat in Ernie's dark room, listening to the radio, which was on a wartime schedule and operated all night long. I was absolutely vacant, and I presume Ernie was, too.

Good news from Stalingrad.

Rommel stopped at El Alamein. Montgomery rolling back the Afrika Korps.

We made no attempt to run. We didn't consider what would happen when the police arrived. I plastered my hand with band aids and returned to the radio. For the first time in our lives we saw a possibility that our enemies might be defeated.

At six we heard the word. O'Brien had been shot to death while routing a bum from his alley. His wife was in a state of shock. She described the bum as middle-aged and heavy. She didn't get a close look. Her husband had surprised him in the alley; there had been a scuffle; and one of Detroit's promising young businessmen was done for.

We again heard the news at seven. Kate Russo had still not mentioned the Gottliebs. At nine o'clock we heard a few details. The police had searched the neighborhood and discovered that the bum had been living in the abandoned shack. O'Brien must have heard him and routed him out, and in the scuffle was shot with his own weapon. Kate Russo identified the gun as his.

Ma called in the late morning to find out where I was.

She hadn't heard about O'Brien. She would never imagine her sons could be the assassins.

The Germans were hopelessly trapped at Stalingrad. There was no way out. Hitler ordered them to perish, and they were ready to oblige him.

The corridors filled up with students, who planned weekend fun. There were dances at the union, drinking at the taverns. They needed relief from the wartime pace. The university had accelerated to keep up. Civvies were being replaced by uniforms.

Ernie finally said to me, "Everything we decide to do we decide together."

I agreed.

"We turn ourselves in or we keep still."

It was difficult for us to part. I was afraid to leave him.

O'Brien leaps into the stage of my mind and performs his dying again, as I'm sure he does for Ernie. I hear the shrill voice. I smell him. I feel the pressure of his arms. I feel, for a moment, that he has real affection for me.

I'm no longer afraid that Kate Russo will pull the veil from the bum and reveal Gottlieb's sons.

A few minutes in O'Brien's house, and we're changed forever. We've left all the landmarks behind. We're not anchored to a grave. Everything's brand-new for us.

Ernie hugged me when I left his room. He told me not to be afraid. "Whatever happens, we stick together."

Later, in Sherry's arms, studying that serene, lovely face, I was comforted by the illusion that nothing had happened.

XXXVII

IT WAS NO MORE SCHOOL for Ernie. He'd jumped off the track, and who knew if he'd land on his feet? But he wanted to throw himself in front of panzers and topple the Third Reich. Evka and I went to see him off to war.

There was a mob at the terminal, a domed hall with gates at one end, ticket counters facing the gates. The hard floor produced ringing echoes. There were lines at the ticket counter, orderly at the head, broadening farther back, spreading into crowds toward the middle of the terminal. A uniformed sergeant led Ernie's group. They were on their way to the Fort Custer Induction Center at Battle Creek, Michigan, to receive inoculations, indoctrination, and GI gear. In his barracks bag he would carry extra boots, field jacket, raincoat, blankets, a shelter half, khaki underwear, khaki socks, a mess kit, canteen cup, wool ODs, summer tans, green fatigues, a wool cap, a fatigue cap, an overseas cap, a helmet liner, a gas mask, and a pack. The recruits would be shown movies to make them dread syph and clap. They'd be tested, their ratings established. They'd go south for basic training. Somewhere along the line, memories of our life together would grow dim for Ernie. But how can he ever forget that night in O'Brien's house? ♠

A loudspeaker—followed by its echo—summons Detroiters to vanish to all parts of America. They leave for Louisville, Atlanta, Miami; Chicago, St. Louis, Kansas City, Los Angeles; Cleveland, Buffalo, Albany, New York. Everyone aboard. ALL ABOARD. I see Ernie among eighteen-year-olds from Hamtramck, Highland Park, Dearborn, the East Side. They already seek common ground. Farewells glue them to a past already discarded. Ernie stands alone.

The boys make strong efforts for a proper farewell, letting dads slug their arms, mommies cling, girl friends preen for the crowds while snuggling close. They want the good-byes ended so that they can get on with the new life.

"You'll write," Evka says. "Remember. I won't be able to stand it if you don't write."

She hung a blue star in the window and waited for the news from her first-born, who didn't write much.

Mothers leak all over Detroit Central Terminal as they suddenly realize that this could be the last view of a son. They produce kids in order to wet them with their tears. So let her weep, Ernie; it'll be over soon.

And how about me? There's nothing false in our embrace. We know that even if this is the last time for us—the afternoon of the fifth of January 1943, Detroit Central Terminal—there will never be a last farewell until we're both in our graves.

The sergeant lines them up; they lift their suitcases. The families are told to stay back. At the gate the sergeant calls the roll. Ernie Gottlieb is there. A non-com leads the double column, another brings up the rear. Shepherds guard their fold. I press against the glass door and watch him descend the ramp, his suitcase swinging out, banging against his leg. I see him at the bottom of the ramp, where the tracks begin. Steam eddies around the column.

There's a sharp whistle, a warning that it may be too late for good-byes. I slip past the ancient guard. He makes a grab, but I sidestep and tell him a soldier boy forgot something. I ignore his warning and run down the ramp. The train stretches for blocks, crammed with soldiers and inductees. I run its length and see him squeezed against the window, already dreaming. I shock him awake for the last time. He may not hear, but I send him the message.

Remember your father. Remember your mother. And remember your little brother, who wants you back.

Titles in the
Great Lakes Books Series

Call It North Country: The Story of Upper Michigan, by John Bartlow Martin, 1986 (reprint)

Freshwater Fury: Yarns and Reminiscences of the Greatest Storm in Inland Navigation, by Frank Barcus, 1986 (reprint)

The Land of the Crooked Tree, by U. P. Hedrick, 1986

Michigan Place Names, by Walter Romig, 1986 (reprint)

Danny and the Boys, Being Some Legends of Hungry Hollow, by Robert Traver, 1987 (reprint)

Discovering Stained Glass in Detroit, by Nola Huse Tutag with Lucy Hamilton, 1987

Great Pages of Michigan History from the Detroit Free Press, 1987

Hanging On, or How to Get through a Depression and Enjoy Life, by Edmund G. Love, 1987 (reprint)

The Late, Great Lakes: An Environmental History, by William Ashworth, 1987

Luke Karamazov, by Conrad Hilberry, 1987

Michigan Voices: Our State's History in the Words of the People Who Lived it, compiled and edited by Joe Grimm, 1987

The Public Image of Henry Ford: An American Folk Hero and His Company, by David L. Lewis, 1987

The Saginaw Paul Bunyan, by James Stevens, 1987 (reprint)

The Situation in Flushing, by Edmund G. Love, 1987 (reprint)

A Small Bequest, by Edmund G. Love, 1987 (reprint)

Waiting for the Morning Train: An American Boyhood, by Bruce Catton, 1987 (reprint)

An Afternoon in Waterloo Park, by Gerald Dumas, 1988 (reprint)

The Ambassador Bridge: A Monument to Progress, by Philip P. Mason, 1988

Contemporary Michigan Poetry: Poems from the Third Coast, edited by Michael Delp, Conrad Hilberry, and Herbert Scott, 1988

Let the Drum Beat: A History of the Detroit Light Guard, by Stanley D. Solvick, 1988

Over the Graves of Horses, by Michael Delp, 1988

Wolf in Sheep's Clothing: The Search for a Child Killer, by Tommy McIntyre, 1988

Artists in Michigan, 1900–1976: A Biographical Dictionary, introduction by Dennis Barrie, biographies by Jeanie Huntley Bentley, Cynthia Newman Helms, and Mary Chris Rospond, 1989

Copper-Toed Boots, by Marguerite de Angeli, 1989 (reprint)

Deep Woods Frontier: A History of Logging in Northern Michigan, by Theodore J. Karamanski, 1989

Detroit: City of Race and Class Violence, revised edition, by B. J. Widick, 1989

Detroit Images: Photographs of the Renaissance City, edited by John J. Bukowczyk and Douglas Aikenhead, with Peter Slavcheff, 1989

Hangdog Reef: Poems Sailing the Great Lakes, by Stephen Tudor, 1989

Orvie, The Dictator of Dearborn, by David L. Good, 1989

America's Favorite Homes: A Guide to Popular Early Twentieth-Century Homes, by Robert Schweitzer and Michael W. R. Davis, 1990

Beyond the Model T: The Other Ventures of Henry Ford, by Ford R. Bryan, 1990

Detroit Kids Catalog: The Hometown Tourist, by Ellyce Field, 1990

Detroit Perspectives: Crossroads and Turning Points, edited by Wilma Henrickson, 1990

The Diary of Bishop Frederic Baraga: First Bishop of Marquette, Michigan, edited by Regis M. Walling and Rev. N. Daniel Rupp, 1990

Life after the Line, by Josie Kearns, 1990

The Making of Michigan, 1820–1860: A Pioneer Anthology, edited by Justin L. Kestenbaum, 1990

Michigan Lumbertowns: Lumbermen and Laborers in Saginaw, Bay City, and Muskegon, 1870–1905, by Jeremy W. Kilar, 1990

The Pottery of John Foster: Form and Meaning, by Gordon and Elizabeth Orear, 1990

Seasons of Grace: A History of the Catholic Archdiocese of Detroit, by Leslie Woodcock Tentler, 1990

Waiting for the News, by Leo Litwak, 1990 (reprint)

Walnut Pickles and Watermelon Cake: A Century of Michigan Cooking, by Larry B. Massie and Priscilla Massie, 1990

.